LOVE

OBEY

&

BETRAY

Copyright ©2012 by Sun Dragon Press
All Rights Reserved

No part of this publication may be reproduced or transmitted in any form or by any means, electronic or mechanical, including photocopy, recording or any information storage and retrieval system without the written permission of the author.

Disclaimer:
All characters in this book are fictitious, and any resemblance to actual persons, living or dead, is purely coincidental.

Cover Photography: Marilyn Kleiber

Library and Archives Canada Cataloguing in Publication

Petru, Maggie, 1942-
    Love obey & betray / by Maggie Petru.

Also issued in electronic format.
ISBN 978-0-9877607-2-2

    I. Title.

PS8631.E866L69 2012   C813'.6   C2012-907982-0

Printed in United States of America

Published by Sun Dragon Press Inc., Canada
www.sundragonpress.com
First Edition, 2012

LOVE
OBEY
&
BETRAY

by
Maggie Petru

DEDICATION

For Vasyl
1927 - 1996
And all the kids
who never got to hear
their dedushka's stories

ACKNOWLEDGMENTS

My sincere thanks to Andre Rocheleau, Dave Carter, and Bob Rutter for their help with the technical bits. If I still didn't get it right, that was my fault. They knew what they were talking about.

Writing news stories is easy. The facts are all there if you just look for them. Fiction, however, is something else. Contrary to popular belief, making up the facts is a totally foreign concept and it took a lot of re-thinking to get the hang of it. So to all those girlfriends and fellow writers who read my manuscript, offered advice, corrected my punctuation, taught me about subjunctive case and generally helped me shape up, thank you, thank you, thank you.

And last, but far from least, a huge note of appreciation to my publisher, Marilyn Kleiber of Sun Dragon Press, for taking a chance on a beginning author and for guiding me through the publication process.

CHAPTER ONE

Returning to the bedroom after brushing his teeth, Vladymyr Horbatsky found his wife laying out her clothes for the morning as she usually did. In the muted glow of the bedside lamp the silky, aqua blouse in her hands shone like a jewel against the navy of the suit it was to accompany.

"Don't wear that!"

The sharp words slipped out before he could stop himself. The instant set to her lips told him he'd made a mistake. She was going to defy him—as usual. Whenever he tried to guide her, it seemed she did the opposite just to spite him.

In desperation, Vlad cast his glance over the clothes in the closet behind Kate and settled on a beige cotton blouse with dark green trim. He crossed to scoop the hanger off the rail and laid the garment against the jacket and pants resting on the back of the bedside chair. "What about this? It will look good with your suit."

It wouldn't, of course. As opposed to the aqua that matched her eyes and accentuated the rose tones of her cheeks, the beige blended with her fair hair, dulled her skin and turned her monotone from head to waist.

That was the point, however. Germans liked their women to look smart and sexy so for her own good she had to look as drab and unappealing as possible.

Kate took the hanger and spread out one side of the blouse for him to look at. "No, Vlad. This isn't fit for work any more. Not with this huge grease stain. It's a house jobby now." She replaced the blouse in the closet, then removed a high-necked, white blouse beside it. "Will this be better?"

Legitimately caught out, he had no choice. He nodded. The white wasn't as eye-catching as the aqua color, but it still suited her much too well. Only how could he protest when she was being conciliatory? Blast it all to hell. Had she guessed his intent? Was she mocking him? Or was she simply trying to placate him? With her, he was never quite sure. She was just too damned smart.

He rounded the foot of the bed, yanked the covers aside, and plopped down to wind the alarm clock. Although she said nothing, he suspected she was as tense as he was. The bloody man was due in the morning. How could she do this to him? Keep it a secret like this for two whole weeks. Or was it three? He wasn't sure when they'd found out that the inspector was a German. Equally frustrating was the fact that his boss, too, had waited until yesterday to warn him that the bastard for whom he was expected to trot out his best smile and most deferential manner was a Kraut.

Moreover, why the hell would they be sending a German anyway? The contract was for the American defense department. Didn't they have any American inspectors?

Discovering her secrecy and the inspector's identity had combined to bring on one of his nightmares last night. Not that having nightmares was unusual for him, of course. Twenty-six years after his escape, he still re-lived scenes from his months in the concentration camp.

Only this one was different. This time the guards stood around taunting him while he made an exhibition of himself with some woman—a thin, dark-haired female. He couldn't see her face. All he remembered were the rude comments she made about his inadequacies. The coloring reminded him of Anna, but that was illusion. He'd lost Anna when he emigrated to Canada at the end of the war. Everyone knew that dreams were based on your fears and it was Kate, not Anna, who had associated all too closely with the Germans.

That would not happen again. He was her husband now. It was his job to protect her—even from herself. She no longer needed to bow to the whims of any German, and he would not allow her to do so.

He felt the mattress dip and then her hand settled in the middle of his back.

"He may not be German, you know." Her voice was soft, her tone the soothing type she used with the kids when they were upset.

The implication that he was being an unreasonable child only infuriated him further. He knew the German way. Hell, he'd grown up among them. No wife of his was going to put out for some smooth-talking Kraut.

"With that name?" he snapped.

"Oh, the name's Germanic. No doubt about that," she agreed patiently. "But the U.S. is a nation of immigrants just like we are. At the time of the revolution, there were so many German colonists in New York State that it was a tossup whether that might be the new nation's official language. We have no idea how deep his American roots may be."

Shocked, he turned to stare at her lying beside him in the bed.

She nodded. "It's true, Vlad. We don't notice these days, but America has a large contingent of long-time citizens of German heritage. Look at Eisenhower, for instance. How German was his name? And yet he led the Allies against Hitler."

Her point was valid.

"Come on. Lie down. Morning's going to come way too soon and you're the head of maintenance. You'll need to be on the shop floor before any of us. You need your sleep."

"Well, you can't go flaunting yourself for some visitor no matter what Gerry says."

She shook her head. "You're missing the point, Vlad. What smart businessman keeps a private secretary who looks like something out of the ragbag? I represent the way management thinks. Presenting a poor image undermines Gerry's competency to meet the contractor's standards. I can't do that to him."

Frustrated, he dragged the covers into place and closed his eyes. He wouldn't sleep, of course, but at least he could try to rest.

CHAPTER TWO

Kate lay motionless, staring into the dark, listening to the February wind whistling around the eaves as a branch squeaked against the bedroom window. She shivered despite the extra blanket. The hollow bonging of the grandfather's clock in the front hall announced it was three a.m. Only six more hours before her world shattered around her.

Beside her, Vlad's deep breathing betrayed the ease with which he had apparently wiped away the disagreement that disrupted their normal bedtime routine.

She hadn't been sleeping well for the past two weeks, and her husband's outburst simply confirmed the tantrum she should expect if he uncovered her secret. Meanwhile, her true victim waited in ignorance of the disillusionment to come. Visualizing the face she hadn't seen in twenty-eight years, tears trickled silently onto her pillow.

Until now, Kate had never known helplessness. Even as a spy behind enemy lines, she had always had choices. Ways to avoid detection. The freedom to run if all else failed. Not this time. This time her home, her family, and her reputation were all vulnerable to the fury of a lover betrayed.

She burrowed deeper into the blankets in search of a softer spot in the mattress and tried to blank out her thoughts. She needed rest even if she couldn't sleep.

For the millionth time in fourteen days she repeated the assurances she had offered Vlad hours earlier. The German surname was no guarantee of anything.

Just who was she kidding? A. Wachter, with a degree in aeronautical engineering? The coincidence was too great. It had to be him despite the years.

As Gerry Clarke's private secretary, Kate had handled the correspondence when Clarke Manufacturing bid on a contract to assemble satellite-based systems to guide the bombs on American warplanes. Both she and Vlad had viewed expanding their market as guaranteeing the firm's continued success and ensuring their own future employment.

Her first inkling of trouble came with the letter announcing the need to inspect the actual physical plant. Even so, the letter said only that an inspector would be sent. The man's name was not mentioned.

Kate rolled over again. Vlad was snoring now, gently, but persistently. It was the last straw. She wanted to apply an elbow to his ribs and push. That might waken him though, and she was in no mood to cope with more of his suspicions. Especially when those suspicions came so close to the truth.

Frustrated, she slid cautiously from under the covers and stuck her toes into her slippers on the sheepskin rug by the bed, then donned her robe and pulled the zipper. Maybe warm milk would help her relax.

She padded down the hallway in the dark, her steps whispering over the gleaming hardwood. As she passed through the family room and into the kitchen, their stocky Rottweiler lifted his black head and blinked sleepily. Moments later, he came to stand behind her, rubbing his muzzle against her leg as she poured milk into a mug. Absently, she dropped a reassuring hand to his broad back.

"Back to bed, Amos," she said softly, trying to erase the question in his intelligent eyes. "I'm okay."

It didn't work. Intuitive and loyal, eight-year-old Amos wasn't leaving. He knew something was wrong even if his mistress was denying it.

Normally the country kitchen with its maple cupboards, avocado appliances and olive arborite countertops filled Kate with satisfaction. Tonight, memories blotted out the warmth of the room she loved. All she could see was the face of the brilliant engineer she had betrayed by passing his designs to the Allies during thirty frenetic months as his secretary at the Nazi rocket research laboratory in Peenemünde.

Since the slightest sound sometimes wakened Vlad, Kate hovered by the microwave while the milk heated. The appliance was new. Although she hadn't wanted it, her husband's eagerness to provide her with the latest appliances had overruled her indifference and she was coming to realize its benefits. With both of them working, they had the money to buy gadgets and little time to waste on time-consuming old methods. When she unlatched the door and shut off the timer seconds before it dinged, steam rose from the mug.

Annoyed with herself for overheating her drink, she returned to the family room, Amos at her heels. She clicked on the lamp beside her rocker, set her cup on the table, and went to the liquor cabinet by the television for the bottle of peach schnapps. A dollop of that would cool her milk, and hopefully, help her to relax.

Framed snapshots on the mantel across the room caught her eye as she settled into her chair. In the gloom, a little blond boy and girl grinned at her from the back of a pony. Now, fifteen years older than they were in the photograph, both attended university in Toronto. Like Vlad, Alexi and Tanya were solid, industrious, no nonsense types, proud of their heritage and looking to their futures. They had no idea how convenience played into their parents' marriage. Nor how heavily that relationship now relied on the comfort of habit. While they couldn't deny she was their mother, learning the truth could cost her their respect.

And the other one, their dark-haired elder sister in the graduation cap and gown. She symbolized Kate's betrayal, not only of Andreas Wachter, but also of all the values her father, Milton Presbyterian church minister Angus Cameron, had preached to his small town congregation throughout Kate's formative years. How would Ruth deal with her birthright if she ever discovered it?

The warm pressure of Amos' head on her foot disrupted Kate's scrambled reflections. The drink was no longer steaming. She took a sip, then drained her cup.

Thoughts of Ruth had undermined whatever soothing effect the drink might have had.

Kate turned off the light, returned to the kitchen to rinse her cup, then headed back to bed.

While her husband was her normal confidant, in any situation involving a German, his paranoia always outweighed his good sense. She had learned never to rouse it unnecessarily. In twenty-three years of marriage, she had come to accept that the family first attitude she had once admired was based on an almost religious dedication to his obligations as a husband. The Eastern Orthodox wedding vows required a husband to be worthy of his wife's obedience. To Vlad, that meant he must lead, provide for, and protect his family, even from things that no one else saw as a threat.

Compared to the husbands of many of her contemporaries, Vlad was a prince. He had a short fuse when defied, but over time, Kate had learned how to avoid outright confrontations. The kids, especially Ruth, sometimes took less than diplomatic approaches in their dealings with their father. They received the full force of his hand in return; however, with her, his outbursts were always confined to verbal skirmishes like last night.

Hiding her fears from Vlad had been a challenge, and ultimately a useless one since Gerry had revealed the inspector's identity the previous day. Now, she had to hope he could control his unreasonable suspicions for the few hours required to complete the inspection.

She wiggled a bit in search of a more relaxing position, without any luck. Her body was still weary, but her mind was racing.

It was two weeks since the letter had arrived. Postmarked San Antonio, Texas, it stated on official letterhead, the exact time and date when aeronautical engineer A. Wachter would arrive to inspect their premises on behalf of the United States Department of Defense. She had been on tenterhooks ever since.

She heard the dog's collar clink on the floor in the kitchen as the clock struck five. Three more hours until she needed to leave for work.

She twisted and turned several more times over the next hour before abandoning further attempts to rest and decided to have a shower.

On her way back to their bedroom, Vlad interrupted his trip to the bathroom to give her a hug and a peck on the cheek. Apparently, he was trying to make up for last night. She'd do her best to meet him half way. Stepping into clean underwear, she threw a housecoat over top and went off to make breakfast. She would finish dressing after Vlad left for work.

When he arrived in the kitchen, their meal waited on the table and she was pouring his coffee.

"Did you sleep well?" Vlad smiled as they sat down together. He didn't wait for her reply, just plunged on. "I've been thinking about what you said last night. You could be right. He may actually be an American. But if his background is German, you still need to watch out for his hands. Germans think they're irresistible. No wife of mine is going to have to fight off some bozo with an attitude no matter where he's from or how wonderful his reputation is."

The warning was typical. Kate forced a smile. "I think I can handle that part. I'm fifty-three, remember? I've gained twenty pounds since I married you and the white streaks are starting to show around my ears. Forget it. Unless the man needs bifocals, he won't be trying to hit on me."

Vlad snorted. "Tell that to the guys at the Legion when we go to their dances. Your eyes are still blue. You're so blonde the white doesn't show. And that bit of extra padding doesn't hurt your figure one little bit."

His attempts to compliment her made her chuckle. "Not every man wants his wife to look like a babushka," she said.

His defensive response was instantaneous. "What's wrong with being a babushka? I loved my grandmother." His expression changed to wistful. "We'd be grandparents by now if your daughter was a natural woman."

Kate headed off the potential tirade about Ruth's interest in her profession and disinterest in marriage. "Most parents aren't in any rush to have their children betray their age to the whole world."

"Most English parents, you mean." He grinned. "I'm a Slav. We're proud of our families."

"I know, I know. Now get out of here." She made a shooing motion with her hands. "Today of all days you can't afford to be late. Since you're responsible for keeping all the machines running he may need to consult with you as much as with Gerry."

Alone again, Kate's tension escalated. She glanced at her watch. Another hour and a half and she'd know.

CHAPTER THREE

Kate set aside her notebook and rose. With the mail sorted and tentative replies drafted, she was temporarily at loose ends. Today, having time to think was not a good thing. It let her traitorous mind recall all those sweet scenes from long ago, a deep voice whispering phrases common to lovers throughout the centuries. Her stomach clenched.

This morning, even her boss was so edgy that he needed to escape. Making an excuse of checking the progress on construction of a new assembly line for the Clean Room, Gerry went down to the shop floor to kill time. While this contract for the American Department of Defense would mean big money for them, it also demanded major changes to the physical plant as well as the installation of previously unnecessary security measures. Experience told Kate this new product must be top secret.

In the office across the hall, the clerk's typewriter clacked, stopped, then started again. Janice looked up as Kate passed on the way to the washroom.

"Relax, woman." Janice grinned. "He's only a man, for goodness sake. You know, puts his pants on one leg at a time. What's he going to do? Complain the coffee's too strong? Forget it."

Kate nodded. Janice was right. Even if the inspector was Andreas, what could he do? She smoothed her hair and examined her face. She was perspiring slightly, her nose shiny, exhaustion painting dark bruises beneath her eyes. She fished her compact from her purse and applied another layer of powder, then grimaced. If she wasn't careful, the creases under her eyes were going to look like cracked plaster. How aging was that? And today of all days, she couldn't bear the thought.

Not that she hadn't changed, of course. It was almost twenty-eight years since she'd fled the rocket research facility while the Americans were evacuating Von Braun's design team. Time had darkened her hair while three children had widened her hips. Her smile was still the same though.

Her hand froze midway through smoothing her hair. What if he didn't recognize her? She rejected the idea instantly. She hadn't changed that much. Had she? She squinted into the mirror again.

Fussing was useless. She couldn't change either her face or her figure. She checked her watch, took a couple of deep breaths, and turned back towards her office. It had to be coincidence even though Wachter was an unusual name and the initial was A. Anthony? Alexander? Adam? There were numerous possibilities.

At her desk, she began placing file folders into separate piles, then rearranging the location of each pile.

Only the tapping of the typewriter next door broke the silence.

Her door stood ajar. The carpeting in the hallway always muffled the sound of approaching footsteps. Suddenly she felt eyes on her back. She turned from the filing cabinet and found their inspector standing in her doorway.

For an instant the aura of power around him took her breath away. He wore a black topcoat and carried a leather briefcase. His elegant mustache and Van Dyke were silver now, and he needed glasses. He had also gained weight with age. The piercing blue eyes and tanned skin were still the same. So were his stance and his instantaneous ability to grasp the nuances of an unfamiliar situation. Tall, erect, handsome and scholarly, he was very much the Andreas Kohlman Wachter she could never quite forget.

"Miss Horbatsky? It is a pleasure to meet you," he said, advancing to stand in front of her desk. He extended his hand.

"Missus, actually," Kate corrected as she walked to meet him, fighting pain. Didn't he know her? "Welcome to Canada, Mr. Wachter. I trust you had a good flight."

He was alive! After all these years, all the tears, all the guilt, all the questions, he had survived. Thank you, God! The sudden stab of disappointment collided with her gratitude, almost choking her. If he didn't recognize her, he couldn't betray her. No one need ever discover what he had once meant to her. She was safe after all.

Relief was quickly followed by a frisson of awareness at the touch of his hand, warm and smooth with the same gentle grip she remembered. The unexpected pleasure shocked her. She felt blood rush into her cheeks. What was she thinking? She was a happily married woman. Throwing her arms around him was not an acceptable reaction. Their past was long behind her even though their daughter was a very real and enduring part of her life.

Rounding her desk with all the confidence she could manage given his appraising inspection of her blush, she detoured to the closet and took out a hanger.

"Let me take your coat. There's coffee in the boardroom if you'd like some. Or we can go straight down to find Mr. Clarke in the production shop."

Before Andreas could respond, Kate's intercom buzzed. It was Gerry from downstairs.

"Any sign of our inspector yet?"

"He just walked in," Kate replied. She could hear the unsteadiness in her voice.

Gerry came immediately to collect their visitor and begin his plant tour.

Kate spent the rest of the morning following dutifully at their heels, recording every question or suggestion Andreas made while Gerry led him around, pointing out an innovative feature of their assembly line here, or a particularly advantageous arrangement of their equipment there.

Even walking near Andreas made Kate shiver. At what point was he going to recognize her? And what would he do when he did?

She fought the urge to develop a sudden flu bug and go home. The last thing she wanted was to make Gerry aware of the history between herself and this supposed stranger.

When the two men broke for lunch Kate declined to join them and slipped out alone for a soup and coffee. The thought of downing solid food under Andreas' watchful eyes made her queasy.

Between sips she fought to order her contrary emotions. Common sense pointed out that she ought to be relieved by Andreas' blindness. As a stranger, she could avoid awkward questions and insinuating remarks. Vlad had no reason to suspect their past. Neither did the family and friends who knew only half her story. Her meticulously-crafted world remained intact. So why did Andreas' indifference hurt so much? What was wrong with her?

Unless he was acting. The sudden thought terrified her. Andreas was definitely intelligent enough to formulate a plan for revenge in an instant. Her disappearance must have hurt him—unless he'd been faking throughout their relationship. Instinct contradicted that thought. In his position there'd been no need for either a proposal or a fake marriage. Yet he'd offered her both.

She returned to her desk even more worried than when she left it.

Her nerves stretched unbearably over the next few hours as the two men resumed their inspection without her. Mid afternoon, they returned to Gerry's office and called for Kate to take more notes.

They were working for several minutes when Andreas stumbled over a word and she looked up to ask for clarification. His gaze was fixed on the scar on her right foot, his jaw tight, his eyes blazing.

Dear God. He knew.

Instantly she looked away, straightened her spine and clutched her suit jacket more tightly around herself. Was it just her imagination or was the room cool? Nerves had raised goose bumps but she must ignore them. She would get through this. One day, two at the most, and Andreas would be off to the next plant.

An accusing pair of icy blue eyes superimposed themselves on her notepad even as the charmingly accented voice resumed dictating at a brisk pace. Feeling Andreas watching her now, she kept her attention fixed on her page, refusing to look up. The moment he finished speaking, Kate scuttled away.

The day was nearly over and she was transcribing her notes when Andreas appeared unexpectedly by her desk.

"I hear you made the arrangements for my hotel room. I must thank you for that, *Mrs. Horbatsky.*"

Despite his deceptively quiet tone, the heavy emphasis on her name shot a chill up Kate's spine. So, she was right. He had recognized her. His silence said he was waiting for her reaction.

That reaction was a desire to scream. How dare he take such a sarcastic tone with her! What had he expected, that she'd remain single? She had expected him to make a new life for himself after the surrender at Oberammergau in 1945. Why should she not have done the same?

It took Kate a moment to master her temper.

"Can I persuade you to have dinner with me this evening?" he continued.

She met his gaze and shook her head. "My husband is expecting me home. Thank you all the same."

Before he could say more, Gerry emerged from his office.

"There you are, Andreas. My wife and I would like you to join us for dinner."

When Andreas nodded, Gerry continued. "There's a good restaurant directly across from your hotel and I had Kate book us a table. How does six-thirty suit you? That will give you time to freshen up a bit and let me collect my wife."

Gerry's distraction was a relief. Kate watched the two men exit together. Needing to compose herself before going home to face Vlad, she finished typing a few more paragraphs before venturing down to the parking lot in search of her own car.

With her mind skipping between men like water droplets on a hot griddle, the drive to their rural home was torture. First Andreas sat across Gerry's desk from her, laying out his vision for their future together. Then Vlad's stern face reminded her how he'd react if she didn't keep her mind on him. She had no thoughts to spare for the potential dangers inherent on snowy dirt roads in the early evening darkness.

Andreas was older, certainly, but all his charm remained. His smile came less frequently but with no less devastating effect upon her senses. She had to get her priorities straight. He no longer had any place in her life.

Supper. What was she going to make for supper? She'd set out pork chops before she left for work. They were easy. A can of mushroom soup over them in the oven, and a Caesar salad. Maybe some chips. Vlad liked fruit. What did she have stashed in the cupboard? Canned peaches? With ice cream and the last of the muffins. It wasn't what she had originally planned, but she could manage it without a lot of concentration. Tonight, concentration wasn't coming easily.

Vlad's truck was still warm when she brushed against the hood on her way through the garage to the back door. Since he finished work shortly after three and it was now five-thirty she wondered what had delayed his return to their house.

The smell when she opened the kitchen door gave her the answer. Chinese food? He'd brought home Chinese food for supper? What had prompted that?

Vlad was lying on the couch reading the paper. "Smells good," she told him as she passed through the family room to hang up her coat in the front hall closet.

Vlad laid the newspaper aside and followed her. "Well, you looked worried enough this morning that I figured you needed a bit of a boost. Supper was the only way I knew to help. So, how did it go?"

Help? If only he knew. Warmth crept over her at his considerate gesture.

"I survived, thank you. He offered quite a few suggestions. Worthwhile ones, I'd say. At least, Gerry's taking them seriously."

"And how does he strike you?" Vlad persisted.

Kate feigned nonchalance. "Serious, knowledgeable, pleasant enough in a no nonsense way." The response was honest, if incomplete.

Vlad nodded. "*Da*. I got the feeling he knows his business. I'm not so sure how much he can benefit us, but if a thumbs up from him is what it takes to keep the Americans happy…well, why not?"

His arms slid around her and drew her back against him. He dropped a kiss on the side of her neck. "Hungry?"

She gave him another smile and hugged him in return. "Yup. Starved. Let's eat now before everything goes cold."

Kate had cleared the table and was loading the dishwasher when the telephone rang. She glanced at the clock and, knowing that cheaper long distance rates kicked in at six, immediately knew the identity of their caller.

Ruth's cheerful greeting brought an instant smile. "Wanted to call before *Ironside* came on," she said. "What are you doing Saturday night? Laura Sabia is speaking at Massey Hall. I have two tickets. Will you come? I can pick you up in the afternoon and we'll have supper together, then go on to the hall. It won't run late. You'll be home early enough to get up for church in the morning."

Kate hesitated. She enjoyed time with her elder daughter. She just wasn't terribly interested in the National Action Committee for Women.

"I don't know, Ruth…"

"Oh for goodness sake, Mom. You're a woman. You need to know what's happening for women these days."

Kate sighed. "I already know as much as I want to."

"No, you don't!" Ruth protested. "Men still run your life. Pop snaps his fingers and you jump. Gerry dictates and you scurry away to follow orders."

"And you don't do what your boss says?" Kate countered. "Come on, now. You know you do, otherwise you wouldn't still have a job."

"Yeah, but it isn't the same. Adam just tells me the finished design needs to do this and this. He doesn't tell me how to design it."

It wasn't an argument either of them would win since they were both right. Kate short-circuited the disagreement. "Yes. You don't have to come for me. I'll drive to your apartment around three. How's that?"

"Great. I've got a new place on Queen Street that I want to take you to. They do the greatest schnitzels. And their tortes are to die for."

Kate laughed. "And I feel size sixteen coming on."

"So? Who are you dieting for? That's what Laura and NAC are saying. Women need to do things for themselves, not worry about what their men think all the time."

Kate didn't reply. What was the point? Ruth lived in a city where neighbors were strangers, immersed in their own lives and totally indifferent to those around them. Staid, old-fashioned Milton didn't operate that way. Kate had grown up with half the town and the other half knew

23

her by reputation. She had raised enough eyebrows by returning to work when the kids entered school instead of joining the sewing circle or volunteering at the hospital. Much more independence and Vlad's friends would be ribbing him about not knowing how to keep his woman in her place.

Vlad turned down the television's volume and watched Kate cross to her rocker and her knitting. "What did Ruth want?"

"To take me to supper in Toronto on Saturday." Kate wasn't lying. She was just editing her response.

"And you agreed?"

Kate shrugged. "Why not? She is my daughter. I don't see a lot of her now that she's working."

Vlad snorted. "What's a healthy woman of her age doing making a date with her mother? Can't she find more appropriate company? Where's her young man?"

"I didn't ask."

"That's the trouble with you," Vlad grumbled. "You never take her to task like you should. As you said, you're her mother. It's your responsibility to teach her about duty. Working's all very well until she marries. Only she isn't showing any interest in marriage. What does she think? Guys are going to want her when she's too old to have kids? I'd understand if she were ugly, but she's not. It's that damn job of hers. She intimidates men."

It was a familiar argument and Kate tried to ignore it.

"Well?"

She shook her head. "Ruth's a big girl. I can't tell her what to do any more. There's no point in trying. It just makes her more stubborn, more determined to go her own way."

"I wonder where she got that from?" Vlad glared at Kate. "At least you knew what was good for you."

"Yes, dear." Kate chuckled as Vlad scowled, and turned his attention back to the evening newscast. "Just hope that Tanya doesn't come to share her big sister's ideas when she graduates. You wouldn't want two independent women in this family."

CHAPTER FOUR

Andreas followed the waiter to a table beside a bank of windows. The Clarkes had not yet arrived. He ordered a beer, leaned back to wait, and gazed indifferently around the half-empty room.

Not many diners this evening. Was that indicative of the quality of food they served here? Probably not. More likely, just the wrong day of the week to find the place full of couples escaping their family commitments in search of a few private moments. It was a small town, after all. Friday was the traditional night for eating out and Milton residents likely retained that habit.

Remembering when he, too, had enjoyed private moments, Andreas again fought back his anger and allowed himself to ponder the afternoon's events. He was still in shock. To find Katrina after all this time.... He'd stopped looking years ago.

When he first arrived, she was just another faceless secretary in another anonymous office. He hadn't really looked at her. Just the same, he berated himself for not recognizing her sooner. How ironic that he ignored the instinct drawing him to her as yet another unwelcome attack of the lust that occasionally surfaced despite his years of celibacy. After his marriage failed he consciously avoided women, convinced that he would never again find the contentment he experienced with Katrina.

All morning he'd felt he was overlooking an important detail, but he couldn't put a finger on it. Then, partway through the afternoon, absorbed in dictation in Gerry's office, she'd slipped her foot free of one shoe, letting it swing on her toe. The shapely curve of her calf caught his eye and he followed it admiringly down to her ankle. That's when he saw it, the white star on her instep. The sight was so familiar he quite literally caught his breath, overwhelmed by memory and pain.

He'd been with her when she got it. An Allied bomb had struck their lab knocking a great hole in the roof and sending structural supports and equipment flying in all directions. When he crawled out from under a section of ceiling, he found her pinned by her desk, a shard of steel through her foot. He freed her and, knowing how overwhelmed their emergency medical service would be, he did the initial disinfecting and bandaging himself. Then he carried her to a safe place in the parking lot before returning to help with rescuing others. How many times in the ensuing months had he kissed that scar when making love to her?

He had looked to see if Gerry noticed his reaction. Katrina's boss didn't need to know about their shared past.

With recognition came the need to examine Kate more critically. Her general shape and her smile remained familiar, but, like him, she had gained some weight. The different hairstyle and glasses had aged her shockingly. In his memory, Katrina was still fresh-faced and young.

He had planned to confront her over supper, but Gerry's invitation had ruined that idea.

The waiter arrived with his beer. Andreas glanced at his watch and took a large swig of the cool ale. It wasn't like German beer, but it was better than the watered-down concoction that passed for beer in the United States.

Turning his face to the windows, he took another sip and returned to his memories. She came into his life innocently enough. As a member of Wernher Von Braun's rocket design team he had used whatever secretary was available in the typing pool when he needed to dictate a report. Katrina first caught his attention when his regular girl was down with the flu. Quickly discovering her superior skills, he singled her out to do his future work, and, despite her protests, to become his mistress. Upon realizing she was truly an innocent, not a coy tease, he became protective, a new and unsettling experience for him. Almost instantly he was as determined to please her, as he was to teach her how to please him. God, how she pleased him!

With no previous interest in long-term relationships, the depth of his new emotions shocked him. He wanted marriage—now—and found her excuses to wait for the war's end frustrating. Between coaxing and threatening, he managed to persuade her to live with him and, for the sake of propriety, pretend to be his wife. She seemed content and apparently wore his ring with pride. Which was why losing her had hit him so hard. Damn it, all! What had possessed her to just vanish?

The realities of war had seldom intruded into their personal world. Allied attacks rarely reached their workplace. Indeed, the greatest upsets resulted from the political machinations of the various megalomaniacs who interfered with their work. Their boss, Wernher Von Braun bore the brunt of that interference.

The big upheaval began in the spring of 1945 when they realized that the Russians were less than two hundred kilometers from their labs. Knowing what their fate was likely to be should they fall into Russian hands, the team agreed to have Von Bruan try to arrange their surrender to either the Americans or the British. Before he could act, two unrelated German authorities devised other plans for them. Himmler's toady Kessler decided to move them all to Oberammergau where they'd be safer from Allied attacks. Simultaneously, some general commandeered them into his army with the intent of sending them to fight at the front. Von Braun felt Kessler's plan was most advantageous to them, despite the dangers of living under continual S.S. surveillance.

Andreas managed to bring Kate with them to the new lab but Allied air strikes provided the excuse for Von Braun to move the team away from the lab into private billets in surrounding villages. Then his brother found an American soldier and surrendered on the team's behalf.

All hell let lose for the next two days. While Von Braun was at American headquarters hammering out an agreement to evacuate his team to the U.S., the S.S. roamed the area, searching for him and interrogating everyone at random.

The morning they were to leave for the American base, the team gathered at the lab. Kate went with him, but he lost her in the confusion of boarding the trucks. No one he asked had seen her. Desperate, he'd raced back to their room. She wasn't there.

Only when he found her wedding ring on the bedside table did he realize Katrina wasn't going to the States. She had left him. All identifiable traces of her presence had vanished. Her papers, the few photographs of her, anything bearing her handwriting, all had gone along with the woman he loved. Except for the ring, it was as if she had never existed.

He told Von Braun and the Americans nothing, of course. So far as his boss and co-workers were concerned Katrina was simply among the missing.

He had carried on, alone and hurting, grieving as did the others who lost loved ones. He'd tried to forget. Sometimes he succeeded. Then something would trigger her memory, wrenching open the old wound, leaving it as fresh and raw as it had been in the beginning.

His mind teemed with questions. Why had she left like that? Hadn't she trusted him to protect her? Where had she gone? How had Horbatsky come into her life? How had she managed to assimilate so well that he could mistake his German mistress for a native-born Canadian?

Somehow, leaving his ring had been the worst insult. It seemed a complete rejection of him and all they shared. Besides, from a purely practical standpoint, why abandon something that could have been turned into cash for traveling expenses or bribes?

Meanwhile, he realized he found her as attractive as ever. Watching her sitting across the desk this afternoon, he had wanted desperately to haul her into his lap and kiss her giddy the way he used to do. Or slap her silly. His actions would depend on the mood her answers created. They'd need to be good answers to erase his years of frustration.

Of course he had no idea how she felt. She was married now and normally he respected that commitment. This, however, was different. She'd belonged to him first. Had she forgotten him or did traces of memory still linger? She was pleasant this morning, and even seemed pleased by his arrival. Damn it! She was going to provide answers before they parted again.

Gerry and his wife, Helen, arrived just as Andreas was draining his glass. Introductions performed, fresh drinks ordered for everyone, and their meals selected, the trio sat back to exchange pleasantries and to build their business relationship.

Andreas had already realized the depth of Gerry's commitment to producing a quality product. It was a business ethic he admired. But his interest was personal. The new version of satellite-based missile guidance systems that Gerry hoped to build for the U.S. Air Force was Andreas' invention. Given that circumstance, he would offer Gerry any professional assistance possible, no matter how fleeting their personal acquaintance.

Gerry began explaining his ideas the moment the waiter deposited their drinks and departed.

"I know you're still designing and that's going to keep you busy. But I also hear you've agreed to oversee compliance for a couple of other suppliers. Could you fit us into your schedule too? We've met military standards in the past, but laser technology is more exacting. I don't want to risk our investment because we can't maintain the quality they need in this contract. I think you could get my guys on track fairly quickly and regular visits would keep them there."

The question caught Andreas by surprise. Retired from active involvement with the American Department of Defense, he still did some consulting for them. These days, with neither financial worries nor family commitments to keep him in Texas, he worked mainly to keep busy.

The proposal met his interests so perfectly he was almost suspicious. Could Katrina have suggested it? That would be too good to be true.

He knew his answer immediately, but prudence dictated that he pretend to consider the matter. Instant acceptance would only make Gerry suspicious.

They were waiting for their desserts to arrive when Andreas raised the subject of Kate's excellent grasp of German.

"I'm intrigued with your Mrs. Horbatsky, Gerry," he said. "The way she was able to pick up when I stumbled into German terms this afternoon says she understands the language very well. I didn't know German was commonly spoken in Canada." He trailed off expectantly.

Gerry grinned. "Kate's Canadian, a Milton native. She once told me she learned to like Germans when she was six. That was when a newly arrived family with a daughter her age moved in next door. They became best friends and taught each other their languages. I forgot she spoke it, actually, she's been home so long."

"Home? From where?" Andreas' interest was no pretense. This time Helen plunged in.

"Kate's one of Canada's special veterans," she said with pride. "She served with the British S.O.E for a time during World War II. By the time it ended, she was widowed and had a little girl."

S.O.E? The British Special Operations Executive? Katrina was one of them?

Only long years of self-discipline prevented him from shuddering physically in revulsion at the monstrous image Helen had created.

A spy. The woman he loved, the ideal to which no other woman had ever been able to measure up, had been a traitor sent to trap him. The realization made him sick.

Helen was still speaking. He forced himself to listen. "When she came home, Kate settled right in to working for Gerry's dad. She was doing a fine job of raising Ruth with no help from anyone until Vlad came along."

"Vlad?" Andreas looked across to Gerry. "That's Horbatsky, I take it. Didn't I meet him this morning?"

Gerry nodded. "Yes. He's the head of our maintenance crew. He was newly arrived from Germany when he started working for us in 1949. I think that was part of the bond between them. He and Kate both had a past to cope with and they seemed to understand each other."

Andreas nodded and turned the conversation in another direction. Through the rest of the meal he only half-heard his hosts' comments as his nerves twitched and his mind churned. S.O.E. So that was why she'd fled. Despite their official alliance, as a spy, she knew being British was no protection from the Russians. Surely she'd have been safe with the Americans.

# # #

Andreas found his mind so consumed by the revelations about Kate that he couldn't face what he had expected would be a pleasant evening. Pleading weariness, the moment the meal ended, he begged off the proposed move to the bar and headed for the privacy of his hotel room.

Alone at last, he stripped off his jacket and tie, broke the seal on a single-shot bottle from his mini bar, and collapsed in the padded chair by the window. His mind whirled as his aching heart battled his shattered pride. He couldn't believe she had deceived him so completely. He'd yearned for her for so long, and now he'd found her only to discover she was an impostor. His fingers twitched with the urge to encircle her throat. How dare she!

He drained the glass in two swallows and kicked off his shoes before returning to the bar for a second bottle.

Her disappearance had driven him to the verge of despair because he feared for her safety. This treachery was far worse. To think he'd worried about her for all these years—rejected other women as unworthy to succeed her—while she had been with him only because he was useful.

Sipping the third drink, he remembered the ploys she used to delay his attempts to force her into marriage. First, she claimed to be already married to a man who was a prisoner in Russia. When that failed, she said they were engaged, but she felt compelled to break the engagement before committing herself legally to another man. At the time, he'd admired her loyalty even as it frustrated him. Now he wondered whether Horbatsky had been that long-ago fiancé she couldn't reject. Yet how could that be? Clarke claimed she was a Canadian. Horbatsky was a Slav of some sort. How could that relationship have predated theirs if Horbatsky only arrived in Canada after the war?

He got up to return to the mini bar and promptly tripped over a shoe. Furious, he grabbed it, hurled it at the hall door, then pitched its mate after it for good measure.

Fresh drink in hand, he stood by the window. Headlights on the nearby highway lit up the night sky and his eyes wandered unseeing over the snow-laden cars in the lot below.

The knowledge that Kate came home with a child poured acid on old wounds. He had always wanted children and his wife tried hard to please him. Lora miscarried six times. At the time of her death in a car accident on an icy highway in 1960, they hadn't shared a pleasant conversation, let alone a bed, for nearly three years.

The more he pondered, the deeper his pain became and the more he raged. How could he have been such a fool, wasting so much emotion on something he couldn't change? He had always prided himself on his rationality.

Yet even now, regret rode him as powerfully as ever. He hated her. Didn't he?

The neat whiskey in his glass made its way to his belly and lay there, burning. Who had fathered Kate's child? Whoever he was, she hadn't wasted any time in finding him. He wondered whether she could have been seeing this other lover while she was living with him. He found he was clenching his fists. Good thing the man wasn't here.

Pacing released some of his tension but not enough to let him sleep. He considered going for a walk, but it was nearing midnight and it was snowing.

After relieving himself, he moved to the basin to wash. He couldn't ignore the face accusing him from the mirror. Healthy. Handsome. Intelligent. Respected by his peers, yet totally enslaved by a sneaky witch who, even now, made his heart race. What was the matter with him?

Disgusted with himself, he shuffled over to the bed and dropped down on top of the covers. The last thing he remembered was a mental image of Kate cradling a bundle in a pink blanket. Again, his churning thoughts questioned who had fathered that child. Where was this man who left her with his bastard?

Awakening late, he reaffirmed his previous decision even as he gulped pain pills for his headache and shaved hastily. He would accept Gerry's job offer, and before he finished, Katrina would pay for her duplicity.

CHAPTER FIVE

When Andreas arrived the next morning, Kate was already at her desk. He ignored her, going directly to Gerry's office and closing the door behind him. They exchanged the normal greetings, and then he announced his decision.

"I can fit you into my schedule but not until I finish a job in Kingston," he said. "I will not be free for at least six weeks."

Gerry shrugged. "The soldering booths haven't even arrived yet and they have to be installed when they do get here. The timing sounds just about right." He rose. "Do you want to come downstairs now and take another look at my layout before you go?"

They were engrossed in discussing improvements to the ventilation system when Kate interrupted them with a message about a customer. Andreas watched her speak to Gerry with the familiarity of longstanding acquaintance while pain stoked the anger he thought he had mastered.

"He says he's leaving the office in a few minutes and he has to know your answer before he goes. He's holding on line three," she concluded.

Gerry sighed and nodded. "I'd better handle it then, or he'll cancel our order. Excuse me, Andreas. I'll take it on Vlad's phone so I don't waste time running up to my office. This shouldn't take long."

He strode away.

Kate turned to leave. Andreas caught her arm tightly. "Does your husband know what you did?" he asked softly.

Her lips tightened fractionally and, lifting her chin, she looked over his shoulder rather than at him. "Of course."

He almost whispered. "And does he know who I am?"

When she remained silent, his fingers gripped harder, biting into her forearm. He knew he was hurting her and took satisfaction in the bruises he was inflicting. He wanted to see her bleed.

Her glance snapped instantly to his. "Should he?"

"Obviously he knows about your child," Andreas continued, louder now. "But does he know who fathered her?" A betraying blink gave him his answer. "So I could claim her."

She gave him a startled look and tried to jerk free. "You wouldn't."

"Why not, *Liebling*? If I had had my way she would have been mine. She and all your children. Just as you pretended to be mine." His voice rose as he continued. "Did you enjoy it, making a fool of the Kraut? Worming your way into my heart, betraying my work to your superiors.

Was it fun, knowing how I trusted you and how thoroughly you were deceiving me?"

She stopped struggling. The color drained from her cheeks and she looked away. He saw her swallow before she met his gaze again and her eyes were moist. She spoke quietly.

"No, Andreas. I took no pleasure in what I did. To be honest, I deeply regret the life we couldn't share. I don't expect you to believe me and it's too late now anyway. However, if it helps, maybe you should know. I loved you very much. Under different circumstances, I would have been proud to be your wife."

The apparent sincerity of her admission shocked him. For an instant, he believed her. Then reality intruded. This was the woman who shared his bed for two years, and his work for months before that. All the while he trusted her she was passing information about his work to the enemy.

He dropped his hand from her arm and stepped back. "What is it you say? Save the tears? Just so you know, somehow I don't believe you." He made his voice heavy with sarcasm as he added, "But it was a good try, *Liebling*."

He pasted a half-smile on his face and watched her leave, threading her way between the work stations, her speed just a fraction below running. He should be proud of himself for making her retreat. He wasn't.

###

When he vacated his office, Vlad had intended to speak to the welder working on the construction at the east end of the shop. He changed his mind the moment he saw

Kate talking to Andreas in the doorway to the Clean Room. They were oblivious of their surroundings, totally absorbed in their discussion. Vlad couldn't hear their words but he could see the rage in the German's posture. He could also see the whiteness of the knuckles on the hand gripping Kate's arm.

His instinct was to challenge the man. In the same instant he realized she was not struggling. Her calm demeanor made him suspicious. He knew she could fight back when necessary. So why was she letting this German maul her?

She was fair and well shaped, the way Germans liked their women. Could he be propositioning her? Vlad expected that behavior of such a man; one with looks, prestige, and money.

Vlad stood by his office and waited. He saw Kate say something to the German, something he didn't like. He spit out a reply and virtually pushed her away. Kate's hasty departure told Vlad she was no happier than the German. Now that was interesting. What could cause a quarrel between strangers? On the other hand, were they strangers? His breath caught on the thought. She had served behind the German lines all those years ago. What was going on?

For the rest of his shift Vlad fretted over what he had observed. He wanted to rush upstairs and confront Kate, but experience had taught him better. The German was due to leave after lunch. The problem, whatever it was, would end with his departure. Their discussion could wait until they were alone. Tonight, he would demand answers.

That evening he pretended to read the paper and watched Kate over the top of the pages. She went about her usual tasks by habit, her motions routine, her mind far away. Although she responded when he spoke, her manner was distant. The German was gone and she should be relieved to have things back to normal. She did not seem to be.

He waited until the evening newscast was over and Kate had picked up her knitting. Amos lay by her feet, his eyes closed, totally relaxed if not asleep.

"So he is gone," Vlad began. There was no need to identify the subject of his comment. "You should be relieved to get back to normal."

She nodded, apparently absorbed in counting a row of stitches.

"So why aren't you?"

She immediately stopped counting, her finger frozen on a stitch. He could tell he had her attention although she had not looked up. He continued.

"Why were you fighting with him this morning?"

"We weren't fighting," she said, her eyes still on her work, her tone remarkably steady.

"The man grabbed your arm and yelled at you. If I did that, you'd call it fighting."

She shrugged and resumed knitting. Obviously she was going to make him pry it out of her, whatever *it* was.

"What did you do to him?"

She took a deep breath. "I betrayed him."

Her tone was soft, almost regretful. It caught Vlad completely off guard. "You betray...what do you mean, you betrayed him?"

"Somehow he's found out that I was a spy. That I was there to feed information to the Allies, information about his designs."

"His designs?" Vlad connected the fragments. "The Kraut was one of the engineers designing rockets for the Nazis?"

She nodded.

"What's he doing here, then? Do his bosses know what he did? How could he have wound up working for NASA?" Vlad couldn't believe the Americans realized they had had a former Nazi working in such a sensitive area as national defense. "Was that it? He was afraid you'd tell someone about his Nazi past?"

Kate shook her head. "No. That's not a problem. That's how he got to America, actually. As one of the chief designers on Wernher Von Braun's rocket team, the Americans welcomed him and his skills. His past is no secret and no threat."

Vlad frowned. "Then what the hell is wrong? How can you threaten him?"

"I don't. I simply infuriate him. Rocket research was secret. Security was very tight at the laboratories. Even the German public didn't know what was going on inside. To think that a spy worked there for three years affronts his belief in their system."

A second fact penetrated Vlad's confusion. "He recognized you. Is that it? He knew you when you worked in the facility?"

Again, she nodded.

"And did you recognize him?" He was getting angry.

"Yes." The admission was quietly made. Her eyes remained on her needles. Her fingers flew. She was not going to elaborate.

"You knew this man and you did not tell me who he was?" It was his job to protect his family from scandal and her silence undermined that effort.

At last she set her work in her lap and looked over at him. "Why should I? I don't tell you every time I meet an old classmate in the street. Why did you need to know that I once worked with this man in a laboratory in Germany?"

His rage spiked. "I have a right to know when someone can threaten you," he growled.

"And exactly how can he threaten me?" She remained calm.

It infuriated Vlad that she should be so blind. "He was far from rational this morning. How will you control his lies about your role in Germany?"

She shrugged. "He won't be talking about our encounters. He's too embarrassed that he didn't realize I was a spy. There is no point getting upset over my past."

"Your past!" Vlad spit the words. "No sensible woman did the things you did. It's a wonder you weren't killed. When did you realize who this man was?"

"When he walked through the office door."

"Not before?" He could hear the suspicion in his voice.

"I suspected it could be him when we got his letter. But I could have been wrong. I saw no point borrowing trouble."

Vlad snorted. "And you knew him well?"

Kate picked up her needles and glanced at her pattern. As though the German was unimportant, she said, "I was a secretary in the office where his reports were written."

"So you saw him every day?" He persisted.

She shrugged. "Yes."

"Did you date?"

Kate dropped her hands to her lap and shook her head. "Do you think I dated Gerry just because we work together? Honestly, Vlad. Listen to yourself. Why do you think I wouldn't tell you about once working near Andreas? I don't need your ridiculous jealousy. It just upsets us both for no reason. Let it be."

He glowered at her in silence for several minutes. She had avoided his question, he noticed. Should he repeat it? Force her to tell him the truth? Her avoidance was an answer in itself, and he wasn't sure he wanted to hear the actual words. When she resumed her knitting and remained silent, he changed the subject. "We've got a choice of hockey or *The Smothers Brothers*." Her look told him not to be so foolish. He knew they never watched sports.

He felt cold when he wakened in the night. Kate was lying quite separate from him on her side of the bed.

Also, she was wearing a long-sleeved flannel nightgown, something she rarely did. Since she complained they were too warm, he suspected she'd donned it to conceal her bruised arm. He cursed the Kraut silently and yanked the covers tighter around himself.

By Saturday, Kate's bruises had faded to dull brown, and Vlad's suspicion to silent, but speculative looks. With a mixture of apprehension and anticipation, Kate drove to Toronto to meet her daughter at her apartment. Something told her that Ruth had more than a libber lecture on her mind.

Future Bakery, a little bakery-cum-delicatessen to which they went for supper, was decidedly European in its presentation. The wire racks bulged with bread of all kinds. The hot table steamed with borsht, cabbage rolls, chicken Kiev and half a dozen fish and meat casseroles. The counter filled with cakes and sweets made her drool. No tablecloths. Heavy crockery. Plain cutlery in buckets where customers picked up their own. No pretensions. Just good food and small village atmosphere.

Nor was the décor geared for the tourist. A portrait of a well-recognized icon jostled for space with photographs of Kiev, and stylized drawings of ox carts, the steppes and Cossack dancers. Corkboard plastered with newspaper stories covered a second wall. While she recognized the Cyrillic letters, Kate did not read the language and knew only that the papers must have been smuggled out of Ukraine so that customers could see firsthand what their relatives at home were being told about the world.

Kate set her well-filled plate on one of the few vacant tables and took her seat. Ruth unloaded her tray, then took the chair opposite her mother. "What do you think?" She grinned. "I told you I'd found a little treasure."

"I'll have to bring Vlad," Kate said. "He'll be able to read the papers."

They had barely begun to eat when Ruth raised the subject of her new home. "I haven't mentioned it before," she said, "because I figured you wouldn't approve of me buying a house on my own."

"Why ever not?"

"You're such a stickler for marriage I expected you to think Martin should buy it."

"And so he should, if you were getting married. Or at least, he should be paying for half of it."

"He's too cheap." Ruth's was stating a fact, not opinion. "He'll never own a house. He thinks the upkeep far outweighs the value of the investment."

"The man's a fool."

Ruth nodded. "Yeah. He's good enough company, well-mannered, that sort of thing, but he's not husband material."

Kate nodded. While Ruth would never say the words, Kate understood the unspoken message. Martin had his uses, and thanks to the advent of the birth control pill, Ruth could enjoy them without marriage.

Pre-marital sex wasn't something that Kate approved, but neither did she favor divorce, and she'd seen what happened to marriages based strictly on hormones.

Then she gave herself a mental shake. How dare she criticize her daughter for following her own example? Martin was no Andreas, she reminded herself. It saddened her to think that Ruth might never know the kind of love in which she had been conceived.

Vlad was the one who'd get genuinely upset once he realized what was happening. He'd see it as yet another affront to his ability to set an example for his family that his step-daughter didn't want a relationship like the one her mother shared with him.

"So why hang around with him? Other men read that sort of loyalty as a hands off sign."

Ruth shrugged. "I'm not that interested in marriage. With the right man, I'm sure I could adapt. But I don't have to live by small town standards. I'm quite happy looking after myself, doing things by myself and for myself."

"So you're buying your own house and tackling the joys of ownership to prove the point." Kate didn't try to hide her sarcasm.

"No." Ruth looked hurt. "I think real estate is a great investment. Right now houses in Port Credit are fairly cheap. Their value will rise over time. If Mr. Right pops up and wants to whirl me away into never-never land, I can always sell. I'm sure I can get my money back at least: probably even make a profit."

"I'm sorry. I should have realized…" Kate stopped herself before she said how much Ruth thought like her father. The inclination to invest for the future was typical of Andreas. "I applaud your courage, and your practicality, Ruth. You're quite right about owning your own home. Married or single, it doesn't matter. You know enough to do your own repairs. And if you can't, you can at least detect a line when some contractor tries to feed it to you. Yes, it's a smart move."

"You mean that, don't you?" Now Ruth looked surprised. "You didn't buy a house when we came home from Europe so I didn't think you'd approve of it."

Now it was Kate's turn to feel hurt. "I didn't have time. Houses were scarce then and men with families got first choice. I had a roof over our heads with Grandma and Grandpa and with you so young, I still needed Grandma to look after you. I was saving for a house, though. I had an account set up and I was working on the down payment. Then Vlad came along and you know the rest."

Ruth's expression changed, grew subtly more respectful. "I never knew that."

"There's plenty you don't know about me," Kate replied, her tone sharp. "We're far more alike than you realize. That's part of why Vlad gets so angry with you."

Ruth grinned. "Oh, is that it."

"And he's going to get plenty angry when he finds out your opinion of Martin," Kate continued. "He'll have a point, too. Continuing the relationship is like posting a keep out sign to other men. Not smart, my dear. Not when there really are such things as good men."

"Like my dad?"

Kate's heart lurched at the question, despite the twinkle in her daughter's eye. She was saved the need to answer when Ruth plunged on to an equally dangerous topic.

"How did Wachter's visit go?" she asked. "There's quite a bit of chatter about him in the industry these days. Over and over I hear about his arrogance and I wondered how you saw him, given that you worked with real Germans."

"Real Germans?" Kate smiled. "As opposed to phony ones like me?"

"Mother. You know what I mean."

Kate grinned and nodded. "I suppose he could be seen as arrogant. But he knows his business and he has no time for incompetence. He projects authority. It's a typically German trait to my mind. What can I say?"

What, indeed, when she had to conceal their former relationship. At the same time, guilt pricked her soul for denying her daughter information about her own father. "Why are you so interested?"

Ruth shrugged. "We're in the same business. I hear he'll be supervising a number of Canadair's suppliers until they get this new plane of theirs up and running. If it's true, he'll be around the area for months. You never know. I just might run into him one day."

Kate almost choked. Ruth and Andreas meet? Dear God! The thought appalled her even though she knew appearances would never betray Ruth's parentage. She was small and dark, completely unlike either of them. Andreas would have no reason to suspect his role in her birth and Ruth believed her father was dead.

CHAPTER SIX

When he left Milton, Andreas wasn't enthusiastic about his upcoming six weeks in Kingston. He felt cheated that he couldn't be in Kate's face daily, sniping at her over little errors, perhaps making her nervous enough to create big ones.

Sadly, it wasn't going to happen. Gradually work consumed him, wearing away at his anger and blotting out his pain. Only in the empty hours between evening meals and the arrival of sleep did he have time to remember. Nor did he find it easy to develop a suitable strategy for revenge.

Destroying her career, after twenty loyal years with Gerry, was an unviable proposition. Nor did he have the stomach to attempt to lure her into an affair. Besides, his own career would be ruined if word got out that he'd tried to seduce a married woman at one of his contract positions. Regardless, he wanted her to suffer as he had.

Then, mere days before he was to return to Milton, the answer struck him. He needed a new girlfriend to make Kate jealous. Someone to fuck and forget. Only, it couldn't be just any woman. That's wouldn't hurt Kate. It must be her daughter. The girl was young, of course, only somewhere in her twenties. Just the same, some women were attracted to older men with money and prestige. He wondered if she was already married? From what Helen Clarke had said, he didn't think so.

Andreas could picture Kate writhing while the residents of Milton gossiped about Ruth. The best part was that Kate could say nothing, unless she wanted her daughter to know about their relationship thirty years ago. Yes, Ruth Horbatsky was the perfect weapon to extract his revenge. He beamed at the thought.

Ruth's venture into home ownership brought back memories for Kate. She had had her own plans for their future when she was discharged. Marriage had seemed unlikely unless she lied about Ruth's birth. She was reluctant to found a relationship on a falsehood.

Envisioning herself as a single mother, she had expected to support herself. Ordinary secretarial jobs were not highly paid, but private secretaries for influential executives made reasonable money. These days she seldom recalled those unrealized dreams. Vlad was a good man and she was reasonably content in her marriage. It didn't offer the rapture she had known with Andreas, but then, she had never expected it would.

First love—puppy love, her parents would have called it—developed on the magic of newness. Common sense told her that subsequent lovers, no matter how skillful, could never recapture that. Indeed, finding a man willing to marry a widow with a young child was in itself a miracle at a time when attractive, single women abounded. Vlad guessed she was no widow, and yet he never threw her scandalous past in her face. Of course, he didn't suspect then that Ruth's father had been her German boss, Andreas Kohlman Wachter. Nor did he realize how she had anglicized Andreas' name. Like Ruth, he thought Kate's lover had been an English pilot named Andrew Coleman.

Only occasionally now did he throw a tantrum that betrayed his Cossack heritage. For instance, he'd been furious with her for returning to Clarke's when Tanya entered elementary school. He professed to understand her need to do something more than laundry, cooking, and cleaning. She knew at heart he thought she should jump into the catty world of volunteer work favored by most housewives seeking escape from the boring isolation of their lives.

While he seemed to have put Andreas out of his mind, she couldn't be sure. There were still moments when she'd catch him watching her with that faraway look in his eyes that told her he was remembering something from his past.

#

Vlad spent the final Saturday morning of March shoveling snow further away from the edges of the driveway. While winter should have passed by now, the weather wasn't following its traditional pattern this year. He was determined to use any good day Mother Nature offered to push back the drifts in preparation for the next storm.

Despite the crush of assignments and studying for their approaching final exams, all three kids came home to celebrate Alexi's birthday. Vlad enjoyed having them around. He didn't share the Canadian notion that each generation of a family should live in a separate house. He wouldn't fight Kate about it, of course, but he planned to insist that Alexi and Tanya move back home as soon as they graduated.

He had to admit, however, that Ruth's absence was a positive thing. He didn't want Tanya developing her half-sister's disrespectful attitudes. Ruth was a perfect example of inherited ills. The two girls had grown up in the same house, with the same influences and yet one was smart and obedient while the other was determined to misuse both her looks and her talents, and mock every family value a proper woman should cherish. Ruth's behavior must be the result of her father's genes.

One side of him was honored to be asked to inspect the house she had just purchased. The other side, however, recognized her request for what it was, a sop to his pride. She had completed the deal without consulting him first. Nor had her boyfriend been involved in any way, something Vlad considered unforgivable until Ruth informed him she did not intend to marry Martin.

"You've been seeing him for three years and he won't marry you?" Vlad was appalled. "How long have you known this?" When she told him the choice was hers, not Martin's, he was even more shocked. "Does he know this?" he asked. When she nodded, he carried straight on. "Then why are the two of you still together—as if I didn't know. I suppose there won't be any *small accidents.*" He emphasized the words heavily. "But that doesn't make it any better. You disgust me, Ruth Coleman!" He drew satisfaction from the fact she didn't use his name any more —at least not professionally, but it was little comfort here where his friends would always think of her as his child.

Alexi's car pulled into the driveway and stopped in front of the garage doors. Tanya was with him. They got out and began unloading the groceries they had picked up in town for their mother.

Vlad glanced at his watch and realized Kate would probably have the meal on the table. He hefted his shovel over his shoulder and headed for the kitchen door.

As he suspected, lunch was almost ready. While Alexi and his sisters unloaded the shopping bags and put away their contents, Kate finished her preparations, lifted the vegetable soup into bowls, and set plates of cold meat and fresh, homemade rolls on the table.

As usual, conversation centered mainly on what was happening for the younger pair. He got the feeling Ruth already knew much of what he was hearing for the first time and it annoyed him. He remembered how he and his brothers had shared secrets. He also knew why they had felt the need to conceal some of their activities. It didn't suit him to realize that his own children might likewise be behaving in ways he would not approve.

They were eating dessert when the telephone rang. The previous Sunday he had agreed to help a couple of the men from St. Mary's prepare the church basement for painting. Expecting it would be his friend Eddie Pasternak letting him know when the work party was meeting, he went to answer the call.

The voice on the other end of the telephone line was low and slightly muffled. At first Vlad wasn't sure he heard it correctly.

"Sorry," he said. "There must be something wrong with the line. I can't understand you. Can you speak up?"

This time the voice was clearer. It was certainly male, but a strange male. Vlad didn't know this voice.

"I asked if you are Vladymyr Horbatsky."

"Yes."

"I am with the Russian Family Fund. We work on behalf of family members trapped behind the Iron Curtain and unable to make their own contact with relatives who escaped. We buy the food or medicines they need in Europe and arrange to get it over the border to the designated individual."

It wasn't a new idea although Vlad had grave doubts about the organization's authenticity. The Ukrainian community had been targeted for scams of all sorts over the years.

"So who are you?" he challenged.

"My name does not matter but you may call me Nicholas if it makes you feel better."

"And where are you calling from, Nicholas?"

"Montreal. But we have a collection location in Toronto. That will be close to you, will it not?"

"What do you want?"

"I am calling for Olga. She is sick and cannot afford her medicine. Drugs are very expensive there. That is why she asked us to contact you. Canadians can afford to help their families. She said you would help us buy her medicine."

Vlad's first thought was to slam the receiver back into its cradle. He took a deep breath to control his anger.

"I don't know any Olga," he said. "And where is *there*?"

"Oh, come, come, Vladymyr. Olga remembers you very well as a little boy playing around the kitchen with her daughter and your father coming in from work at night and bringing you both a sweet. I will not tell her you have forgotten her. It would hurt her too much to think the colonel's son would forget his responsibilities. She is a family responsibility, you know."

"No." Vlad's voice was sharp. He thumped the receiver back into its cradle.

For a long moment, he stood in the hall staring at the wall by the clothes closet. His mind had slipped directly to his childhood and the kitchen in their Berlin apartment overlooking the park.

It was a large apartment, full of sunshine. He could see himself running in from school looking for a snack. Nadia was there ahead of him and she was hungry. Olga was peeling an apple for her daughter. She washed one for him, but didn't peel it because he preferred his with the skin on. His own mother came out of the bedroom in her uniform, ready to go to their restaurant. Dimitri was already gone. He went in early every day to supervise the menu and go over the books. The two women ignored each other although the children could approach either one of them when they needed something.

The man on the phone was right in a way. The Horbatskys did have a responsibility, but it was to Nadia, not to her mother. Olga had married and moved out of their home before the war.

It was little Nadia who should concern him, his younger half-sister with the big brown eyes and the wavy, dark hair. If he had to help anyone, it should be her. Of course, sending money to help care for her mother could be seen as helping both Nadia and Olga.

Laughter penetrated his memories and he turned towards the sound. His wife and children were sharing a happy moment. He should be out there with them, not here fuming at the subtle threats of some con artist looking for money.

The man hadn't made any specific demands. Vlad had slammed down the phone before that happened, but he had no doubt the demand would have been made. Vlad wasn't about to pay anything for an old woman who was probably already dead.

The puzzling part was why anyone would try extortion now. He hadn't seen Olga in nearly forty years. Why should they think Olga would be his weakness?

The answer hit him like a slap in the face. Wachter. Of course! Andreas Wachter had lived in Germany. He could still have access to records or to people who had access to records. Wachter wanted Kate. If he could disrupt their life with extortion, he stood a better chance of coming between them.

Wachter had money. Perhaps he thought Kate would look on him more favorably if they were having financial problems because Vlad was paying Olga's bills. Then Wachter could step forward and provide Kate with luxuries beyond Vlad's means.

Well, it wouldn't work, he vowed. Kate was his wife and he would provide for her and their children.

He returned to the table, determined to conceal the caller's identity and purpose. Ruth's house and her relationship with Martin had already put Vlad in a bad mood. No one needed to know about his new worry.

CHAPTER SEVEN

The morning of the first Friday in April began normally enough. Kate sorted the mail and took it through to Gerry, then returned half an hour later to receive instructions about his replies.

Just before lunch, she brought back the letters requiring his signature. When she rose to leave, he stopped her.

"Dig out one of the standard contract forms, will you?" he said. "Andreas has agreed to join us on contract to train the Clean Room production staff and I want the papers ready for his signature the day he arrives."

Kate almost stumbled. Andreas was coming back? She managed to sound calm as she turned and asked when that decision had been made.

"I asked him the night I took him to supper," Gerry replied. "He came in the next morning and agreed. We worked out the price and terms but he figured it would be at least the end of this month before he finished his previous commitments. He called last night and gave me a start date of April sixteenth."

So the bastard had known he'd be back the morning he'd accosted her in the Clean Room.

"How long do you expect he'll be with us?" she asked, her shocked mind pleading for a short time frame.

Gerry shrugged. "Three months should do it, maybe less. But it might be smart to give him an option for an additional three months in case there's a problem we don't foresee."

Three months? What kind of damage could he do in that time? How was she going to keep him away from Vlad for three whole months? She could feel her heart thumping in panic.

"So he'll handle the start-up?"

"Yes, and the initial adjustments. Once the machines are operating properly and the men are trained, we should be able to keep them going. Vlad's good. He can handle the on-going maintenance, but it isn't fair to expect him to set everything up when he's never even seen these machines before."

Fair? What was fair about shattering her life, Kate wondered distractedly as she returned to her desk and collapsed into her chair. How was she going to tell Vlad? He'd think it was her doing, that somehow she had encouraged Gerry, maybe even suggested Andreas for the job.

The rest of the day, she struggled with her problem, handling her regular tasks in a daze and trying to ignore the complications posed by their planned outing to Future Bakery that night for supper.

Although Andreas had not been mentioned since he left, she had sensed Vlad watching her. He'd been even more attentive than usual during the past six weeks, for instance, insisting that he drive her when she went to the mall in Brampton to shop for her mother's birthday gift. He'd even volunteered to accompany her to Toronto for a craft fair she attended annually. That was the giveaway. Other years he'd shown no interest when she'd made the trip by herself. This year he ensured she had no opportunity for a secret meeting with Andreas.

So how was she going to tell him that Andreas was due back in just over a week? Indeed, should the message come from her? It would certainly sound more innocent coming from Gerry, and she had no doubt he would tell Vlad eventually. But when? Should she prod Gerry to do it now? No matter how she plotted, she could devise no plausible excuse for asking Gerry to break the news to Vlad, short of the truth. That was a bad idea.

By the end of the day she accepted the inevitable. She must tell Vlad herself.

Vlad was reading the paper when Kate arrived home after work. He waited patiently while she refreshed her makeup and changed her shoes. Then they headed back to her car for the drive to Toronto.

He had always tried to keep Kate happy. It was his duty if he expected her to make him happy. It was also part of his father's early teaching that a happy wife is a contented woman and a contented woman brings peace and harmony to the home. So far, Vlad felt his success on that score was even greater than his father's. However, Wachter's appearance in their lives worried him and prompted him to increase his efforts at fulfilling his obligation to be a helpful, loving partner.

All week he'd been looking forward to supper at the Ukrainian bakery-cum-restaurant to which Ruth had had taken Kate during the winter. Both women praised the food and he'd heard good things about the place from a couple of friends at church. He'd enjoy tasting the familiar dishes again. Kate was a good cook but the traditional foods were unfamiliar to her and her results didn't always match his boyhood memories.

Traffic wasn't bad for a Friday night and they arrived shortly after six. The place was already full, but the aroma wafting from the kitchen and scanning the papers from home tacked to cork-boards along one wall compensated Vlad for the short delay until a table became vacant.

Delighted at the assortment available on the buffet, he heaped his plate, picked up his cutlery, and seated himself. He was well into his schnitzel before he realized Kate's plate was half empty and she was just picking at its contents.

"You okay?" he asked, concerned by her uncharacteristic disinterest in the food. He'd always thought she liked Ukrainian cuisine. That's why he'd suggested coming here. She'd certainly seemed enthusiastic enough when he suggested the trip four days ago.

She nodded. "Yup. Just not very hungry."

"Not sick?"

"Nope." She smiled at his skeptical glance and stabbed a fresh piece of cabbage roll. "Guess I'm tired. It's been a long week. Good thing you're doing the driving."

She managed to clean up her plate and showed more appetite for the blini with fresh strawberries and cream that he brought her for dessert. Even so, her meal was scanty.

"You aren't dieting on me, are you?" he questioned when she refused a second helping. "Because if you are, you can stop right now. I like a good armful in my bed, you know."

She shook her head and managed a small grin. "I know that. But this stuff would be deadly if I ate much of it. You'd have more than one armful in no time."

Despite her denials he was sure something was wrong. She lacked her usual sparkle and she was too quiet. He'd need to keep an eye on her. If work were too much for her he'd be happy to have her home again full time. Extra money was useful with the kids at university, but not that useful. He'd call on Ruth to contribute if necessary. Kate's health was more important.

They arrived home shortly after nine and settled in front of the television. The evening newscast was ending when she set her knitting aside and began speaking.

"Gerry gave me some interesting news today. I don't know if he's told you yet, but I think you need to be warned."

He looked up, then closed his newspaper. He'd been right. Something was worrying her.

She continued. "This morning he asked me to prepare a three-month contract for Wachter. He's bringing him back to set up the new machines in the Clean Room and train the staff to use them. He's due to start April sixteenth."

The bastard was coming back. She'd sat there all through supper denying her knowledge of this impending disaster. Anger burned through him as he fought for control.

"Congratulations." He gritted the word through clenched teeth. "You managed very well, you and your lover. Of course, we know what a sucker Gerry is. The least suggestion from you and he falls into line like a well-trained pet."

He rose and began to stalk about the family room, ignoring her protests. Her denial was only natural. She had enjoyed some sort of relationship with the Kraut back then and saw no danger in renewing it. What was wrong with her that she could never understand how easily gossip started and how completely it destroyed a family? He had given her his all—money, home, devotion, children—everything a man could give. Still it was not enough. She hankered after the excitement of this…this German bastard.

The longer he paced, the louder and more infuriated he became.

As the tirade escalated, Amos moved closer to Kate's feet, keeping a wary eye on Vlad as he did so. He was a big animal with the aggressive instincts of his breed. He didn't like loud, excited voices. Officially, he might be a family pet, but experience had taught him when to be wary and who might need his protection. He ignored the soothing hand Kate set on his head, his eyes glued to his agitated master's every move.

The tantrum lasted the better part of an hour before Vlad screamed a parting insult in Ukrainian and stormed out of the room.

Kate heard the bedroom door slam and set her knitting on the table, tension draining away. *So much for attempting to be reasonable.*

While Vlad's short fuse grew shorter with age, the episodes came less frequently. Over the years, she had learned to let the words wash over her and ignore them since reactions of any other sort were viewed as a challenge to his judgments and exacerbated his rage. Even so, she avoided conflict whenever possible.

Much as she tried to placate him, she was never truly frightened by his outbursts. S.O.E. had trained her to handle threatening situations, and although she had not used those skills since her discharge, neither had she forgotten them. She knew that Vlad's size and strength would be no match for her speed and training if he ever forced her into a showdown.

She had to hope that time would take the edge off his temper. Regardless of how well Vlad handled himself in public, she knew that in private she would face three rough months full of suspicion and accusations.

Nor would Vlad be her only problem. Since Andreas, too, was furious with her, there was no telling what punishments he might devise. He didn't know about

Vlad's jealousy—yet. How long would it take before he discovered that weapon? With his mind and his knowledge, she had good reason to fear that his revenge could cause her more than mere embarrassment.

"Men!" she muttered in disgust, turning off the television and getting up. "Come on, Amos. Let's take a walk. We both need to unwind."

Vlad threw his work clothes into the laundry hamper and turned on the shower. Normally bathing was part of his morning ritual. Tonight he hoped the warm water would soothe him, otherwise, there was little chance he'd get any sleep.

He lathered thoroughly and scrubbed hard, doing his best to think about something—anything—other than Wachter. Only his wife knew the true extent of his hatred for Germans. He had always made a point of avoiding the town's few German families. If Wachter were going to be lording it over Clarke's staff, keeping his distance might well be impossible.

He knew others would find his loathing to be irrational. Most Canadians had such convenient memories. With the war long past, it was easier to forgive their former enemies than to live with the constant reminder of the threat they once posed. Not Vlad. He would never forgive the Germans for collaborating with Lenin, a move that culminated in the October Revolution, and the rise of Communism that had ultimately cost his family their homeland. Nor would he forgive them for blindly tolerating a dictator whose hatred for Slavs saw them rounded up into camps twenty years later to die of overwork and starvation.

Now with the phone calls, he realized Wachter had his minions working on a scheme to cripple Vlad financially. He had told Kate nothing about the original call, nor of the second one, three days ago. This time Nicholas had made his demand, one hundred dollars sent to the Russian Family Fund by money order and mailed to a Toronto address. That amounted to almost a week's wages. Vlad would lay odds the call wouldn't be a one-shot plea. It would gradually become a systematic whine, akin to blackmail. He wouldn't be making any contribution, but he suspected that wouldn't stop the calls.

Unbidden, his mind formed an image of the big man standing in the Clean Room doorway, his hand on Kate's arm. The arrogance of his stance, the power in his expression, the clipped voice issuing orders—Vlad could picture it. Most distressing of all was how readily Kate obeyed those commands. He, too, would be expected to take direction like a well-trained puppy.

Clean and toweled dry, Vlad crawled into bed, hoping to lose himself in the imaginary world of the novel he had begun reading several evenings earlier. He propped pillows behind himself and picked up Fleming's latest James Bond adventure from the night table. Living with a real-life spy highlighted the absurdities of the fictional variety. All the same, Vlad found Q's imaginative gadgets fascinating enough to outweigh the fantasies Fleming spun to challenge his secret agent.

He awoke with a start, looking frantically for the source of the explosion. His heart was racing. He was unbelievably warm. The odor was wrong. Amid all that charred wood and twisted metal he should not be smelling lemon. Lemon? Lemon polish.

It took him a moment to realize he'd been dreaming. He wasn't cleaning up a bombed Polish railway station in 1943. He was safe in his own bed in 1973. There'd been no explosion.

He took deep breaths to calm himself, struggling to push away the nightmare. Although he hadn't experienced this one in years, the passage of time had not dulled his memory. They were near Danzig that winter afternoon when they stumbled on two young girls in an abandoned shed beside the railway line. There were twenty men in the work party clearing away the debris of the bombed station, and six German guards.

Laughing and joking, the guards split up. Two kept their rifles trained on the ill-clad, starving prisoners struggling to haul aside the timbers and wreckage blocking the tracks. The other four men went inside, stripping off their greatcoats as they went. They didn't bother to shut the door.

He had not wanted to watch what happened; had not wanted to know. Then one gut-wrenching scream broke his resolve, and he glanced into the shed.

What he saw almost pushed him to use the board in his hands on the skull of the guard beside him. Only a sharp word from another prisoner nearby made him look elsewhere. That was when he saw the second guard's rifle pointed at his chest.

It was no use. Even with odds of twenty to two, the prisoners were too weak to overpower their guards. Besides, the girls were already beyond help with injuries they could not survive. Deaf and dead-eyed, the prisoners continued with their task until no more sounds came out of the shed.

Calmer now, he heard the sound of violins from the family room. So she was playing her damned records. She only played classical music when she was upset. Good. She deserved to be upset for trying to deceive him.

He had no doubt that she was as genuinely concerned as he about how Wachter might affect their future. They simply viewed the problem differently.

CHAPTER EIGHT

Andreas settled into life with Clarke's staff as though he had always been part of it. It was the sort of workplace where employees spent their whole working life. Everyone knew everyone else and more than a little about each other's business. They talked openly about their families and Andreas figured he'd soon be able to ask questions about Ruth without raising suspicion. He just needed to find someone who knew Kate well enough to know her children too.

During his first week on the new job he concentrated on learning to blend in. He needed acceptance if he hoped to get the information he sought. He deplored cultivating patience.

He was also busy with the telephone book and maps of the town. Vlad was the only Horbatsky listed. Andreas picked up a copy of the town's history at the library, then discreetly followed Kate home from work one night. It was a small enough community that he had its geography figured out inside of two weeks. Finding Ruth Horbatsky, however, was not so simple.

He was finishing his third week in Milton when Janice Kane approached him carrying a sheet of paper.

"Whatcha doing this weekend?" she began.

Andreas shrugged. Janice was Gerry's Girl Friday, receptionist, general secretary, and extra hands for the upstairs staff. He'd been warned she was single and usually on the prowl.

"Nothing much," he replied. "What's on your mind?"

Inside of five minutes she had him roped into partnering her for the company's annual fundraising car rally for cancer. He would drive and she would navigate. They'd use her car. He spent the rest of the day wondering just how smart the move had been. He had no desire to dawdle with her when his sights were set on Ruth Horbatsky.

Since the office was the rally's starting point, Janice collected Andreas on Saturday morning and they drove to Clarke's. The number of familiar faces milling about waiting to pick up their sheet of directions told Andreas the rally was a popular one. At the appointed time, Janice snatched up their sheet and raced back to join him.

The morning was bright and clear and road hazards were limited to the few places where melting snow swamped the area's natural drainage. They made good time for the first couple of hours, then took a wrong turn at the Forks of the Credit and wasted almost an hour discovering their mistake and getting back on track.

Janice proved to be less of a chatterbox than Andreas hoped. She spoke of joining Clarke's eight years ago and readily praised Kate's help in settling into the position she still held. She made several comments about Kate, even explaining that she and Vlad had probably laid out their route.

Their destination turned out to be a secluded restaurant in Huttonville called Someplace Else. It was set back from the road by a long lane way winding up a hill and surrounded by trees. Not until they saw Gerry's station wagon in the parking lot were they confident they had reached the correct goal.

Andreas was pleased to discover they had made a respectable showing. Only four of the twenty participating teams arrived before them. Janice hugged him in delight.

"If I hadn't gotten us lost at the Forks, we'd have won," she told everyone. "Andreas is a great driver, and I'm going to invite him back next year no matter where he's working."

Andreas hoped his smile was indulgent rather than smug.

Over the ensuing hour, as they waited for the laggards to arrive, Andreas bought Janice a couple of drinks. By the time they sat down for their celebratory meal, Janice was much more relaxed. She revealed that Clarke employees respected both the Horbatskys, but Vlad was treated with caution.

"He's touchy about anyone trying to get close to Kate," she confided. "One guy tried to dance with her too often at the Christmas party a couple of years ago. Vlad broke his nose and would have done worse if Kate hadn't stopped him."

"Is she that flirtatious?" Andreas feigned surprise. "Does she give him cause for such jealousy?"

Janice shook her head. "Nope. Never. Kate's dedicated to her marriage. Probably the result of losing her first husband. Can't have been easy trying to raise a kid on her own. Especially in the forties with all the other widows around. She was lucky to catch Vlad's eye."

Andreas bit his tongue. Something told him Janice wasn't all that much younger than Kate. She, too, must have faced a dearth of appropriate males when she reached marriageable age.

"I think Gerry mentioned Kate's child. A girl, wasn't it?"

Janice accepted the question as casual curiosity. "Ruth's a really bright kid. She did a degree in engineering and works for one of the plane makers around the airport."

A female engineer? Now that was interesting. They would have more in common than he expected.

"Engineering? That's an odd field for a girl. What does her husband think of that?"

Janice shook her head. "No husband. I hear Vlad's not happy about it, but Kate doesn't seem to be worried. Doesn't need to be, I guess. Ruth's a cute enough kid. Kid? What am I saying? She must be closing in on thirty. She's no kid any more."

Smugly, Andreas tucked away this nugget of information. A female engineer working for one of the aeronautical manufacturers shouldn't be hard to find. It was a tight community. His contacts at Canadair would know about any female engineers in the business regardless of their specialty.

When Andreas called his friend, Harry Lennox, to arrange to meet him for lunch the following day, Harry agreed readily. Before hanging up Andreas casually asked whether there was such a thing as a magazine catering to their branch of engineering.

"I'm working up here so much these days, I was thinking of subscribing to it. I might even want to join the association."

Harry was enthusiastic. "Sure. We can always use good men. I know you're approaching retirement, but we have lots of work for consultants, and the magazine is a great place to find those opportunities."

"Yeah, well, find me a gal in our field and maybe I'll consider moving here too." Andreas continued in a joking tone. "This bachelor life gets lonely sometimes."

Harry groaned. "I only know two and you wouldn't want either of them. Grace Warrington is a real bitch with two ex-husbands who live the life of the walking wounded, and Ruth Coleman is more interested in her job than in men. Although, come to think of it, I think she already has a guy in her life. Besides, she's under thirty, too young for you. At least I assume you don't want to worry about diapers and two a.m. feedings."

Kohlman? Andreas' heart thumped. She'd given the girl his name? What had prompted that, he wondered.

Andreas said, "You never know. A pretty girl on your arm is always good for the ego. Where do I find her?"

Harry laughed. "Over at MacDonnel-Douglas. She's part of their wing design team."

Smiling, Andreas set the receiver back in its cradle and found the telephone directory. In addition to Milton, it showed listings for Oakville, Brampton, Mississauga, and several small towns in the surrounding area.

There were two Kohlmans in Brampton, one in Mississauga and none in any of the other communities. G.R. Kohlman in Brampton, the only customer with the right initial, turned out to be male and sounded ancient enough to be Andreas' father.

Disgusted, Andreas ended his call and sank back in his hotel-room chair, cursing Kate. Giving her child his surname seemed like a calculated insult. Had the real father not been willing to accept responsibility for this bastard? Or was theirs a fleeting relationship? The next poor sucker she'd duped into betraying the Fatherland. A married man, even? He was so frustrated he wanted to punch someone.

One thing seemed obvious. He must approach Ruth through work. But how? What inducement could he offer to persuade her to their first meeting?

After a couple of hours of contemplation, he decided to offer her work. If she were as ambitious as he suspected, she'd pay any price to advance her career. Now all he needed was a way to concoct a believable story about how he'd heard of her skill. He'd pump Harry over lunch.

He dropped into bed, tired but elated. For the first time in weeks, his plan seemed to be coming together. Kate Horbatsky would regret naming her bastard after him. He'd see to that.

###

By the Friday of his second week on the job Andreas finished supervising the setting up of the last piece of Clarke's new equipment. Everything was in the appropriate location now. Safety switches functioned properly. The vacuum designed to guard the entrance to the Clean Room was hooked up and operating. It all worked. The four men transferred from the main line to handle the specialized operation would begin training on Monday. Andreas was ready to sign off on the initial phase of his assignment.

From habit, he powered up the first machine, picked up the goggles and laid two pieces of wire on the soldering bench. He always did a test run on everything before beginning to train greenhorns. Gerry had assured him the men were skilled operators but every piece of equipment had its own idiosyncrasies. To be truly proficient, these men would need to start from the beginning as though they knew nothing, and learn the behaviors of their specific machines.

Andreas did his test piece, then hit the off switch, satisfied with the operation. The second machine heated up, zapped the wires on command, and shut down as was its design. He did his third test, shut down and then proceeded to the fourth. It, too, performed as specified. In turning to close down, he brushed the adjacent soldering booth, then cursed, and jerked his hand back. His whole arm tingled from the jolt of electricity that shot through it.

The equipment was supposedly shut off. What was wrong with it? He began checking immediately, systematically examining each component—the switch, the motor, the heating element. It took nearly an hour to find the culprit. The insulation on the vacuum attached to the booth hood was defective. He could repair the faulty wiring, but that would void the warranty—not a wise thing to do with new equipment.

He went up to Gerry's office and laid out the problem. The hood needed replacing, but getting the supplier to do it could prove time consuming.

"At this hour on a Friday the installation crew will already be gone for the day and the boss mentioned that they start a new job in Cornwall on Monday. They won't be delaying that just to fix our hood."

"But we need to get into production," Gerry protested.

"I can dismantle the hood myself and take it back to the shop," Andreas offered, "but you're going to need to raise Cain with their sales manager to get that authorized."

Gerry nodded. "I'll call Fred. If he can have someone here on Monday morning, then we'll leave it for him. Otherwise he'll give us written permission to handle this problem ourselves, or lose a chunk of his commission."

Andreas could tell Fred wasn't happy, but Gerry was determined. The conversation ended as he had predicted. He replaced the receiver with a satisfied nod.

"He'll square it with his boss and have the new hood waiting for you. He wants to do it without the crew finding out though, so that means you have to get to the shop to pick up the replacement before noon tomorrow. The shop's hard to find, on a back street in Barrie and you'll need something bigger than your car to transport it. I'll get Vlad to take you. He's used to our delivery van and he's been to Hoffman's with me before."

Andreas returned to the Clean Room to finish dismantling the faulty hood. Instinct told him the trip to Barrie was going to be long and the atmosphere chilly.

CHAPTER NINE

Kate was putting supper on the table when Gerry called. Vlad stomped back from the telephone looking like a thundercloud.

"I've got to take Wachter to Hoffman's in Barrie in the morning," he announced. "Seems they sent us a faulty hood for one of the soldering booths. Wachter is dismantling it now and we're to return it and pick up a replacement before noon."

Kate knew that spending more than half a day with Andreas would stretch Vlad's patience to the danger point. She could think of only one alternative, but that wouldn't be popular either.

"What about asking Ronnie to go in your place?" she asked, pinning on the most innocent smile she could manage. "He owes you a favor or two and he is your lead hand."

His expression grew even darker. "No, of course not. He'd expect to get paid overtime. Besides, he doesn't know where Hoffman's is."

Kate turned back to the stove to hide her frustration.

So much for trying to give Vlad a way out of a distasteful chore.

"Good thing we had no plans for the morning," she said. "I'm supposed to help Mom make sandwiches for the lunch at the church after the Kelly funeral. The Ladies Aid is catering so I'll be busy most of the morning. I'll have supper ready early though, so we can still get to the concert at St. Mary's on time."

Vlad stared at her so often during the evening that Kate wanted to slap him. He was obviously dwelling on questions about her acquaintance with Andreas and just as obviously he didn't like the images he was conjuring up. Served him right. A sensible person let the past go.

Kate left Vlad to watch the late news and headed for the shower. She was waiting for him in a low-cut silk nightie when he shut off the television and arrived by their bed. She saw the sparkle in his eyes as he crawled in beside her and immediately snapped off the light. She knew how to distract him from gloomy thoughts and he knew exactly how to reward her efforts.

###

Andreas had the hood dismantled and the pieces laid by the Clean Room door when Vlad brought the Clarke van into place. Loading was simple enough with two men to share the lifting. They were on the road ten minutes later.

Cold air blasted out of the air conditioner. Tension filled the cab like a third body.

Over the years, Andreas had learned that Americans were uncomfortable with extended silences. But, like himself, Vlad was European. Five long minutes later, when they reached Highway 401, still without a word spoken, he decided to initiate conversation.

"You've been with Clarke for a while," he began.

"Twenty-four years," Vlad answered. There was no small talk, just a response to a question.

"And were you always their head of maintenance?"

"It took a year to get there." Again the words were crisp, not friendly.

Andreas found getting conversation flowing was akin to pulling teeth. It took mention of Viet Nam before Vlad began unbending.

"So how will the peace in Vietnam affect things?" he asked. "A general decrease in military spending, or just switch it all into cold war hardware?"

It was a topic about which Andreas was confidant. "They'll shift. Maybe some of it will go to the space program, but the Russians haven't gone away. The Secretary of Defense still wants to find their bomb factories and missile silos. Your contract won't be cancelled."

"You do not see the Russians as a threat?"

Andreas shook his head. "Oh no. That wasn't my point. They're dangerous all right. It's just that so much of our economy revolves around defense spending that the government doesn't dare cut back. Nixon's popular right now because he got us out of Nam. He won't risk that popularity by scaling back on defense contracts. It would put a lot of manufacturers out of business—jeopardize thousands of jobs."

Vlad snorted. "So you are a cynic."

"I design planes. I'd like to see my work used for civilian purposes. In nearly forty years of designing, that's never happened. The innovation must have a defensive use first if it's ever to be transferred to civilian aircraft. I came to terms with that years ago."

They fell silent as Vlad maneuvered around a couple of big rigs, then changed lanes to continue their trek eastward towards Highway 400.

"Did I detect a dislike of the Russians in your earlier comment?" Andreas asked as they settled into a straight stretch free of heavy traffic. "I have to plead ignorance but your name sounds decidedly Slavic to me. I'd have thought you might sympathize with them."

"No." Vlad's voice was tight. His knuckles showed white on the steering wheel. "I am Ukrainian."

The statement apparently told it all. In fact, it merely confused Andreas. While he recognized the hatred in Vlad's tone, he had no clue to the cause. The silence stretched while Andreas sought a response.

"That must have been quite a handicap growing up under Communism," he managed at last.

"I grew up in Berlin. Hitler was no kinder than Stalin."

Andreas nodded. "I'll bet!" Christ! He couldn't win. He wondered how Vlad regarded Germans in general. Did he separate the population from their leader or did he suspect them all of hating Slavs? The man had survived a great deal by the sound of things. In a way, it explained Kate's loyalty. It also explained Gerry's comments about them having experiences in common which drew them together.

#

The man beside him faded into the morning sunshine as Vlad pushed east towards Toronto.

I am Ukrainian. For Vlad, the statement was the foundation of his being, the explanation for his very existence. From infancy the Motherland had been the family's focus. His earliest memories were of their home in Kiev, Mamma supervising the kitchen staff, Papa coming in with his uniform dusty, and smelling of horses. He had rarely smiled.

Then the Communists came. Vlad didn't remember the fighting, just the adults sitting around the dining room table, absorbed in earnest discussions he was too young to understand.

His world was in turmoil. All the women were crying, the men were sober, even glum. Papa was giving orders. Vlad's brothers were sorting possessions and packing their trunks. They didn't even say goodbye to Babushka. His father and brothers mounted their horses while he was hustled into the carriage with his mother and sister and Nana.

The journey to Berlin had seemed long and unpleasant, full of tense moments when he must remain perfectly still and silent in his hiding place, then climb out, cold and hungry, and resume the bumpy, exhausting ride.

Only later did he understand how the Communists had toppled the free Ukrainian government and begun to hunt its members. Like all high-ranking Ukrainian army officers, there was a price on Dimitri Horbatsky's head and his family was destined for Siberia if they were captured.

Thanks to the detours and disguises, separations and concealments, the trip to Berlin took the better part of a month. Even then, Communist agents made two attempts on his father's life and succeeded in wounding him severely in the second attack.

In 1926, Lenin's minions murdered his mother's brother, Nikoli, for daring to object to the collectivization of the family estates. He was pushed under the ice with his hands bound behind him.

Six years later, his father's mother was one of the early victims of Stalin's contrived famine. Ruthless and cunning even in his early days, Stalin—or Uncle Joe as the West liked to call him—starved the last remnants of resistance out of Ukrainians and forced their submission to Russia. Babushka had been expected to harvest her own food and cook her own meals like any common peasant. Her devoted servants would have cared for her if they could, but waiting on an aristocrat would have cost their own lives. Since she was already ninety-three, they opted to save themselves and abandoned her to fend for herself.

A loud blast from a disgruntled trucker jerked Vlad back to the present. He was blocking traffic; going too slow when he should be merging into the northbound lane.

"Bloody trucks," he muttered. "I hate the city. Too many trucks. Too much speed."

Andreas nodded, relieved to hear Vlad's voice return to normal. "I'm just starting to get the hang of the place after making so many trips across it in the last couple of months."

#

They arrived at Hoffman's shortly after eleven and were on their way home with the new hood by the time Andreas began to feel hungry. Food seemed a safe enough topic so he suggested they stop to eat. Vlad nodded agreeably and pulled in at a roadside diner a few minutes later.

They were waiting for their order to arrive when Andreas raised the issue of Slavic heritage institutions around the Milton area.

Vlad explained about the cultural centre that had grown up around St. Mary's Ukrainian Orthodox church in Oakville.

"The kids speak and read our language and Tanya belonged to a dance group when she was younger. Alexi took *bandura* lessons there. We were lucky to have the larger Ukrainian populations in Toronto and Hamilton close by. It gave us a wider range of opportunities that way."

"Bandura?" Andreas asked

"It's our form of guitar, only larger and upright like your harp."

"Does your wife speak Ukrainian, then?" Andreas asked a moment later.

Andreas could feel Vlad's sudden tension. Had he said something wrong? They both knew she spoke German. It seemed an innocent enough question.

Vlad shook his head. "No, but she insisted the kids learn it, even though she could not get the hang of it herself."

"That surprises me, given how fluent she is in German."

"Good enough to fool you?"

The remark was casual and Andreas kept his affirmative reply the same. He remembered Janice's comments about Vlad's jealousy.

"She was an extremely efficient secretary," Andreas said. "No one ever suspected she wasn't one of us."

"Not even when she talked in her sleep?"

Such a simple statement, yet so loaded. For an instant, Andreas was tempted to torment him. Honor won out. Kate was his target, not Vlad.

Andreas shook his head and shrugged. "Does she talk in her sleep?"

He could feel Vlad wrestling with the desire to confront him directly. Somehow, he managed to restrain himself. Was he afraid of the answer; was he warning Andreas that he knew about their former relationship; or was he simply fishing?

The moment passed and the arrival of their order gave them an excuse to remain silent for a time. Having established his position as Kate's husband, Vlad seemed content to drop the issue. When the conversation resumed, it was about Andreas' other contracts.

#

Kate sank back into her folding chair and tried to relax, glad they hadn't been late. The turnout for St. Mary's annual spring concert was larger than usual. A few more minutes and there might have been no more free seats.

Her day had been busy. Vlad returned late and in a bad mood. He'd helped Andreas to get the new hood in place when they got back to Clarke's. As a result, she'd had to delay supper. While they ate, he watched her with that speculative look that told her something must have happened between him and Andreas. So far she had no idea what. She could only hope he'd get over it quickly. Hearing his own language would help, and she loved the dances.

The concert began as always, with two of the youngest dancers performing the official greeting. It tugged at Kate's heartstrings to watch the tiny pair. The girl, her fair hair carefully braided and crowned with a wreath of flowers, the flowing sleeves of her blouse embroidered in great red roses, calf-high red boots encasing her little feet, carried the traditional bread covered by an embroidered cloth. Behind her, an equally small boy used two hands to balance a bowl of salt on a plate as they trod dutifully from the rear of the auditorium, down the centre aisle between the banks of chairs, and up the steps onto the stage.

That was when the fringed red sash wrapped around the lad's waist tangled in the bulky pantaloons tucked into the top of his tall black boots and he tripped. Kate could hear the gasp from the adults around her. Catching himself without dropping his bowl, he stepped up beside the girl, shot her a smirk, extended the bowl, and bowed. A collective sigh of relief rippled through the crowd. The boy grinned, the gravity of his task forgotten.

Shaking his head at the near catastrophe, the Master of Ceremonies stepped between the youngsters to make his welcoming remarks.

The first performers were from the Hamilton Cultural Association's dance troupe. A choir of older women from the Toronto Cultural Centre followed the dancers.

At the intermission, Vlad led Kate out to the hall where the Society's female members had set up two tables of baking in front of the bar. While he bought their drinks, Kate purchased poppy seed cake for both of them.

A touring troupe of Winnipeg dancers were the special guests for the event. Their set spanned the entire second half of the concert, starting with women doing a circle dance with ribbons and followed by several regional dances representing different parts of the homeland. The performance ended with the *Hopak,* the traditional celebratory dance of victorious Cossack warriors showing off the acrobatic leaps and whirls, splits and handstands which dazzled their vanquished enemies.

Vlad's mood had lightened by the time they left the church. Hearing his native tongue spoken all around him, tasting the familiar foods and watching the athletic displays of the boisterous young men had soothed him. He could never go home as long as Communists ruled Ukraine, but, at least for tonight, he could share his pride in his nation with understanding, and equally nostalgic compatriots. Even as an outsider, Kate could empathize with them. Her time in Germany had taught her to value home and tradition.

Illogically, amid calls of *Do zvidaniya* between departing friends, her mind flew to a gasthaus near Berlin and an accordion player belting out a polka. Andreas' arms were around her again and her legs ached from dancing to the energetic rhythm.

She reached for Vlad's hand, feeling the strong fingers wrap around her own and draw her closer as they walked toward the car. She must not let her memories overshadow the good things in her present, she reminded herself. The past was gone. Vlad was her reality now.

CHAPTER TEN

Andreas finished installing the new hood by mid morning and tested the machinery one final time. He would begin training Clarke's new production staff after lunch. He had an hour to call his own before that. No one would question his absence. He left the Clean Room and headed for his car.

Back in his room, he picked up the paper on which he had written the MacDonnel-Douglas number and dialed. It took several rings before the switchboard operator answered. The fact that she knew Ruth Kohlman's extension without hesitation suggested she must get a lot of calls.

"Coleman."

It was a pleasant voice, crisp, clear, businesslike. Andreas needed to swallow before he spoke.

"Miss Kohlman," he began. "My name is Andreas Wachter. You don't know me but a friend of mine suggested you might be just the person I need for a contract I'm considering. Harry Lennox works for Canadair. Perhaps you know him."

Andreas was gratified by the moment's silence. At least she had the wit to consider her answer.

"I'm sorry, Mr. Wachter. I'm afraid your name is more legendary in this field than Mr. Lennox's. I'm flattered you've even heard of me when I'm just a beginner. How can I help you?"

"I'm bidding for a job with a company in Virginia. They're looking for a new type of executive jet. The boss is a woman. I suspect using pink upholstery won't quite meet the goal so I'm looking for a female's advice."

Her laugh was fresh and genuine. There was a touch of Kate in it. Andreas liked it in spite of that. He could hear her catch her breath.

"You're right. I suspect pink upholstery won't be the answer," she replied. "What sort of modifications do you think she'll want?"

"I don't know. That's why I want to talk to you. Do you have a free night this week? May I take you to supper at the Four Seasons on Airport Road to discuss it?"

Again there was an instant of silence before she agreed, naming a time on Wednesday evening as most suitable for her. Andreas hung up wearing an enormous grin.

The rest of the week sped by. His trainees learned quickly, despite the fact they were mature men and would ordinarily have been overlooked as too old to learn new skills. He was well satisfied with his progress when he heard the loudspeaker on Wednesday morning.

"Telephone call for Mr. Wachter," Janice's voice announced, then repeated the message three times.

The nearest phone was in Vlad's office. He went to it and was relieved to discover the place empty.

"Wachter here."

"Hi." The voice was so hoarse he barely understood the words. "It's Ruth Coleman. Sorry to call at the last minute, but I don't think I dare to meet you this evening. I'm so sick I'd probably give you the cold too, just being in the same building with you, never mind at the same table. Can we re-schedule for next week without making a total mess of your submission?"

The tone was right, not pleading but certainly interested. He'd hooked her. Now if he could just make up enough phony details to be convincing, the rest would fall into place. He didn't want to delay, but he must unless he wanted to seem unkind and arrogant.

"Sure," he replied. "How about the same time and place next week? That should let you get over this bug."

"You're very understanding. Thank you. I will look forward to it."

Damn. He replaced the receiver and turned to leave. Vlad stood in the doorway, his face stern.

"Getting stood up?" he asked.

Could he have overheard Ruth? Andreas didn't think her voice had been loud enough for that. If he heard, would he tell Kate? Andreas didn't want her to know until after he and Ruth had met. He needed to lay a foundation with the girl before Kate tried to interfere. Once Ruth perceived a professional advantage, Kate would have trouble talking her out of his grasp.

"Yeah," he told Vlad with a smile. "But only delayed, not discarded."

Mother's Day found the three Horbatsky children home for the celebration. As always, they were heading for the elder Cameron's house and a late lunch after the morning church service. Although retirement excused Kate's father from preaching the service, that didn't mean he could sleep in or his family could neglect their Christian duty.

Vlad had not gone to St. Mary's Ukranian Orthadox Church in Oakville as he usually did. Instead, he had driven the family to Knox Presbyterian Church in Milton to attend service with Kate's parents. Walking down the aisle in the familiar church, surrounded by worshipers she had known most of her life, Kate felt at peace. She loved her family and they returned her affection.

She slipped her hand into Vlad's and edged slightly closer. He was a fine man despite his momentary lapses. She knew he missed his own parents and siblings at times like these. That was why he willingly joined her family for special occasions. They had become as much his family as hers.

A few minutes later Kate stood on the church steps and glanced around, basking in the glories of the warm May morning despite the stiff breeze. Vlad had gone to get the car and her father was talking to an old friend.

She saw Andreas in a doorway across the street. He was wearing a black trench coat, hanging open in acknowledgement of the sunny weather. His head was bare and his attire suggested he, too, had just left service. While he had never been particularly devout, she remembered him attending mass occasionally.

A playful gust whipped around the corner and tugged at her jacket. Even as she reached to button it, she heard her father's exclamation and saw his hat do a somersault and skip across the pavement. Two more cartwheels and it landed at Andreas' feet. Kate watched him reach down, pick it up, dust it briefly with one hand, and begin crossing the sidewalk towards them.

He was going to speak to them. Damn. No, he wasn't. He was coming directly to her. Damn, damn, and, triple damn. She glanced around nervously, expecting Vlad to show up at any moment, and braced for his reaction.

Andreas leaned against the doorjamb of the store and watched people streaming from the Presbyterian church across the street. Since coming to Milton, he'd taken to attending mass again as a way to avoid spending long Sundays alone in his hotel room. When today's service was cut short because of the priest's laryngitis, he decided to intrude on Kate's peaceful family time, give her a taste of what it felt like to be spied upon.

He'd been watching the congregation emerge when Vlad and Kate appeared in the doorway. They came down the steps and Vlad split away, heading for the parked cars while Kate ambled towards the sidewalk.

She looked disgustingly content with herself, surrounded by her community, shielded from the damage she had done to him. As he watched, she stopped a couple of feet behind a white-haired man in a dark coat talking to an equally elderly couple. Something in her stance indicated that she knew this man. A young fellow with Vlad's build and coloring came and stopped beside her. He must be her son, Andreas decided.

Seconds later the wind skimmed the hat off the old man's head and tossed it across the street towards Andreas. He had been taught to help his elders and that childhood training kicked in automatically. When the hat landed at his feet, he picked it up, and prepared to return it. He was already walking before he realized the opportunity this presented him to humiliate Kate. In seconds he was standing before her, hat in hand.

"Good morning, *Kati*," he said. "Are you going to introduce me to the owner of this hat?" He could see the tension in her eyes.

Before she could respond the old man stepped around his friend, his hand outstretched. "Thank you, sir," he said. "I believe that belongs to me."

With an innocuous murmur, Andreas nodded and gave him the hat, then turned his gaze back to Kate, waiting patiently for an introduction. Her cheeks flushed and she took a deep breath.

"Andreas, this is my father, Reverend Angus Cameron. Dad, Andreas Wachter, the consulting engineer Gerry hired to get the Clean Room into production."

She stepped back and laid a hand on the young man at her side. "And this is my son, Alexi Horbatsky." He read both pride and defiance in her tone.

A minister? Then he recalled what Gerry said that first night. As he shook hands with both men, Andreas caught sight of Vlad pulling the car to the curb beside them. His frown told Andreas that he was angry. Gleefully, Andreas realized Kate would be in for trouble later. He was bracing to offer Vlad a pleasant greeting designed to increase his bad mood, when a small, dark-haired, young woman passed Kate and grabbed the old man's arm.

"Where are your keys, Granddad? I'll go bring your car around for you. Then we can leave as soon as Tanya and Grandma get out here."

The voice—that voice—it was the one he'd heard on the phone. This was Ruth Kohlman. Her coloring. Her build. The shape of her face. She was the spitting image of his mother! Andreas stood stunned, watching Rev. Cameron hand over the keys she requested. In moments, she was gone.

His daughter. He had a daughter. The realization shot through him like an arrow, mixing searing pain with singing joy, making him dizzy. He couldn't move. He couldn't breathe. His eyes traced her path through the throng until she disappeared.

The old man's hand on his arm broke his trance. "Are you all right?"

Andreas realized Rev. Cameron was speaking to him. He looked concerned.

"What? Oh. Yes. Thank you. I'm fine." He was stuttering like a teenager on a first date. He had to get away. He needed to think. He forced his mind back under control and managed a smile at the older man. "Just distracted for an instant. Really, I am fine. I must not intrude. I must go."

He turned and found Kate in front of him, her face pale, fear flooding her features. She stared at him, her eyes pleading for understanding. Understanding? *Guter Gott!* To think he had trusted her. Adored her. Laid his future at her feet. She'd had almost four months to confide her secret. This was how she treated him?

"*Guten morgen, Fraulein,*" he murmured, his voice like ice, and turned away. Although his car was parked on a nearby side street, the walk seemed to take an age. The day's warmth and light had vanished. He was cold, remembering how he'd planned to use Ruth against her mother. Shame welled up. He hadn't known, he reminded himself. His hand shook so badly he had trouble fitting the key into the ignition.

He recalled the fear he'd seen on Kate's face in February when he suggested claiming her daughter as his. At that point, he had simply been venting his anger. Seeing Ruth changed everything. His claim was no longer an idle threat. She *was* his daughter.

As he drove, an image of Ruth gnawed at his mind. In his apartment in San Antonio he had a picture of his mother holding him outside their Vienna house on Bergenstrasse when he was a toddler. Her hair was dark then, like Ruth's, and she had the same engaging smile. Ruth wasn't very tall, and her hand on her grandfather's arm was fine-boned, like his mother's. They shared dark eyes and a high forehead. Even their lips were the same shape. The physical similarities were too numerous. He couldn't be wrong. He couldn't be imagining it—just because he had always wanted a child with Kate. Ruth must be his daughter. If he was angry before, now he was furious.

Andreas went straight back to his hotel, too upset even to consider food. He needed to think. He went up to his room and changed into cords and walking shoes. He must burn off this rage.

He threw on his jacket, grabbed his wallet from the dresser, and set off to walk the streets of Milton until he calmed down.

The rocky prominence looming over the town caught his eye as he came out the hotel's main exit. As a young man he'd loved to walk in the mountains. The Niagara Escarpment was far from a mountain but it was the closest to a replacement he would find here. Crossing to his car, he headed off along Derry Road, following the signs for Rattlesnake Point. Where the dirt road ended, he pulled off, got out and began to clamber through the trees.

The air seemed clearer here, free from the exhaust fumes of town. He found himself surrounded by a scattering of wildflowers and snatches of song from unseen birds. Here, the trees were old but not primeval. An open area to one side, dotted with saplings, showed nature at work reclaiming the void. Beautiful as he might once have considered the scene, at that moment its charm vanished beneath his anger.

A chipmunk, cheeks bulging, tail erect, raced down the trunk of a dead elm to his right and skittered across his path. Having reached the top of a suspiciously regular stone arrangement that hinted at the remains of a pioneer's fence marching along the perimeter of a long-abandoned field, the tiny creature froze and assessed him cautiously. Then, deciding he posed no threat, it dashed along the rocks and dove into a hole between them.

Nature going about its business. Usually it was a soothing sight. So why had he not been allowed to be part of it? His mind's eye saw a small child racing through the trees ahead of him, dodging behind a dark trunk, then poking her head out, and calling mischievously for him to come and find her.

Fighting tears, he started forward, breathing deeply, hurrying despite the steepness of the slope and the berry canes that grabbed at his pant legs. He didn't want to think. He wanted to grab Katrina's shoulders and shake her.

How dare she keep him from his child! What did she think he was? The enemy? Bitterly, he acknowledged that was exactly how she must have seen him—as the enemy from whom her daughter must be shielded at all cost.

But even now? It was almost thirty years since the war's end. Surely she had outgrown that hatred. They talked in February; they saw each other almost daily now for three weeks. Despite Vlad's jealousy, there must have been some way she could have gotten a message to him, arranged to meet him privately so she could tell him about their child. Yet she had avoided the subject. He couldn't ignore the obvious. She hated him.

The faster he walked the faster the questions arose. They seemed to run in an endless circle. Why didn't she tell him about the baby? Why must she hide the girl now, after all these years? Why did she still hate him?

The higher he went, the rockier the terrain became. Soon he was breathing heavily and beginning to perspire. An awkward step on the point of a rock protruding from the forest floor almost upset him. He crashed into a maple to his left and grabbed the rough trunk to keep from falling, massaging the ankle he twisted in the process. Cursing silently, he caught his breath, and resumed his climb. Now he moved more slowly and gave his full attention to his surroundings. The last thing he needed was a broken bone.

By the time he emerged from the trees a few feet from the actual edge of the escarpment, his hair had curled and his shirt was stuck to his back. He mopped a sleeve across his face and, finding a stump with a reasonably flat top, sank down to catch his breath. The breeze he'd been denied under the trees swept over him.

Just beyond his feet the world plunged away, revealing gently rolling farm fields, more trees coming into their early spring foliage and an occasional vehicle wending its way along Appleby Line.

High over the tranquil landscape, a single turkey vulture soared on the updrafts in search of its daily meal. The loneliness of the bird caught at Andreas' emotions, reminding him that even in nature, not all creatures have a mate.

As his breathing returned to normal and his heart rate slowed, his thoughts turned again to his daughter and to their impending dinner. The wisest course of action might be to call the whole thing off. Certainly, he must drop the fiction about a job offer. Yet, he couldn't bring himself to give up their date. He needed to make Ruth's acquaintance. He wondered what had she been told about her father.

Four hours later, although the sun was still high, the wind had developed a fresh bite. He was glad to be back at his car in one piece. His legs ached and any jolt on the uneven terrain shot pain into his instep and through his ankle. His anger had settled into a dull ache. Although he was still wrestling with part of his dilemma, at least his mind was made up to confront Kate.

By the time he arrived back at the hotel the dining room was open. He ordered dinner and tried to ignore Ruth's image as he picked at his food.

In his room once again, he stripped and showered. However, instead of soothing him, the water had a rejuvenating affect. Now he was wide-awake and restless again. He glanced at his watch. It was not quite seven o'clock, much too early to consider sleep. It was still light. A new idea crossed his mind. He went to his bedside table and found the telephone book. The Milton section was small and listed only a handful of Camerons, including Rev. A. Cameron on Kingsley Court.

Picking up the town map he'd purchased when he arrived, he headed for the door. Common sense kicked in before he reached the lobby and he turned back. What would he accomplish by driving around town tracking Ruth down like a jealous lover?

He took a bottle from the mini bar and made himself a drink. Sitting by the window, sipping and watching the darkness close in, he reconsidered his original intention to tackle Kate in the morning. If he didn't want her to interfere, he should delay their confrontation until after his dinner with Ruth.

As the hours passed and the drinks trickled down, the alcohol mellowed him so that pain drowned his anger. Over and over, he questioned why Kate had hidden her pregnancy from him. She couldn't help but know how much he loved her. He'd made it so damned obvious.

He was on the verge of sleep when a new thought jolted him awake again. What if her parents knew about him? Since she had returned with his baby, she must have made up some story. Gerry had referred to her as a war widow. Had she pretended he was the man to whom she was married?

Surely she would never have revealed his name, not when he was an enemy. Still, plenty of Germans had emigrated to American. Her fake husband could have descended from one of them, he speculated. That would let Ruth be called Kohlman. Did she fear his name would be recognized?

When she introduced him to her father this morning she'd called him Wachter. Kate was the only one here who knew he had once used both his father's and his stepfather's names. It still made no sense.

Then another suspicion popped into Andreas' slightly fuzzy thoughts. Vlad was so jealous, had he gone checking on Andreas' emigration papers? Had he somehow discovered that Andreas had dropped the Kohlman part of his name when he emigrated? It would certainly explain

Horbatsky's hatred. He'd be justifiably furious if he thought Andreas had a legal claim to Kate. No man wants his marriage invalidated by the appearance of a former husband, real or imaginary.

Now that would make for an interesting situation. He relaxed and pulled the blankets more firmly around his shoulders.

CHAPTER ELEVEN

Supper was over and the younger Horbatskys were in their rooms packing up to return to the city. Alexi was working in a law firm, gaining experience before beginning his law degree. Tanya, too, had a summer job, working in a veterinarian's office.

Nor was Ruth staying the night. Struggling to shake the remnants of her cold, she was leaving for her own house as soon as she finished helping her mother clear the table.

"Got a big date Wednesday night so I need to be back in shape," she said, then grinned. "Well, it's not a date, really. He wants to talk to me about a plane modification and I already put him off once because of this cold. I need my sleep if I want my head working properly."

Kate was curious about this opportunity for Ruth to expand her work experience but a day of Vlad's pointed stares and clipped comments told her an explosion was imminent. It was hard enough to deal with his rages when they were alone. The kids' presence always escalated the difficulties because they tried to mediate on her behalf. Ruth in particular, brought out the worst in Vlad.

"Why don't you get out of here now?" she suggested, trying to hurry Ruth's departure. "The food's put away and the dishwasher takes care of the tedious part. Go on. Get your rest. Then call me Thursday and tell me all about this new assignment. Okay? Scoot. Take care of yourself."

Ruth's car had scarcely started up before Vlad stalked into the kitchen and took up a stand by Kate's elbow.

"I see he could not leave you alone even for the weekend," he began, making no explanation for who *he* was.

Kate concentrated on slotting plates into the dishwasher rack. She kept her voice calm. "Just in the neighborhood, I expect. Probably attending service."

"I did not see him in the church."

"You wouldn't." The words fell into suspicious silence. Kate wanted to kick herself. If she knew Andreas' religious denomination, obviously, she knew him rather better than she'd implied. She straightened up and shut the appliance door.

Vlad was looking at her, making a beckoning motion with his hand. "Come on. Explain to me how you know he is not Presbyterian."

Here we go, she thought. "Andreas is Austrian and Catholic," she said. "I used to see him in the church in Peenemünde when I attended mass."

"You went to mass?" Alexi had entered the kitchen unnoticed, his suitcase in his hand. His face mirrored absolute shock. "You?"

Kate shrugged. "I was supposed to be a good little German girl, remember? Church was a logical place to go if I wanted to fit in."

"And Wachter was there." Vlad wasn't asking; he was stating a fact. "So he must have been shocked to discover you are protestant and your father is a minister."

By this time Alexi was more than a little curious. "Wachter? Are you talking about Wachter the engineer? The guy we met after church this morning?"

Kate nodded.

Alexi turned to his father. "And why would you think he's interested in Mom?" He stopped and shook his head. "Now that was a dumb question if I ever asked one. What do you think? He was Mom's boyfriend?"

Kate tensed, fearing Vlad would strike their son.

Vlad's eyes flashed and he colored slightly. "He may well have been. In fact, the way he is hanging around after her, I am sure he was."

Alexi groaned and rolled his eyes.

"I worked in the same office with Andreas when I was in Germany." Kate began to repeat the sanitized version of her story for her son. "I saw him on a daily basis. Of course he knows me—or thinks he does. He's furious to discover that the woman he trusted to type reports for him was a traitor. It affronts his self-confidence. He thinks he should have seen through me and discovering he did not shakes his faith in himself. In other words, Hon, I'm not on Andreas Wachter's Christmas list at the moment. Okay?"

"So that's why he wanted to be introduced to Granddad. He wanted to meet your family."

"Or to embarrass me."

Alexi nodded thoughtfully. "I suppose. Only that would indicate he is interested in you."

Kate shrugged and pushed buttons on the dishwasher to start it. "I won't deny he's interested. He'd like my head on a platter. That's not the romantic interest your dad imagines."

Vlad grunted. "He wants your butt in his bed."

"Vlad, don't be a fool," Kate snapped, her cheeks flushing with embarrassment that he would express his suspicions so bluntly before their son.

Her husband snorted and shook his head. "Who's the fool? He may well be annoyed with you but he still wants to sleep with you."

"Give it a rest Dad," Alexi sighed wearily. "You've been accusing guys of eyeing Mom ever since I can remember. And even if it were true, just because some guy has the hots for her doesn't mean she returns his interest. You know better than that, for goodness sake."

Vlad shot his son a contemptuous look. "Lawyering will suit you; you're good with words. You think you can talk her way out of any infidelity."

Alexi clenched his fists. Kate grabbed his wrist.

Fuming, Vlad marched into the family room, turned on the television, and dropped to the couch. All of a sudden, he snatched an ashtray off the adjacent end table and heaved it at the stones of the fireplace. There was a loud crack, followed by the tinkle of falling crockery.

Alexi cocked an eyebrow at her questioningly. Kate shook her head, then made a shooing motion with the other hand. The worst was over now and the sooner the kids left, the sooner calm would return.

#

Andreas was so nervous he felt nauseous by the time he actually got to his dinner meeting with Ruth. He wanted desperately to get acquainted with his child, and to build a friendship with her if at all possible. He also needed to know what Kate had told the girl about him. The trouble was if she were as smart as he expected her to be, getting information without betraying their relationship would not be easy.

He barely had time to find a seat in the hotel lobby before Ruth walked in. He rose and watched her cross to meet him. Dressed in a smart beige pantsuit with dark brown accessories, she looked very professional without losing a speck of her femininity. She reminded him so much of his mother, Eva Kohlman Wachter, but with Kate's confident manner and easy smile.

Resentment welled at how Kate had deprived him. He should have been there to see their daughter grow up. Instead, he was meeting her as a mature woman. He pushed the regret away and held out his hand.

"It is a pleasure to see you again, Miss Kohlman," he began. "I trust you are feeling better than last week."

"Oh, goodness. You're the man at the church on Sunday. I had no idea who you were. Please forgive my bad manners." She gasped and grasped his hand firmly, then fell into step as he led her towards the dining room.

The waitress showed them to their table and they took their time placing their order.

Still dithering about how to raise the issue of Ruth's childhood, Andreas decided to eliminate the easy problem first.

"I must confess to luring you here under false pretenses," he began. "I found out yesterday that I didn't get the contract. But since I raised your expectations I felt I owed you dinner. I hope you'll forgive me. Besides, I'm always interested in what's going on in the industry, and what my colleagues are doing."

He relaxed as she waved her hand in a dismissive gesture.

"I appreciate the face-to-face explanation. Saves me those self-doubts about being secretly rejected." She grinned. "It also gives me the chance to ask how you heard about me in the first place. Mr. Clarke?"

Here we go, he thought, and determined to be as close to honest as possible.

"Actually, Janice mentioned you during the car rally. Females are scarce in our field so I was very curious. Then the jet contract came up and it seemed a perfect excuse to meet you."

Their wine arrived and Andreas went through the tasting ritual, then turned the conversation to what had prompted Ruth's interest in airplanes.

She shrugged. "Maybe the fact my dad was an engineer. Maybe the fact Mom got me summer jobs at Clarke's and they were doing plane components. I started university with the idea of going into teaching—maths and sciences, actually. But biology turned me off. Physics caught my interest. And the rest is history, as they say."

So Kate had confided his occupation to Ruth. He'd follow that clue as innocently as possible. "Vlad is an engineer? I didn't know that."

"Vlad Horbatsky is not my father." Her voice was clipped.

Ashamed of him, Andreas wondered, or disliked him? "Sorry," he murmured.

Immediately she changed the subject. "What about you, Herr Wachter? What put you into plane design?"

"Curiosity," he replied promptly. "My father died in World War I and my step-father was an engineer. Our house in Vienna was full of tools and drawings. My younger brother and I were always welcome in his workshop. Anton is ten years younger than I am, so we didn't share a lot of projects but Papa encouraged us both and helped me to teach my little brother. For a while I thought I might want a career in education, but I, too, changed my mind at university when I got into physics. The war was building up then too. When I met Wernher Von Braun, I got hooked on his work with airplanes and rockets."

"Von Braun? With NASA and John Glenn? Wow."

Andreas forced a smile. She knew about Von Braun but not about her own father. He felt rejected, jealous.

"I knew there was a reason for your reputation," she continued. "Were you also doing fuel research or were you always involved with the engines?"

So she admired the program, not the man. Substance mattered more to her than celebrity. He was growing to like her more and more.

"Strictly hardware."

She nodded, then took yet another tack. "And your family? Do you have sons following in your footsteps?"

"No." *But I have a daughter in the field.* "My only son died a few hours after his birth. Then my wife was killed in a car accident several years later."

"Life's a bitch, isn't it? My parents only had a short time together. Dad didn't even know Mom was pregnant when he disappeared. Yet she loved him so much she took years to get over his memory."

Could that be true? Shame swept him as he remembered Kate's assertion she would have married him under different circumstances. He took a sip from his glass to hide his confusion.

"Your mother told you this?"

Ruth shook her head. "No, but I was old enough to see how hard Vlad had to work to persuade her to marry him. She almost didn't, you know. I guess I helped him there. I remember whining about wanting brothers and sisters like other kids had."

Andreas had to choke back the lump in his throat at the picture Ruth painted. It was so unlike what he expected, so much more than he had dared to hope.

"And are you close to your brother and sister?"

"They're younger of course, so our interests always differed. But I expect we'll get closer now that they're out on their own. At least we've always shared our love for home and family."

"Kati would have insisted on that."

Instantly, her expression changed. The pleasant laugh vanished. Her eyes went sharp, hard almost, as they examined his face. She was making no secret of assessing his motive in seeking her out. "How do you know that?"

Again, he trod the edge of truth. "Has your mother ever talked about what she did during the war? About going to Germany as a spy?"

Her expression remained tight. She nodded slightly, obviously braced for a shock.

"Kati and I worked in the same research facility through most of the war."

He could see Ruth was puzzled. She had expected more. When he added nothing, she prompted him. "And?"

"And I admired her very much. She was smart. She was kind. She was beautiful. We didn't have actual private secretaries at Peenemünde but your mother came as close to that for me as our system allowed. She was my right hand."

Prepared or not, he could tell that was not what she had expected to hear.

"We lost touch when I was brought to America at the end of the war, so naturally I am interested in what happened to her after we parted."

There was a long silence. Then she asked, "Did you know what Mother was doing at Peenemünde?"

Andreas shook his head. "No. I only found out when I came to work for Clarke's. I asked Gerry how your mother learned to speak my language so well and he told me about her career as a spy."

"And you can still think well of her?"

He grinned. "After I got over wanting to rip her throat out, I realized how brave she is, and how smart. All the same, I won't be spreading around any tales of our time together. Others don't need to know what a fool she made of me because she was a damned good spy."

The waitress appeared with their plates and Andreas steered the conversation to Ruth's work at McDonnell-Douglas. By dessert, their conversation was flowing almost like friends rather than the strangers they truly were.

She was listening intently to him and responding intelligently. He was flattered to have such a bright daughter. Beautiful, too. Kate had done him proud.

As the evening progressed Andreas concentrated on absorbing the new information Ruth provided and storing it carefully for later contemplation. She was giving him much to think about starting with the possibility he had misjudged her mother. All the same, the question persisted. If Kate didn't hate him, why hide Ruth's existence from him?

CHAPTER TWELVE

Vlad was barely down the driveway on Thursday morning before the ringing telephone interrupted Kate's routine. She was surprised to hear Ruth's voice.

"What's wrong?" Kate demanded immediately. "You never call at this hour."

"I never have news like this," Ruth shot back. "Vlad's gone, isn't he? You can talk?"

"Yes. He just left. What's wrong?"

Ruth sighed melodramatically. "I think I'm in love."

"What? Ruth, be serious. What's going on?"

"I am serious. Well, I'd like to be." Ruth paused, then added, "Only, I don't think he is. Not about me, anyway."

"Okay. Now that you've got me thoroughly confused, what the heck are you talking about?" Then Kate remembered Ruth's big date. "You had a business dinner last night, didn't you? Is that it? What happened?"

"Yeah, I did. And nothing happened. Well, nothing work-related. He didn't get the contract so there's no job for me. But wow, Mom! Why didn't you warn me? He is gorgeous." She enunciated each word with extreme precision.

"Warn you? About what?" Suspicion rippled through her, and Kate shivered. "Who did you meet, Ruth?"

"Andreas Wachter, the NASA contractor that Gerry hired. Why didn't you tell me you knew him?"

Kate's knees went weak and she had to lean on the counter for support. Andreas had talked to Ruth. *Dear God, what did he tell her?*

Tears clouded her vision and her hands shook. She felt like she was racing up a hill. She couldn't catch her breath. She hesitated before speaking, fearing the tremor in her voice would betray her.

"Mom, are you there?"

"What happened?"

Ruth sounded annoyed. "I told you, nothing happened. He was a perfect gentleman. But that's it. When do I meet a gentleman, let alone the kind with European manners, cultured interests, and knowledge of aerodynamics? I swear, if he'd made a pass I'd probably have accepted it."

Kate gasped. She couldn't help herself. "You can't mean that."

"Oh, I mean it, but relax. I saw the light before the evening was over."

"Light? What light?"

"You. He's crazy about you."

Ruth's assertion rocked Kate's composure more than Vlad's accusations. Fear pressed harder. Kate found her hands were damp, slipping on the receiver she held. "And just what did he say to give you that impression?"

"He said you were as close to being his private secretary as the system would allow."

Kate's heart thumped so hard she expected Ruth to hear it all the way down the phone line. "That's true. So?"

"So, I think he was sweet on you. Was he?"

There it was. The question she didn't want to discuss with anyone. The question she'd avoided for twenty-seven years. The answer to which could destroy her marriage, her family, and her reputation. While she wanted desperately to lie, Ruth deserved the truth. Or at least some of it. This man was her father, after all. Apparently she liked him. She might never meet him again. Surely, she should be allowed to see something of the loving man Kate had known.

Kate took a deep breath and plunged in. "Yes, Ruth, he was sweet on me. In fact, he wanted to marry me."

There was a long silence. "He's still in love with you, you know," Ruth said.

"I don't think so. He loves the woman he knew, not the woman I am."

"Are you sorry you refused him?"

"I beg your pardon?"

"Your life would have been very different with him. More money, a prestigious husband, travel, no irrational jealousy, no rages, a peaceful home. Do you ever wonder if you made the wrong choice?"

She forced a cold tone, hoping to discourage her daughter from pursuing the idea. "No. I had no choice, Ruth. I was a spy, remember?"

"But afterwards. The war was almost over before you left. You could have stayed in touch. You could have gone to him after he got to the States. You were on your own for several years before you met Vlad. Why didn't you contact him after we got home? Weren't you in love with him?"

Kate's mind seized up in panic. Admitting her love would point Ruth to the obvious conclusion. If she had already reached that conclusion, denying it would negate everything Kate had always preached to her children about honesty.

"Are you questioning my morals? The morals of a spy?"

Instead of answering, Ruth switched directions. "So it wasn't because of me? He wouldn't have objected to you having a child?"

"No. Never. I told you. I was a spy. Love wasn't an option for me." Kate wanted to yell at Ruth to drop the subject.

"And that's it?"

"Yes." What more did she expect?

Ruth was silent for a moment, as though figuring out how to continue. Then said, "So, you won't be upset if I want to date him?"

Kate almost choked. She knew Ruth was just feeling her out. She wanted her suspicions about Andreas' identity confirmed, and Kate's evasion had forced her onto another path. Two could play that game.

"Of course not. I don't interfere in your social life," Kate replied, fighting the inclination to scream. "I'm just surprised you'd chase a man of his age, especially if you think he's got other interests."

Ruth made her excuses in a flat voice, and hung up. Fuming, Kate resumed her morning chores, clearing the table, filling the dishwasher, setting out meat to thaw for supper. Her mind churned, alternating between fury with Andreas for intruding into Ruth's life and cold fear that she had misjudged the point of Ruth's call. What if she really didn't know her father's identity?

# # #

Kate's temper did a slow boil as she drove to work through the late spring sunshine. How dare Andreas approach Ruth? What had he been plotting? An end run around her efforts to protect her family? Now she was left to do the explaining.

And pretending he still cared about her. How stupid did he think she was? He couldn't help knowing how he upset Vlad. Was that his revenge, wrecking her marriage?

She needed to have it out with him. She wouldn't tolerate any more of this sneaking around.

When she opened the factory door, Gerry was in the front entry with a bundle of mail in his hands. "I just had a call from Gus," he said. "Bring your pad straight to my office. I need to get a reply off to him immediately. Come on." He handed her the letters and whipped off towards the stairs.

Kate bit down on her anger and raced after him. Andreas had received a temporary reprieve.

As she was leaving Gerry's office with notes for the reply to Gus, she almost collided with Andreas in the doorway. He stepped back to let her pass.

"We need to talk," she muttered through clenched teeth. "Lunch. Marg's Diner on Martin Street. Eleven forty-five."

"Shall I drive?" His words were curt.

"Separate vehicles would attract less attention."

He nodded. "If that is your wish. I will be there."

The morning dragged. Janice's sudden need to chatter grated on Kate's frayed nerves. She still had no plan of attack when she hurried down the stairs and drove off to meet Andreas.

She arrived at the diner just ahead of the lunch crowd and chose a booth near the kitchen where the noise of banging pots and shouted orders would cover their conversation from any would-be eavesdroppers.

She was staring at the menu when Andreas eased onto the bench across the table from her. He shrugged out of his jacket, waved away the menu the waitress offered, and ordered a hot beef sandwich and coffee.

Kate ordered soup, then sat back, toying with a glass of water. She began as soon as the waitress departed. "What's the big idea of offering Ruth a made-up job?"

"Who says it's made up?" he countered.

"I do. You were just looking for a way to meet my daughter, weren't you?"

"Your daughter? You gave her my name."

"Not really."

"I know she's my child, Katrina. What I want to know is why you didn't tell me you were pregnant."

"At the time you left, I didn't know." Andreas stared at her, then raised one eyebrow. "Her birthday is February second," Kate explained, then fought the urge to slap him as he held up his hand and counted off nine fingers.

"All right. You didn't know then. But later, after I was settled, you could have contacted me. I would have looked after you. I wanted to marry you, for God's sake. I would never have turned my back on you, much less on our child."

"And now that you've found her, what are you planning to do? Tell her that you're her father?"

"Would that be a sin?"

Kate gripped her water glass, fighting the desire to dump it on his head. "Almost. At the very least, it would be a very bad idea."

"Are you sure? I got the impression last night that she just might like to have me in her life."

"That's it, exactly. She finds you attractive."

"She what? Oh, hell. No!" He looked stricken. Kate was stunned to see the blood drain from his face. He was taking Ruth's reaction as seriously as she did.

"Yes. She was so excited about meeting you that she called me this morning to talk about it."

"I didn't do anything. I swear it. I didn't...damn!" There was a long pause before he asked if she wanted him to stay away from Ruth.

Kate could see real pain in his expression. In spite of herself, she felt sorry for him. She sighed. "No. That would hurt both of you. In fact, I suspect Ruth already knows who you are. I think she was digging, trying to get me to admit to our relationship. I think I should tell her."

"But you just said...I don't understand."

"I wasn't sure whether you cared about Ruth or just wanted to get back at me."

He glared at her, then grimaced. "I guess I deserved that. I admit I was very angry when I discovered you had a child. But when I realized she is my child, my baby girl..."

"Yes, I could tell that by the look on your face Sunday. How did you know? She certainly doesn't look like you. Or me either, for that matter."

"She's the image of my mother at that age. Same coloring, same size, same facial features. I couldn't miss it." He brushed the question aside and returned to his original point. "Why, Kati? Why couldn't I have been her father? I loved you. I wanted our children."

"I realize that." Kate looked away, suppressing tears. "I knew you were supposed to go to the States, but I certainly couldn't follow you. You thought I was German. Daughter or no, how would you have reacted when you found out what I was? Nor would the Americans have accepted my phony papers. Even knowing the truth wouldn't have pleased them much. A spy's a spy, and since I'd obviously been fraternizing with the enemy, they wouldn't trust me."

Damn. She hated sounding like she was making excuses. She was, of course, but it was the truth. "I had no way of finding you and by the time Ruth was old enough to hear the truth, I was married to Vlad."

Kate reached for her coffee to cover up the tremor in her voice.

"Bull," Andreas protested. "The team's surrender was only kept secret for a few months. We arrived in the States in June and the public knew all about us by early October. We weren't hidden away."

"But I didn't know that. I was still in England then," she pointed out, setting down her cup, irritated by how desperate she sounded to herself. "The Brits didn't care who the Yanks had scooped up. All that mattered to them was whether their boys had survived and when they were coming home."

Andreas leaned back while the waitress served their food. When she departed, he continued. "But your family must have heard about us. They were here, listening to the American news broadcasts."

Kate ignored her food. "I doubt it, and what they did hear didn't mean anything to them. They never knew where I was or what I was doing. Even today they don't understand what I actually did as a spy."

"But Vlad knows."

Kate shrugged. "Only that the S.O.E. put me in a rocket research facility and I was there from 1942 until the collapse in 1945."

Andreas persisted. "He knows Ruth is my child."

She shook her head. "He thinks I was a widow. That Ruth belonged to a serviceman named Andrew Coleman who disappeared."

"Andrew Kohlman." He repeated the name, his eyes softening. "You must have felt something if you gave her my name."

"Coleman. C-O-L-E-M-A-N." Kate spelled the name. "The English spelling, Andreas."

His face reddened with anger. "You lied about her name? About her identity?"

Anger flared again at his tone. Didn't he understand yet what it meant to live in that never land between enemies?

"I couldn't very well tell the truth, now could I? I mean, you were an enemy combatant. And fraternizing, regardless of my mission, made me a traitor. My family and my community would all have seen me that way, and Ruth as well. I couldn't put that sort of burden on a child. Her very life might have been in danger if the truth came out so soon after the war."

"So you were protecting her?"

"I needed to consider my parents, too. My father stood in the pulpit every Sunday preaching about virtue and honor and honesty. What do you imagine it would have done to his reputation if it got around that his daughter had a child out of wedlock? And with a German at that."

Andreas pointed an accusatory finger at her. "That was your fault. I wanted to marry you."

"No, that was Hilter's fault. What was the first step in any marriage in Germany in those days?"

Andreas frowned. "Getting permission, and calling the banns."

Kate nodded. "Now think about what you just said."

Andreas frowned and softly repeated the words.

"Part of that permission involved a check of your family by the state authorities," she reminded him, curtly.

"So?" Andreas challenged, picking up his cup, then replacing it, slowly. "Your background." The startled expression on his face told Kate he finally understood her dilemma.

"Yes. My background. My non-existent background. By the time they were finished checking me out, they'd know I wasn't Jewish. But they'd also know the family I claimed to have never existed. Nor did I—officially."

"You would have been executed," he said.

"And you, too."

"What? But I..."

"You were consorting with an enemy. That was a treasonous offense—even if you didn't realize what you were doing. Remember how they arrested Von Braun for a casual remark at a party? His position was far more crucial to the war effort than yours was. I couldn't risk your life as well as my own."

Andreas looked as though she'd struck him. "You were protecting me?" He shook his head in frustration. "You said you loved me. If that's so, why couldn't you have told me about Ruth when I arrived in February?"

"After you gave a good imitation of wanting to rip me limb-from-limb for being a spy? I don't think so."

"Oh." He dropped his head and toyed with his coffee cup.

"And then there was Vlad spitting fire if your name even got mentioned," she continued. "Exactly how do you think I'd manage to arrange a few moments to speak to you privately? In your mood, had I tried, you'd probably have announced to the whole world that you were too busy to take a secret meeting with a spy."

"Kati, that's not fair."

"No? You aren't being very fair either." Hurt and anger boiled over. Probably she shouldn't admit her feelings, but she had carried the guilt for so long she felt compelled to tell him the truth. It wouldn't change anything, but at least it would clear her conscience.

"I've always wanted to tell you about our daughter. I'm sorry I needed to deceive you in Germany. I can only say it was never personal. I was there to get information, not to destroy you. In fact, if you recall when I first arrived at Peenemünde, I tried to avoid you. Only you wouldn't leave me alone. It would have compromised my mission to protest more than I did. I couldn't let that happen so I stopped fighting. I knew I'd hurt you and I certainly hurt myself. Unfortunately, I couldn't avoid it. I wasn't at all sure you'd want me once you knew what I'd been doing. Canada couldn't deport me because I'm a citizen, but you'd have had no future here in your field. If you gave up your career because of me, over the years you'd come to hate me. That's why I decided to just disappear. One clean break seemed to be the kindest way to end things. I made that decision before we went to Oberammergau, before we were even sure you could surrender to the Americans. Before I got pregnant."

Andreas' grim expression turned into a scowl. "You should still have told me. We could have found somewhere to start over together."

Kate bit her lip to hold back the tears, all her anger gone. Painful memories welled up of lonely nights during which she wrestled repeatedly with her dilemma. She could read the hurt in Andreas' eyes.

"Where would that have been?" She challenged him. "Believe me, I considered every country with even a rudimentary industrial base. There was no place that would accept me as a spy and offer you anything in your field. I knew you'd want the baby and I wanted desperately to share her with you. But a child would only increase the burden. So I stayed silent."

Andreas' anger was blazing again. "Being noble, was it? Depriving me of my daughter in exchange for my career? Thank you so much for making my decisions for me. I'll try to put in a good word for you with St. Peter when I get there."

Kate shook her head in disgust, her nostalgia gone. "Oh, get off it. Feeling sorry for myself had nothing to do with it. I was too busy making a life for myself and Ruth."

"So you turned yourself into a war widow and waited for a good offer. But Christ, couldn't you have found someone better than Horbatsky?" Kate could again see pain in his expression.

"No." she snapped. "I wasn't some sweet little housewife who served her country running a machine somewhere so her man could go off to war and get killed. The things I saw weren't things I could talk about. Vlad understood that. He also followed the European attitudes and value systems that were totally foreign here at that time. The lifestyle you taught me. Remember?"

"So you're saying I taught you to appreciate Vlad?" Andreas shook his head in disbelief and took another sip from his cup.

Kate couldn't tell whether he didn't believe her or just rejected the connection.

He changed the subject. "So now you want to tell Ruth who I am. She's my daughter, too. Why can't I be there when she finds out?"

God, men could be thick at times. It would be hard enough telling Ruth the truth without him standing there gloating over her confession.

"Because it might be embarrassing for all of us. She's going to have a lot of questions. She might be more comfortable asking them if you aren't around. You might be happier not knowing some of my answers."

He glared at her, then nodded. "I suppose. But tell her I'm proud of her and it would make me very happy to call her my daughter."

Kate swallowed the last of her drink and nodded. "I'll tell her. And I'll let you know when we've talked. Then you can call her yourself and speak freely."

CHAPTER THIRTEEN

As he was coming out of the washroom, Vlad saw Kate hurry up the stairs. He wondered where she'd been. She hadn't mentioned needing to do any errands when they talked at breakfast. By evening, routine problems had driven all thoughts of her lunchtime absence completely out of his mind. His suspicions did not return until Friday afternoon when he sat down in the Charles Hotel beverage room with co-worker Tim Haskins for their weekly beer after work. The decade-long routine had seen them share numerous ideas and attitudes over a brew. Tim knew how protective Vlad was of his marriage.

They were chatting casually, the way they always did, when Tim asked Vlad if he'd had a fight with Kate the previous weekend.

Vlad's hackles rose instantly. What had his wife done now? As the family matriarch it was her duty to be a community leader. As the focus of the local gossips she opened the family to ridicule. He would not tolerate that. Maintaining his unruffled façade, Vlad looked at Tim and shook his head. "No. Why?"

The younger man looked embarrassed as he

explained about his wife seeing Kate having lunch with Andreas at Marg's Diner on Thursday.

That Kraut again! Vlad's anger escalated. He might have known Wachter was involved if Kate was behaving inappropriately. He took a fresh swallow of beer, using the interruption to get a firmer grip on himself, then nodded. "Could be, I suppose. I never know what she's up to from one day to the next." He already knew the answer but he had to ask the question if he were to conceal his suspicions from Tim. "Was it a business lunch? Was Gerry with them?"

Tim shrugged. "Freda said they were alone. She walked right by them and Kate didn't even see her. She was too busy talking to Wachter."

Seething under his poker face, Vlad made a dismissive gesture. "I'll have to ask her. I'm sure it was nothing, but thanks for telling me. The last thing we need is people gossiping."

Privately, he vowed this was the end of his tolerance for her antics with the German. There would be no more placating efforts on his part. Since she refused to see the damage she was doing, he would take stronger measures. She was his wife and she was going to behave that way if he had to force her compliance. Removing the Kraut would be the best way to ensure that.

Vlad steered the conversation to construction of the new assembly line and Tim dropped his questions about Kate. When his glass was empty, Vlad wished his buddy a good weekend, and excused himself to do his banking.

Having Tim confirm his suspicions about Wachter set Vlad to raging. Normally he would have stormed home and demanded answers, but he knew she'd only lie about it. He knew how men looked at his wife. He also knew when she was making a fool of him. Hadn't his father been sleeping with Olga while his mother was carrying him?

The question was what to do about it? He had tried ignoring the man. That didn't work. He'd told Kate what the fat prick was up to. She didn't listen. He wouldn't just step aside and let the German take up where he'd obviously left off. No Kraut was going to take away his wife and destroy his family. This was Canada. Vlad was a citizen. He had the same rights as anyone else. No smug arse-hole was going to ruin his life here. They'd already done enough to him. It was going to end. Now.

#

Vlad stewed over Tim's remarks in silence throughout Friday evening. After Kate left to visit Ruth on Saturday morning, he continued to brood about the secret meeting as he went about his chores.

He kept remembering Kate's remark that no one knew she and Wachter were old acquaintances. She denied that Wachter could threaten her but Vlad didn't believe her. Former co-workers did not sneak off to have lunch together to discuss business—especially not thirty-year-old business.

So how could Wachter compromise her now? There must be something. Everyone knew she'd been a spy. Everyone knew she'd had a baby out of wedlock. He stopped mid-thought. Didn't they? Was that it? Did

Wachter know the identity of Ruth's father? Was that the secret Kate wanted to keep hidden?

No matter how Vlad twisted and turned his thoughts, it was the only answer that made sense. Kate feared Andreas would reveal her lover's name.

Originally, Vlad had suspected Andreas of being that lover and probably Ruth's father. Now, deliberating the matter over his midday sandwich, he changed his mind.

Wachter must have heard Ruth mentioned at some point since his arrival in Milton, yet he'd made no attempt to meet her. When they did run into each other the previous weekend, he ignored the girl. Vlad couldn't imagine a father ignoring his own child.

The answer struck him mid afternoon, while he was cutting grass. Did Wachter know Ruth was not his child? That possibility halted Vlad in his tracks. Then he shook it off and returned to pushing the mower.

Wachter couldn't be sure Ruth was not his unless he had some knowledge to the contrary. Only one circumstance could provide such proof—that Kate and Wachter had never been lovers. Vlad couldn't accept that; not when Wachter looked at Kate with his feelings visible for all to see.

Vlad's mind continued along the path. If they had been lovers, how did Wachter know Ruth wasn't his? Ruth bore no trace of physical resemblance to the Kraut, of course, but that didn't mean much since she didn't look like Kate either.

He was washing up for supper when the answer came to him. Ruth must look so much like her father that

Wachter recognized her. Which meant that Kate had become pregnant at the rocket research facility in Germany. If Wachter wasn't the girl's father, then one of his cohorts was.

That explained many things. Like why the girl was so arrogant and disrespectful. She was a typical German. No wonder he hated her.

Vlad strode to the refrigerator and took out the casserole Kate had left for him. He put the dish into the microwave and took out a plate while the food warmed. As he sat down to eat, he began wrestling with his new problem.

He really didn't need to know the identity of his wife's former lover. It was enough to know the man was German. He didn't need to hear Kate's explanations—or denials.

Obviously she was ashamed of her behavior—and so she should be. That was beside the point. He was her husband now and it was his responsibility to protect her from men like Wachter. To protect his whole family, in fact. The Horbatsky name was old and distinguished, part of the Ukrainian military nobility. No one mocked them or dishonored their women, least of all, a filthy Kraut.

The question was how to silence the German before he forced Kate back into his bed. Because it was obvious that was what he wanted. Vlad had known that all along. The part he hadn't understood was what ammunition Wachter could use.

# # #

The morning sunshine failed to lighten Kate's mood as she drove east towards Ruth's new home in Port Credit.

She wondered if Ruth suspected the circumstances surrounding her birth were different from what she had been told. If so, then hearing the truth might be a relief. Especially if she liked Andreas as much as she intimated.

Still, their mother-daughter chats had always followed old-fashioned moral lines based on chastity. For Ruth to discover Kate had stepped outside the bounds she preached would present an entirely new picture. Hypocrisy. That's what Ruth would call Kate's attitude. And she'd be right.

Then again, kids tend to see their parents as asexual, and view their own birth as the result of some sort of immaculate conception. Discovering the reality might severely strain their relationship.

Kate tried to tell herself she had had no alternative, given the times and her circumstances. It didn't help. These days, extra-marital affairs and unwed mothers barely drew any notice. But when Ruth was born? Times were different then, Kate mused, thinking of an old classmate.

Jeannie had become pregnant in the spring of their year at business college. While they weren't close friends, they were well acquainted having been in the same class throughout high school.

Several times in the cafeteria, Kate had noticed and ignored Jeannie's pale face and puffy eyes. It seemed ill-mannered to push, and when polite inquiries were brushed aside, she carried on with her life and left Jeannie to her own devices.

Less than a month after graduation the town was horrified to learn Jeannie was dead. She'd taken her father's car into the most deserted part of the township one night, rolled up the windows, plugged the exhaust with a potato, and let carbon monoxide end what she obviously saw as the ruin of her future. Even today her parents' contemporaries occasionally cast pitying glances toward Jeannie's mother, bit their lips, and shook their heads in disapproval of the girl who had so shamed her family.

Ruth met Kate at the back door. She was dressed in jeans and a ratty t-shirt. Her smile couldn't hide her strained posture as she stepped back to let her mother enter. Ruth's obvious discomfort roused Kate's protective instincts, temporarily overshadowing the nerves knotting in her stomach.

"What did you do to yourself?" she demanded, making the obvious connection with the garden fork leaning against the wall by the step.

Ruth half-shrugged, then winced. "I pulled something in my back trying to work up the flowerbed." She forestalled her mother's questions with an outstretched hand. "No, I haven't seen the doctor. I'm trying the rest cure. Instead of doing all the chores I planned this weekend, I've distracted myself with cooking."

She turned towards the stove and began stirring the soup. "So, what was it you needed to talk to me about?"

Kate's stomach did another flip. Just as she suspected. Ruth knew this was no casual visit. Ignoring the question, Kate dropped her purse on the counter and sniffed. "Smells good. What's on the menu? Borscht?"

Ruth nodded. "Yes, with a salad and bread pudding for dessert. Now what…"

Kate cut her off, determined not to allow Ruth to question her until her tension was back under control. "I was going to suggest taking you out to compensate for your bad mood. But not after all this preparation. Guess I'll owe you some digging instead."

Ruth looked at her, then shook her head. "I don't need bribing to have my mother for a visit. I can take a hint too. I know the rules at our house. Food first. Talk later." She took bowls from the cupboard and filled them. "Pull up a chair. I'm hungry."

Kate kept up a steady stream of chatter during the meal, but received only monosyllabic responses. She couldn't tell whether Ruth was in pain or offended by the delay. Finally, with their plates empty and their appetites satiated, she sat back and toyed with her teacup.

"Since you know this isn't just a social call, I may as well start." She hesitated, refilling her cup and adding sugar, then stirring it, killing time while she made one last effort to settle the errant butterflies. Then, she set down her spoon and plunged in.

"You asked some pointed questions Thursday morning that I didn't want to answer over the phone. I also wanted to talk to your father first."

Ruth was looking down, concentrating on her cup. Her rigid posture told Kate that she was listening intently.

Kate continued. "You've already figured it out, haven't you? That Andreas Wachter was my lover and your father. Andreas Kohlman Wachter, the Austrian aeronautical engineer you found so attractive, is the Andrew Coleman I said was your father."

Ruth looked up, her eyes blazing. "So I was right. All that drivel you shot me when I was a kid—about saving myself for my husband—was just a bunch of crap. You didn't want me stuck with a kid out of wedlock like you were. You never wanted me, but you had no choice. Abortions weren't available in 1945."

The accusation rocked Kate like an unexpected blow. She had never once imagined this reaction from her daughter. Her denial was instantaneous.

"Of course I wanted you. You were the only tangible link I had with your father after we separated."

She could see Ruth's expression darkening. Kate's heart thumped. *What now?*

"Daddy's parting gift, was I? Gee, thanks, Mom. It's great to know where I always stood in this."

Kate could see the hurt in Ruth's expression. Damn. Now how did she explain this? Honesty might not help. All the same, it was all she could offer.

"I don't think I ever stopped to consider it that way," she said. "When I found out that I was pregnant, I was shocked. I'd been on the road for three weeks, ducking Allied troops, German troops, civilians, DPs. Getting to the British lines was no fun. Most of the time I was hungry, and all of the time I was scared. I missed Andreas terribly and I worried for him almost as much as for myself. It never even occurred to me that there was a reason for the missed period. Not immediately, anyway. I guess it was early July before the penny dropped. I was secure at British HQ by then. I was eating regularly again and I didn't have to watch over my shoulder all the time. Apart from missing your father, I should have been back to normal. Only I wasn't. As I said, it was a shock and no, initially I wasn't keen to take on the burden of raising a baby alone. But I couldn't bear the thought of losing my last link with your father. Not then, anyway. And by the time you were actually born, you'd taken on a meaning of your own. I could have given you up, you know. A lot of women gave up their kids. But I never even considered it."

Ruth shot her a black look, still not buying the argument. "Uh huh. And if he was such a great man that you missed him so much, why didn't you marry him? You told me yourself that he proposed. Didn't you love him?"

Not love Andreas? The implication made Kate so angry she wanted to slap Ruth for suggesting it. She held herself back, realizing that so far, physical relationships were the only kind her daughter had experienced. Love, such as she had shared with Andreas, was still an unknown for Ruth.

"Try again. No one raises a child unless the relationship had serious meaning. It's just too much work." She realized her voice was rising and forced herself to calm down. "Of course I loved him. Very, very much. I told you that. I think the hardest thing I ever did was refuse him when he wanted to marry me. But I was a spy. I didn't dare accept him."

Ruth shook her head. "Why, for heavens sake? If you loved him that much, why would you let ideology get in the way? No one knew what you were doing."

Although Ruth's tone was softer, Kate could still see anger in the set of her jaw. They were so alike, Ruth and her father. Neither of them understood the word no.

"No one knew what I was doing, but they certainly would have if we had applied for permission to marry." Kate explained about the background checks required to weed out Jews and ensure the purity of the master race.

Ruth shook her head. "That's sick."

"Maybe. But remember, as a spy standing in the middle of it, I was in no position to challenge the system."

"That's still no excuse for not telling him afterwards. The war was over. If you loved each other that much you could have followed him. Gone to the States and married him there."

Was it only three days since she'd had this exact same conversation with Andreas? Reliving the memories of her own turmoil wearied Kate. She repeated the explanation she'd given Andreas and hoped Ruth would understand.

"I had to be practical, Ruth," she concluded. "No matter how we cared about each other, if I destroyed his career there was a good chance that over time he'd turn into a bitter man and take his anger out on both of us. I felt a clean break was best."

Ruth wasn't satisfied. "Maybe you were right. Still, that's no reason why I couldn't know my father was still alive. Why did you lie to me all these years?"

Was Ruth hurt or just angry? Kate couldn't tell. Her voice shook despite her efforts to sound calm.

"I told you. The only way to save our reputations at first was to pretend your father was dead. And later, I couldn't go changing my story if I didn't want you looking for your father. So I kept quiet."

"What? You figured he'd want me? Was that it?"

Kate nodded, remembering Andreas' casual comments about their future and the children they'd have. "I had no doubts about how much he'd want you. Or about the lengths to which he might have gone to find you."

"And what would be wrong with that?" Ruth glared at her. "Why did I have to be stuck with Vlad?"

There it was. The animosity in Ruth's tone said it all. As a child, Ruth hadn't minded her *Pops* as she'd called Vlad, but they began butting heads during her teens. Since her university days they had been virtually at war. Now Ruth blamed her for their discord.

"You aren't using your head. If Andreas had found out about you, he'd have demanded his rights as a father. Vlad would have fought that tooth and nail. You know how he hates Germans."

Ruth snorted in disgust. "He's a possessive bastard, all right."

"That's not quite fair," Kate scolded gently. "You enjoyed Vlad and the kids when you were young. He always treated you as though you were his own."

"His slave to be ordered around, you mean," Ruth fired back. "Either I jump to his orders or I'm no good."

"You don't know life would have been better with Andreas," Kate countered. "I'm sure he'd have been just as strict a father a Vlad was."

"At least he lives in this century." Silence fell as Ruth sat thinking. "So you kept us both in the dark and hoped we'd never meet. Only it didn't work out that way. He said he was pretty angry when he found out you'd been a spy."

"I think that's a bit of understatement," Kate said, remembering the confrontation in the Clean Room, his face hard, his jaw set, his fingers biting into her arm as his furious words exploded inches from her face like bits of shrapnel.

"Apparently your existence was a big part of his anger in February. Originally, he thought I'd lied about my feelings for him. I must have or I couldn't have turned around and hopped into bed with someone else so soon after we parted. Then he saw you and realized who you were. It devastated him. If he were the violent type, I'd have been in big trouble."

Ruth stared at her, open-mouthed.

"I'm not kidding, Ruth. He handled the notion of me being a spy much more easily than the thought that I'd lied about loving him."

"But what about your marriage? He…Dad… Andreas…shit. What am I going to call him?" Ruth shrugged and plunged on. "What's he going to do about the fact you're married? He's still in love with you. You still care about him, don't you? Are you going to leave Vlad?"

Kate shook her head. She'd made her decision years ago and nothing had changed. She still had no alternative. Marriage was for life. So why did it still hurt?

"No. I married Vlad knowing full well that Andreas was somewhere down in the States. I can't turn back the clock now. Yes, I still love him. But only as a friend. A very, very dear friend, but just a friend. Nothing changes for me, Hon. Except that I won't have to lie to you about your father any more."

"But Vlad's a total prick. He orders you around like some kind of servant. There's no reason for you to put up with that. Not in this day and age."

Kate shook her head and rose from the table. "You're wrong. A bit of hot air is no excuse to walk away from a marriage. He's never struck me and he does his best to keep me happy. I can't ask more than that from any man, Ruth. But there's nothing to stop you from treating Andreas like a father, if that's what you both want."

Kate began gathering the dishes. "Now, first we clean this up and then I tackle that flower bed. Just exactly how much did you want to dig up?"

CHAPTER FOURTEEN

Vlad was washing up his supper dishes when the telephone rang. He expected it to be Kate and ignored the call. He didn't want to listen to her excuses for spending an entire day with her daughter.

Finally, frustrated at the caller's persistence, he answered on the tenth ring. "*Da?*"

"I dragged you a long way."

For an instant Vlad didn't recognize the bland male voice. Then he did, and his anger soared. "You cannot understand plain English?" His voice gritted through clenched teeth. "I said no. I meant no. How many times does it take to get the message through your thick skull? I will not pay you."

"But Olga needs the help desperately. Her heart is bad and without her medicine she is in great pain." The caller's tone changed, and he began to plead. "You are not a cruel man, Vladymyr. At least, she says you were a kind little boy. Good to her daughter. Just like the colonel was good to her. Have you changed so much?"

The comment stung. Had he changed that much? What if Olga really were in pain?

"What is your name, Nicholas?"

"You don't need to know my name."

"Then you do not need my money," Vlad snapped back. "Why should I trust you if you will not even tell me your whole name?"

There was a long pause. "Tartarinov," the man replied softly.

For a moment the name struck Vlad dumb. Tartarinov? He had not heard that name in twenty-three years. Not since her last letter in the spring of 1949. Three months after he began working for Frank Clarke. Vlad pushed aside his memories and returned to the present. Despite the name, there could be no connection between Anna Tartarinovska and Nicholas Tartarinov.

"Thank you, Nicholas Tartarinov. Now, tell me Olga's address. If she needs money, I will send it directly to her."

"Don't do that." Panic tinged Nicholas' tone. Then he added, "The nurse will keep it from her."

"Directly to Olga, or not at all," Vlad repeated.

"But the nurse…"

Vlad cut the connection before Nicholas could manufacture another lie. Not that Olga's nurse couldn't be stealing from her. If she were sick at home and depending on hired help they might well be robbing her. Only Vlad had no reason to suspect she was still alive. Not at her age.

He returned to the kitchen and added detergent to the dishwasher. His hands worked on autopilot while his brain wrestled with painful memories.

Anna's name had been Tartarinovska, the feminine version with the *ska* suffix, but males would use the masculine form of Tartarinov. Some dim memory said she'd had at least one brother, although Vlad had no clue what his Christian name was. Anna had rarely spoken about her family other than to say they were in Warsaw. At the time, Vlad had seen no reason to probe.

Now he wondered if it were possible that Nick Tartarinov was Anna's brother's child.

When Vlad had first met Anna Tartarinovska, he was sixteen and she was a waitress in his father's restaurant. Dark of hair and eye, slim and vivacious, his family had first ignored, and then condemned Vlad's infatuation with the Polish peasant whose heritage could not match his own. Their relationship was heading for a collision with his father's disapproval when the Horbatsky men were marched off to the work camps in 1941.

When Vlad returned to Berlin in 1945, he was already in the American army. The city was in shambles. Russian soldiers roamed the streets like gangs of thugs, preying on the helpless and hungry survivors struggling to meet their daily needs in the rubble of their homes.

Their old apartment had been blown to bits as had their restaurant, the *Jar am Zoo*. It was only when he found the priest that Vlad learned his mother was alive and secreted in a couple of rooms in a shattered house in an old suburb. She wasn't well, the priest warned him, but at least the girl kept her alive. He didn't know the girl's identity.

Vlad worried who the mysterious girl might be and what she might want from him until he walked into the draughty kitchen of his mother's new shelter. There was his Anna at the stove, stirring a pot while his mother lay on a couch nearby, covered in blankets and old coats. Even now he remembered the rush of joy at finding her alive. So few of his friends had survived that he had resigned himself to life without Anna. When she threw her arms around him and began to cry with joy, his own emotions almost got the better of him.

One glance told him how readily his mother now accepted Anna's help. Whatever divisions existed for them before the war were now gone, erased by pain and hardship endured together.

He had been assigned to work with the Americans as a translator at the naval war crimes trials in Hamburg and would be in and out of Berlin until the job finished. There was no way he could bring his women with him, but at least with Anna to look after her, he knew his mother would be well cared for in his absence.

Over the next three years, he had visited when he could and shared his pay packet with them. Anna haggled, traded and stole to keep them fed and sheltered, while her engaging smile, quick wit and excellent marksmanship kept out the roving bullies and rogue soldiers. This time there were no protests when Vlad announced his intention to marry his devoted sweetheart.

Receiving permission to marry took time, however, and before it arrived, word came down that the regiment was returning to the States. Wives would come later and sweethearts must apply through regular immigration channels after their men were settled.

Therein lay the problem. Vlad suspected he would get no chance to settle. Everyone would get a brief furlough, and then they would be shipped off to various army bases across the nation. That suited him fine so long as peace held. Except with the Communists dominating North Korea and the Americans helping the South, he feared there'd be no peaceful future for him in the military.

He made up his mind. He had had enough of war. The army could transport him to America but once he hit New York he was going to disappear. There was no way he was going to spend any more of his life following orders, dodging bullets, and sleeping in the mud.

He had some sympathy for the Koreans in their battle against Communism and Uncle Joe. But Koreans were just another bunch of slant-eyed gooks like the Mongols. Vlad's family had suffered as much under them as under the Communists.

Anna knew he planned to cross into Canada and seek refuge as a displaced person. Since his mother was very frail by this time, Anna agreed to stay as long as Tatiana needed her. Then she would come to join him.

Vlad purchased the forged papers he would need to establish his new life and was days away from embarking with his regiment when his mother died. While her death freed Anna, there was neither money to buy her transport to America nor time to arrange the journey.

Anna accepted the separation better than he did. Vlad would find work more easily if he were alone and free to move around, she said. She would wait until he was settled and sent for her as they had originally planned.

His forged documents did their job and by August of 1948 he was starting his new life in Toronto. He worked his heart out at three jobs, saving every penny he could. Meanwhile, they exchanged letters faithfully. When he wrote to her in April 1949, he had moved to Milton and begun working at Clarke's. Once his probationary period was done, he would have the money for her passage on a ship to Canada. He told her to go to the authorities and start the process so her papers would be ready when his money arrived.

He received no reply. After two months of silence, he sent the priest to find her. He, too, was unsuccessful. Anna had quite simply vanished.

Vlad had been frantic at first, feeling his whole life was shattered. By September, when she still hadn't been found, he began drinking himself into a stupor each night in order to forget. He saw Kate Cameron for the first time at the Clarke Christmas party.

Kate knew nothing about Anna. Vlad had been insecure enough about his background without revealing that, on top of all his other deficiencies, he wasn't man enough to hang onto the woman he loved.

Although she was no Slav, Kate had turned out to be a suitable replacement. She gave him two fine children and—until now—made him proud to be her husband.

For an instant he wondered how much better his life would have been had he married Anna. Then he shoved the thought away. He had not married Anna. He was married to Kate. He must cope with the life he had, not the one he had once planned.

That life was getting pretty miserable now, what with Kate scoffing at his concerns while he braced for the Kraut to make his next move.

And what a move it was. Hiring someone in Germany to dig up skeletons like Olga with which to threaten him. Well, this was the end. His would make no more attempts to reason with Kate. It was time for action.

He wondered if this was how his Cossack ancestors had felt when the Mongols had overrun the steppes. Warriors to a man, they resisted the golden hordes from the east until they were mown down and ground into the dust. Since that time, many of his ancestors gave their lives to prevent a repeat of that humiliation at the hands of assorted foes—Turks, Poles, Russians, Muslims. The source of the threat hadn't mattered. In times of danger the Horbatskys had stood up to the enemy. Now the family honor was in his hands and no damned Kraut was going to ruin it.

Vlad was watching television when Kate arrived home. He glanced at her, then returned his attention to the program. He was only vaguely listening when she announced that she was tired and needed a bath. He gave her an acknowledging nod and she disappeared.

His decision had been reached and there was nothing to be discussed. Kate didn't need to know the lengths to which he would go to protect the family reputation. The man threatening their peaceful existence was about to have an accident. A fatal accident.

###

At the end of the day, Andreas came out of the lunchroom and saw Vlad leaving through the back door.

Normally he left by mid afternoon. Andreas wondered what had delayed him today. Zipping his jacket as he retraced his steps through the plant, Andreas realized the day shift was gone and the afternoon crew was already on the floor.

Although he had no idea what was going on, his instinct said something was. He had felt Vlad's eyes watching him at least half a dozen times during the afternoon. It wasn't that he was worried exactly. It was more a case of listening to that small, inner voice. Old habits prompted caution.

He hadn't come to like Horbatsky any better with exposure. Nor had Ruth's guarded comments done anything to encourage friendship with her stepfather. The man was living what should have been Andreas' life, and insisted on treating Andreas as though he were the interloper. Andreas was doing his best to see Vlad's perspective but, given Vlad's manner, it was hard going.

At this hour, with employees already on the job or gone for the day, Andreas knew Vlad could well be waiting for him in the deserted parking lot. As he passed his toolbox Andreas picked up a slim wrench and slipped it into his pants pocket. If he didn't need it, he would put it back in the morning.

He exited through the rear door into the late afternoon sunshine, then paused at the end of the walkway to the parking lot, glancing around. Vlad's truck was in its usual spot. The motor was running but he wasn't in it.

Andreas' eyes automatically went to where he had parked his own car. A half-ton parked beside it blocked his view. Andreas moved on stealthily, being careful not to step on loose gravel or debris that would make a noise. If Vlad were tampering with his car, Andreas was determined to force a showdown.

He cut through the row ahead of his car so that he could approach from the front. He was almost at his vehicle before he saw it. The hood was up and Vlad was bent into the engine compartment.

Andreas smiled grimly. He wasn't paranoid after all.

He didn't stop to ask questions. He came up directly behind Vlad. Then stepping to the side at the last second, he dropped the hood onto Vlad's shoulders and saw him go limp. The heavy metal knocked the breath from him. Andreas heard the metallic clatter of an object bouncing off engine parts before striking the pavement below. So Vlad had been tampering with something.

Andreas put his hand on the hood and held it down. Only Vlad's lower body was visible. After several seconds Andreas could feel Vlad regain his breath and brace for action.

"Don't even think about it," Andreas said, leaning a touch more weight onto the hood. "What do you think I am? Stupid? Yes, Katrina and I worked together. But no one else knows that and no one else will know, provided you leave me alone."

Andreas waited a moment, letting his message sink in, then raised the hood and stepped aside.

Vlad moved back and straightened up. Briefly, he stood flexing his shoulders and glaring at Andreas.

"She is my wife." He squeezed his words through clenched teeth. "I will not let her go."

Although Andreas had known that their dislike was mutual, the fury he saw in Vlad's eyes came as a shock. There was no rational reason for such hatred. All the same, it was there and couldn't be ignored. This time he'd caught Vlad attempting sabotage. Next time he might not be so lucky. Groping for a way to prevent further attacks, Andreas remembered his will.

After meeting Ruth and talking to Kate, he had written a new will and sent it to his lawyer. His aim had been simply to ensure that Kate understood his love had not changed despite her marriage. That, however, was not how he'd explain it to Vlad.

"You may not want to let her go. Then again, it may not be your choice in the end. Kate knows I loved her, wanted to marry her. I have changed my will. If anything happens to me, she gets everything I own. She would be free to follow her instincts. And being the honorable person we both know her to be, if she found out you were responsible for my death..." His voice trailed away.

Vlad took another step back, stretching his shoulders yet again to ease the pain.

Andreas glanced at his motor, but could see nothing wrong. He'd stop and check more thoroughly when he got away from the parking lot. He slammed the hood shut on his car. "Do I make myself clear?"

Vlad grunted.

"Is everything okay?"

Both men looked around, startled by Gerry Clarke's voice cutting into the silence between them. Gerry's car was stopped behind Andreas'. While concentrating on Vlad, Andreas had not noticed Gerry's arrival.

Andreas nodded and smiled. "I believe so—now. Thank you."

He took a couple of steps along the side of his sedan and unlocked the door. Gerry wasn't pulling away so he got inside and started the car. No warning lights lit up on the dash panel. It appeared that Vlad had been interrupted before he had the chance to inflict serious damage.

Andreas nodded and waved, then waited. Gerry touched his horn lightly and moved off. Andreas gave him a few more seconds, then put the car in reverse. Vlad stood glaring at him as Andreas backed out of his parking space. Pausing to turn to follow Gerry's winking brake lights, Andreas saw a grey sliver of metal lying on the asphalt several feet in front of Vlad. A file. The perfect tool for rupturing the brake lines at the brake fluid reservoir.

CHAPTER FIFTEEN

Vlad's back ached so badly he could barely lift his arm to eat supper. He tried to relax, but the run-in with Wachter had left him far too angry for that. How dare the Kraut include Kate in his will! She was Vlad's wife and her future rested with him, and only him.

While he was still convinced Wachter was not Ruth's father, the will confirmed Vlad's suspicion that Wachter had once been Kate's lover. It also said he still cared for her. Cared so much, he wanted to make up for the man who had left her pregnant and unmarried. Filthy bastards, Vlad fumed. Spouting all that propaganda about their Aryan women being the mothers of the pure race. He'd heard it all in his teen years. Growing up a Slav among the master race, his inferiority had been pointed out to him repeatedly. Well, he'd show Wachter who was inferior. He'd find a way to eliminate the Kraut. A way no one would expect.

For the moment, however, he had to conceal both his pain and his anger if he were to avoid Kate finding out about today.

Her unwillingness to understand the threat Wachter posed and the measures required to neutralize that threat frustrated Vlad. Which was ironic, given that it was her spying career that created the whole problem in the first place.

The suppertime newscast was barely over when Vlad headed for the shower. "I feel like I'm coming down with a flu bug," he told Kate. "My shoulders are aching like mad."

He rejected her offer of a hot toddy and soaked for a long while before seeking the comfort of his bed. Although he usually slept in his shorts, he opted to add a t-shirt that night. It bolstered his flu story and covered the bruise Kate must not see.

Kate could tell he was still sore when he rolled out of the covers the next morning. She wanted him to take a sick day to rest and fight the bug. Vlad shook his head. He wouldn't give the German the satisfaction of knowing how badly he'd been hurt. Nor would he leave Wachter free access to Kate. She must not hear the story from his viewpoint.

Working would be difficult but sitting around aching would be no less taxing. He needed to keep his mind off his pain, especially when he wasn't genuinely ill and painkillers weren't helping. Besides, work occupied his conscious mind and left his subconscious free to design a solution for this problem with the Kraut.

All day he kept a wary eye on the Clean Room door, half expecting Wachter to come bursting out and run up to tell Kate. Later, over supper and throughout the evening, he braced for Kate to question his encounter with Wachter. The next day, too, he waited for someone to say they'd seen what happened in the parking lot. No one did.

He had to give up on his flu story after a couple of days but it took almost a week before the pain left his shoulders. The bruise persisted for nearly two weeks, so long in fact, that Vlad feared Kate would become suspicious of his sudden modesty. All the while he waited for Wachter to tell her about the attack. Waiting was almost as unnerving as being caught tampering with the car.

Despite his intentions to remain silent, when nothing had happened by the second weekend, he made another attempt to talk sense into Kate. They were planting petunias in the flowerbeds lining the driveway when he asked how things stood with Wachter. "He's still drooling over you," he told her.

"Don't be silly, Vlad. He's being civil. Nothing more. You're just overreacting because he's German."

No matter how reasonable he tried to be, she would hear none of his arguments. Wachter was no threat, she insisted.

"And you won't believe me when I tell you the man is determined to get you into his bed?" Vlad concluded, exasperated. "I should just tell Gerry you are leaving."

"You're going to pay for two kids at university as well as meet all the household bills?" Her eyebrows rose speculatively. "Don't be ridiculous. I enjoy working. The housework gets done just as well as it would if I stayed home. You wouldn't like the grouch I'd become if I were isolated here all the time. No, Vlad. I will not give up my job just because you've got a bee in your bonnet about a man I used to know thirty years ago."

"And if I insist?"

Kate looked at him in silence for several moments. "That would be very foolish," she said at last, her voice icy calm. "I do love you, but I will not allow you to dictate to me. Especially when those orders are founded on unreasonable jealousy."

So that was it. He had tried again and once again she had refused to obey him.

In the old days, it would have been his right to kill her for such willfulness. Sometimes he wished the old ways still applied. Not that he really wanted to be free of Kate, he reminded himself. Her bastard child, yes. But not Kate. It was just her inappropriate notions about a wife's place in a marriage that frustrated him unbearably. She was his wife, damn it! She belonged to him and she had no business flaunting herself for some bloody Kraut to drool over.

He wondered yet again whether Wachter intended to tell Kate about the attempted sabotage of his car. Then he remembered Wachter's comment. *No one knows we knew each other and no one will so long as you keep quiet.* Well, Vlad certainly wasn't about to tell anyone.

Three weeks after the incident, life seemed to have returned to normal. Vlad's bruise was a brown smudge; the pain was gone. All that remained was the firm conviction that the German had to be eliminated in such a way that no one suspected it was deliberate.

The morning he found his solution, Vlad awoke before dawn, sweating and shaking from a dream he had not experienced in years. The real event had been murder too, but the culprit was never found. It had happened in 1934, when Vlad was in his last year of secondary school. The Nazis were relatively new to power but Hitler already had his agenda mapped out. One of those aims was to ensure that youngsters attending Berlin's private schools received the same indoctrination as their public school contemporaries.

Like Vlad, pupils attending the Russian School were the offspring of Slavic families who had escaped from countries overrun by the Communists during and after World War One. They had all been raised to understand propaganda and indoctrination and how to resist it.

Whether the Nazi educational bureaucracy saw signs that the young Slavs were likely to be subversive or whether it was just a standard precaution, no one knew. However, in Vlad's final year, a new history teacher was added to the staff.

He was not vetted and approved by the parent-board as other instructors had been in previous years. Nor was he accepted into the staff social circle as new teachers had always been. He just appeared. A hard-eyed, weasel-faced individual with prominent teeth, Herr Kuehn spoke with a lisp that made him the butt of many pointed comments when he was not quite out-of-earshot.

His assignments were extraordinarily long and intricate and his punishments were more frequent, more extreme, and earned much more easily than with any other instructor in the school. No one had to tell Vlad and his classmates that this man was a Nazi spy planted among them to ensure everyone—from tiniest Kindergarten tot to governing principal—towed the party line.

The Russian School was housed in a stately old brick mansion with skylights illuminating the immense, central stairwell connecting the building's three floors. On the main level, centered within the square of staircases, was an attractive arrangement of potted palms, settees and end tables.

That year the weather turned unseasonably warm in early March, and the first graders had planted spring bulbs as part of a science assignment. With no greenhouse to enhance the growth process, the caretakers helped the tiny scientists to set their heavy clay pots on the wide ledge of the banister surrounding the stairwell on the top floor where they would catch the most sunlight.

At the end of recess each morning, the little ones made a trip to inspect their bulbs. Some were so small their teacher had to lift them to look into the big pots where the bulbs had been planted in groups of five or six.

After recess, the students from several classes traded rooms, while other classes stayed put, and their instructors scurried among the rows of moving pupils to get to waiting students.

Vlad had been on the stairs coming down from the third floor with his class when he heard the young girl scream. Instinct stopped him and he turned to look over the railing.

Two floors below, Kuehn lay on his face just inside the edge of the stairwell. A pool of blood spread under clumps of soil from the base of a shattered earthenware pot that lay partially on the top of his skull. Obviously, the pot had fallen from the banister three stories above.

A class moving along the corridor behind where Kuehn lay, stood frozen, staring at the fallen man. One girl, her face covered, was sobbing loudly.

Soon, several girls began to cry and teachers began appearing in the halls and on the stairs. Everyone was immediately returned to their rooms to await the arrival of the authorities.

The investigation lasted until school broke for summer vacation. It was obvious the police had their suspicions. However, with so many people on the move and only the tiny ones proven to be near the pots, no culprit was ever identified. The whole affair had to be written off as an accident.

That, Vlad concluded, was how Wachter's death would be seen. As an accident. Unfortunate, of course, because it would cost Gerry a lot of money. It was his own fault, though. It had been his decision to hire the German. Had he picked a Canadian for the job, the whole situation could have been avoided. However, he chose a Kraut and now he was going to pay for that stupidity.

Organizing the accident would take no special equipment; just careful planning. Vlad knew exactly how to manipulate the components. Timing would be the tricky element. The Kraut had to be in the Clean Room because that was next to the gas cylinders. Vlad would need to be the one working with the welder. He'd either pick a day when the assistant was sick or manufacture an errand to take him off the job for the morning so Vlad could take his place. That would give him access to the hoses.

#

Normally, the steady hum of the machinery on the shop floor filled Vlad with satisfaction. Gerry trusted him to maintain those machines. Equipment failure was a rare thing at Clarke Manufacturing because of Vlad's skill and careful attention to detail.

This morning was different. His heart thumped loudly, so loudly he was sure those around him could hear its nervous rhythm.

Over to his right, on the north side, steel groaned as a saw cut away specified sections. Behind it, a brake press clanged as it slapped down on a metal sheet, bending it to a new configuration. In the center, people on the line maintained a steady rhythm. Screw on the nut and turn the part over. Repeat the process. Place the finished piece on the belt and pick up a new part to start again.

Vlad knew that in the Clean Room along the front wall, four men were aligning the wires precisely in tiny metal cases, touching them with solder and pressing again with a hot iron to permanently attach them in the correct location. Earlier in the morning he'd checked to be sure the German was in his usual place wandering amongst his trainees, checking that their work was up to the standard demanded by the contract.

Vlad was careful to avoid looking at the room. Others must not notice him focusing there. When it was over, no one must remember any suspicious actions on his part that might connect him with the event.

Vlad knew what could happen to those four other men and considered their fate was insignificant compared to his need to eliminate the Kraut. It might be unfair, but it was their fault for agreeing to work for the bastard. Vlad remembered the German's warning and smiled privately. Kate would never suspect his involvement in an industrial accident.

Keeping his attention to his own task was difficult. Instinct said he needed to watch the Clean Room door to ensure that the German didn't leave. It would never do to spring his trap when his target was elsewhere. He wouldn't inflict such damage for no purpose.

Vlad gripped a pipe and felt it slip in his hands. Despite his sweaty palms, he was icy cold. People and things seemed to swim in a haze as his mind grappled with his fear of what might go wrong.

From the corner of his eye, he saw Ted Grayson return from his smoke break and go to the wall rack to pick up his cutting torch and welder's mask. Checking for passing forklifts, the young man headed across the floor. He was assembling the pipe frame along which the new assembly belts would be mounted. This morning Vlad was moving the pipes for Grayson.

Vlad knew it was only moments away now. Anticipation coiled his gut into a tight knot. All morning he had fought stomach cramps as he alternated between hauling long pipes to the saw and carrying the cut pieces to the new line for Ted's torch. He must not hurry. Nor dare he flinch. His location must seem appropriate if he were to avoid awkward questions.

He saw Ted flick the switch to ignite the gas. He watched the flame shoot white hot. The spark would quickly follow the gas fumes back along the line to the regulator. The acetylene tank was only twenty feet away. He forced himself to begin walking towards the rack of piping by the east wall. Acid backed up in his throat yet again. He swallowed and began to count mentally. One, two, three...

When it came, the boom sounded hollow across the room, almost like an echo. Shrapnel-like bits of steel from the tanks flew in all directions. The blast caught Vlad before he reached his destination, knocking him off his feet. Smoke and dust billowed from where the exploding gas tanks had blown a hole in the Clean Room wall.

Pieces of asbestos tile hung down, obstructing the opening. Flames licked at the paneling of the ruined wall and ceiling. Just inside, a soldering booth lay tipped over, a foot protruding from one edge.

Despite his efforts to brace for the explosion, the sudden change in air pressure blocked Vlad's eardrums. Both his balance and his hearing were out of kilter. He couldn't seem to move.

His mind dropped back thirty years in a single leap. Straight back to a hot June day in a barn near Trezcianka. Again, he listened as Germans battled Allied tanks in their relentless trek northward. Shells flew overhead and machine guns rattled somewhere to the east.

Once again, a young, dark-haired woman sat on the floor beside him, holding a little girl in her arms. The lower torso of a boy, probably two years older than the girl, lay on the floor beside her. The boy's head and arms were nowhere to be seen. The girl's face was bloody and there was a long tear across her scalp where something had struck her.

The woman was a stranger, already in the barn with her children when, during the early morning hours, he had slipped through the door and tucked himself behind the remains of a pile of straw. Now, several hours later, the battle had come too close. He could not escape. He could only hope the opposing armies would sweep by without checking for snipers hidden inside the ruined structure.

Then the woman began to scream. It was hard to believe that a human throat could produce that sort of cry: high-pitched, agonized, unnatural. Before his eyes she hugged the lifeless bodies to her and wailed, going on and on until Vlad thought he would never forget the sound. If it weren't for the heavy rattle of gunfire and the roar of passing vehicles she would surely have attracted someone's attention.

But it was too late for the children. And for their mother too. She was completely mad with grief. Three hours later, when he cracked open the door and slipped away into the cooling summer evening, she was still sobbing and rocking her dead children.

CHAPTER SIXTEEN

The floor shook as the explosion reverberated through the building. Kate almost fell off her chair. It was nearly thirty years since she had heard that sound. She recognized it instantly even though the cause was a mystery. In tandem with the old memories came the immediate frigid sensation of fear. There was a routine to follow after explosions and following it kept panic at bay.

She collected herself and stood up just as Gerry burst from his office yelling for her to call the fire department and the ambulance. The hall door bounced against the wall as he flung it open on his way to the stairs.

Kate's hands trembled as she dialed. She managed to convey the pertinent details, then set down the receiver and followed Gerry. Bewildered, Janice and the accountant stood in the hall, gazing about uncertainly. As she passed them, Kate ordered them out of the building. Her thoughts on the confusion below, she only vaguely registered the sound of their steps following her down the stairs.

Automatically, her mind was obeying the old routines, remembering to walk quickly rather than to run.

She felt remarkably calm. One glimpse conveyed the gist of the situation.

Smoke filled the north end of the shop and flames flickered around the corner of the Clean Room wall. Several employees were shaking their heads or holding their ears. Fire wardens were marshaling people towards the doors at each end of the main floor. The chaos was orderly. Seriously injured individuals were conspicuously absent. She saw no sign of Andreas.

Almost unconsciously she recognized Vlad standing by the pipe rack. His face was grimy, and he looked dazed, but he appeared unhurt. She went to him, automatically saying his name as she approached. When he didn't respond, she reached out and shook his arm to get his attention.

"Out," she told him. "We need to get out of here. Do you understand me?" No response. "Vlad, come on." She grabbed his arm and began leading him towards the north doors. He followed, robot-like, oblivious to his surroundings.

She caught up with one of the fire wardens and put Vlad's hand on his arm. "I can't get through to him," she said. "Can you get him out? I'm going back to look for others."

She turned away before the man could respond.

The confusion in the main room seemed to be subsiding but there was still no sign of Andreas. The Clean Room was the most seriously damaged area. Heart in her throat, Kate headed towards it, terrified at what she might find; body and mind encased in ice.

The door from the main room was sitting partly open, jammed by a toppled chunk of ceiling stud. Kate ducked around it and entered the smoke-filled room where Andreas worked with his four trainees.

"Tom!" she called. "David, Jack, Bill! Are you in here?" There was a muffled voice, and coughing to her left. "Who's in here?" she called again. "Keep talking so I can find you."

"Over here."

It was Andreas' voice. Relief flooded her. She took a deep breath, regretting it instantly as thick smoke stung her throat. She moved towards the sound, bending low. The smoke thinned slightly. She saw him supporting David Cox at the extreme left of the room, almost beside the emergency door.

"Where are the other three?" Kate asked.

Andreas shook his head and winced. He too, was black-faced and breathing with difficulty.

"The door is this way," she said, moving cautiously around a piece of ceiling tile dangling off a stud and stepping over something she couldn't identify in the smoke. "Take my hand."

The door opened without difficulty and she slipped David's other arm across her own shoulders to help Andreas support the badly befuddled man as they left the plant. Without a word they stopped to breathe deeply in the clean air, then walked several yards from the building before seating David to await the arrival of ambulance attendants.

Now, where were the other three? Her own safety seemed secondary at the moment. She turned back only to have Andreas catch her arm.

"Where do you think you're going?" he demanded, suppressing a cough. "It's dangerous in there."

"We can't leave the others."

"No." He nodded, then winced again. "Damn headache. Stay out here. I'll go."

"Not alone, you won't," she snapped, chilled once more at the idea of him returning to the smoky scene. "We'll get help. We've done this before."

She turned, and seeing several men milling around near the south doors, she waved to them and yelled. "Hey, give us a hand. We've got three men still missing in there."

She turned back towards the half-open door in time to glimpse Andreas stepping through the opening. Damn the man, endangering himself when he, too, probably had a concussion. She dare not wait for help in case he passed out and couldn't be located in the gloom.

The smoldering ceiling tiles exuded heavy, acrid smoke. Debris and toppled equipment littered the floor. Kate concentrated on breathing and tried not to trip. She had caught up with Andreas by the time he located Bill. His hand was trapped inside his protective inner booth. He appeared to be concussed by the blast and too confused to extricate his ensnared hand.

They freed Bill in moments and began leading him back towards the door. Before they got there, her lungs were burning and tears streamed from her stinging eyes.

The moment they got outside helping hands took Bill from them and walked him away.

Still gasping, Kate turned appraising eyes to Andreas. He looked haggard, and almost on the verge of collapse. His face was a blackened mask made almost comical by the pink streaks on his cheeks cleared by tears from his red-rimmed eyes. His normally immaculate coveralls were ripped near one knee and sooty particles speckled his chest. Blood stained a rip in his left sleeve. She felt his eyes examining her and knew she probably looked just as bad. Kate had no concern for herself. She knew she was unhurt.

Her breathing was almost normal again when Andreas turned away. She didn't need to hear him say he was going back inside. Two men caught up with them as they approached the doorway.

"Who's left?" one man asked.

"Tom Keegan and Jack Olsen," Kate answered immediately.

"Tom was next to the end wall," Andreas added. "Jack's off to the east somewhere, about half way in."

"We'll find them," one man said, as they all filed inside.

Almost instantly, her eyes resumed watering and her nose clogged shut in an effort to close out the stench. She began breathing through her mouth and choking on the fumes. Afraid she might lose him in the haze, Kate put a hand on Andreas's shoulder. They fought their way across the tangled floor until they were almost beside the flames. The heat, added to the smoke and stench, set Kate's heart racing. What would Tom's condition be when they did find him?

It didn't take long for Andreas to locate the toppled Plexiglas booth. Tom was on the floor, trapped inside, his arms entangled in the inner soldering chamber just as Bill's had been.

As Andreas worked to free Tom's arms, Kate stooped to feel for a pulse. It was there, but just barely. She followed the contours of the booth with her hands and wound up on her knees, using her fingers to replace her useless eyes. She felt sticky, wet fluid along one edge. Then she touched a foot. She felt Andreas attempt to lift the unconscious man. She put her hand on his arm to stop him.

"His leg's caught," she said, guiding Andreas's hand to Tom's trapped foot. The effort to speak immediately set off a spasm of coughing.

"We need to lift the booth," Andreas told her. She felt him reach along Tom's body to check the location of his arms and other leg. "This side is clear. Maybe we can roll it."

Kate stood up and moved to where the booth lay on Tom's leg. The heat seemed worse and the flames licked closer. Breathing was growing increasingly difficult. Perspiration rolled down her back. She could hear Andreas wheezing beside her. He squeezed her fingers as a signal and they began to pull.

They tried three times without success. Kate realized they didn't have the strength to move the heavy booth. Just as she gathered her breath to shout for help, she felt the presence of others around them. Several pairs of hands reached to assist. Now it took only one mighty heave to roll the booth away. Other hands gathered Tom up and carried him back towards the door.

Andreas groped for her hand and clung to it as they stumbled along in the wake of Tom and his rescuers. By the time they reached the doorway Kate found herself supporting him. Once outside, helpful hands immediately grabbed Andreas and eased him to the ground a few feet from the building.

Kate stood to one side while she cleared her eyes and lungs. Andreas was safe. She could relax. Firefighters were on the scene now, taking care of the flames. Ambulance staffers were collecting the injured.

Reaction set in. She began to shake so hard she had to lean on the nearest car. It was over. She willed herself to calm down reminding herself she was full of smoke, but not seriously so. The Clean Room was a mess, but not irreparable. So far as she knew there were no fatalities. It could have been worse, much worse. Memories of other scenes flashed through her mind's eye. This was a minor explosion despite how Gerry might view it from the sheltered perspective of one who had never seen combat.

###

Vlad batted away the hand at his shoulder and tried to focus on his surroundings. He was sitting on the rear bumper of a car. A woman in a dark blouse was talking to him.

"What's your name?" she insisted, waving her hand before his face and stooping to get a good look at his eyes.

"I am fine," Vlad muttered, recognizing the technique she was using to check for concussion. "Go look after someone who's hurt."

"You're not in that great shape," the woman protested. "Shock's sneaky. You can pass out at a moment's notice. We'll be taking you to the hospital, too, when we've got everyone ready."

Hospital? He didn't need a hospital. Vlad started to rise, then reconsidered the motion as his world spun and his ears shot pain into his skull. Perhaps he should rest a few minutes. Then he'd go and find Kate.

He leaned back against the trunk and scanned the parking lot behind Clarke Manufacturing. It teemed with people, some standing, some milling about, all staring at the plume of smoke billowing through a hole in the factory wall.

The explosion had obviously damaged the Clean Room as he had planned. Now all he needed was confirmation that Wachter was dead.

Kate's bright blue sweater caught Vlad's eye. She was by the rear doors, leaning on a car as though trying to catch her breath. Catching her breath? Surely not. She hadn't gone into that mess to try to rescue Wachter, had she? Dear God, no. He hadn't even considered the possibility she'd do that. Vlad wanted the man dead but he hadn't meant to endanger Kate in the process.

As he watched, Kate turned and crossed to where two men were bent over a body curled on the ground. The men stepped aside and Kate knelt on the pavement beside a figure in navy coveralls. Vlad watched her speak to someone, then reach out to the injured individual. She turned to one of the men standing beside her and he hurried off towards an ambulance attendant. His departure gave Vlad a clear view of the man receiving Kate's attention. The size and white hair identified him immediately.

Unable to tear his eyes away from the scene, Vlad watched Kate lean over Wachter, her hand caressing his head, her whole attention focused on comforting him. Vlad saw her pull something white from her pocket and wipe Wachter's face. Two men appeared beside her with a stretcher. While Vlad could not hear the conversation, he could tell that Wachter was not co-operating. Kate appeared to say something, then he allowed her to help him stand.

Wild with frustration, Vlad could only watch. Supporting Wachter with an arm about his waist and his arm across her shoulders, she walked him to the ambulance. Not only had Wachter survived, his injuries seemed minor.

Vlad couldn't believe it. All that planning. All the risks. All the damage to the plant. It would cost Gerry thousands to repair this. And for what? Wachter was alive. The damned son of Satan had survived. What magic did he posses to escape justice no matter what Vlad did?

"We're ready for you now," a man said from beside Vlad.

Caught unawares, Vlad looked up to see fire warden Oliver Kirkness holding out a hand.

"The bus is ready to take people to the hospital," Kirkness repeated. "Come on, Vlad. It's just a precaution. Don't argue about it. Gerry's not going to be happy until he's sure everyone has been examined. If you're as good as you think, the doctors will just send you home anyway. Gerry will need you in shape when they start the repairs."

The determined hand under his elbow forced him to his feet. About to reject the command, he changed his mind when his world did a slow somersault and pain once again cleaved his skull from ear to ear. Maybe a short hospital stay would be a good idea. He needed time to think and Kate needed reminding about the proper placement of her priorities.

###

Kate remained at the scene until the fire department left. While the explosion had not touched the upper floor, smoke had reached all parts of the building. They'd need restoration crews up there just as they'd need someone to rebuild the damaged Clean Room.

As soon as everyone was safely accounted for, Gerry began sending staff home. "We'll be back in production by Monday," he assured them.

Kate knew that Ministry of Labor investigators required time to do their job. Should Tom's injuries prove fatal, the police might also have to be involved.

Kate found Gerry standing beside his father's car at the south end of the building. Amid the commotion, she exchanged greetings with her former boss.

Frank Clarke was as blunt as usual. "You look like hell, if you'll forgive me saying so. Why aren't you in the hospital with the rest of the smoke victims?"

"I'll be fine," Kate replied. "I just need some fresh air and a good bath. Besides, they may be sending Vlad home later and I'll need to be available to collect him."

"He was one of the concussion cases then?" Gerry asked. "I wasn't sure whether he went."

Kate nodded. "He was badly confused when I saw him. I don't know if it was concussion or war-related. Since you were too young to serve, you wouldn't know, but between the smoke and the blast, it was a lot like a battle zone in there. It may have triggered memories that they have to bring him out of."

The elder Clarke nodded. "That can happen."

"So what's next?" Kate turned to Gerry.

"For you, home." He was firm. "I'll stick around to talk to the fire chief and the Ministry of Labor investigators. There's probably nothing for you to do for at least a day. If I need you Friday, I'll call. Okay? Otherwise, all we can do is wait."

And pray for Tom. None of them needed to acknowledge the worry they shared.

CHAPTER SEVENTEEN

Too keyed up to rest, Kate went straight to the shower and scrubbed away the smoke and grime. Despite her protests that she was fine, Kate knew the late morning blast had shaken her far more seriously than she was revealing.

Over and over, she heard the explosion and smelled the smoke. It wasn't the first time she'd known the heart-stopping fear that accompanied such a sound. She'd been through it several times when Allied bombs struck the facility at Peenemünde. Only those explosions had killed people.

How many times had she searched the rubble praying she would not find Andreas among the dead while battling fear the bombers would return for a more successful strike on the gas tanks beside the research laboratory. Then when they did find each other they would cling together, tears streaming down their cheeks, thankful just to be alive and together.

Kate called the Milton hospital early in the afternoon. Vlad was resting comfortably but they would keep him over night to ensure his concussion was not serious, the nurse at the station on his floor assured her.

Andreas, too, had been admitted for observation and would likewise be released the following day, provided nothing serious developed.

She was loath to ask the condition of the Clean Room team but knew she must. Andreas would want answers about all four men when she visited him.

Only Tom was serious, the nurse assured her. Thankfully, the booth had just shattered his leg without severing the main artery. Barring complications, there'd be no permanent damage.

With the relief came weariness, but she couldn't rest. Her mind was busy turning the puzzle over and over. Clarke's had experienced no serious accidents in more than three years. Why now?

It was even more disturbing to contemplate the cause of this morning's instinctive reaction. She thought she'd put her past behind her, yet when disaster struck, she had unhesitatingly abandoned Vlad to others and rushed to Andreas. Perhaps Vlad had more reason to be jealous than she had realized.

An hour later, still tired and worried, she dressed, made herself a light meal, and drove to the hospital.

Vlad looked pale when she arrived. He'd been cleaned up and fed, but his expression was wary. Was that a remnant from some wartime memory stirred by the blast, Kate wondered. Or was he unsure of her reaction to his performance during the morning's accident?

"Well, you look better than you did," she said, trying to keep her tone neutral as she pecked his cheek. She moved back to sit on the chair by the window. "How do you feel?"

He shrugged. "A little ashamed, I suppose. I do not recall anything and I gather it was quite a mess. I should have been helping."

Kate, too, shrugged. "Well, you did catch the same blast as others directly in front of the explosion. Why should you have survived better than anyone else? Come on, Vlad. Don't be so hard on yourself."

"Is everyone else okay?" he asked.

Kate nodded. "Mostly. Ted Grayson's got a burnt arm and a concussion. Tom's got a shattered leg where the soldering booth tipped over when the wall blew into the Clean Room. They're the only serious injuries. The other four are fine despite the amount of smoke they inhaled and their scrapes and cuts, in addition to their concussions, of course. They got the worst of it in there. And you're as serious as anyone out on the main floor."

"And Wachter?"

"Scrapes and bruises and a cut on his arm," she replied. "He's in here like the rest of you being treated for concussion."

Something about his tone left Kate wondering if Vlad had seen her helping Andreas. She hoped not. Given his propensity for violence whenever he felt threatened, Andreas could be in danger if Vlad had seen them together.

They talked a few minutes more and Kate promised to collect him the next day when he was released.

Obediently, she kissed him again and set off to find Andreas.

He was dozing when she entered his room, and she was reluctant to waken him. She laid her coat over the back of the chair by his bed and sat down to wait. He looked pale and his right arm, swathed in bandages, lay atop the covers.

No matter her connection to Vlad, a part of her ached to touch Andreas. She needed to be sure he was going to be all right. How foolish could she be? It was over between them. It had to be. All the same, his injuries roused her protective instincts.

A nurse arrived bearing a blood pressure cuff and thermometer.

"Ah, you must be Mrs. Wachter." She launched right in before Kate could correct her. "Your husband will be fine. He's lucky, actually. The arm took quite a gash but no major nerves or blood vessels were cut so he shouldn't have any long-term damage from this. He'll cough and splutter some for a few days, but that won't last long, either. You can take him home tomorrow."

Home? Kate suppressed the inclination to giggle. If Vlad were showing signs of jealousy before, she could just picture his reaction if she brought Andreas to their house. All the same, the notion of looking after him held a certain appeal.

Andreas surfaced to the sound of a woman's voice. His eyes felt heavy and he didn't bother trying to open them. In the first seconds he didn't know where he was. It annoyed him to be awakened for no good reason just when he'd been about to kiss Kate in his dream.

"Come on, Mr. Wachter. Your wife's here. Don't make me out to be a liar. Open those eyes and reassure her that you're as well as I've been saying."

Her hand was stroking his cheek, trying to waken him. He saw the thermometer through half-closed lids and opened his mouth obediently. He felt her wrap the blood pressure cuff around his arm and begin to pump it up. Becoming more alert by the moment, Andreas had his eyes open by the time he felt the restriction on his bicep released.

"You're going to be fine," the nurse told him as she tucked her stethoscope back in a pocket and headed for the door. "I just told your wife she can take you home tomorrow if you continue like this."

Behind the woman's back, Andreas smiled. Once she left, he said, "You see. Even strangers picture us as a pair. And we know how well we work together. Did I thank you for staying with me this morning? I'm not sure I'd have managed to get myself out of there the last time without your help."

Kate shook her head. "You'd have made it. You're tough."

Seeing her sitting there, he remembered her courage. Old memories flooded in. He wanted to hold her. He'd known for weeks that he still cared. Nor was that only because of Ruth. Kate herself was the source of both his pain and his pride. Today, she'd risked her life for him as much as for the men he worked with. Surely that was significant. Sensing unease in her posture, he knew better than to raise that issue and inquired about his co-workers instead. He was relieved to hear that Tom's injuries while serious, were not life threatening.

"And Vlad?" he asked, hoping his animosity didn't show.

"Concussion, but nothing serious. He'll be home tomorrow, just like you."

"So, have you heard what caused the accident yet?" he asked.

Kate shook her head. "No, but it's early. I left before the investigators arrived, and Gerry hasn't called me with any news. I'm not sure I will hear anything until I get back to work on Monday."

Andreas nodded. "*Ja.* It takes time to go through the wreckage. But what exploded? It must have been something heavy."

"Oh, I know that," Kate told him. "It was an acetylene tank. And, since it was chained to the wall beside an oxygen tank, it went up too. Ted Grayson burned his arm and suffered concussion in the blast. He turned on his torch to cut some pipe and everything went boom."

"Acetylene. Of course." Andreas nodded. "There must have been a break in the line so when he turned it on, the spark lit the accumulated gas and traveled back along the hoses to the tank. The fire would go right through the regulator into the tank and acetylene is highly flammable. It would go up in seconds once the operator lit the burner. But they check those hoses daily to prevent accidents…" His voice trailed off thoughtfully.

"Yes, they do." Kate nodded solemnly. "I've seen them doing it. So what happened?"

"I don't know," Andreas said, closing his eyes as though thinking. It was only two weeks since he'd caught Vlad trying to destroy the brakes on his car. Kate didn't know about that, however, and Andreas dare not tell her. She'd accuse him of being as jealous as Vlad. And she'd be right. He was jealous. Except after this morning he suspected her attitude was changing. She'd left Vlad to others and come to help him. Surely that meant something. He'd need to tread carefully though if he didn't want to scare her off. Had she realized yet what she'd done?

Vlad pushed away his tray and lay back in his bed. The man in the next bed groaned and called for a nurse. He wore a wreath of bandages around his forehead, and his right arm was in a cast. By the look of the stitches in his cheek and the swelling around his eye, Vlad presumed the man had been in a car accident.

He felt no sympathy. The man had made no effort to eat his soup and he was complaining because his tea was cold. Whatever his injuries, he was not going to help himself by lying around whining. Vlad gritted his teeth and blocked the repetitive cries, hoping the man's sedative would take hold soon.

Closing his ears against the feeble moans, Vlad concentrated on the morning's explosion, seeking the flaw in his scheme. Where had he erred? Every detail he examined had worked as expected. The more he analyzed, the more puzzled he became. He'd made no mistakes, and yet, Wachter had survived.

As the younger man's moans diminished to an occasional whimper, Vlad turned his churning thoughts in a new direction. Given the failure of a complex plan, would a simple one succeed? His target was nearby. Why not just hunt him down and smother him? Milton hospital was small. Wachter couldn't be that difficult to find.

Timing was the issue. He'd be seen if he tried anything now while staff was hustling around collecting trays. Visitors, too, would be coming and going for another couple of hours.

When he caught himself drifting on the edge of sleep, he decided to get up and check out Wachter's location. His roommate's eyes were closed and he'd uttered no sound for at least fifteen minutes. Vlad was sure the man was asleep.

He eased upright, then stretched his toes to the floor. Standing up brought yet another spear of pain through his ears. He grabbed his tray table, stood still and waited. Gradually the pain eased. It didn't disappear completely, but it was bearable. He hung onto his bed-table until he was clear of the foot of the bed, then struck out for the door.

The hall was empty. Vlad discovered it was hard to maintain a casual appearance when his feet were bare and the tail of his hospital gown flapped open with every other step. He got to the neighboring room unobserved and peeked around the doorjamb. Failing to recognize either of the occupants, he moved on slowly, leaning against the wall.

He heard voices in the second room and recognized one as George Edwards from the shipping department. The answering voice also seemed familiar, although he couldn't place it. Since he was in no mood to talk to anyone from the plant, he continued his unsteady progress towards the third doorway. All was silent here. He placed his hand on the frame and started to peek inside.

"Mr. Horbatsky. You shouldn't be out of bed alone." The nurse's sharp voice startled him so badly he wobbled as he turned. The woman grabbed his arm for support and succeeded in further disrupting his balance.

"Back to bed with you. Right now." She gripped his upper arm firmly. "Do you want to fall? How do you think we'd get you back up?" Her peevish tone conveyed her anger without putting it into words.

"Linda," she called. "Come and help me with this stray."

The second nurse laid a hand on Vlad's back. He wasn't exactly sure where she'd come from, probably the room he'd been about to enter.

"I just needed to stretch my legs," he protested.

"Then call me," the nurse named Linda said. "I'd rather walk with you than find you on the floor. Okay?"

It was *not* okay. But neither could he say so. Vlad pretended to be cowed and fumed internally all the way back to his bed. He could only hope for solitude later in the evening. Perhaps the nurses would relax their vigilance after visitors left and the sleeping pills were administered.

Love, Obey & Betray

Just when he hoped to make another foray into the hall, his roommate began demanding attention again. His ceaseless complaints and repeated use of the call bell disrupted the midnight shift change and kept nurses running in and out of their room for more than an hour. By the time the man's fresh pain medication took effect, Vlad was exhausted. He couldn't believe how wearying it was to feign sleep. Unable to help himself, he dozed off.

He came awake with a start. The room was dim, the doorway a bright rectangle to his right. He glanced at his wrist. The illuminated dial of his watch told him it was after three. He lay listening for several moments. He could hear his roommate breathing heavily behind the curtain separating their beds. There was no sound from the hall outside. He dare not assume the nurses had all gone on coffee break together, but if he moved quietly and quickly...

He slid out of bed and shivered at the cold of the floor beneath his bare feet. Out of the blue, a loud snore from a room down the hall disrupted the stillness. He waited a moment to be sure no nurse was going to respond to the sound. Reassured by the ongoing silence, he struck off for the door, then turned to his right. He was surprised at how shaky he felt, but at least his headache was almost gone.

He paused in the doorway of the adjacent room. The bed beside the door was empty. The curtain was drawn between the beds, concealing the man by the window. Vlad moved forward quietly. He didn't notice the bed-table behind the curtain until his big toe connected with one wheel and slammed it into the side of the bed.

Stifling a gasp of pain, Vlad jumped back as the sleeping patient jerked awake with an exclamation. He waited, afraid to move, until the man sniffed softly, turned over and rearranged his covers. It was not Wachter. In seconds the patient's breathing had resumed its deep, regular rhythm and Vlad, too, relaxed, then turned and crept back out of the room.

The two remaining rooms in this section of corridor were empty. Vlad crossed the hall and halted in the first doorway. It was a ward with four beds. Each one was full. He scanned the occupants. None had Wachter's bulky frame and white hair.

Although the next room was designed for two patients, the bed by the window was vacant. The covers on the other bed were tossed back, and the occupant was absent. Vlad looked around, puzzled where the man could have gone in the dead of night. Then he heard the toilet flush in the ensuite washroom. He stepped back to flee, but not fast enough.

The door opened and Andreas emerged. The two men eyed each other in silence, both startled, neither prepared to back down.

"How do you think Kate will react when I tell her you visited me at this hour?"

No reply was needed. They both understood the ultimatum. Vlad could feel Wachter's eyes on his back as he turned and walked out into the hall. At the door to his own room a worried-looking nurse rushed out, almost colliding with him.

"Linda said you were a wanderer," she scolded softly, relief warming her expression. "Do you need a pain pill?"

"No."

"Just can't sleep?"

Glad of the proffered excuse, Vlad nodded.

"Well, let's go for a walk together then," she murmured, putting a hand on his arm.

He was in no position to protest as the nurse patiently walked him up and down the hall for the next five minutes, then led him back to his bed and watched him settle down.

Frustrated and exhausted, he gritted his teeth until the woman turned away.

"Nurse," his roommate called through the closed washroom door.

So that was why she had been in their room. Vlad suppressed the urge to strangle the man. He'd deal with him later.

"Nurse."

She opened the door and Vlad heard her speaking softly to the man. In seconds the toilet flushed and she reappeared, supporting his roommate. Once he was back under the covers, the woman disappeared into the hall.

Vlad didn't hear her return until she slid the curtain aside. He opened his eyes and found her standing beside him, a syringe in her hand. Before he could protest she pushed aside the sleeve of his hospital gown and administered the injection.

"There. That should let you rest comfortably." She smiled, straightened the curtain and walked back to the end of his bed. Already he had to struggle to keep his weary eyes from closing. How the hell was he going to get back to Wachter's room in this condition?

CHAPTER EIGHTEEN

Vlad returned to work with everyone else on the Monday after the blast. It was surprising how quickly order could be restored to a disaster scene. Investigators had made their inspection, taken their samples, questioned witnesses and gone away. It would be weeks before their report arrived. Vlad knew their findings would not incriminate him. He'd used no suspicious materials. Even if the cut in the hose were discovered, there was no way of determining what sharp edge had made it.

While part of him regretted causing Gerry the expense of repairing the damage, he still blamed Gerry for making the explosion necessary. Mostly he just fumed at his failure. He felt no compulsion to discuss the blast with others. He was much too busy wrestling with the problem of forming a new plan. His mind sifted through his options even as he supervised removal of debris and construction of a new Clean Room wall.

He caught Wachter watching him occasionally and braced for interrogation. He expected Wachter would want the police to connect the blast with the attempt to tamper with his car and Vlad's thwarted hospital visit. It didn't happen. Vlad had no idea whether Wachter stayed silent or whether the police just ignored him. Either way, it was a warning. Next time he must be truly ingenious.

Kate, too, seemed strangely silent about the explosion. While he hoped she would confront him if she were suspicious, he had a niggling fear she might not. He was haunted by the knowledge of how cunning her spymasters had taught her to be.

The new answer to his dilemma struck late one June evening when he received yet another call from Nicholas Tartarinov. It was his fifth plea on behalf of the Russian Family Fund and Vlad understood the pest was not about to take no for an answer. So why not use him?

If Wachter could try to blackmail Vlad with this fake Russian organization, why not turn the tables? Why not make it look as though Wachter had Communist connections? Even though he was just a contractor now, it would shake up his American employers to think Wachter dealt with Iron Curtain countries. His reputation would be shot and his security clearance revoked. With a little luck, the German might even be deported.

#

Vlad waited by the rear doors of St. Mary's until he saw Eddie Pasternak come up the basement steps and exit the building. A staunch member of the congregation and a long-standing member of Oakville's Ukrainian community, Vlad had been acquainted with the Bell Telephone technician for many years.

The wizened little man turned with a start when Vlad called his name, then smiled and waited for Vlad to catch up. They exchanged small talk as they proceeded into the rear yard away from the rest of the congregation heading towards the parking lot.

When they were well out of earshot of others, Vlad began to explain about the calls purportedly on Olga's behalf.

Eddie stopped short and turned to scowl up at Vlad. "Where are they coming from?"

Vlad shrugged again. "That's just it. I don't know. This Nicholas says he's in Montreal but somehow I don't think so."

"You can always ignore him."

Vlad nodded. "True. Only if the need is real... well...maybe I should help out."

"Is it likely she's still alive?" Eddie asked.

Vlad shrugged. "I don't know. Probably not. She'd be in her eighties if she were. That's not very likely, given conditions in Poland."

"Ah." Eddie nodded. "Well, we can always see if we can track down your mystery caller. There'll be records at the switching station."

"I was hoping you'd say that. Do you think you can get me his number?" Vlad stopped, letting Eddie consider the request, then added the bait. "I need to be sure it's an honest claim. I may need to go over this guy's head to be sure of that, talk to his boss."

"I'm not supposed to do this, you understand. But if there's a chance the old lady is alive and in need of help..." Eddie shook his head. "It's just not right the way the Commies treat people."

Vlad didn't like using his friend but he did need his help to get a number for Nicholas' handler. Once he had that, he knew what to do. He'd set a trail that led right back to Texas. That smug clown would look good behind bars. If he were serving a prison sentence for selling American defense secrets, Kate wouldn't be so quick to defend her precious German.

Like all of Clarke's staff, Andreas returned to work the week after the explosion. During the first few days he turned his hand to whatever job he could find to do. At the back of his mind lay a vague idea of seeking the source of the *accident*, as everyone called it. The notion was ridiculous, of course. Ministry of Labor investigators had been all over the place. What could he find that they had missed?

All the while, Andreas kept seeing Vlad's expression the night he appeared in his hospital room. Pure hatred. Just like when he had caught Vlad monkeying with his car. Vlad was the man who inspected equipment throughout the plant.

Instinct told Andreas there was a connection. Common sense denied it. Whatever else he was, Vlad was a smart man and no smart man risked killing so many just to get one. Besides, Clarke was a friend as well as his boss. Surely Vlad wouldn't destroy a friend's business, never mind risking his own future if he were caught.

Then there was Kate. What Andreas had told Vlad in the parking lot was true. Kate was not the sort to stay silent about criminal activity. Were she to learn that Vlad had caused the explosion, she'd turn him in. Wouldn't she?

Andreas puzzled over the issue repeatedly. Given her own espionage background, betraying her husband seemed hypocritical. Yet, at heart, Andreas knew Kate was a moral individual. Much as he would like to think otherwise, he acknowledged that her anger would arise from Vlad endangering anyone, not from fear for him.

So, should he tell her about the tampering incident? Tempting as it was, he restrained himself. Kate was loyal. Tattling like a pre-schooler would only diminish him in her opinion. That was certainly not his intention.

What was his aim? He found the explosion had solidified that for him, too. His anger at her betrayal was a surface reaction. He had loved Kate for years and meeting their child only reinforced it. That was the idea behind his new will. Then, finding her beside him in the crisis underscored the correctness of that original decision. Katrina Horbatsky should be his wife.

Only she took her marriage vows seriously, he reminded himself. She wouldn't go skipping off into the future with him no matter what he promised her. Not unless she had a genuine reason to break with Vlad. Suspicions about the explosion wouldn't be enough to prompt such a break. He'd need concrete proof. Even that might not shake her loyalty.

By the middle of the second week after the explosion Andreas had made up his mind. He was going crazy concocting make-work projects for himself. There was no way he could do the job for which he was being paid until the Clean Room was operational again. He had a small contract waiting for him in London, which he was scheduled to deal with when he finished at Clarke's. Why not switch? Go to London now and come back when Clarke was back on track. He'd feel more honest about taking Gerry's money then and he'd lose nothing in the process.

It would also reduce the temptation to make an inappropriate approach to Kate. She'd known him as an honorable man. That gentlemanly image was one of the few cards he still held. If the investigation found Vlad responsible, he'd be around to support her. If Vlad's guilt were never uncovered at least he'd still have his pride.

Kate was alone in the office when Andreas dropped off his last report before leaving for London. "I presume Gerry told you I'm off to Kerry Tool and Machines on Monday," he said, laying the report on her desk.

She nodded. "Didn't surprise me, knowing how you hate to stand around pretending to work."

Yes, she did know him. "How are things? Vlad over his concussion?"

Again Kate nodded. "Short term headaches. What about you?"

"The same. I was fine again by Monday although I confess I was gulping Aspirins much of the weekend."

"And the arm?"

He shrugged. "The stitches are starting to itch. You know how that goes. I should get them out in another week."

When Kate reached to pick up the report, Andreas laid his hand over hers. "Be careful, *Liebchen*. Call me if you need any help."

Her expression didn't change but Andreas felt her eyes searching his face. He shook his head. "No, I don't know anything. I just don't like this accident. There's more to it than we know."

"And you think I'm going to need a friend?"

"Maybe. I can talk here without being overheard, so I'm telling you. I was angry, Kati, but I'm over it. I want you to know that you can always turn to me for anything you need—a sounding board, money, shelter, whatever. Is that clear?"

He saw her surprise before she looked away. He waited, but she didn't ask. He didn't need to say the only strings attached to his offer would be those of her choosing.

"I couldn't do that, Andreas. I've already taken advantage of you. Way, way too much advantage. It wouldn't be fair." She picked up his report and rose. "I'll see Gerry has this before he leaves for the weekend."

He nodded and turned away. It was going to be a long summer.

#

The early afternoon sun was warm through the car windows as Vlad headed east along Steeles Avenue towards the shopping center in Brampton. He tingled with anticipation. Kate was planning to do something with Ruth and paid no attention when he said he would be busy with errands for most of the afternoon.

Nor would Korczak easily identify Vlad should he be questioned about the meeting later. He had made a stop at a gas station rest room on the edge of Huttonville to don the white wig and goatee purchased a few days earlier from a theatrical supply house in Toronto.

Now, with his upper body padded and his blue eyes shielded by horn-rimmed reading glasses from the local drugstore, a casual observer might not recognize him. Should anyone show Korczak a picture or provide a verbal description of Andreas Wachter, Korczak could easily misidentify the man who arranged to sell him designs for the U.S. Defense Department's bomb control system.

The meeting wouldn't take long. The time-consuming part had been tracking down his contact. Eddie was good. Vlad had to give him credit for that. He'd found Nicholas' number within a couple of days of their conversation.

When Vlad called Nicholas Tartarinov and pretended to have re-thought his refusal to help Olga, the man swallowed Vlad's bait. He hadn't been happy about passing on Vlad's message, but he'd been left with no option. Unless Korczak called Vlad, there'd be no money for Olga.

The trickiest part of the exercise for Vlad had been concealing his plan from Eddie while still getting him to reveal Korczak's Toronto location. Then a telephone directory provided the number he needed to cut Tartarinov out of the loop.

When Korczak called, Vlad kept his message brief and pointed.

"I think we could do each other some favors," Vlad had told him. "I hear you are collecting funds to benefit infirm citizens in the Motherland. I will not be sending you any money. But maybe—just maybe—I could arrange a way for you to earn the money they need."

At first Korczak blustered that he knew nothing of the Russian Family Fund. Vlad's reference to Tartarinov silenced his protests. When Korczak wanted an explanation, Vlad said he had goods Korczak might be interested in selling. Cautiously, Korczak agreed to meet Vlad at the mall. Vlad knew he'd do more checking, but he wouldn't find solid answers.

Vlad parked and entered through the mall's front doors. He collected a coffee and picked up a newspaper at one of the stands on the main corridor. He resisted the temptation to glance around. If Korczak were watching, he must not realize Vlad was nervous. Vlad found a place to sit near the entrance to the largest clothing store on the ground floor.

He spotted Korczak almost as soon as he left the store. He was a big man, heavy set, needing a shave and leaning on a cane. Vlad wondered if Korczak, too, was in disguise. It didn't matter since they would never meet again.

Vlad tossed a section of the paper towards the end of the bench on which he was sitting and pretended to be engrossed in reading as Korczak shuffled over, sat down and picked up the paper.

"Good game last night," Vlad offered, giving Korczak a chance to recognize his voice.

Korczak nodded. "Yeah, but I prefer golf."

Vlad recognized the accent and smiled. "Perhaps, if you have a desire to beat in someone's brains. Otherwise it is just an excuse to wander around in the sunshine when you should be at home doing chores."

Korczak looked at him. "You like to work more than to play?"

"That depends on what you call work. Me, I'm an inventor. I can spend a whole day tinkering with an idea and never think I am working."

"Ah." Korczak nodded. "I can see that would perhaps be less work than some other things. What do you make?"

"Targeting systems for the air force."

Korczak's expression sharpened. "That is a lucrative business, I understand."

"I hear people in Czechoslovakia are interested in our bomb guidance systems," Vlad said. "Unfortunately, my boss is not interested in supplying to them."

"Your boss?" Korczak was puzzled.

"The American Defense Department."

Korczak nodded slowly in an effort to cover up his surprise. "I see. Indeed, some of our friends claim North American designs are superior to what their engineers produce in Russia and Hungary."

"Then they might be interested in buying plans for a new type of guidance system used on NATO bombers."

Korczak nodded again and unfolded the newspaper. "I believe they would. The trick would be to supply those plans for them."

Vlad smiled. He could sense Korczak's interest, even though the man was pretending indifference.

"That is no trick," he said. "The plans go to manufacturing plants that supply the finished products to the Defense Department."

"But that sort of stuff is heavily guarded. How do I know you can get it?"

Vlad just smiled. It wasn't a pleasant smile, and Korczak understood the message.

"So that's your problem. Of course. The issue is your commission rate. What are you looking for?"

"Not much," Vlad said. "I only ask that your buyer realizes more might become available. It depends on how unhappy I get with my superiors. I'm not looking for much money. I'll set up an Austrian bank account for my mistress and you can make the deposits into that."

Korczak's eyes narrowed as he stared at Vlad. "You are a generous lover."

Vlad grinned and shook his head. "No. I think my daughter's mother has earned a reward for her dedication."

Korczak changed the subject. "And if my people are not interested?"

Vlad knew the man was bluffing. Two could play that game. He shrugged. "Then I guess our friends at home will have to do without their superior guidance system," he countered, pretending indifference to the value of the sale.

He rose and bundled up his newspaper as though he were preparing to leave. "I'll give you two weeks before I call for a progress report. You can tell me then how to get the plans to you."

Korczak also stood up. "Very well. I will make inquiries. Then I will call you."

Vlad shook his head. "I will call *you* in two weeks."

Korczak nodded, then turned on his heel and limped towards the clothing store.

Vlad bought another coffee and headed back to the parking lot. He had to work at keeping the smile off his face. The sun was indeed shining on him. It would take time for Wachter's superiors to find out what he had done. Selling the right plans to the right buyer would put Wachter squarely on the wrong side of the law. Oh, he'd plead innocent, and he would be. Only he wouldn't be able to prove the plans were stolen. Nor would he know who had done the deed.

Yes, Andreas Wachter would eventually regret threatening a Cossack. When his reputation was in tatters and he was facing a prison sentence for selling stolen defense secrets, then Kate would have to admit that her precious German was a fraud.

CHAPTER NINETEEN

The fourth Monday in July, Kate's mind wandered as she drove to work. Summer had come reluctantly this year. The nights were still cool and crops were slow in starting to ripen. It rained before dawn and the air was still damp.

She had arrived in Peenemünde on a day like this.

With thoughts of Peenemünde, quite naturally, came memories of Andreas. Tall and solid; his jacket over the back of his chair; his tie unfastened; bent over a drafting table; pacing restlessly around the workshop; absent-mindedly munching sandwiches she brought to him late in the evening while he tinkered with a finished engine.

Of course, the past weeks had provided her with a whole new set of memories. For the first time, she's seen Andreas' temper. Unlike with Vlad, however, there was logic behind Andreas' reactions. Likewise, she had seen him accept reasonable actions even if he disagreed with them. Most importantly, he'd made it plain that he could forgive. He was keeping his distance and letting Ruth's importance to them both remain their secret. Rather than straining their bond, this new image somehow made him more precious.

Ruth said he loved her, and Kate could interpret his recent offer in that light, but that would be foolish. She was married to Vlad and she wasn't going to change that. This interlude was putting a comforting end to her relationship with Andreas.

The accident had scared her, but things had settled down since Andreas' departure. The repairs to the Clean Room were progressing well. Life seemed to be back to normal.

Unfortunately, the strain on her marriage had started her treacherous mind to playing with the *what ifs*. What if she left Vlad? What if Andreas asked her to move to the U.S. with him? What if Ruth's parentage were discovered?

She scolded herself, knowing such thoughts could destroy a marriage. Andreas had simply called a truce. What kind of fool was she to embellish it into anything more than that?

She parked in her usual spot and ignored the familiar racket from machinery on the assembly lines as she climbed the stairs to the offices.

She realized the door was already open because it swung in when she tried to put her key in the lock. Odd. Gerry must have come upstairs first rather than going directly to the plant floor to talk to his foremen as he usually did.

She stowed her jacket in the outside office closet, then stepped aside as their Girl Friday, Janice, arrived behind her. The two women chatted a moment, then went their separate ways.

With her first steps into her own office, hairs tickled on Kate's arms, although there was no obvious cause for unease. Her desktop was undisturbed. Her chair was in its place, shoved against the desk. Her typewriter was still covered on the side console. No drawers stood open and the lights were off as usual.

Despite the lack of evidence, she was sure someone strange had been there. A new cleaner? Possibly, but that shouldn't be setting off wary sensations. As she stood thinking, Janice appeared at Kate's door.

"You've got to see this," she said, beckoning Kate to follow her back down the hall to her desk. "I wouldn't believe it if I wasn't seeing it myself."

Kate's first glance revealed little. Then she realized what Janice meant. The top drawer of her file cabinet sported a neat hole where its lock had been. The missing mechanism rested on top of the cabinet. The rest of the room showed no signs of being disturbed.

"Petty cash?" she asked quietly.

Janice nodded. "I checked. It's empty."

"How much?"

"Eighty-five dollars and change. The exact amount was on the slip I did before closing up last night. But the slip's gone so I can't be absolutely certain."

"Peanuts," Kate said. "What else is in there?"

"Just copies of letters from would-be suppliers. The other drawers have reports Gerry brought back from conferences over the years. Mostly background material about manufacturing; general info he wanted me to keep for him about banking programs for small businesses. That sort of thing."

Nothing a burglar would want.

"Come on." Kate turned and headed back towards her own quarters. She went directly to Gerry's office and found that door, too, was unlocked. Janice stood behind her as she pushed it open and looked around.

Again, a casual observer might have noted no obvious signs of an alien presence. Further examination revealed subtle hints. Gerry's chair was pulled back from his desk, and when she went to look, there was a small daub of mud on the carpet beside it. The lock on the top drawer was broken and the middle drawer was open a crack. Pulling down her sweater sleeve to cover her hand, she eased the top drawer open. Gerry kept his keys in the front of it. They were gone.

Determined not to panic, Kate turned to the middle drawer and pulled. Even she was surprised at the jumble of junk it contained—including the missing key ring nestled atop a pair of leather gloves.

"I don't believe this," she told Janice. "Gerry wouldn't break into his own desk. And he never puts his keys in the wrong place. We've been burgled. We need Gerry up here and we'll have to call the police. We shouldn't touch anything until they give us the okay."

Accountant Wanda Page stood in the hall doorway as they came out of Gerry's office. "Someone broke into my office," she announced before Janice could tell her about the theft. "My desk has been rifled and my file cabinet is hanging open. So is the supply closet. But I don't see anything missing."

The rest of the morning saw Clarke's office staff accomplishing very little as police combed their section of the building and identification officers dusted surfaces all over the area in a vain search for usable fingerprints.

Shop employees were of no help to the investigators. No one had seen any strangers or heard any unexplained sounds during the evening. It was almost as if an apparition had melted through a wall, took what it wanted, and then slipped back out again.

When the police left in mid afternoon, the detective inspector in charge of the investigation could only speculate about the event.

"Looks like an inside job," he said

That evening over supper Kate told Vlad what she had found. "The police suspect someone brought someone to work with them," she said. "But if that were the case I'd think someone would have spoken up, or pointed out who brought in a stranger."

"They're all friends," Vlad reminded her. "Nobody rats on a friend. Especially if the friend brought along his son or his grandson, or maybe his nephew, and the kid didn't seem to disappear at any point."

"I suppose we're lucky that the intruder didn't try to remove any of the office machines. Even at a fraction of their original value they'd be worth more than what they got out of the cash box."

"Yeah. But that would tip off the person who brought him in. Unless it's a former employee, of course."

"It's months since anyone was fired," Kate mused. "I can't remember the last time anyone was mad at us when they left."

Vlad pretended to hesitate before suggesting the former employee might not have been fired.

"Left voluntarily?" Kate was puzzled. "In that case why would they rob us?

Vlad shrugged. "Well, you won't like it if I draw the other obvious conclusion."

Kate stared at her husband in shock, her temper rising by the second. When she spoke her voice was sharp with the strain of controlling herself. "What could Andreas possibly gain by doing something like this? Especially when he's coming back in another couple of months. No. It's all in your head."

"I suppose it could have been someone hired by a competitor to get bidding figures for them on a specific contract." Vlad tone suggested that he didn't believe that for an instant. He gave her a pitying look and left the table to turn on the television. *Good.* He'd planted the seed of doubt. *Now let it fester.*

He'd had a panicky moment when he went to photocopy the plans the previous night and found the machine out of toner. Hunting down the chemicals had led to creating a mess he couldn't cover up. Faking a burglary had obviously concealed his dilemma whereas actually taking the plans would have revealed the real theft. It would also have opened the question of it being an inside job. Nope. His staged theft was a tactical success.

As Kate cleared away their meal, her mind worried Vlad's suspicions round and round, despite the lack of logic behind them. Why would Andreas care about Clarke's bidding figures? The only possible connection would lie in revenge and if that were the case, Andreas himself, not the Clarke files, held all the necessary information.

Two weeks later, Gerry announced they'd lost a longstanding contract with a firm in Ohio to some newcomer who had undercut their bid.

"Guess I need to look up some of our old customers," he said as he turned towards his office.

So Vlad might well have been right, Kate decided as she began digging through her files. Accidentally right, of course, because Andreas would certainly not have hired anyone to interfere with a contract.

With the plans for the guidance control system passed into Korczak's sweaty hands, Vlad relaxed. He wouldn't hear when the sale was completed. He didn't care. His commission, when it was earned, would be sent directly to the new Austrian bank account established in Kate's name. He reveled in the knowledge that trouble would come eventually and Wachter would be firmly in the middle of it.

After a few days, however, his conscience began to bother him. Even knowing the Russian Family Fund was a scam, he couldn't quite get Olga out of his mind. If she were still alive, she might truly need financial aid. Also where were her daughters? He hadn't heard from them since 1945. Nadia at least, was part of his family. Perhaps he should see what he could find out about her.

The only way he knew to do that was through the church.

The Eastern Orthodox Church has been the repository of Ukrainian nationalism for more than four centuries, ever since the Czars decided to claim the Steppes all the way to the Black Sea and outlawed the Cossacks who had been the land's previous protectors. From that time on, no matter who were the Motherland's allies and who were her enemies, Ukrainians had found themselves in the middle of the battle. All too frequently when the smoke and dust settled, they were also its principal victims.

Then came the Communists and the Russification of Ukraine using spies deliberately planted in congregations to betray any nationalists. Through it all, the church remained the information highway helping families reconnect with their missing relatives.

Tired of fretting, Vlad called Father Darcovich and arranged an appointment to talk about Olga.

Father Darcovich had been St. Mary's priest for nearly twenty years. He was an older man with deep experience of human nature. Like the Horbatskys, the Darcovichs had been uprooted by the Communists at the end of World War One. Unlike the Horbatskys, the Darcovichs had chosen Canada as their refuge.

Mrs. Darcovich answered the door and fussed like a mother as she took Vlad's coat and showed him to her husband's study.

It was a cramped room, overflowing with books, piles of paper, and framed photographs. In the middle of the confusion, two overstuffed chairs faced Father's wooden desk. Behind it, his padded rocker threatened to unbalance precarious piles of files or strike over one of the haphazard mounds of old newspaper on the floor to its left.

It wasn't quite like Vlad remembered his own father's office, but there was a comfortable feel to the place. Father Darcovich exuded compassion and understanding as he offered Vlad a seat, settled back in his own nest, and lit up his pipe.

"So, how can I help? You said you needed information about family left behind when you came to Canada. I don't know what I can find out for you, but I will help if I can."

"Thank you, Father," Vlad said. "And that is exactly the point. I do not know if you can help, but I have to try every source I can think of. I am coming to you to see if we can find out what happened to my father's former mistress, Olga Danilewski. She would be in her early eighties if she were still alive. The last I heard about her was in 1945 when I brought her daughter out of Poland. Olga and her husband stayed behind.

"I would also like to track down my half-sister, Nadia. She was using the name Danilewski at the time I brought her back to Berlin, but she might have married since that time. Or she might have decided to use the name Horbatsky since she was my father's child."

Father Darcovich showed no surprise. Mistresses might not be publicly acknowledged in North America, but they were common among the more affluent and influential circles in Eastern Europe, especially in pre-war days.

"You have taken your time about this." Father scolded gently. "She could well be dead."

Vlad nodded. "I suspect she is, actually. But I'd feel better with a definitive answer. You see, I've been getting calls from a certain fellow telling me Olga is sick and she wants me to send her money to buy her medication because she's too poor to buy her own."

The old man nodded and puffed. "Typical. Typical. But all the same we can't dismiss it completely. You realize there is an extortion network here just as there is in many nations where our people have settled?"

Vlad nodded. "I suspected it. That's why I haven't sent any money. Still as you say, until I know Olga's situation I can't quite dismiss it either."

A smile twitched one corner of the priest's mouth. "I'm glad to hear you are being sensible about this. All too many of our people knuckle in to the callers and send them money. We all realize that things are very bad at home. Some of our people seem to feel guilty at achieving success when their relatives left behind have not."

Vlad shrugged. "I suppose I, too, have a certain sense of guilt. But mostly it's because I never tried to help Nadia or Olga. I just ignored them."

Father nodded. "You were busy. You had your own family to raise. Kate is a good woman but even so, you would not have wanted to talk about your father's mistress. Canadians don't understand what so many Europeans take for granted."

Vlad nodded. "My parents were happy, yet somehow my father needed to prove he was beyond the ordinary man in that he could look after two wives."

Vlad remembered his first encounter with Olga. It was in Kiev. The family was leaving the church when a pretty woman in a heavy coat stepped off the walk in front of them and turned her ankle. She went down in the snow, knocking over a little girl walking beside her. The child let out a cry of surprise, then jumped up and began brushing herself off. It wasn't until the woman failed to rise that the child looked frightened. She went down on her knees and spoke to her, then jumped up and looked about. The child's eyes fastened on Vlad's father and immediately she broke into a huge smile.

"Papa," she exclaimed and ran back towards him. "Mama hurt," she said, grabbing him by the hand and pulling him towards the woman.

Vlad had instinctively reached for his father to protest the girl's possession. His big brother Mikhail had grabbed him, shaking his head and dragging Vlad back into place beside him.

Bewildered, Vlad had looked to his mother for an explanation only to find her glaring at her husband's back, her chin elevated and her lips scrunched into a tight line. Instinct warned against questioning her and he looked back to see his father lift the woman and summon their driver. The elder Horbatsky placed the woman on the front seat beside the driver, then lifted the child in beside her and tucked the robe around them both.

While the Horbatsky family struggled on though ankle-deep snow in full view of their neighbors, their driver turned the sleigh around and disappeared towards the hilly, eastern section of town with the strange woman and her pretty daughter.

When the driver left without needing directions, his mother had clamped a possessive hand through his father's arm and begun walking on. Her expression dared anyone—including Vlad—to question her actions and his brothers and sister stared straight ahead as though the incident had not happened. It was only later, when they were retiring, that Mikhail told Vlad that the woman was "Papa's friend, Olga."

"Olga was not my father's wife," Vlad explained, "but he set her up like a wife and lavished gifts on her as freely as on my mother. I was still young when the Communists routed the patriots and Father had to gather us up and run. He insisted on bringing Olga and Nadia with us.

"She shared our apartment in Berlin for a time so she was very much a part of the family, even if she did not have my father's name."

Father shook his head. "Poor Mamma."

Remembering his mother's set face and silent anger at the announcement of their living arrangements, Vlad nodded. "Poor Mamma, indeed. Most men do not expect their wives to accept competition in their own homes."

The priest nodded his balding head and smiled. "No, they do not. The surprising part is how few of the women ganged up on their men. Can you imagine what would have happened if your mother and Olga had done that?"

Father's suggestion made Vlad laugh. The mere idea of Dimitri Horbatsky bending to the will of any woman was ludicrous. Yet, he had danced attention on them both for several years. That is, until Olga got tired of taking second place to Mamma and found a husband of her own.

"The authorities are investigating the various funds supposedly set up to help our people," Father continued. "So far I have not heard that they have hard evidence to make arrests. But it will come. Someone will make a mistake somewhere and they'll find out who is behind them. Personally, I'd bet on the KGB. They use whatever means they can find to get foreign money into Moscow."

Father wrote down the information Vlad gave him pertaining to Olga Danilewski and warned him it could take months to learn anything about her. On the other hand, they might never track her down.

Vlad drove home with his mind still skipping through a sun-filled kitchen sharing cookies with a dark-eyed girl clutching a stuffed gingham dog.

CHAPTER TWENTY

Although it was only midmorning, the office was already hot and sticky when the deliveryman knocked on Kate's door.

Her heart thumped in trepidation when he set a huge, paper-shrouded crystal vase on her desk, then fished a padded envelope from his pocket and set it beside the bouquet. A tiny envelope with a card from the sender was already pinned to the paper wrapping the floral arrangement.

She thanked the man, then waited from him to leave before opening the card. The message was brief and unsigned.

Thanks for the memories.

She didn't need a signature to know the sender's identity or the reason for the gift. What did surprise her was Andreas' poor judgment. He knew Vlad temper. He should also realize nothing ever remained a secret at Clarke's.

Her fingers trembling with excitement, she removed the green wrapping paper and counted thirty roses. One for every year since she and Andreas had set up their own apartment ten blocks from the factory.

She never spoke of the significance she attached to August third. Andreas knew though and shared the impact that day had had on both their lives. She wadded up the wrapping and dropped it into her wastebasket.

Torn between annoyance and joy, she slit the padded envelope and removed its contents, a thick, heavily engraved gold band. The sight of the ring brought tears.

Although she had refused to marry him, it was their secret. Andreas had insisted she wear his ring to prevent tongues from wagging until such time as they could make their relationship legitimate. She had felt compelled to leave it behind when she fled Oberammergau. The significance of his gesture tore at her heart. That he had kept her ring said more plainly than words how deep his feelings had been. That he was returning it reinforced his message about forgiving her.

While she had no right to wear it, neither would she return it. She would put it away and give it to Ruth one day. But not yet. She couldn't part with his gift just yet.

She opened her purse and stowed both the ring and the tiny card inside. These were mementos she could treasure at her leisure.

Even as the fragrance of the flowers seeped into every corner of the room, her worry deepened. How was she going to explain them to Vlad?

When Gerry passed through her office on his way to lunch, the bouquet drew a smiling *congratulations*. Kate opened her mouth to contradict his assumption, then asked him for a favor.

"Will you take these home to Helen?" she said, pointing to the flowers on her desk.

"You're sure? I wouldn't want to get in the middle of something. From the size of the bouquet, Vlad's pretty contrite, whatever he did."

Kate just smiled. "Helen could use a nice gesture. Just tell her she's doing me a favor if she accepts them. And let on downstairs that you had them sent here for you to take home with you. Please, Gerry?"

His smile faded. "These aren't from Vlad?"

Kate shook her head. "No. I don't need his jealousy set off over a kind gesture."

Gerry just nodded and scooped up the vase.

When they sat down to supper, Vlad's flushed face and snappy sentences told Kate he had heard about the roses. They weren't mentioned, but the meal was quieter than usual and Kate could feel her husband's anger radiating across the table.

The telephone rang just before bedtime. Kate kept her eyes on her work, stitching meticulously as she finished the heel on a sock she was knitting. Vlad, who had been watching television, went to the hall to answer it.

Kate could hear him speaking in Ukrainian. At first, she thought it was someone from St. Mary's. Then she recognized the hostility in his tone even though she couldn't understand the words. The brief conversation ended with him slamming the receiver back into its cradle and returning to the family room.

"What was that all about?" she inquired, keeping her own voice neutral and her eyes on her knitting.

"Same old thing," he snarled, punching the off button on the television. "You can just tell Wachter it won't work."

Realizing Vlad was resurrecting his ongoing argument, she said nothing. She couldn't understand how a Ukrainian speaker was connected to Andreas, but neither was she about to exacerbate Vlad's already foul mood.

"So you finally see what he is up to," he went on. "Sent you flowers today, did he not? What was that all about?"

"Yes, he sent me flowers," Kate nodded. "But you notice, I didn't keep them. I sent them to Helen. Satisfied?"

"No," he growled between gritted teeth and came to stand over her. "No, I am not satisfied. What the hell does he think gives him the right to send you flowers? You are my wife, not his."

"And since when does one need an excuse to send flowers?" Kate replied steadily. "It's his money. If he wants to waste it, I can't stop him. All I can do is hand the flowers to someone else. Which is what I did."

"That is not good enough. I want it stopped." Vlad's voice rose. "I do not want you speaking to him. I do not want you writing to him. I do not want you seeing him. Is that clear? It is over between you two."

Kate just stared at his furious face and sighed. These accusations were getting beyond annoying. His tone was threatening. She clung to the calm façade she always used when his temper flared.

"This is the first I've heard from him since he left, Vlad. I did not initiate the contact. He'll be back to complete his contract when the Clean Room is operational again in a few weeks. I can't avoid seeing him then without creating a lot of questions. Neither of us wants that so I won't be avoiding him. Understood?"

Carefully she wove the last end into the sock's heel, removed the needle and folded everything into her knitting bag. She rose and turned off the light beside her chair. "The subject is closed. I am going to bed."

Kate sensed Vlad behind her as she stood by the night table removing her earrings. His fury was a tangible thing in the room. She was angry herself. How dare he accuse her of impropriety! She had struggled for weeks now to put Andreas behind her. She'd done a reasonable job of it too, until today.

She might have realized Andreas would remember this date. For all his scientific bent, he had a sentimental streak. He remembered the date of her birthday, so it was only natural that he'd remember their anniversary. She should have expected the flowers, too.

After all, the anniversary was a shared event. They both had reason to remember the night Andreas brought her to live in his apartment, the date when their relationship went from an affair to a marriage.

She didn't admit it aloud, but there was no way to deny the truth of Andreas' claim to be her husband. Only time and a scrap of paper made Vlad's claim superior. This ceaseless, irrational jealousy eroded her acceptance of his right more deeply with each outburst.

Ignoring Vlad's brooding silence, Kate kicked off her shoes and stripped to her underwear. She gathered up her clothes, then pulled her nightgown from under her pillow, and went to the bathroom to brush her teeth.

Vlad was already in bed when she returned. The heap of clothing on the mat by his side of the bed was as indicative of his bad mood as the grim set to his mouth. He didn't stir as Kate turned off the overhead light, went around to her side of the bed and slid under the covers.

Hoping that reading would calm her, Kate turned on the bedside lamp and picked up the mystery novel she had placed on the night table the previous evening. Before she even had time to remove her bookmark, Vlad yanked the book from her hand and flung it across the room.

"Do not think you can ignore me," he yelled as he jerked her onto her back and held her there with a painful grip on her shoulder. His leg thrown across hers trapped her beneath him. The fingers biting into her flesh told Kate that Vlad was out of control. Jealousy and reason had battled and reason had lost.

"Let me go, Vlad." Kate kept her voice low. She wanted to strike out, knock him away. Only she knew that would just increase his anger.

"No." His manner exuded violence even if he spoke more quietly. "I will not allow you to think about him when you are with me. I am your husband. And you are going to remember that."

As his mouth came down, Kate turned her head to avoid it.

"Stop it, Vlad," she snapped, her own anger breaking through her control. "I am well aware of your place in my life."

One of his hands closed painfully around her throat as the other moved from her shoulder to tangle in her hair and prevent further attempts to escape the mouth that now ground against her own.

Pain knifed into her lip as it split and she tasted her own blood. An instant later Vlad's hand grabbed the neck of her nightgown and she heard the fabric rip away even as his mouth began trailing a series of harsh bites down her throat to her breast.

Instinctively, she tensed to resist. Then common sense prevailed. She willed herself to relax. His thinking was already irrational. Rejection would only inflame it. They were too evenly matched. If she fought back, the contest would turn deadly. She needed to placate him.

She forced herself to lie still as his mouth moved. Only when he bit a nipple, did she tense and dig her nails into his shoulder to push him away.

Feeling her protests, Vlad drew back and slapped her. Once was enough to knock the breath out of her. Never before had he struck her.

One of the holds she had learned in her special training flashed through her mind. Again, self-preservation asserted itself. Using it would simply increase her danger.

His knee was between her thighs now, forcing them open and pinching her skin painfully against the mattress in the process. She tried to console herself with the knowledge that the bruises wouldn't show.

Her passive resistance seemed to infuriate Vlad even more. He didn't strike her again but it was domination and rage, not love, that drove him. He was determined to imprint himself on her and eradicate all thoughts of Andreas in the process.

Ironically, his violence hurled her mind back to precisely the memories he wanted to erase. As Vlad thrust into her limp body, she remembered that first night with Andreas. How gently he had made love to her. Indeed there had been passion, but Andreas had ensured it was mutual. He had taken time with her, caressing her sensitive spots, teasing her until she had reached for him. Now, thirty years later, her husband, the man who claimed to love her, was breaking the vows Andreas had never been allowed to make.

When Vlad rolled away from her, Kate got up and marched to the bathroom in a fury. She pulled the bathmat from its place on the edge of the tub and threw it on the tile floor, then turned on the tap to warm the water.

She bunched up her ruined nightgown and pitched it into the laundry hamper. She'd never wear it again, but it would make a rag for washing floors. Methodically she laid a small towel on the vanity, then placed a large one beside it.

She focused on each task individually, separating herself from her emotions as her S.O.E instructors had trained her to do.

"Think about the job," they'd said, "not about what caused it or what will come next. You can get angry later. Right now, you need to do your job."

Checking the water temperature with one hand, she switched to the shower and stepped into the warm spray. The water erased the scent of Vlad's anger. It did nothing to ease hers. She stayed under the stream until the water ran cold.

She could forgive his jealousy. She had forgiven his verbal abuse. She had gone out of her way to be honest and loyal, but by subjecting her to physical abuse, Vlad had succeeded in tipping the balance. Their marriage was dead.

Very deliberately, Kate wiped mist from the tiled walls before ripping the rubber mat loose and hanging it over the rail at the end of the tub. She stepped onto the fuzzy bathmat and wrapped the small towel around her head to dry her hair. She began rubbing the large towel down her legs, then stretched it across her back.

Kate could hear Vlad snoring in their room across the hall. She returned to their room, donned her robe and slippers, and collected clothing for the morning, then went to Ruth's old room. The bed was made up and she crawled between the fresh sheets. It was the first time she'd slept alone since their wedding night.

Too angry to sleep, she lay in the dark, fuming. She had no wish to publicly humiliate him. All the same, neither would she put up with more abuse. He was going to apologize and drop his accusations, or he was going to find himself without a wife.

The house was quiet when she awoke. She wondered whether Vlad was still sleeping or waiting for her to get up and make his breakfast. She rose cautiously; very conscious of assorted bruises, she showered again in hopes the hot water would ease her sore muscles.

As she dressed, she determined she would not be the one to bring up the subject of last night. She'd just carry on as usual until bedtime. Then she'd go to Ruth's room. With the kids both working in Toronto for the summer, no one would be the wiser about their changed circumstances and only Vlad would be affected by her decision.

When she arrived in the kitchen, she discovered she was alone. She ate, then returned to the bedroom to finish dressing. She took Andreas' wedding band from her purse and put it on a gold chain, then fastened it around her neck. How Vlad felt about her previous relationship no longer mattered. She treasured her memories, and he had forfeited the right to object to them. She was going to wear Andreas' ring, and Vlad could damn well get used to it.

CHAPTER TWENTY-ONE

In mid-August, Vlad received a call from Father Darcovich. He sounded well pleased with himself.

"I was luckier than I expected," he told Vlad. "One of my old friends in Paris has a brother serving a church in southern Poland. Our congregations there tend to be small and close-knit. Anyway, Father Paul remembered an old lady named Olga Danilewski. He did her funeral mass about two years ago. He asked me to track down her family because he hasn't been able to find them to pass on the message that she's dead."

Vlad felt his excitement building. He was right. She was dead so there was no need to worry about helping her. The calls were strictly extortion and he was justified in sloughing them off.

"Thank you very much for this, Father," he said. "I felt all along that she would be dead. Now I don't have to worry when the calls come in."

"It gets even better," Father continued. "Since she had no family, the church handled her burial and the nuns sorted out her belongings. They found pictures of two young couples. The names written on the back were Nadia and Joe Dymitruk and Ivana and Klaus Tartarinov. There were dates too. Father figured they were wedding pictures. Am I right in thinking the women were probably Olga's daughters?"

Caught off balance by the name Tartarinov, Vlad nodded, then realized the priest couldn't see the gesture across the telephone lines.

"Yes, Olga's daughters were named Nadia and Ivana," he said.

"That's what we assumed so I put out the word here since Father Paul said one of the men was in some sort of military uniform. There is a Klaus Tartarinov attending St. Sophia's Cathedral at The Pas in Manitoba. The priest there is new and he couldn't tell me whether Tartarinov is widowed or divorced. All he knows is that the man seldom attends mass and when he does, he comes alone," Father Darcovich concluded.

"Well, it's a place to start," Vlad replied, repeating his thanks for the old man's information. "I won't be happy having to pass on word of her death, but I'll start making inquiries. If he was married to Ivana he would at least know who Olga is and he may be able to tell me how to find Nadia."

Deep in thought, Vlad thanked the priest yet again and returned to the family room. Kate was in her rocker, watching television as she embroidered a tablecloth for Ruth's new house. She was getting a lot of pleasure from the work and Vlad envied her that contentment.

"Who was that?" She turned and looked at him.

He shrugged carelessly. "Just Father Darcovich. They need someone to fill in cutting the grass next week while Eddie's on vacation."

She nodded and turned her attention back to the program.

Vlad dropped back onto the chesterfield staring at the television with unseeing eyes. Could there be a link between Nicholas and this Klaus Tartarinov in Manitoba? Could Nicholas actually be Olga's grandson?

###

Summer heat had come to Prague with a vengeance over the past two weeks, sinking into the old buildings like rain into a blanket.

Mikhail set his calculations to one side and leaned against the wall behind his lab stool. The little black box on the counter before him went silent, its display unit showing zeroes when he disconnected the receiver designed to read the target location as determined by triangulation with the satellite signal. So they really did have it, a guidance system that allowed bomber pilots to locate their objectives despite natural barriers like fog and trees. Russia had a system too, but nothing as accurate as this.

The scientist chewed his lip, his thoughts whirling. He had another day at most before his superior demanded results from the tests. Once he confirmed that the black box worked, it would be taken away. He would be given another project. If he wanted to sell information about this new technology to the Israelis, it must be done tonight.

The sound of footsteps in the hall sent a chill up his spine. *Foolish to be so nervous at just contemplating a betrayal.* He ran his hand over his hair and glanced at his watch. It was after six. Quitting time. Nothing unusual about people passing his door at this hour.

The prospect of returning to his stuffy apartment near the Danube held no appeal. Here, in the lab, he enjoyed air conditioning. At home, the late July sun would have raised the temperature through the day and even opening all the windows for the night would bring him little relief from the clinging humidity.

He sat forward, picked up his pencil, and flipped to a fresh page on his pad. The circuitry was complex. While he could draw it out over time, he didn't have time. Nor would he dare hurry. Speed encouraged error, and no one paid for incorrect information.

Mikhail set the pencil down again and walked to the supply cupboard above the sink. In the midst of five shelves of electrical components, he had made room for a small tin of instant coffee, a jar of powdered milk, another of sugar, and a package of musty biscuits. His miniature Minox camera was concealed behind a loose section of the tongue and groove paneling lining the rear of the cupboard. He kept his film supply behind a similar loose panel beside the air conditioning vent.

A window to his left provided plenty of light. He set the circuit drawings in the full glare of the early evening sun and went to work. Each exposure captured a page of the plans. In minutes, he recorded all the details his superior had provided. Perspiration beaded his lip as he shot off the remainder of the roll of film, ran all the tiny celluloid frames into their protective canister, then loaded that into the hollow space in the screw lid of his hip flask.

With the camera back in the cupboard, he collected the papers from his bench and locked them in the top drawer of his desk. It wasn't much security, but it was the best available to someone in his position. Given that the plans were probably stolen in the first place, it amused him to think of anyone trying to steal them from him.

He wiped his face with his handkerchief and started for the door. The man in the security booth by the front entry nodded at him. After twenty years in his position, Mikhail was a familiar figure in the lab. Only rarely now, was he searched on entry and exit. No one knew about his special relationship with the import/export broker from Tel Aviv—the relationship that had founded a bank account in Switzerland that would eventually fund his retirement in a warmer climate beyond the borders of the great Motherland.

Instead of going home, he went to a sidewalk café in the heart of the city. He ordered a meal, then took out his pad and pencil and began to doodle. While he made no pretense of being an artist, he and Izak had long ago worked out a communication system based on drawings.

With a few strokes he created a cartoon pilot's head draped in goggles and headphones. The speech bubble above it said "twenty feet to the right". Beneath the head, communication flashes zigzagged between the antennas of a cartoon bomb and an equally stylized orbiting satellite bearing a series of numbers indicating the price for Mikhail's information. Even if the message weren't crystal clear, Izak would easily link a bomb, a satellite, a pilot and a high value figure.

When the waiter approached, Mikhail slid his little sketch into his shirt pocket and tucked into his food.

The evening was still hot when he left the café to purchase a bottle of the kosher wine Izak supplied to the merchant a few blocks from Mikhail's apartment. As always, the wine was out of stock. Mikhail filled in the order form and laid it on the counter along with his money. The shop owner informed him a shipment was expected by the end of the week and Izak would deliver his order to his home when he arrived.

Outside once more, Mikhail wandered down to the river near the docks. The breeze from the water encouraged people to stroll and he stopped to lean against a lamppost and smoke, his eyes scanning his surroundings. Reassured, he went to their special telephone by the warehouse where Izak stored his merchandise and dialed a non-existent number. In the process of collecting his refunded change, he slid his drawing into the crack between the phone and the coin return chute.

Mikhail's name on the list was Izak's hint to check for a message. Delivery of his order told Mikhail his payment was in the bank. He could place his film in the cavity behind the coin chute of the telephone in the box at the end of his own street. While the system was complicated, it succeeded despite the presence of KGB staff and informers everywhere.

He turned and walked away. Regardless of the humidity, he felt good. He'd leave his flask on his bedside table and take its twin back to the office in his pocket in the morning. Another five years and he could begin looking for that retirement villa in Greece. Or Malta, perhaps. Izak could probably help him with that, as well as arranging his escape over the Czech border.

In the weeks since Kate moved into Ruth's old bedroom Vlad had left her alone, expecting her to return any night. She hadn't moved though and he hadn't issued any invitation.

Wachter was due back in another two weeks and Vlad was willing to give her until then to get over her sulks. He disliked laying down the law, but this time she'd gone too far. She must apologize and acknowledge that she was wrong. If she refused, he'd insist that she give up her job and her car. He couldn't allow her to continue flaunting herself in front of that bastard. She must stay home where she belonged.

Milton fall fair fell on the last Saturday of September. They always attended the event, and since it had not been discussed, Vlad assumed they would be going as usual.

Right after lunch, he went to the bedroom to change while Kate cleared the table. When he returned to the kitchen, he found her at the sink pouring scalding water over a basin of peaches. The canner, filled with jars for sterilizing, was already sitting on the stove's largest element.

He was annoyed by her decision to stay home and even more annoyed that she hadn't consulted him about it.

While it was perfectly normal for a working woman to handle household tasks on Saturday, he decided not to let her away with it. He would make her accompany him.

"You cannot go to the fair looking like that," he said with a frown.

"I know, but the peaches won't last until next weekend, so I'm staying home to do jam today."

As Vlad opened his mouth to take her to task, the telephone in the hall rang. If this hadn't been the weekend the contractors were moving the new equipment into the Clean Room, he would have ignored it. Shooting her a frustrated look, he went to answer it.

"Hi." Eddie Pasternak sounded almost breathless. "We need to talk. When are you free?"

Vlad hesitated. "We were just heading for the fair."

"Good. How about meeting at the heavy horse exhibit around three o'clock?"

"Sounds good," Vlad agreed. "What's up?"

"Not on the phone. See you at three."

Puzzled, Vlad hung up and returned to the kitchen. Now busy with her peeling knife, Kate didn't question the phone call. The determined set of her jaw said that trying to change her plans would result in a battle. The excitement in Eddie's tone combined with his low voice made Vlad suspicious. It seemed wiser to attend the fair alone.

It was a perfect day to be outdoors. Vlad was forced to park six blocks from the fairgrounds because several hundred other people shared his opinion. He wandered around for an hour, repeatedly checking his watch until it was time to find Eddie.

They exchanged a few pleasantries before Vlad's curiosity got the better of him. "So what is this all about that you don't want to speak on the telephone?" he asked.

Eddie's voice dropped and his expression turned conspiratorial. "Keep it under wraps. That Tartarinov guy you had me find? It sounded funny so I talked to one of our fraud boys. They tapped his line and you were right. It is a scam. I hear they've handed it off to the Mounties. Looks like they'll bust him for telephone fraud. Probably pull in his boss and the whole network, because you can bet he won't be their only canvasser."

"Well, what do you know? That should be a relief to his victims." Vlad didn't have to fake his surprise. His mind racing, he changed the subject before Eddie thought to ask whether the Horsemen had contacted him.

"Did I tell you we found out my acquaintance died a couple of years ago? Father managed to track her down through a priest in Poland. He also got me a lead on her daughters. I'm looking for them now."

Vlad couldn't let on how Eddie's news had shaken him. If the Mounties were closing in on Tartarinov, then he, too, was in danger. He didn't trust Tartarinov to conceal Korczak's identity. Nor did he expect that Korczak would keep his mouth shut about Wachter's plans if he were caught. He dare not take a chance. Maybe he should just take a little drive up to Timmins to visit Tartarinov. What should he do? He needed time to sort this out.

Timothy Ford leaned against the railing and gazed down into the street. The morning sun was already hot and he hoped David would be on time. Ford was due to meet with the ambassador before lunch. He couldn't afford to be late for that.

Seconds later, the junior clerk from the Ministry of Defense puffed up the stairs and halted by the wall, breathing heavily. With his rumpled shirt and dark skin, sporting a day's growth of beard, he looked more like a hawker from a stall in the market than a government official.

That, of course, was David Segal's cover. He contacted people from all walks of life. By dint of a shave and a crisp suit he was a respectable businessman. Add robes and a full beard and he could walk any Middle Eastern city street unnoticed. His costume this morning suggested he had further meetings once he finished talking to the American diplomat.

Ford returned to a table bearing a tray of glasses and a sweating pitcher of fruit juice sheltered by a colorful umbrella. He pulled out a wrought iron chair and gestured for the Israeli to join him.

"The lemonade is cool, David. Have some and catch your breath." He poured two glasses and sat back while the Israeli crossed the balcony towards him.

Back in control, David set his glass aside and got down to the reason for the meeting. "We just picked up an interesting new device from a contact in Czechoslovakia. The boss thinks Washington might also be interested in it."

"From that source, of course we're interested," Timothy said. David's superior was the Israeli Minister of Defense, but Timothy knew that authorization to share

Russian technology would have come from higher up, perhaps the Prime Minister himself.

"Actually, it's not their work," David continued. "They picked up this fire control system from somewhere in the West."

Timothy's attention went from serious to intense. "The West?"

"Yes, my friend. We have no indication of the original source, but English language words on the circuits told us that it wasn't theirs in the beginning."

"You mean it could be our stuff coming back to us?"

David shrugged. "Maybe. Who knows? Researchers work on military designs in England, Canada, Australia, even South Africa. All of you would detail the specs in English."

Timothy nodded, shocked. It wasn't unheard of, of course, for the Russians to get their hands on some American military invention. It was simply that he had received no recent warnings of betrayal.

"Ours or theirs, it doesn't matter," Timothy said. "When do I get it and how do we repay you for the help?"

David removed a folded envelope from his shirt pocket and slid it across the table. "I am sure our superiors can work out the details," he said. "For now, it's enough that your country knows who its friends are."

CHAPTER TWENTY-TWO

The first Friday of October, Kate arrived home with a full workload ahead of her. Monday being Thanksgiving Day, both Alexi and Tanya were coming home from Toronto, and she needed to get her weekend cleaning done tonight. She would throw the laundry into the washer as she vacuumed and dusted. Since she was using Ruth's old room, she hoped they wouldn't notice she had moved out of their father's bed. They'd have to be told eventually, but she was in no hurry to reveal the split.

They would probably show up after lunch, but she could bake and talk to them at the same time. Then she would be ready for Ruth and the rest of the family to come for dinner on Sunday. Her plans well in hand, Kate pulled into the driveway, opened the garage door, and parked her car.

Although she was surprised that Vlad's truck was not where she expected it to be, she didn't give it much thought. He was probably getting a haircut. He was always meticulous about his grooming and he knew they had company coming, even if it was just family.

She put the ingredients for a casserole together in a pan and set it into the oven before starting the wash. That way they could eat when Vlad got home. She found no note saying where he was or when he would be back. That, too, was odd, but since the separation his actions were increasingly unpredictable. There was always the chance he was having a beer with someone because he wanted to stay out of her way. He might even be getting back at her, trying to make her worry. He hadn't stooped to that level before, but there was a first time for everything.

With the floors shining, the furniture polished and the last load of washing in the machine, Kate decided against delaying supper any longer. It was after eight and her stomach was grumbling.

She ate without tasting her food, her mind consumed by conflicting emotions. One half of her wanted to shrug off Vlad's disappearance; the other side warned her the move was totally at odds with his suspicious nature. He'd never leave her unsupervised for an evening, especially not while their disagreement remained unresolved.

When he was still absent at nine, she broke down and called Gerry to inquire if some emergency had arisen at work. Gerry, too, was puzzled.

"That's not like him," he muttered. "He's so dependable it has to be serious if he's disappeared."

"That's why I called you," Kate replied. "I'd feel awfully stupid checking the hospital for accidents only to find out later that he was at work."

Gerry tried to reassure her. "It's got to be truck trouble. He'll turn up soon."

Pretending to share his opinion, Kate hung up. She couldn't tell her boss about the estrangement. The thought of Vlad committing suicide flashed through her mind and disappeared as quickly as it came. While they still had not discussed the attack, seven weeks of increasingly icy silence told Kate Vlad's thinking had not altered. In his eyes, if Andreas felt free to send her gifts she must be encouraging him. Vlad would most assuredly not be leaving her free to join Andreas.

Off the phone, she wandered around for several minutes more, then glanced at the clock. If she was going to call Father Darcovich to find out if Vlad were involved in any church work, she needed to do it now, before it was too late.

The priest, too, saw Vlad's unexplained absence as unusual, but, like Gerry, brushed it off. Kate let him, satisfied to eliminate one more logical explanation for her husband's absence. She stood by the telephone for a moment, debating whether to call her mother, then decided against upsetting her and dialed her brother's number instead.

Her sister-in-law, Rachel, informed her that neither she nor her husband had heard from Vlad. "And I just got back from picking a basket of tomatoes from Mom's garden. He wasn't there and they weren't expecting him," she finished. "Sorry, Kate, but I don't think we can help you."

"Don't worry about it, Rach. He's probably in somebody's back yard having a beer and oblivious of the time," Kate soothed. "I shouldn't worry, only it's unlike him to just fail to mention it when he plans to be late coming home."

Before she began calling his co-workers, Kate went to the bedroom closet to eliminate the last possibility. There she discovered that his weekend case, three sets of underwear, his favorite sweater, a shirt and work pants, his razor, and assorted toiletries were missing. The message was disturbingly obvious. His departure had been planned and looking for him would be a pointless exercise. He'd show up when he was ready—not before.

Furious, she returned to the family room and collected Amos for his evening walk. As they strode down the gravel road in the dark, she debated whether her concern stemmed from habit or from some lingering remnant of the love she had once felt for her husband. Unable to answer the question, she turned instead to pondering whether she should call the police. Given that he had taken his suitcase, bringing in the authorities seemed inappropriate. She could see no alternative to waiting it out.

Finally, at midnight, Kate dragged herself off to bed and tried to sleep. Every vehicle that came down Appleby Line set her waiting to hear it slow and turn in their driveway. None did. Sensing her uneasiness, Amos came to sleep by her side of Ruth's bed instead of in his usual spot on the kitchen mat. Some time near morning exhaustion got the better of her and she fell deeply asleep, only to jerk awake in the terrifying aftermath of a nightmare.

She couldn't remember the details, only that she was running and Ruth was with her. Physically drained, she turned and looked at the clock. It was barely six. She needed more sleep if she were to achieve the things she planned for today. Another hour of tossing about convinced her that wouldn't happen.

She took a long, hot shower, then choked down dry toast and coffee heavily laced with cream and sugar. Since it was still too early to go for groceries, she set to work mixing the ingredients for the hamburgers she'd feed her children at noon. Pounding breadcrumbs into the meat at least let her vent some of her frustration.

Right after breakfast her brother, Rob, called her. "What's this Rachel tells me about Vlad disappearing? Where was he?" he demanded.

"I don't know. He hasn't come back and he packed a bag."

"Packed?"

"Yeah. I didn't realize that when we talked last night. I only thought to check before I started calling anyone from work. His razor's gone as well as a couple of sets of underwear and one set of work clothes."

"So he deliberately went somewhere without telling you."

"Looks that way." Kate could hear the anger in her voice.

"What's going on?"

"Don't know."

"Kate." His tone was a mixture of scolding and coaxing.

Rob was just two years Kate's senior and they had always confided in each other. She had only ever kept one secret from him and that, too, might need to come out if her marriage to Vlad didn't get back on track.

Reluctantly, she outlined the situation with Andreas and the resulting problem with Vlad's jealousy. Confessing that Andreas was furious when he discovered she was a spy, she avoided any reference to Ruth or the reason Andreas forgave her. Instead, she passed off the flowers as a peace offering. She did not, however, attempt to conceal Vlad's reaction to the gift.

"He accused me of encouraging Andreas and attacked me. I moved into the spare bedroom and our relationship has been hands-off since mid-July," she concluded her explanation.

There was a long pause. Kate could practically feel her brother's legal mind whirling.

"Have you discussed separation, divorce or anything else that would set him off?"

"No."

"Are you thinking along those lines?"

"No." Kate hesitated. "Well, not like that. I'm not interested in any reunion with Andreas, despite what Vlad thinks, but neither am I prepared to put up with harassment and abuse. I can continue the life we have right now, but I have no idea whether Vlad will tolerate it. We haven't discussed it."

"Haven't...Kate, how does a couple live together for weeks without talking about something like this?"

She snorted. "Very easily if you're married to Vladymyr Horbatsky. He started this and until he's prepared to raise the issue, the problem is all mine. He's probably waiting for me to crawl back and apologize. Since I don't intend to do that, there's nothing to discuss."

"So this disappearing act could be his way of scaring you into line?"

"Maybe."

"Does he have any friends, relatives, or—perish the thought— a girlfriend?"

"Not that I know about."

"So he's holed up in a motel somewhere for the weekend?"

"Could be. But it isn't like him. First, he's not the passive type. If he's that mad at me it would be more in character for him to throw a screaming fit and start ordering me around. Second, he's too cheap to waste money on a motel."

Rob chuckled. "Now that's more like my little sister. Cheap? God, Katie. He really does have you ticked off, doesn't he?"

"I can't help it, Rob. I'm fed up. I ought to hate the jerk but this is so unlike him, I can't help being a bit worried."

Rob was instantly all business. "Okay. This is from Robert Cameron, the lawyer. Since police won't see a man leaving on his own as any sort of emergency, let alone suspicious, they won't put high priority on their search if and when you do file a missing person report. Give him time to come home on his own. If he's gone too long, then notify the police. He packed a bag, so he intended to go. He had enough clothes to last until at least Monday. So wait that long, minimum."

He tried to offer some comfort. "It will be hard on you—and even harder on the kids—but hang in there. He needs to remember that you can handle your own life. I'm sure it wasn't his plan, but he just might discover he's the vulnerable one. He's going to think twice about dishing out orders if he finds you don't need him."

"At least he might realize I'm serious when we actually do talk about this separate living arrangement," Kate concluded.

As expected, the younger kids rolled in shortly before lunch, dragging laundry and full of chatter about this year's university courses. They were even more shocked than their mother by Vlad's inexplicable absence and just as bewildered about his possible destination.

"It's not as if he had other family members he could visit," Alexi said. "Even when he's mad at the world, he never has had a place where he could go to brood."

Tanya wanted to call the police despite her uncle's advice. Her brother intervened.

"If Uncle Rob says wait, we should listen," he insisted. "He knows the system. We don't. I know you're anxious. We all are. But talking to the police won't change that unless they have answers—and they don't. If they had, they'd have called us already. So, you start on the laundry and I'll tackle the lawn. Being busy won't fix our problem, but it will help us to cope with it."

#

Sunday morning Kate took one look at the dark rings under her eyes and decided to skip church. Her appearance was a dead giveaway that something was wrong and she wasn't up to making excuses.

Ruth arrived just before lunch. While she was as puzzled as everyone else by her stepfather's disappearance, she questioned whether her mother had called Andreas.

Startled, Kate looked up from peeling potatoes and shook her head. "Why would I do that?"

"We all know Vlad's jealous streak," Ruth replied. "He didn't know you and Andreas were acquainted when my father arrived in February. But he does now. Would he drive to London to try to threaten Andreas into not coming back to Clarke's?"

For an instant Kate was too shocked to respond. Ruth didn't know about the cold war that had enveloped the house. Even so, her idea made perfect sense.

"I didn't consider that," she admitted.

"Should you?" Ruth challenged.

Kate was torn. She wanted to reject the idea instantly, but…"I can't just call him up and casually ask whether Vlad came by in the last couple of days," she protested. "They weren't friends. He'd think I was crazy."

Ruth shook her head. "He knows Vlad's jealous. He also knows Vlad will do anything to keep you two apart. He wouldn't see your question as the least bit crazy."

When Kate hesitated, Ruth offered to make the call.

"And if he hasn't seen him?" Kate asked, watching Ruth head for the phone.

Ruth shrugged. "Then he'll at least know he may be in Vlad's line of fire. What's wrong with that? Andreas isn't the type to go blabbing about your fears."

Her daughter was perceptive. Correction. Ruth knew Vlad's temper. Only once had she crossed him, and Vlad had slapped her so hard Ruth's cheek had carried the bruise for three weeks.

Although neither of them mentioned Vlad's hatred for Germans, Ruth had seen Vlad's reaction on Mother's Day. It was enough to underscore the obvious.

Kate nodded. "Okay, but you make the call. I'd probably break down trying to explain and that would just give him the wrong idea."

Kate was putting the lid on the pot of potatoes when Ruth returned from the telephone. "He hasn't seen Vlad and he was just as understanding as I expected. Says he's had a glitch of some sort that will hold him up for a day or two. Even so, if you need him, he expects you to call. For sure he'll be in Milton by the start of next week."

Kate's parents arrived early in the afternoon. One look at their daughter's strained features when she met them at the door told them she had a problem. Mrs. Cameron began questioning her even before their jackets were hung in the closet.

Knowing it was pointless to try to cover up Vlad's absence, Kate stated the fact directly. "Vlad took off after work Friday and I haven't heard from him since."

"Took off? For where?" her mother demanded.

Kate shrugged. "That's the trouble. We don't know."

Ruth interrupted before her grandmother could continue. "We haven't a clue what's going on, Grandma. So don't bother grilling Mom. It won't help." Her smile was designed to take the sting from her pointed remark.

Mrs. Cameron looked bewildered, then turned her attention to Amos, giving him an affectionate pat and letting him lead her to the family room.

Rev. Cameron offered no comments. Long exposure to families in crisis had taught him to recognize the symptoms of stress. He would speak to Kate later, in private.

Rachael, Rob and their children arrived for the family dinner late in the afternoon and ignored Vlad's absence beyond a perfunctory "No word, huh?"

As they rose from the table Rev. Cameron took Kate aside. "I need to talk to you. Ruth and Rachael can look after your mother. Let's go to the garden."

His questions were gentle but direct. Kate felt no hesitation in telling her father about Vlad's disappearance and Rob's advice concerning reporting it.

"So he's gone and you don't know what prompted it?" he concluded when Kate fell silent.

"I won't pretend, Dad. We had a major fight over Vlad's jealousy, but that makes no sense as an excuse for him to walk out on me. In fact, I'd have expected him to be hovering over me even more than usual to ensure I wasn't seeing someone."

"What sparked his jealousy this time?"

Kate was prepared for the question. She could give him part of the story without lying.

"Do you remember meeting Andreas Wachter on Mother's Day? The guy who brought back your hat?" Rev. Cameron nodded. "I worked with Andreas at the research lab in Peenemünde when I was with S.O.E. Vlad can't handle that, suspects Andreas wants to start up our old relationship and all that crap."

The retired clergyman's gaze was somber. "And does he?"

Kate knew that her father's world was far from the sheltered, highly moral place many imagined it to be. He'd seen humanity with all its faults and foibles and understood its motivations in all their ugliness.

"I'm married, Dad. Andreas knows that."

Rev. Cameron raised one eyebrow. "But does he accept it?"

Kate sighed. "In 1943 Andreas wanted to marry me. It's not 1943 any more. Vlad's the one who refuses to accept how things have changed."

Rev. Cameron nodded. "He seemed like a nice man."

"He was…" Kate stopped to correct herself. "He is a gentleman. In different circumstances he would have been your son-in-law."

The old man smiled sadly. "I won't tell your mother that, Katie. But thanks for telling me."

CHAPTER TWENTY-THREE

It was a quiet neighborhood, full of modern buildings, industrious professionals, and mobile executives. Residents paid little attention to their neighbors. So long as the rent was paid and private lives remained private, landlords asked no questions and nodding acquaintances were satisfied just to recognize familiar faces on the street and in the hallways. No one wanted friends living next door.

Igor Lukanovich lay back in the lounge chair on his balcony. His coffee, like the early morning temperature, was cool. Below him, traffic hummed down the street of the Paris suburb in which his apartment was located.

The man sharing Igor's telephone conversation was sitting in an equally discreet apartment in an equally nondescript city neighborhood half a world away.

Frederick Korczak had immigrated to Toronto in the 1960s as a professional photographer specializing in magazine illustrations. His mediocre skill with a camera earned him admission to assorted industrial and commercial establishments but not enough money to provide his living. It was his link to the backgrounds of numerous former Soviet citizens that raised his income level from subsistence to substantial.

Former classmates at a private Parisian school for children of Slavic émigrés, Igor and Frederick had shared a common heritage and a common taste for luxuries. The fact their backgrounds had once boasted aristocratic connections only provided access to the social world of their compatriots. It didn't put sports cars in their garages or francs in their bank accounts. Most of these families had lost their money along with their power when they fled the Communist takeover of their homelands.

What lifted the pair from their impoverished backgrounds was a not-so-accidental encounter with KGB agents within their own community during their university days. From these mentors they learned the secrets of preying on their fellow émigrés. At the same time, they established their own connections in the Motherland.

Since it would have horrified their parents to discover their sons had embraced the very ideology that had driven them from their estates in Russia and Ukraine, Frederick and Igor rarely visited their families. They preferred to foster the belief they were busy pursuing careers in some nameless international trade.

In a sense, Frederick's move to Toronto was exactly that. Since many members of the Parisian community had relatives and former friends in America, the move gave the transatlantic partnership a much-expanded base of operation.

"I don't know what to recommend," Igor told his old friend. "There is no question that Gaston is efficient. He has never been suspected, let alone charged. And you are quite right in saying Tartarinov's thefts must be stopped. But can you take over his call list? Some of his people make substantial monthly donations. We don't want to lose that. Besides, if they stop hearing from us, they may start asking questions."

"I don't seem to have a choice," Frederick grumbled. "I dislike turning to people like Gaston, but discipline is necessary. I would not have believed the little weasel could skim off five bills a month without us noticing."

"You say it began a year ago. Are you sure?"

"Oh, yes, my friend. The letter was explicit. The donor wanted a picture of his new nephew to prove his donation was providing the supplies the child needed. He stated the amount of his contribution and I know we received only a portion of that. In fact, Tartarinov could be taking even more than I suspect. I may not have found all his contacts yet."

Igor sighed. "Unfortunately that is one of the dangers of a good solicitor. They can set up their own operation because they know how the system works."

"What worries me is whether Tartarinov has any accomplices."

"Well, there was Horbatsky," Igor suggested. "We know he traced you through Tartarinov. If he could figure it out, who else may have done so?"

"Yes, he bothers me too," Frederick said. "The sale went well and Ibstein would take more plans from us if we could get them. But that disguise concerns me. Why did he go to such lengths to pretend to be Wachter? Makes me wonder what he's up to."

"*Da*," Igor agreed. "He may have been trying to keep us from identifying him. Then again, he may have thought we'd prefer to deal with the real designer."

Frederick answered impatiently. "Who knows? Who cares? The only answer we need is whether he is involved with Tartarinov. I suspect he is, and I vote to remove him while we're at it. Eliminate all risks."

"Why not?" Igor agreed. "If he is a danger to us, and I am inclined to agree with you, my friend, that would end both potential problems at one time. I will have a talk with Gaston. You have the pictures he will need in order to identify them? I have the background information. He should be on a plane for Canada within the week."

By Monday, Kate was fed up with her children's pointless fussing and speculation. Ruth understood her mother's frustration and left Sunday night on the pretext of attending to her own household chores. Tanya and Alexi had not taken the hint. Right after breakfast, Kate overrode their protests and shooed them back to the city, reminding them that their classes resumed the next morning.

Tuesday, Kate left for work in a quandary. Vlad had neither come home nor phoned. While she was still annoyed, she was also growing more worried than she wanted to admit. She could only presume that he would be at work when she arrived.

He wasn't.

Gerry came out of his office while she was placing her purse in her desk drawer.

"Vlad didn't show up this morning. Have you heard anything?"

There was no point evading the question. She shook her head. "Nope. Not a word. I expected to find him here when I got in, but obviously I was wrong."

"And the police haven't been able to help you?"

"I didn't call them." Seeing his puzzled frown, she explained about the missing suitcase and her brother's recommendation that she delay making any call until after the long weekend.

"Obviously he planned to go since he packed a case. What are the cops going to think? We had a fight and he took off to cool down? Or he's got a little something on the side that I don't know about? He took enough clothes for the weekend, possibly a bit longer. I can be plenty angry and worried, but I can't say anything's wrong. Not yet."

Gerry shook his head. "I don't get it. He doesn't do things like this. I mean, he's so damned reliable... There's got to be something wrong here, Kate."

"Oh, I agree. I just have no idea what it is."

Vlad's maintenance crew knew their routine and fell into it without prompting. Kate urged Gerry to talk to the men.

"You never know what he may have said. He could have told one of the guys what he planned, where he was going."

The men were as puzzled as Kate and Gerry. Vlad had mentioned nothing to any of them.

When Vlad had still not shown up by midweek, Kate decided to go to the police.

The interview went much as she expected with the bulk of the questions centering on recent disagreements, financial worries and potential girlfriends. The officer taking her report seemed to consider she had waited a long time to begin searching for Vlad.

"And exactly how would it look to you for me to say he was missing when he took a suitcase, a change of clothes and his razor? That tells me it wasn't a kidnapping or an emergency. He planned to leave."

The cop shrugged. "Yeah, it does. So why get excited now?"

"Because he's been gone too long. He only took enough things for one weekend. I have no idea what's gone wrong, or why, or where. I just know something is wrong and I don't know any other way to deal with it except through the police."

The officer nodded, accepted the missing person form she had filled out, and promised to call as soon as they had any information.

###

Although Gerry had already told her that Andreas would return Monday, Kate saw no sign of him until the day ended. She was putting the cover on her typewriter when he appeared in the office doorway.

He glanced around, checking that they were actually alone, then crossed to stand before her desk. "How are you?"

"Fine." She kept her answer short. He mustn't learn about her breach with Vlad.

"Everything's okay? No lawn mower problems? No neglected garden work? No leaky faucets?"

Kate smiled and shook her head. "Nothing I can't handle."

Andreas nodded. "Yes, I should realize that, shouldn't I? You're so damned competent you don't need a man." He looked away and sighed. "Sorry. That came out much more bitterly than I intended." After an awkward pause, he continued. "Have you had any word?"

"No."

"The police have nothing to offer?"

"Only one thing. Apparently, Vlad set up a separate bank account in May. The day he left, he cleaned it out. But that's all we know."

"A secret account? Now that's interesting." Andreas raised his eyebrows and whistled silently, then changed the subject. "I know this could be misunderstood, but I need to say it anyway. Any help you need, call me. I'm not trying to come between you, I swear. But I've been through this suspense thing. Do you understand?"

Understand? Oh yes, she knew the pain. In a flash she was back in London, lying in a cottage hospital with their newborn Ruth beside her. How scared she'd been. How badly she'd wanted him. She had let him go without any hope of ever meeting him again.

It hurt to see how he, too, had suffered over their parting. She fought her desire to take him in her arms and hug him. He was a good man. Vlad's irrational insecurities weren't Andreas' fault. He didn't need to get tangled up in their mess.

"I can't tell you how much I appreciate your offer, 'Dreas, but you know I can't accept it. It would damage your reputation as much as mine. This is no time to destroy a lifetime of hard work."

"Reputation? At our age? Katrina, for God's sake. Do you think I give a damn what some gossip says? You were my wife. Ruth is my daughter. I should at least be allowed to support you, even if you won't live with me."

His face flushed and he turned away. "I'm sorry. That was uncalled for."

"No. I'm the one who should apologize. I never meant to drag you into something like this." She laid her hand on his arm, then dropped it. "*Won't* doesn't come into it."

"Then, don't push me away," he replied sharply. "Don't force me to find out what's going on via Ruth. Tell me yourself. Is that too much to ask?"

She shook her head. "No. No, I can keep you up to date if that's what you want."

"Good. Now come on. We're going to supper. There's a decent restaurant near Mill Street. That shouldn't compromise us, eating in a public place."

Kate shook her head and sighed in exasperation. *Give the man an inch...*"Yes. All right. But that's it. Tonight and no more."

He nodded. "I'll drive," he said as he shepherded her towards the stairs. He remained silent, concentrating on the road as he worked his way through the early evening traffic. They found a table at the small restaurant and placed their order before Andreas mentioned Vlad again.

"You haven't told me how he reacted when I sent your ring back. Could that be what's behind this disappearance?" Andreas asked.

Kate shook her head. "I don't believe so. He was furious. I expected that. We had a serious disagreement. I won't deny there was tension between us, but I never felt he wanted a separation."

"Could he have been planning to leave and just not let on?"

Kate shrugged. "He planned enough to take a suitcase. But when he only took one changes of clothes, I'm sure he didn't expect to be gone this long."

"So you think he'll come back?" Andreas made no effort to conceal the surprise in his tone.

"I don't know. I thought so at first. But now..." She shrugged.

"In that case, I suppose the important question is what you'll do when he does return."

Her smile wasn't happy. Looking at Andreas across the table, all the old feelings were simmering just below the surface. She must be careful or he'd see her conflict.

"What should I do? He's my husband. Nothing's changed about that just because he pulled a disappearing act."

"What if he were dangerous? Would that change things?"

Kate took a deep breath. Her voice flattened. "I've always known he could be dangerous. He was four years old when his family first fled the Communists. He was twenty-five when the Nazis left him for dead. His whole life has been a battle for survival."

"And I'm just one more threat."

Kate nodded. "A different kind, but yes."

"So killing me would be logical."

"Killing you?" Pain jolted through her. She should deny the notion, and yet she couldn't. "What makes you think he wants you dead?"

"The fact I caught him tampering with the brakes on my car two weeks before the Clean Room blew up."

Kate's hand trembled as she reached for her water glass. "What did he say?"

"That I wouldn't have you. You belonged to him."

The response was so typical she couldn't doubt it. "I see. And you said?"

Andreas sighed. "Apparently, I was very stupid. Instead of saying I don't live in the past, I told him I've changed my will. I warned him that if he killed me, you'd have sufficient money to live comfortably on your own. Then I said you'd probably leave him if you suspected him responsible for my death." The deafening silence lasted several moments. "You wouldn't have made the connections if I'd died in that explosion."

Hearing Andreas voice the suspicion she had denied for weeks felt like being dunked in icy water. Kate gasped and shuddered. "No," she whispered. "He didn't do that. He couldn't."

Andreas reached for her hand. "Why are you so sure? Do you know someone else did it?" When she didn't answer, he continued. "He had access to the hoses and the tanks. He did the regular inspections. Clarke employees aren't careless. If someone ran over a hose, they'd know it was serious. They'd report it. It wasn't an accident. It was deliberate."

"The Ministry inspectors didn't think so." Her response was automatic.

"They weren't looking for sabotage," Andreas reminded her. "Why should they when an accident seemed so much more logical?"

Pain and anger flooded her, driving her on. "How could you have been so stupid? You know how jealous he is. Telling him about the will was a red flag to a bull."

Andreas nodded, his face grim. "You think I don't realize that now? It scares me to death to understand how I endangered you. I never once suspected he'd do something that rash..." He let his sentence tail away, his implication obvious, then resumed. "He's unstable, Kati. You aren't safe around him."

The waitress arrived with their order. While she rattled crockery into place and refilled their coffee mugs, Kate wrestled with the new information. The will changed everything. No wonder Vlad suspected her of encouraging Andreas.

When the woman left, she continued, her voice angry. "Why did you do it? Change your will, I mean."

His answer stunned her.

"You gave me a child. You raised her. You have earned anything I can give you." He held up his hand before she could protest. "You weren't looking for a reward, I know. But I feel indebted to you."

Shaking her head, Kate picked up her fork and began to eat. Was he trying to say he still loved her, or was he just consumed with guilt at abandoning their child? Her plate was empty before she finally gave up attempts to be Machiavellian and blurted out her question.

"So what do you want in return for your money?"

He frowned. "The money has nothing to do with it. That was just a precaution. Even if I was furious, I still owed you. Now, I've tamed down. I want to resume our life together." He waved his hands to ward off her protest. "I realize this is not the time. You still don't know where you stand. We'll wait, together. At least I can be available for you to lean on when you need me."

It annoyed her to hear Andreas repeat the line Vlad uttered frequently. She didn't need looking after. She tried to ignore the tiny voice reminding her how comforting she had always found Andreas' care to be.

CHAPTER TWENTY-FOUR

Gaston pocketed his passport, walked briskly out of customs, and crossed through the international terminal at Malton airport into the early October afternoon. Although this was not his first trip to Canada, he had done only a few jobs here. Wherever he went, he started the assignment in the same way.

Walking with purposeful strides, he entered the parking garage and looked around as though seeking a vehicle he had left there some days before. The handful of fellow travelers absorbed in their own search, took no notice of a man in khaki slacks and navy windbreaker.

Gaston carried his duffle bag in his left hand and fingered the clip leads in his right pocket. His eyes roamed the rows, assessing the most common makes and models. Then, seeing a three-year-old beige Chevrolet next to the back wall, he crossed to it and tried the door. It was unlocked. Most encouraging of all, a time-stamped parking ticket peeked from above the driver's-side sun visor.

He tossed his bag on the floor in the back seat and unzipped it. The hold-all's front pocket contained his roll of tools. Dropping the roll over the back of the front seat, he got in and closed the door.

With equipment specifically adapted to the task, he had the ignition punched out of the steering column, the leads clipped into place, and the hot-wired Chevy backing out of its parking spot mere minutes after he entered it. He passed the ticket to the attendant in the booth by the garage exit, and waited patiently while the man tallied the cost. Gaston had come prepared and removed the appropriate Canadian bills from his wallet as though he knew he owed the parking fare. With a curt nod, he accepted his change, pocketed it, and pulled onto the highway. It was less than an hour since his plane from Paris had landed.

He was in no hurry to find his target and finish his assignment. Canada was a great place to hide after the contract in Greece that he had completed less than a week before receiving Igor's call. All the same, Igor wanted the work finished quickly so he dare not dawdle. Perhaps he would take a couple of weeks on the west coast when he finished. Let the heat in Europe die down before flying home.

A few miles north of the airport, he gassed up and bought an Ontario road map.

When he stopped for his evening meal at a family restaurant an hour later, dusk was settling in. He reviewed his route as he waited for his food. His original calculations seemed right. It would take a solid day of driving to get to Timmins.

Since flying wore him out, he considered finding a motel for the night. First he needed to dump the car's license plate if he didn't want some bright-eyed cop figuring out his wheels were stolen. He was close to Barrie. According to the map, the city should be large enough to have a bar or two. It would be dark by the time he arrived.

It took a bit of driving around to find the sort of place he needed, one with a dimly lit parking lot and several empty spaces near the street. He chose a vacant spot near the back, under a tree, between a half-ton and a station wagon. He knew that new customers would fill those inviting front places first, thereby giving him the privacy to make his switch.

He stuffed the handle of his screwdriver up his sleeve and walked to the back of his car. The screws holding the license plate in place were badly corroded. He returned to his tool kit for the can of lubricant he carried for such problems. Even so, he was swearing quietly by the time he had the screws worked free. He wasn't going through that again, he told himself.

Back on the highway, he relaxed. So long as the wagon had plates, its driver was unlikely to notice that they were the wrong ones. Nor would police, looking for a beige Chevy, stop him when his tags didn't match those on the missing car. For safety sake, he'd do a switch every week until he abandoned the vehicle.

An hour north of Barrie, he found a roadside motel and checked in. He'd be on the road before eight, which should get him to Timmins by early afternoon.

He'd give himself a day to scout the place and determine how best to accomplish the necessary accident. After that, with the photo and address he'd been sent, he should have no trouble locating Tartarinov. The first half of his contract should be over by the weekend. Then he could head south to find Horbatsky.

That job should be even easier, given that Horbatsky apparently lived in the country. No neighbors to hear a shot and a good long drive to and from work where he could easily have a fatal accident. One way or another, the whole thing could be wrapped up within a week.

Gaston settled himself on the single bed and rolled into the blankets. Morning would come early.

Kate was just finishing the dishes after her evening meal when Ruth let herself in the back door. It was more than a week since Vlad had disappeared and she was glad to see her daughter. All the same, she wasn't sure the visit was an innocent one. Although they'd spoken on the phone every other day, those conversations were brief—comforting rather than probing. Kate's facade had worked with Alexi and Tanya because they were engrossed in their own lives and their studies. Ruth was more mature and saw her mother differently.

Ruth dropped her knitting bag on the couch and continued into the kitchen to pick up the tea towel. "This sitting around with nothing more strenuous than walking Amos in an evening could get boring. I figured you might need a distraction and I'm it."

Kate smiled and they began discussing the day's events at their respective jobs as they finished tidying the kitchen and settled in front of the television with their knitting and fresh coffee.

It wasn't long before Ruth raised the subject of Vlad's disappearance. "How is Gerry taking it?" she asked.

Kate shrugged. "How can he take it? Vlad isn't here. No one knows where to look for him. We have no idea when he'll be back. We'll just have to muddle along."

"But how will they keep things working properly?"

"Well, for a few days the guys can cover for him. He has them pretty well trained on the regular, everyday maintenance. We'll only have trouble if something unexpected happens."

Ruth nodded, flipping her needles to start a new row on the sweater she was knitting. "I can't understand it. All my life Pops was so insistent on us keeping our word, living up to our obligations. It doesn't make sense for him to just vanish like this."

Kate shrugged. "No, it doesn't. But then, a lot of things haven't made much sense with him of late."

"Yeah, I wondered about that." Ruth kept her eyes on her needles. "What was going on that you were sleeping in my room? Oh, I know I wasn't supposed to notice, but I've seen your stuff in there twice now. The kids don't know, do they?"

Kate brushed the question aside with a shake of her head. "It's not important."

Ruth protested. "Mother, it isn't *nothing* if it's serious enough to force you into a separate bedroom. For heaven's sake. What do you think I am? Did my father do something that made Vlad go violent?"

"How could he do that? He was gone for ten weeks." She could feel Ruth watching her. She snipped the end of yarn and pulled it through the last stitch to finish her mitt.

Ruth wasn't about to let Kate get away with avoiding the issue. "I know Vlad has a temper, Mom. And I know how ridiculously upset he's been ever since my father showed up. Did Andreas set him off somehow?"

Kate shook her head. "No. It's not Andreas' fault, Ruth. It's Vlad. He's completely irrational where Germans are concerned."

"So he has been going at you. Did he hit you?"

"Not really." Kate tried to pass it off, suppressing a shudder at the memory of Vlad's furious face the night he attacked her.

"Not really? So how do you get hit without being really hit? Come on, Mom. This is me, remember? The kid who sported a bruise for three weeks for talking back to him over Donnie Marshall on prom night?" Ruth looked grim, referring to the long ago disagreement about curfew. "So if he didn't hit you, what did he do to upset you that badly? It's not in your nature to move out like that."

"Oh, for heaven's sakes, Ruth, leave it be. I don't want to talk about it."

"Mother, I can't just ignore it. I need to know. Are you in physical danger with Vlad? Because if you are, you need to get out. I mean get right out. Leave. Come and stay with me. Go to Grandma and Grandpa's house. Do something. You can't just wait here for him to come back and start knocking you around again."

Kate heaved a sigh. "Okay, okay. I give up. We had a huge fight and Vlad attacked me. I moved into your room and our physical relationship has been non-existent ever since. I'm not afraid of him, Ruth. I'm just not prepared to be a wife any more if he doesn't trust me."

Ruth nodded, satisfied that she had heard the truth. She continued. "Is that what's behind this disappearing act? Is Vlad trying to teach you a lesson?"

Kate shrugged. "I don't know. Maybe. Then again, he's had these weird phone calls. Only a couple, mind you, but I noticed. I did question him casually, but he wouldn't talk about them. That's not like him."

"Have you told the police?"

"No. I can't even prove they were happening."

"How is Andreas taking all this?"

Kate shook her head, unwilling to talk about Andreas' offer. "He's doing his job."

"Nothing more?"

"No."

"Darn." Ruth almost pouted.

"What did you expect?"

Ruth shrugged. "I don't know. I just didn't expect him to sit on his duff and do nothing. Not the way he feels about you. Have you told him about Vlad attacking you?"

Kate stared at her. "Of course not. Why should I?"

She could imagine the row that would precipitate. If he didn't insist on moving her to his hotel, he'd take up residence in her spare bedroom. Wouldn't that just cause hell on wheels when Vlad came back.

"He'd protect you from Vlad."

"Your father can do no wrong in your eyes, can he?"

Ruth shrugged. "I just like the man. Isn't that okay?" She paused, then getting no response from Kate, continued. "Okay, fair enough. Just don't stay here and let Vlad bully you. You have every right to walk away if he's mistreating you. He might come to his senses if you went out the door."

"Well, for the moment at least, it's a non-issue. He's the one who went out the door. And what about Amos? I'm not walking away and leaving the house empty."

"But you will walk if the problems continue after he comes back? Promise?"

Kate shook her head and laughed. "You know, you're as stubborn as Vlad. Yes, Ruth. I'll keep your advice in mind. Now, finish your coffee and I'll get us another cup."

# # #

Light snow was falling, melting on contact, darkening the already-black pavement. His headlights cut twin paths into the night. Around him, the pines enclosed the highway heading west from Thunder Bay. Apart from a few trucks, the road was empty.

When he was looking to make time, Vlad preferred driving at night. He could push his speed without fearing the cops would pick him up. The weather annoyed him. He hadn't prepared for snow when he left and they wouldn't be getting any in Milton. He twisted the heater knob on the dash and cursed yet again at the steam clouding the truck's rear window. God-forsaken wilderness. He'd need to stop in Winnipeg to pick up a winter coat and boots.

The truck was behaving itself now after the delay in South Porcupine to install a new fuel pump. It had cost him a whole day, but it was a necessity. Besides, he didn't think it would matter since Nicholas wasn't expecting him anyway.

Compared to the three days lost in arguing with the mine's personnel officer and Nicholas' landlady, the truck was a minor problem. He'd been damned lucky to run into Nichols' old roommate.

His task had seemed simple enough when he left Milton. He would go to Timmins and explain what the Mounties were up to. Then he'd offer Nicholas money to get out of the country.

Only it hadn't turned out to be that straightforward. The mine office had been shut down for the whole long weekend and when it did open, he'd wasted another day waiting for the personnel office clerk to provide him with Nicholas' home address.

Then, when he finally located the place, Nicholas' landlady refused to tell him anything. He'd been about to leave when Red Castonguay came down the stairs and, despite the old woman's angry glare, asked for a lift into town. Always quick to grasp an opportunity, Vlad agreed immediately. On the short drive Red told him about the telephone call on Sunday afternoon two weeks earlier. The next day Nicholas paid up the money he owed Red and said he was heading home to Sudbury. His parents' old house had just sold and he had to look after the paperwork.

Vlad arrived in Sudbury only to run into another delay. The house had indeed been sold. However, it took him another two days to track down the realtor responsible for the sale and bribe Nicholas' forwarding address out of her. That address was in The Pas, Manitoba, at least two hours north and west of Winnipeg.

It couldn't be pure coincidence that Nicholas was going to the same community to which Father Darcovich had traced a possible connection to Olga's daughter, Ivana. All the same, he was getting tired of all the driving. He consoled himself with the thought of returning to Milton within a week.

He missed Kate's comforting presence. Despite the strain in recent weeks, just knowing she was there, handling the little chores, was reassuring. He wondered yet again how she was managing in his absence. Was she worried? She should be. Life alone would be no picnic. The bills would eat up her salary and keeping up the house and the yard would exhaust her. She needed to realize how much he did for her. Surely this would scare some sense into her. He wanted to call, but thought better of it. Let her stew. His silence would reinforce the lesson. Besides, if they did talk she'd demand answers he dare not provide.

Wachter would be back in Milton by now. Vlad remembered Kate going into Ruth's old bedroom and shutting the door on him the night before he left. His lips tightened into a grim line and he stomped on the accelerator. He needed to get home before she let that Kraut fill the void in her life.

The radio in his truck played softly as he sped through the night, his mind drifting to the old days and the woman connected to Nicholas' calls.

He hadn't seen Olga in what—forty years? Not since she married Danilewski and had her second daughter. The whole family had moved to Poland in the mid 1930s.

During the war Vlad was too busy keeping himself alive to spare any thought for his half sister. That didn't change until he returned to Berlin in 1945. When his mother handed him the two-year-old letter from Olga begging them for help, he tried to refuse. His mother, sick as she was, would hear none of his excuses. It didn't matter that Poland was behind the Russian lines. Nor would she make allowances for what might have happened in the period since the letter was written. As the only surviving male in the family she insisted it was his duty to help his sister.

In the end it was not his mother but Anna who had persuaded him to make the trip. She pointed out how Nadia had been a part of the Horbatsky family as a toddler, how his mother saw her almost like her own child. Now, with only Vlad left of her family, it was understandable that his mother wanted Nadia back, Anna said.

When he got to the address on Olga's letter, only Nadia was still living there. If you could call it living, given that the house was little more than a shell full of rubble and rats.

He never asked about Olga. Nor did he ask Nadia how she was surviving. He didn't want to know and she didn't say. She had simply bundled up the blanket she was using for a bed and followed when he said he'd come to take her back to Berlin.

It was a long walk. Sometimes they hitched a ride on the back of a cart or in an army truck. Vlad pretended not to notice when some soldier got a hand up her skirt or offered to share his rations if she'd step into the back of the truck to help him find them.

They had a relatively easy trip despite the miles involved. Only once, at a farm near Slaska, had they encountered real trouble. The Russians had stationed a large force there and interrogations were lengthy and serious when anyone stumbled into the place.

Knowing Nadia's charm wouldn't get them out of this, Vlad took charge. He told the sentry they were heading for his family at Frankfort. He let on Nadia was his fiancée and they were to be married when they reached his parents' farm.

It was a thin story, but for some reason he never understood, the sentry accepted it. Maybe the man thought they looked too scared to lie. Maybe he was just so sick of fighting that he understood the need to settle down and rebuild a normal life. Whatever the reason, he waved them through.

Vlad had taken Nadia to the church in their old neighborhood in Berlin where she could find food and shelter in the remains of the Ukrainian community. Then he left.

He'd become immersed in translating for the Americans at the war crimes trials. What free time he got was spent with Anna and his mother. When his mother died three years later, he had already applied to emigrate. He never heard from Nadia or Olga again. Now Olga, too, was dead.

CHAPTER TWENTY-FIVE

Tom Kelly rose from his desk and began to pace. There was no doubt that the circuits on the printout before him were identical to the ones currently in use to build guidance equipment for American bombers. The design was new, less than two years old, actually. Worse, he recognized the telltale initials worked into the drawings. They were the signature on all designs produced by his friend and mentor Andreas Kohlman Wachter.

Andreas had been an old hand at inventing equipment for military planes when Tom joined Lone Star Logistics. The difference was that Andreas preferred his lab and the thrill of overcoming a problem, while Tom realized early in his career that his creative talents were limited. He was better at administration than innovation. He used his authority deftly, ruffling as few feathers as possible, and came to the attention of the defense department as a result. It was Andreas who had encouraged him to move on when the opportunity arose.

"Red tape is as much of a problem for researchers as lack of funds," Andreas had told him. "You can help us all by cutting through that bureaucracy. So go. Do it."

Despite the move from Texas to Washington, Tom and Andreas kept in touch and when Andreas retired three years earlier, Tom attended his going away party.

Tom had been the one to sign the funding approval when the contract was let for the updated guidance design. He had personally congratulated Andreas for his continuing contribution to the nation's defense.

So how did the Russians get their hands on the circuit drawings for Andreas' design? He didn't subscribe to the prevailing theory that Andreas had double-dipped, selling to both Washington and Moscow. He was personally acquainted with the man and he'd have bet his life on the German's integrity. What other explanation was there? Where did their security system break down? Who could have betrayed them to the enemy?

Determined to track down the breach, he returned to his desk and punched numbers into his telephone. Although military types liked to conduct their own investigations, they also liked to protect their own. He had connections at the CIA. If he wanted a thorough and unbiased examination he'd do better to call in help from outside the system.

Vlad pulled up in front of the small house on the outskirts of The Pas and checked the name on the mailbox. K. Tartarinov. According to the telephone directory Klaus was the only Tartarinov in the community and this was his address.

The place was neat enough, but there was a certain faded look to it that suggested the owner had lost interest in his home. The thought crossed Vlad's mind that this was how his house would appear if he lost Kate. He pushed the thought away as quickly as it came. He wasn't going to lose her. He'd beat the Kraut at his own game.

Klaus Tartarinov arrived home just after dark. Sitting in his truck down the street, Vlad saw the old car disappear around the heap of snow at the end of the driveway, then reappear as its driver stopped to open the double doors on the wooden shed that served as a garage. Moments later the doors closed and a dark figure moved towards the house. In seconds, light shone from a rear window.

Vlad gave him five minutes to dispose of his outdoor clothes and begin unwinding from work before he entered the back shed to rap at the door. The stillness stretched for several minutes and Vlad raised his hand to rap again. Abruptly, the bare overhead bulb flickered on, and the door groaned in protest as it opened. A woman, wearing a cranky expression, peered around the edge of the door. Startled, Vlad inquired the whereabouts of Klaus Tartarinov.

"He ain't here," the woman told him. As she stared, her frown disappeared and her eyes showed interest. "But you're welcome to come in an' wait."

Surprised, Vlad hesitated a moment then stamped the snow from his boots and stepped through the doorway. His eyes swept around the kitchen in an instant. It was untidy without being dirty. Dishes filled the sink and cupboard doors gaped open. Nothing like the way Kate kept house, he thought.

He turned to speak to the woman and caught his breath. The clingy robe wrapped tightly around her ample torso, and the bare legs below its calf-length hem, suggested she was naked. He felt his face flame and reached awkwardly back for the doorknob. "Sorry. I... was...looking for Klaus. I'll come back later," he mumbled.

"Oh, don't be silly." The woman smiled. "I was just heading for the shower. It can wait. Give me your coat."

Vlad felt the woman's hands at the buttons of his jacket and automatically stepped back to escape. The move trapped him against the wooden door without deterring her. When he lifted a hand to brush hers away, he accidentally touched her breast. The immediate softening of her smile told him she knew the havoc she was creating. No, he was not going to get tangled up with some woman. That wasn't why he was here. He had to keep his mind on his objective.

"I'm sorry to intrude. Really. Just tell me when Klaus gets home and I'll come back then."

"Relax. There's no rush. Klaus doesn't have to know you were here. The neighbors don't notice when we have visitors. Come on. Give me your coat and sit down. By the way, I'm Millie. Can I offer you a drink? How do you know Klaus?"

Millie turned away and draped his jacket over the back of a chair behind the table. Then she walked to the cupboard by the stove. "Now what do you like: beer, rye, rum, vodka, scotch?"

Reluctant to risk touching her, Vlad found himself following meekly towards where she had placed his coat. He settled cautiously on the edge of the chair.

"Coffee will do." His voice croaked in his ears.

The look she shot him said she knew he was trying to distract her, keep her busy. The corner of her mouth twitched. She dug out a glass percolator from the back of the counter, dumped its cold contents into the sink and filled its drip trap with fresh grounds.

"So, I ain't heard Klaus mention you before. You new to town?"

"No. Just passing through. Actually, it's Nick I'm looking for. I expected to find him here, but when I didn't see his car out front, I figured his dad would know how to get in touch with him."

"Nick?" The woman's expression changed, hardened. She slammed the pot onto the stove and turned on the burner. "He ain't here no more and he won't be comin' back if I can help it."

Unsure how to proceed, Vlad tried to change the subject. "You think you should put some water in that perk?"

"What?" Millie glanced around. "Oh, yeah." She grabbed up the pot, and holding it under the tap, turned her attention back to Vlad. "What would you want with that ungrateful little bastard?"

"He helped me out. I owed a guy, the kind it's not good to owe. I figured on paying Nick back, but when I got the money together he wasn't there to give it to him."

The woman stared hard at him for a moment, then

went to the refrigerator and removed a bottle of beer for herself. She popped the cap and leaned on the counter. Her expression was skeptical.

"He gave you money? That little weasel? I can't believe he'd have two cents to give anyone. Yeah, yeah. I know he may have a good enough heart. He just ain't got a brain in his head. Every time he turns around he's looking to Klaus for money to bail himself out of somethin'." She tipped the bottle to her lips and swallowed slowly. "The idea of him loaning money to anyone…just…it don't add up."

"That's not the kid I know," Vlad said, then added, "but I didn't know him that long. I suppose I could have been wrong."

Her smile returned and she nodded. "He's like his mother that way. Ivana could always put up a good front. That's how she snagged my Klaus, all sweetness and hard work until she got over here. Then she turned into a first class bitch, want, want, want. All the time complainin'. And by then they had kids."

"Oh?" Vlad didn't need to pretend ignorance. He hadn't seen Olga's younger child in more than thirty years.

The single word was sufficient. Millie launched into a tirade on Ivana's deficiencies that lasted until the gentle burbling of the percolator caught her attention. Then, bringing Vlad his coffee, she laid her hand on his shoulder and leaned across him to reach the table. Her housecoat gaped, exposing a large breast. A warm leg pressed against his. Vlad shunted back in his chair, trying desperately to stay out of her reach. Years of devotion to Kate had overcome any sense of satisfaction he might once have experienced from casual encounters. Besides, unlike Kate, Millie was flabby and starting to show her age. Whatever appeal she might once have possessed was gone. She really needed that shower.

She was his ticket to Nick, though, and Vlad couldn't afford to offend her. "Mighty good coffee, Millie. You been with Klaus for long?"

"Nine years now. I knew him before Ivana left though. He and my Gord worked together at the mill. We used to skidoo together. Then, when Gord got sick…. Ivana'd been gone a couple of months. Ya need company, ya know? And what about yourself? Nick was working in Ontario. That's a long way from here."

"I'm heading west to visit my kids. Seemed only right to stop and pay Nick back on my way through, when I'm coming this way anyway. So, where did he go?"

Millie shrugged. "Don't know. He said he was goin' to see his sister. Ya never know. He might have gone there. They were close. Might think he could help her, Sandra bein' widowed an' all."

"And when was that? That he left, I mean."

Millie wrinkled her brow and took another swig from her beer. "I guess it was a couple of weeks ago. Don't remember, exactly. Klaus might know. He'll be home later. He's working the afternoon shift."

Millie got up and went to the stove. "Time I got supper on. You like fish and chips?"

Vlad wasn't hungry and neither the state of Millie nor her kitchen did anything to whet his appetite. Besides, her sudden attempt to distract him suggested she had other ideas for passing a few hours during Klaus' absence.

He shook his head. "I'm not hungry but thanks for the offer. I need to keep going. I only have two weeks vacation. But I'd still like to repay Nick. Can you give me his sister's address?"

"Gotta think about that," she replied. "I'm not sure where Klaus keeps that address book of his."

Vlad waited in frustration as she fussed about with a frying pan and a deep fryer, deliberately loosening her hold on her housecoat as she set the package of frozen fish on the table beside him, then clutching the garment, shut it again as though the move were accidental. Dumb broad. Did she think he was going to get all excited at a glimpse of her sagging belly?

Truth be told, her pale skin did affect him, although most assuredly not as Millie hoped. Rather, it reminded him of how long it had been since he'd held Kate in his arms, let alone shared her bed. Too long, damn it. That had to change. He'd get this Nick matter settled, then he'd go home and settle that Kraut too.

Maybe he should call Alexi to check up on Kate. Not that a call would help much. The kid would only say his mother wasn't seeing Wachter. What did he expect? The boy was his mother's son. He'd swear black was white if she told him to.

"More coffee?"

Vlad snapped out of his introspection to find Millie standing way too close again, this time with her coffee pot poised over his cup.

"You can warm it up." He smiled at her. "Remember where that address is yet?"

Topping up his mug, she set the pot back on the stove and returned to Vlad. Before he could move or protest, she had settled on his outstretched knee, draped both arms around his neck and nipped his earlobe.

"And whatcha gonna give me if I get it?"

For a second Vlad was too startled to know how to react. Was he flushing again? He decided playing Millie's game was the most likely key to success. He couldn't quite bring himself to fondle the breast practically rubbing his chest when what he actually wanted to do was straighten his leg and dump her on the floor. Instead he grinned and ran a finger along her cheek.

"Aren't you a married woman?"

Millie looked startled. "What's that got to do with anythin'?"

He shrugged. "Nothing, I suppose. But slow down a little, honey. Relax. It's more fun that way, slow and steady. Everything in its own good time."

Millie practically floated up onto her feet and back to the stove. "Sure, sweetie. Ain't no rush. We got all evenin'. Now, as I said, how do ya like your fish?"

Vlad shook his head more emphatically. "Sorry, Millie. I ate an hour ago. There's no room yet, but don't let me stop you from eating. I'll just work on this coffee."

"If you're sure."

Millie returned to the stove, chattering away as though she hadn't had anyone to talk to for days. By the time she finished eating and stacked the dishes into the sink, Vlad knew far more than he wanted about Millie Dupois and the Tartarinov family. Her grin told him Millie was getting impatient. So was Vlad, although for a different reason. He took control before she could point them towards the bedroom.

"Okay, Millie. You've been patient and I'm getting mellow. Now, where's that address?"

"But…" she started to pout.

"But nothing." He scolded gently with a big grin. "I want that address and I know what you want. So, fair's fair. Where's the address?"

Millie laughed and headed towards a corner of the counter where the telephone sat. She opened a drawer beneath it and rummaged around for several seconds. "Ta da," she announced and held out a battered blue notebook. "Now, ya got a pen?"

She rhymed off the name, address and telephone number while Vlad scribbled frantically to keep up. While she jammed the book back into the drawer, he tucked the paper with its precious information into the breast pocket of his shirt.

"Okay, buster. Now it's your turn." Her face was already flushed.

"So it is." Vlad smiled back at her. "You said you were heading for a shower when I interrupted you. Want to do that now?" She looked puzzled. "What? You've never shared a shower?"

Comprehension dawned and her bewilderment shifted to wonder. "Wow. Together? Really?"

"Sure, why not?"

"Why not, indeed! Right this way." She held out her hand to lead him towards the bathroom.

Vlad followed her to the door, then shook her off. "Go start the water. I've got to get something out of my coat." He winked suggestively and she continued into the hallway. He could still hear her giggling as he grabbed up his coat, stepped into his boots, and moved softly towards the outside door.

CHAPTER TWENTY-SIX

Officially, Robert Cameron's office was closed for the weekend when Kate rattled the knob on the outer door. His receptionist looked up, then smiled as she came across to unlock it.

Her brother's office was at the back of a converted brick house on Market Street West. He was one half of Cameron and Daley, Attorneys at Law.

"Sorry, Mrs. Horbatsky. I almost ignored you. We're always getting stragglers after hours."

"I know. That's why I called Rob earlier to see if he'd be here when I finished work. Does he still have clients with him?"

The young girl shook her head. "He said to send you straight back."

Kate nodded and started along the narrow corridor to where her brother's open door indicated he was expecting her. He looked up from his paperwork as she walked in.

"Ah, there you are." He smiled and set the file aside. "Grab a chair. What's up?"

Kate draped her coat over the client's chair and dug two papers out of her purse, then tossed one on the desk in front of Rob.

"You tell me," she said, pulling the chair closer to the desk and sinking onto it. "This came Tuesday and I marked the numbers I originally thought were an error because I was going to call and complain. Have them removed. Then this came on Wednesday."

She handed over September's credit card statement with one item circled on it from the South End Garage in South Porcupine. The telephone numbers, she had learned, were for a Timmins hotel and for someone in Sudbury.

Rob examined both papers, then leaned back. "Okay. So what have we got here? A clue to where Vlad went?"

Kate shrugged. "That's my guess. But am I right, or am I just reaching? Hoping?"

Her brother nodded his dark head. "I understand your hesitancy, but I think this time there's reason to be optimistic. You never call either Sudbury or Timmins, do you?"

Kate shook her head.

He continued. "Both calls were placed just the day before the garage bill was paid. Who but Vlad would use his credit card at a garage and bill calls to your home phone number? No, Kate, this certainly looks like we've got something happening. Have you told the police yet?"

Again, Kate shook her head. "Not yet. That's why I'm here. I need some unbiased advice. I do need to pass this on to Inspector Davies at some point. I'm just not sure how much I should tell him."

Rob shoved his glasses onto the top of his head and got up to close his door. Then he leaned against it and gave Kate that elder brother look. "I thought there just might be more to this than you were letting on. I can't be your lawyer, you know," he warned. "If you need one, we're going to have to go somewhere else for you."

Kate waved off his caution. "No. At this point, I don't need a lawyer. At least not to defend me. I need advice to keep myself out of trouble. I know you're my brother, but I'm still going to ask for lawyer/client confidentiality on this. Please. For now at least, I don't want Mom and Dad to know this. Or the kids."

Kate watched Rob's lawyer persona settle into place.

"I'm scared that Vlad caused the explosion at the plant in June," she began. "Earlier this week Andreas Wachter told me he caught Vlad tampering with his car two weeks before the blast. When Andreas tried to scare him off by telling him he'd made a new will leaving everything to me, Vlad threatened him."

Rob leaned forward and threw up a hand. "Whoa up a minute. This guy is leaving you everything in his will? Why?"

Kate took a deep breath. "Because he's Ruth's father."

Kate watched her brother's jaw clench. Then he caught himself and relaxed. "Does Vlad know?"

She shrugged. "No one has told him, no. Still he knows Andreas and I worked together in Germany."

"And this will would confirm it for him," Rob said softly.

Kate nodded. "It would certainly increase his suspicions. And his position gives him the perfect opportunity to monkey with equipment. If Andreas had died in an industrial accident, no one would have suspected a thing, including me. I can't prove anything, of course. I'm not sure I want to. But neither can I quite ignore the possibility."

Rob scowled and walked back to drop heavily into his chair. "There's still more, isn't there?"

"Yeah." Kate nodded. "Vlad got odd telephone calls starting in March. He never talked to me about them, but they disturbed him. Then one night after getting one of those calls, he accused Andreas of trying to extort money from him. The calls continued until..." She hesitated, thinking. "The last call I know about came in late September. Vlad and I were arguing about me going to the fall fair with him when the phone rang. When he came off the phone he was distracted, forgot all about the argument and went off on his own."

"And you have told this to the police. Right?" Rob asked when she stopped.

"No." She shook her head.

"Kate, that's obstructing," he scolded, scrubbing his face with his hands. "You're asking them to do a job with their hands tied. You could get charged."

"Well, that's my problem. And to top it off, Andreas has made it plain he's not just going to walk away now that I could become available again."

"Oh, Christ." Rob groaned and dropped his head against the back of his chair. "Wachter appeared in your life in February, didn't he? Then began his contract at Clarke's in early April. The explosion was in mid June. Vlad's calls start in March. He threatened Andreas in May and set up his hidden bank account around the same time. You two have a virtual split. He gets another call. And then he disappears."

Rob's expression was frighteningly serious. "Could he have been trying to arrange a hit on Andreas? Presuming that his own attempts failed, could he have hired a professional to finish the job?"

Hearing her fears put into words brought Kate to the edge of tears. "I don't know," she whispered. "It crossed my mind, but I couldn't take the thought seriously at first. After Andreas told me Vlad knew about the will…" She stopped and threw up her hands. "I just don't know, Rob."

Her brother got up and came around his desk to squat beside her chair and take her hand. He held it for a second, then circled an arm around her shoulders and squeezed. "I'm sorry, kid. I don't mean to pry like this. I know he's been good to you. But he's changed. I've seen him watching you. We can't ignore the possibility he's gone off the deep end."

Kate breathed deeply, getting herself back under control. "It's okay. I'm just angry with myself. I may have driven Vlad to this."

Instantly Rob protested. "Hey, cut it out. You didn't drive Vlad anywhere." He stopped. "Did you? Have you been seeing Wachter, encouraging him, wishing you could get back together?"

Kate sighed. "No, I haven't. Of course I have my memories. And there are times when the calm I knew with Andreas looks pretty good compared to the turmoil Vlad can create. But actively encouraging Andreas? No. He was so furious when he discovered I'd been spying on them in Germany that I was a tiny bit worried he'd attack me. Then he saw Ruth on Mother's Day. He cornered me three days later, and after a serious discussion about the implications of his move to the U.S., and my status as a spy with an enemy child, he tamed down. Apparently that's when he made the new will. I never mentioned Andreas to the police because I don't believe he's involved. I certainly can't prove Vlad attempted to injure Andreas. I can't even prove Vlad was getting phone calls. But with Andreas planning to stick around, the police are going to be suspicious no matter what I tell them. So advise me. What do I say? Obviously, these bills should be turned over, but what else do I tell them and what can I leave out?"

Kate watched Rob deep in thought, massaging the back of his neck with one hand. Then he looked up.

"No help for it, Kate. You're going to have to tell the cops everything and show them these bills. Davies is a reasonable guy. He's not going to spread it all over town. Meanwhile, I can always call Louis Belanger in Timmins and see who he knows that might be able to do some snooping for us."

Puzzled, Kate kept quiet while he scribbled numbers and names off the bills, then grabbed a card file and began rifling through it. When he finished, he explained.

"Louis and I took a couple of law courses together at university. We both went home after graduation, but we stayed in touch. He'll know if there's anyone up there competent to do some private investigation for us."

Assured her brother would call as soon as he had more information, Kate left the now-silent building and went to Marg's Diner for her evening meal.

Vlad returned to the darkness and trudged through the cool evening to his truck. This trip to find Nicholas was turning into an odyssey. It had looked so simple when he left Milton. Just a couple of days up to Timmins and back, a week at most. However, one week had turned into two and he was still no closer to his quarry. Now he was heading even further away.

The only positive thing about this extended trip was the opportunity it gave him to reconsider his first plan. He could probably persuade the little pest to go, especially if he knew the Mounties were onto him. However, Nicholas would be back as soon as he realized he had facts with which to blackmail Vlad. That must not happen. Nicholas must disappear permanently.

He should have told Kate what he planned. She understood how important it was to protect family. Once he explained the threat Nicholas posed she'd have accepted his reasons for eliminating the problem.

He had not told Gerry he was going either and he was more of a worry than Kate was. When he got back Vlad would need a hell of a story to keep his job. He shrugged. Time enough to figure that out once he disposed of Nicholas.

His real concern was not being able to call Kate. He refused to admit—even to himself—how much he missed her. He also needed to know she was behaving. That Wachter was not sticking his nose in. For now, he must content himself that the silence would frighten some sense into her. Make her realize what life would be like without him. He needed to straighten out the Tartarinov problem first. After that, he would deal with her separate bedrooms nonsense.

Vlad stopped to eat at a diner beside a service station, then returned to his truck. It was getting late but he wasn't tired. He had slept in his truck most of the afternoon waiting for Tartarinov to come home. He should be able to drive until morning. He would be across Saskatchewan by then.

The road was clear of snow and relatively free of traffic. Moonlight picked out shadows on trees and boulders along the ditches. The radio alternated between a Winnipeg rock station and static. The signal seemed to be weak up here.

The stillness of the night reminded him of Slovenia in the winter of 1944. The night he left Jana and Milos had also been cold and clear. Milos had provided him with his heaviest pants and a thick sweater to wear under his threadbare coat. Even the boots were borrowed, left behind when the Germans took Milos' father.

How young he had been then. How much he had already seen. The day he collapsed, the air was so cold at midday that his breath formed clouds when he breathed. The guards from the camp had moved his work party off, leaving him alone to die by the side of a rutted, dirt road that January afternoon. He was starving and he had pneumonia.

He could not remember Jana and Milos finding him. He woke up in a feather bed in Jana's attic, wrapped in blankets and goose down comforters beside the chimney where they could keep him warm.

He remembered the pain too. Just breathing hurt so much he almost wished they would not feed him soup and fresh bread. Nevertheless, they did, and gradually the pain eased.

It took three weeks of Jana's food and nursing before he was strong enough to venture out of the house. Then, for a month, he helped Milos feed their cows and clean stables. It took ages to get his strength back. All the while he dreaded being seen. He kept close to the house and raced back up to the attic whenever anyone knocked at the cottage door.

Even now, thirty years later, Vlad admired the boy. He was only eleven but he had taken a man's place around the farm, helping his mother with the animals and tilling the fields the way he had seen his father do. Milos' father had been taken to work in a factory when the Germans occupied Slovenia. There had been no messages from him since that time, and mother and son could only pray for his safe return.

Meanwhile, they helped those they could, feeding neighbor children whose families were even poorer than they, and sheltering the occasional passing stranger. Vlad was the first prisoner they had helped, but he had no doubt they would have risked their lives again if the need arose. Only they had been given no further chances.

Jana's husband had caught up with Vlad in Berlin just before he emigrated. The man wanted to talk to Vlad about his wife and son because he had learned that Vlad was the last person to see them alive.

He told Vlad that someone had betrayed them. Vlad had left the farm in the early evening. When a neighbor arrived looking for food the next day at noon, he found their bullet-riddled bodies in the farmyard where the S.S. had left them as a warning to others who sheltered prisoners marked for death.

The information had shaken Vlad, guilt cutting deeply into him for destroying two gentle, generous people. It took him years to accept that their deaths were not his fault.

He had left their house just after dark and walked for miles that night, hiding behind bushes whenever he heard a vehicle approaching. By morning he was in a big city and he stowed away on a freight headed for Germany. Military police were checking the trains, so he had to keep jumping off before they stopped at stations and sneaking back on as the train started up again. It was difficult, but it was easier than running from the Gestapo on foot.

That was when he began to treasure his Slavic adaptability and his native's grasp of the German language. The German reverence for authority worked to his advantage as he lied and improvised his way back to Berlin. Since their own army was the last place the Germans would look for an escaped prisoner, Vlad used a phony name to enlist as a dispatch rider. It was getting late enough in the war that papers could not always be checked. Although he knew he looked much older, he pretended to be eighteen and no one could prove otherwise. With the tremendous need for recruits, authorities were too happy to ask indiscreet questions when they found a volunteer. He was safe.

Learning to handle a motorcycle was relatively easy. It was learning to ride horses that almost exploded his cover. As the son of a military man, Vlad had begun riding at the age of four. When the training officer introduced the new recruits to horses, Vlad forgot the difference between German and Ukrainian riding techniques. He walked up to the horse quite fearlessly, grabbed its mane and swung himself into the saddle.

"What the hell do you think you are? A Cossack?" The drill sergeant thundered the supposed insult at him.

Vlad's heart was in his throat. Cossacks mount from the right; Germans, from the left. In his haste he had forgotten his German disguise.

Luckily, the rule-obsessed man just considered Vlad a complete idiot and never questioned the possible accuracy of his own words. Nevertheless, the blunder taught Vlad caution. Never again did he relax and let his natural inclinations govern his reactions.

CHAPTER TWENTY-SEVEN

Gaston crawled back behind the wheel of his beige Chevy and relaxed, thankful he didn't mind driving. This would be his third trip in a week over the same damned road. All this jerking around annoyed him. He'd come to do a job, and now the bloody target had decided to get cute. In their discussions, Igor's low opinion of Tartarinov's intelligence was obvious. Gaston had come to a different conclusion.

It didn't matter, of course. When he took a contract he finished it. That's why he took the money. It was good money, with plenty to cover his expenses even if it did take longer and involve more running around than initially expected.

The telephone chat with Tartarinov's realtor revealed that the Sudbury house had been sold. It didn't matter that the woman refused to say where the money was going. The records in her office would disclose all he needed to know, including the new address of the former owner.

He glanced at his watch and re-started his car. He'd have a quick meal, then find a quiet parking lot where he could snooze for a few hours. He'd already seen the office and knew the area would be relatively quiet once businesses closed for the night. He should be able to pick the back lock, check out those records, and be gone within the hour. By morning, when the entry was noticed, if it were noticed at all when nothing was taken, he'd be miles away.

Kate received Rob's invitation to discuss the investigator's report less than a week after the man was hired.

When she knocked at the back door of her brother's home and let herself in, Rachael was setting the table.

"I hope Rob was telling the truth when he said you were expecting me," Kate said as she hung her coat in the closet. "Men don't always think how inconvenient they can make things when they issue invitations."

Rachael grinned and hugged her. "Too true, but this time he did it right. He checked with me first." She turned to the refrigerator. "What would you like? A pop? Tea? Dinner won't be long—depending on when Rob shows up. Grab a chair. We haven't talked in days. How are things going?"

Declining the offered beverage, Kate dropped onto a stool by the counter. "They're going. What can I say?"

Returning to chopping vegetables for a salad, Rachael nodded. "That good, huh? Well, in that case, let me add to your list of wonderful surprises." The vehement whacking of the knife onto the cutting board warned Kate something was wrong. "How would you like to hear that you've got a new boyfriend? Wachter, I think his name is." She waved the knife in frustration. "Whoever that American engineer is that Gerry hired last spring. It's all around town that Vlad left because you're stepping out with this other guy."

Kate sucked in a breath, too shocked to speak.

Rachel shook her head in exasperation. "Exactly. As if Vlad hasn't given you enough to worry about, the good Christian women from Knox Presbyterian Church Ladies Aid are trashing your reputation with abandon."

Kate felt tears of outrage fill her eyes. "Who?" she demanded.

The disgust plain in her voice, Rachael snapped out the names of two of Kate's former high school classmates. She could see their faces still: Elizabeth with her overbite and Lynda with her receding chin and coke-bottle lenses. They'd been jealous of her then, so they'd be exacting real satisfaction out of running her down now after having to wait thirty years to do it.

The injustice of it made Kate furious. She had worked so hard to protect her parents from insinuations when she brought Ruth home that hearing them now, when they were untrue, really hurt.

While Kate fought down her temper, Rachael poured juice, then set the glass beside Kate. "Ready to help me call them liars?"

Kate took a deep breath. "That depends. What started this anyway?"

"Apparently you were seen having supper together at The Muddy Duck at the beginning of the week."

Kate nodded resignedly. She should have expected it. Even an innocent meal would raise speculation.

While she and Rachael had shared secrets like sisters for years, that had never included her history with Andreas. Even now, she was loath to talk about it. Still, she knew she'd need help to battle the gossip.

She plunged in. "Well, if having supper with an old friend makes an affair, then I guess I'm having an affair. You see, Andreas Wachter used to be my boss in Germany. He's concerned about Vlad and wants to help."

Rachael began placing plates and cutlery on the table. After a moment she said, "If he's a friend you should have no trouble making him understand why you can't be seen together right now."

Kate took a calming breath. Obviously Rachael needed to hear all of it. "Oh, he understands, Rachael, but you see, Andreas is Ruth's father."

Rachael dropped the handful of cutlery with a crash and turned to stare at Kate. "Ruth's... So what about your...Oh, boy." She stopped. "Does Vlad know?"

Kate shook her head. "No, but he never needed facts to manufacture his own scenario."

"So that was the fight." Rachael nodded knowingly.

Kate sighed. "Yeah, sort of."

"But there's more, isn't there?"

"I suspect he tried to kill Andreas."

"What! My God, Kate! Have you told the police?"

Kate shook her head. "Told them what? You need proof for accusations like that, Rachael. I have no proof. I just know Vlad's mindset. No one ever takes anything away from a Cossack, especially not a German."

"That's crazy. You can't stick around if he's that unbalanced. He might attack you."

"He already has." Suddenly the tears were rolling down her cheeks. She couldn't stop them. The mixture of hurt, anger, and shame got the better of her. She felt Rachael's hand on her shoulder.

"Let it go, Kate. You can't keep something like this bottled up."

Rachael reached for the box of tissues from the top of the fridge and set it beside her on the counter. She waited while Kate blew her nose and mopped her face before speaking again.

"If Vlad has already attacked you, you need to go to the police. Even if you can't prove your suspicions concerning Andreas, you know what he did to you."

Kate shook her head. "A man can't rape his own wife, remember? What can the police do for me? Bringing them in would only set him off worse than ever."

"Well, you can't stay with him. You're in danger."

"That's what Andreas says." Kate felt herself tearing up again.

"Well, I don't know him, but my guess is that he's right."

After a moment's silence, Rachael went to the stove to check on her spaghetti sauce. She stirred quietly for a time, then turned to face Kate. "What are you going to do?"

Kate shrugged. "I don't know."

"Well, you can't stay with him. Not after that."

Kate shook her head. "I can't just walk away. He wouldn't allow that."

"You could divorce him."

"Could I? How do you think the kids would handle me leaving their father?"

Rachael grunted. "Badly, if I know Tanya. But we aren't talking about little kids here. They're almost on their own. You have to think about your safety, not their vanity."

"Uh huh. And what about Mom?"

"Yeah, there is that. But your safety is paramount. When it comes to your life versus her pride, even Mom would support you."

"And the bitches at the Ladies Aid? Come on, Rachael. She'd never be able to face them down if their gossip turned out to be true."

"One step at a time. Getting a divorce isn't the same thing as starting over with someone else."

"I realize that, only I'm not sure I could refuse Andreas again if I were really free."

"Again?"

"He wanted to marry me. I ran out on him before he found out I was an Allied spy."

The back door banged and Rob called a greeting as he hung up his coat. "Smells good," he announced as he walked into the kitchen and pecked Rachael's cheek. "I see you made it, Sis."

"Yes, and we were having a good yack," Rachael told him, obviously frustrated by the interruption but unable to continue the conversation. "Go and wash up. Everything's ready to be lifted."

Rob waited until they finished eating and moved to the living room with their coffee before explaining how Joli had tracked Vlad to the mine office in Timmins, his visit to Nick's boarding house in Schumacher, the truck repair in South Porcupine, and eventually the conversation with the Sudbury realtor.

"So now what?" Rachael voiced Kate's thoughts when Rob finished summarizing Joli's report.

With a sheepish smile he glanced towards Kate. "I know I should have asked you first, but I told Joli to head for Manitoba."

"Good." Kate agreed immediately. "You say the realtor saw Vlad more than a week ago? That should be plenty of time to get to The Pas and back. So where is he? And where does Tartarinov fit into this? We need to know."

"You might want to tell Davies about this," Rob suggested, then stopped. "Or maybe not. First, let's see what Joli turns up in Manitoba. Then the police may be willing to check further if we can offer them something solid to start with."

#

Between Prince Albert and Jasper alternating weather fronts served Vlad a mixture of snow, rain, freezing rain, and ice pellets. He regretted his decision to take the northern route across the prairies. The trip that should have been accomplished in less than two days stretched into three. By the time he reached Jasper, he was so tired he broke down and rented a room and slept for almost eighteen hours.

As he checked out the following afternoon, he was told the snow had come early this year and a slide had just closed the highway beyond Yellowhead Pass. There was no help for it. He would have to go south to Kicking Horse Pass and take the highway through Field to Kelowna and then head north again to reach Nicholas' sister in Prince George.

When he crossed through the pass that night, Vlad found the weather west of the Rockies had cleared. He drove to a hotel tucked away on a hilly back street in the north end of Kelowna before taking his next rest stop. Traveling north would be more challenging, partly because snow arrived earlier in the season at that elevation, but also because much of the traffic consisted of heavy trucks that beat holes in pavement as fast as road crews fixed them.

On the desk clerk's recommendation, he ate in a Greek restaurant a few blocks from the hotel. Stars twinkled in the night sky and the unseasonably early snow squeaked under his boots as he walked back to his room. The air had the crisp feel common to cold temperatures and Vlad turned his collar up around his ears. All around him the mountains reflected moonlight on snow-crusted peaks while evergreens girdled the lower elevations.

He felt the cold biting into his ears and nose. As he stepped over frozen slush to cross a road, he wondered if it was snowing in Milton. If it were, how was Kate coping with clearing the driveway and changing to winter tires on her car? Those were his jobs, normally. Resentment boiled at the answer that immediately came to him.

She would call on her old friend, Wachter. He could picture her sidling up to Wachter with that teasing smile of hers, asking him for a favor. Vlad wanted to slap her for even considering such a thing. She would too. He had no doubt about that. The moment his back was turned, she'd be chasing after the German with his fancy words and his university degrees. And his money. Why wait for Wachter to die if she could get it while he was still alive?

The German would accept the invitation. That, also, was a certainty. Nor would Kate be slipping off to a separate bedroom as she had with Vlad in the last few weeks. With Wachter she'd be all sweetness and light. The perfect example of femininity, warm and giving, the way she had once been with him, back in the beginning, when she'd set out to trap him into marriage.

He should have known better, of course. Should have realized she'd spread her legs for some Kraut. She had the child, after all. That was pretty significant proof of her morals.

Unfortunately, there had been lots of legitimate widows around in those days, too. How was a man supposed to weed out the honest women in that situation?

To be fair, she'd been a good mother. Taught the kids to value family, encouraged them to learn his language, attended church with him, worked hard to keep their home clean and tidy. Usually, she'd deferred to him the way a wife should. Other men had been kept at arm's length, too, properly, the way a virtuous wife should behave. Yes, until Wachter interfered she'd kept her deceitful nature under complete control.

So what had changed? Did she really fancy him? Was Ruth really his child? Or did Wachter just know the identity of Ruth's father? Not that it mattered. A proper wife would have told her husband the truth, turned to him for protection from the intruder. Kate preferred to deceive everyone with her pretense of virtue and integrity. She had fooled them all with this image of hard-working wife and mother, pillar of the community, dedicated right hand to her employer.

Except for him. He knew better. Give her an inch and she'd be off chasing after the Kraut, turning her back on everything Vlad had given her over the years.

By the time he returned from supper, Vlad was so worked up between memories and imagination that he went to the telephone booth in the hotel lobby to phone home.

He dialed the necessary numbers to make the collect call. Hearing the telephone ring over and over again, he fumed. When Kate had not answered after several minutes, he cursed silently, and hung up. Was she out with the Kraut, in his hotel room, perhaps?

Conversely, what would talking to her prove? For all he could tell, the German might be standing behind her in their living room while they talked.

He opened the door of the phone booth and began to walk away. Then he turned back. He'd call his son. Alexi would know if the Kraut had moved in with his mother.

Again Vlad dialed a number. Yet again, he listened in frustration as the line hummed and buzzed, then began the series of familiar ringing tones. He counted twenty rings before hanging up. Alexi, too, was out.

 He railed at the silence, then remembered it was Friday and glanced at his watch. Recalling the difference between Eastern Standard and Pacific Time, he realized there was nothing unusual about his son being out with friends at ten o'clock on a Friday evening. But what about Kate? Where was she at this hour?

CHAPTER TWENTY-EIGHT

With breakfast finished and his case repacked, Vlad checked out of the hotel and headed north. The weather was still clear but local forecasts promised snow later in the day.

He pushed himself through the morning, stopping for lunch at a small place near Hundred Mile House. The view from the dining room was stunning. Long vistas across a meadow at the bottom of a valley. On both sides, the mountains rose slowly as though cupping a natural treasure they wanted to protect.

The sun broke through as he finished his meal, beckoning him back onto the road. It was growing grayer by the moment as he neared Quesnel. Not only was late afternoon shutting down the light, the predicted storm was approaching rapidly. Small flakes of snow skittered before the wind, glancing off the hood and the wipers before perishing on contact with the warm glass of the windshield.

The storm set him to thinking about the stories his parents told him in childhood. His mother's tales were about the family's large properties in Poltava, Ukraine where the serfs who worked the land shared her father's big house with various branches of the family.

He had been fascinated with the dogs they kept to ward off wolves. In winter, she said, they earned their keep, running by the troikas, protecting both horses and passengers from the wild creatures of the steppes. In his mind, he could hear the bells on the horses' harnesses and the rattle of ice pellets on his windshield sounded like snow hissing under the sleigh's runners.

Of course, the sleigh drivers did their part, too, carrying long whips with lead balls tied into the thongs at the end. A thump on a wolf's head from one of the weighted tips could split its skull. If it weren't already dead when it fell, the dogs or the wolf's ravenous contemporaries would finish the job the whip began.

His father's stories had centered on the Cossacks' horses and the bond between horse and rider. How the rider couldn't survive in the cold, but if he protected his horse the animal would get them both through bad times. While the man couldn't eat the frozen grasses, the horse could. Then the man could cut a tiny slit in the horse's neck and using a straw, sip a little of its blood to share the nourishment the horse gained from grazing.

The horse would keep his master warm, letting him curl tightly against its side during the sweeping blizzards that raged across the open steppes just like the storm he was fighting now. It was the sturdy horses' capacity to endure hardship that had allowed the Cossacks to defeat Napoleon. They hovered just beyond his reach, and drew him away from Moscow across the frozen wastes in the dead of winter. Termed ghosts because of their silent maneuvers, they had burned everything that might provide food or shelter to the retreating French troops. Through it all, their horses had provided for their masters.

Vlad had neither horse nor dog to help him with this storm. All he had was his inherited Cossack cunning. All the same, he'd beat his enemy. The Kraut would never take Kate away from him.

The prospect of continuing in the dark in strange countryside held no appeal. He found himself a room in Quesnel and holed up for the night.

Near morning Vlad awoke to find himself reaching for Kate and dreaming of her kiss. As he willed himself to relax, he wondered how well she was sleeping in her lonely room in their Milton home. When he returned, they'd sort out this foolishness of hers, this nonsense of sleeping in separate beds. Her place was with him and he'd teach her that once he got home. He'd knock that fat prick from her mind once and for all.

Morning sunshine was freeing the blacktop from the traces of snow at the edge of the roadway by the time he finished breakfast. He crossed the trestle bridge over the railway track at the southern edge of Prince George in the early afternoon. He checked into a hotel first, then struck off for a late lunch.

He found a telephone directory in the desk in his room that provided Sandra McLeod's address. A map of the town on the back of a complimentary menu from a nearby steak house showed the street's location.

It was late afternoon and long shadows crept out from buildings and greenery. He decided to scout out the location of the McLeod home, then return later so as not to interfere with the evening meal.

The modest clapboard bungalow was set close to the road in a neighborhood of older homes. Giant evergreens flanked a small gate in a wire fence around its tiny lawn. The driveway curved around to a detached garage at one side of the property.

The curtains were open and Vlad could see a fireplace through what appeared to be a living room window. Light also shone from a small window in a room closer to the back of the house.

Then a youth appeared in the doorway with a hockey stick over his shoulder and a large bag in one hand. He went as far as the gate and stopped. From his parking place across the street, Vlad watched a van pull up moments later. The teenager got in and the vehicle disappeared around the corner.

If that was Sandra's son, he was off to a game or a practice. That would mean supper was either already over or on hold until his return. This was probably a good time to make his call if he wanted to avoid involving the boy. Vlad shut off the truck's engine.

Sandra McLeod's expression grew puzzled when she saw Vlad on her doorstep. The big husky at her side was obviously her protector and stood his ground suspiciously while Vlad introduced himself. The fact he neither growled nor bristled convinced his mistress that the stranger was no threat, and she invited Vlad in.

He stepped out of his boots in the foyer and followed her to the living room. It was comfortable and showed signs of family life: a pair of socks by an armchair, a text and notebook open on an adjacent end table, an empty pop can on the floor by the chesterfield.

"I'm not sure I can help you," Sandra McLeod said. She cast a glance towards the back of the house as she settled into the wingback chair. "You say you're looking for my brother, Nick. Why would he be here?"

Vlad fell back on the story he had told her father's girlfriend, ending with a question about whether she had been warned to expect him.

"No. I haven't talked to my father since early summer. When he took up with Millie…" She stopped speaking and shook her head. She had none of Millie's garrulous nature. "Now, he only calls for Christmas and my son's birthday."

Vlad pressed her. "So was she right? Is your brother here?"

"He was, but he just stopped for one night. Then he left to see Mom in Vancouver."

The grey husky had wandered closer to Vlad to sniff his hand and hint at his willingness to accept petting. Vlad obliged absently, scratching behind the animal's ears.

"Is he still there?"

She shrugged and glanced toward the hallway. Vlad could see the edge of a pile of clothes on the floor beyond the doorway. "I don't know. I rarely hear from my mother either, so I have no idea where Nick is now."

Careful to keep his tone neutral, Vlad asked for Ivana Tartarinovska's address. "I've come this far. I hate to give up now if he may still be with your mother."

Caught in the middle of doing laundry, the need to finish her chores overrode any fleeting suspicion she might have harbored concerning the authenticity of Vlad's errand. Quickly, Sandra rhymed off her mother's street address and telephone number.

With a new destination marked down in his notebook, he slipped it into his shirt pocket, offered his thanks, and returned to his hotel for an evening meal.

He was frustrated to hear that Nicholas had gone to Vancouver. Not that four more hours of driving mattered, given that he'd already been on the road for three weeks. It was the fact that his goal kept eluding him that grated on his short temper.

Nicholas had no business putting himself in such jeopardy. The longer it took Vlad to catch up with him, the more chance the Mounties had of reaching him first. That was unthinkable. Where Vlad had suspected Nicholas' integrity before, now he had seen Nicholas' background and the treachery it bred. He was sure one threat from the Mounties would be enough. Nicholas would blab the whole scheme.

While Korczak was probably made of sterner stuff, he, too, was likely to take advantage of any bargain the Mounties might offer. If that meant sacrificing Vlad, Korczak would do it without a qualm. Vlad's disguise might have worked. Then again, it might not. The only way to protect himself was to eliminate Nicholas, since he was the one person who could link Vlad to Korczak.

Sandra's indifference angered Vlad. It wasn't right for a grown woman to care so little for her family's safety.

Or was her callousness an act? What if she were covering up her own involvement in Nicholas' scheme? In that case, she was stupid. She had no idea what Vlad planned and she'd just betrayed her brother's whereabouts.

What of her mother? How would Ivana react to learning her daughter had handed over her address to a stranger? To Vlad, such indifference to your family's welfare was unforgivably selfish. Olga hadn't been like that. On the other hand, it did match his childhood impression of Olga's lout of a husband.

Reflecting on the Tartarinovs drew his thinking around to his own family. Until recently he would have seen no comparison. Now, with Wachter in their lives, things were different. Not only was Kate betraying him, their son would, too. Vlad should have been able to rely on Alexi to protect the family honor. He knew he could not. If Vlad had reached him the previous night, Alexi would have lied to protect his mother. He'd have insisted that Vlad come home instead of admitting his mother's involvement with Wachter. The thought of his son's duplicity cut like a knife. In the old days a traitorous child, like an unfaithful wife, would simply have been executed.

He finished eating and called Ivana Tartarinovska from the pay phone in the hotel lobby. He wanted to confirm Sandra's information about her mother's location and re-visit her before leaving town if she had tried to deceive him.

Ivana answered on the second ring. Her heavy accent confirmed her as a genuine immigrant and her cautious replies suggested more concern than her daughter had displayed about his proposed visit. Only by pretending to be a priest with a message about Olga was Vlad able to convince her to allow him to visit her at her apartment the next afternoon.

Despite the fact she enjoyed her brother and sister-in-law's company, Kate headed home early, supposedly because Amos needed his walk. In reality, she was beginning to feel the strain of Vlad's absence and the additional chores that now fell to her. Tonight, she just wanted to crawl into bed and collapse.

Amos was waiting for her at the door. He did want his walk, but he seemed to sense Kate's exhaustion and let her keep it brief.

She was barely back inside, when the telephone rang. Eddie Pasternak admitted they weren't well acquainted, but he felt they needed to talk. He wanted to see her tonight and despite her fatigue, Kate agreed to a meeting.

Kate had the coffee pot on when Eddie arrived. Amos settled watchfully by her feet as she and Eddie sat down by the fireplace to talk.

She could tell Eddie wanted to get something off his chest, but he seemed at a loss to know how to begin. "I'm pretty much shock-proof, Mr. Pasternak," she said when he'd made a couple of false starts, then stammered to a halt. "Why don't we just get down to it and worry about the consequences later? You wouldn't have come this evening unless you thought it was important."

Eddie took another sip from the coffee cup in his hands, and gave her a sheepish grin. "It's just that I don't like to talk behind Vlad's back. But now that he's been gone for weeks and no one seems to know what's happened to him, I admit I'm worried. Did you know he was getting calls from someone in Timmins?"

Kate shook her head. "I knew he was getting calls. Has been for six months or more. I didn't know who was calling though, or what the calls were about. Vlad would never tell me."

"I wondered," Eddie nodded. "You see, he was getting calls about this Russian Family Fund that he figured was a scam. Just to be certain, he wanted me to get the guy's number for him. Turned out he was from Timmins."

While Eddie had made the Timmins connection for her, Kate still needed clarification. "Russian Family Fund? What's that?"

Eddie set down his mug and started to apologize.

"You don't know about the extortion, then," he said. "The caller wanted Vlad to send money to the Fund to pay for Olga's medicine. Only Vlad wasn't about to do that because he suspected she'd be dead. He was right, apparently. When I told him the Mounties were about to close in on the guy, he made some comment about being glad he'd never sent them any money. That was the last we talked about it."

Kate's mind raced. Extortion? No wonder Vlad was upset. So who was Olga, and why would the extortionist think Vlad would pay money for her benefit?

"Okay, Mr. Pasternak. I'm not angry about your efforts to help my husband, so please don't misunderstand my question. I'm just trying to figure things out. Who was Olga?"

Eddie shrugged. "I don't know. But Father Darcovich might. I think that's how Vlad found out she was dead."

Kate nodded. "Given how the church conveys information for families on both sides of the Iron Curtain, that would make sense. Now, second question. Was one of the guys named Tartarinov, by any chance? Nick Tartarinov?"

Eddie gave her a suspicious look. "I believe that was his name. I didn't pay a lot of attention. Once Vlad got what he wanted, I turned the information over to our own fraud squad. They looked into it and turned it over to the Mounties. They've dug up a whole ring of extortionists preying on our people."

"When did you tell Vlad about the Mounties having information about Tartarinov and his cronies?"

"At Milton Fall Fair," Eddie answered promptly. "You weren't coming, Vlad said, so we agreed to meet and talk there."

Kate nodded. "Well, I'm still not sure how this fits into the puzzle, but now I think I need to ask another favor of you. I'm going to pass this on to Inspector Davies at Halton Regional because we talked about the phone calls last week. At that point I couldn't tell him anything beyond the fact that the calls were happening. He may want to talk to you in person rather than getting information second hand through me. If that happens, don't hold back to protect either Vlad or me. This situation has gone well past the need for privacy, Mr. Pasternak. Vlad has been gone far too long."

Kate didn't mention her private detective. She just thanked Eddie and reassured him of the value of his information. Then, when he left, she picked up the telephone and called Father Darcovich. She hoped he would still be awake.

Father, too, seemed reluctant to talk about Vlad's investigation into the telephone scheme. However, since Kate already knew about the Russian Family Fund and the request for money to pay for Olga's medication, he relented.

"Olga Danilewski was Vlad's father's mistress," he began. "She and Vlad's half-sister shared the family home in Berlin until Olga married someone else and took her daughter away. I believe that was before the war."

"That would make Olga quite elderly," Kate said.

"That's why Vlad suspected she would already be dead," Father replied. "And she is. I told him the priest in Warsaw conducted her funeral service a couple of years ago and wanted us to find her daughters for him since he had never been able to contact them about their mother's death."

"When did you tell him this, Father?" Kate continued.

The priest had to think. "Late August, maybe a bit earlier. He didn't know where the daughters were, but he seemed to think he might be able to track them down."

"And do you recall the names of Olga's daughters?"

"Yes, Vlad's half-sister was Nadia. But the other one..." His voice trailed off as he searched his memory. "Ivana, I think. Ivana...Loshenko...Evashuk...no, Tartarinov. That's it, Ivana Tartarinovska. The feminine version of the name," he explained.

Kate's breath caught at the coincidence. Or was it? Had someone in the family deliberately decided to take a swipe at Vlad because his father had taken advantage of their mother? No, that would be their grandmother, since Olga apparently only had female offspring.

With her appreciation properly expressed to the priest, and her mind still reeling with the new information, Kate hung up and called her brother. He applauded her intention to call Inspector Davies and shared her bewilderment over Vlad chasing down Tartarinov.

"Unless he figured he was one of Olga's grandchildren and he couldn't see him go to prison," Rob said. "But given the guy was trying to shake him down...I don't know, Kate. Vlad never seemed to be that forgiving. I can't quite see him trying to keep Tartarinov out of jail just because he was a quasi nephew."

Kate had to agree with her brother. "But what else could be going on?" she questioned. "Both Father and Eddie said Vlad wasn't paying into the extortion scheme. So if he wasn't paying, why did they keep calling him?"

"And what's the connection between Vlad finding out about the Mounties' plan to scoop up the ring and his leaving?"

Kate hadn't considered that until Rob pointed it out. "Right. He was getting the calls all along, wasn't he?" She thought aloud. "Then when he hears the ring is about to be shut down, he disappears. If I didn't know better I'd think he was involved with them somehow."

"That's my reading too," Rob told her. "Only, it can't be. Not with Vlad. He hated Communists as much as he hated Germans. If the ring is operating here, then its information comes from behind the Iron Curtain. He would never work with them."

"Unless..." Kate hesitated. "When Vlad was emigrating, his godfather was a professor at the University of Winnipeg. He warned Vlad not to go west because there were still so many Communists in the Ukrainian community out there. In fact, the pro-Communist network was so strong at the end of the war that Vlad's godfather went back to Berlin because he couldn't tolerate what he saw happening in Winnipeg."

"You have to be joking!"

"Oh, no, Rob. It was no joke, apparently," Kate assured him. "That's why Vlad settled in Ontario, to stay away from the Communists in the west. I suspect that changed as people got to see what Stalin and his Communists were really like. I mean, the engineered famine in Ukraine in the 1930s has to have opened some eyes. Then, what the Communists did to the escaped nationalists in Germany at the end of the war was nothing short of criminal. Word of that has to have circulated in the community."

"What was that?" Rob was fascinated.

"Did Vlad never tell you about the Allies giving in to Stalin's demands that Germany's Slavic émigrés be repatriated?"

"No."

Kate nodded, and began to explain. "In 1945 the Brits and the Yanks were so determined not to wind up in a slanging match with one of their buddies that they caved in when Stalin demanded his people be sent home. Vlad was in the American army by that time, so when the Russians came to take his mother back, he was sitting on her doorstep in an American army uniform with a thirty-thirty across his knees. They decided not to force the issue, and moved on to the next house.

"The next morning he saw the convoy of trucks heading out for the border to Poland. They were covered in barbed wire so people couldn't jump out. And there were tarps over top to conceal the way they were forcing repatriation. The people inside were singing hymns and in the distance, a couple of miles or so across the border, out of reach and sight of the Allies, he could hear the machine guns firing as they liquidated all the nationalists who had opposed them and escaped years before.

"Even the idealists must have begun to see the difference between what the ideology says and the reality does," she concluded. "My guess is that these days you won't find many western Ukrainians admitting to the beliefs they once held."

"If this Tartarinov is from The Pas, could he be a holdout from that crowd?"

"Now that's a thought. But it wouldn't explain why Vlad would try to see Tartarinov. I just can't imagine him trying to convert the man, semi-related or not."

"I have to agree with you," Rob said. "Something else is going on here, but we still don't know what it is."

"Regardless, I think you should warn Joli the next time he reports in. He may see or hear something if he knows to make the connections."

CHAPTER TWENTY-NINE

Deep in thought, Andreas was driving to the restaurant for supper when the host of the Toronto radio show interrupted a discussion about psychic phenomena to make an emergency public announcement.

"Just got a call from Halton Regional Police," he said. "This is for listeners in the Milton area. Three men broke out of Maplehurst Correctional Centre a couple of hours ago. The hunt is on, of course, but homeowners are warned to make sure doors and window are locked, garages, workshops—all the usual places where someone on the run could hide. Drivers too. Be extra cautious of hitchhikers this evening. Although the three men escaped together, police have no reason to think they'll stay together. While the men are not believed to be armed, police still recommend residents take extra care until the escapees are caught."

Escaped convicts? He'd been aware of the jail, of course, but Andreas realized he had never before given any thought to criminals running loose in the community. Not that he had reason to worry. They wouldn't be coming anywhere near a hotel.

Then Kate crossed his mind. He had never visited her home officially, but he'd driven past it. It was out in the boonies, to use the Canadian expression. It was also several miles on the other side of town from Maplehurst. Surely, she would be safe.

Of course, if he were trying to escape, an isolated house miles from the nearest major road might seem a suitable hiding place.

Kate was a resourceful woman. All the same, he needed to be sure she was safe. He'd just drive out and check on her. Vlad was still gone. No one would see him. It should not cause her any trouble if he just showed up at her door, had a brief chat, and drove away again.

Long shadows framed the edges of the dirt road as he headed along Steeles Avenue to Appleby Line. The leaves were beginning to lose their brilliant fall colors and Andreas enjoyed the scenery as he drove. Having spent most of his years in America in the South, the spectacle was not familiar. Nor had he enjoyed this sort of display in Europe. Now if they just had real mountains…

The Horbatsky house seemed deserted when he stopped in front of the garage. Flowerbeds lined the driveway and edged the front of the grey brick bungalow. Although the plants had not been removed, they were already dark and drying. Only a few spots of color remained where hardy chrysanthemums persisted despite the temperature and wind.

He walked to the front door and rang the bell. The silence was such that he could hear the chimes echoing beyond the oak panels. Several rings, accompanied by two applications of knuckles to wood, convinced him Kate was absent.

He retraced his steps across the front porch and followed the sidewalk to the back of the house. There a second entrance opened onto a large area paved with concrete slabs and surrounded by raised planters full of still more dying perennials. Vine-laden trellises created a roof of sorts over the patio and Andreas could imagine Kate sitting in the shade sipping lemonade on hot summer evenings. At the moment, the empty redwood table and chairs looked desolate despite a flash of scarlet plumage among the tall cedars that surrounded the entire rear yard.

Just in front of the evergreens, remnants of a vegetable garden emphasized the home's isolation. Heaps of dirt in straight rows marked where Kate had dug up some root vegetables. Beside them, overgrown spikes of lettuce, yellowed cucumber leaves, and dried corn stalks waved in the wind. A couple of cauliflower and half a dozen mature cabbages contrasted with the dark earth. Only tomato plants were still in production and Andreas saw a couple of pinkish fruit peeking through the dying foliage.

The sight told him he should insist on helping her prepare for winter since Alexi had obviously not stepped into his father's shoes after all. That she was capable of digging and composting by herself, was no reason she should do it. He could use the exercise, and she could probably be talked round, given the size of the task and Vlad's continued absence.

He crossed the patio and started down the other side of the house towards his car. Out of nowhere a large black

Rottweiler appeared in his path. The animal's teeth were bared and Andreas could hear a hostile rumble low in his throat.

Shit! Where had this protector come from? No one had ever mentioned a dog.

"Kate," he called, hoping against hope that she was nearby. Even when he heard her voice behind him he wasn't sure he dared to turn his back on the dog. Obviously she'd recognized his car and circled around the house in search of him.

"It *is* you. Okay, Amos. He's a friend. Relax fella. Come here."

The dog looked at him suspiciously and crowded past him on the walk to reach his mistress. Andreas turned to see Kate in a casual jacket and jeans, her hand on the top of the beast's broad head.

"What brought you here at this hour?" she asked.

"The announcement about the escapees. I was just checking to be sure you were all right." He glanced at the dog and grimaced. "Guess you've got an even better body guard than me."

Kate smiled. "I don't know if he's better, but he's definitely good. Most people would think twice about facing him down."

Andreas nodded. "I can believe that. So where were you?"

"Taking our nightly walk. I prefer to do it in daylight if I get home in time, especially when there are bad guys on the loose."

Andreas watched her hesitate, then come to some sort of decision. "Come here," she continued. "You need to get properly introduced to Amos."

Andreas walked up to Kate and took her outstretched hand. She held it out so that the dog could smell it while she repeated the word friend several times.

Andreas saw the dark eyes examine his face carefully, then the big beast sat down in front of them and looked back at his mistress as though awaiting her next order.

"That's it?" he asked. "I'm free to go?"

Kate smiled. "Yup. He is obedient so long as he knows the rules." She dug a key from her jacket pocket and headed for the back door. Amos trotted after her, then looked back at Andreas. He wasn't sure whether that was an invitation.

With the door open, Kate asked whether he'd had his meal. "I have a casserole in the oven. There's plenty for two."

"And the right-hand man there will let me in?"

"Oh, yeah. If I don't object, he won't."

"Then you're on, lady. I heard about the escapees and got side-tracked from dinner, so I'd love some of your cooking."

Amos stood aside and let Andreas follow Kate into the kitchen. He could feel the dog's eyes on him as she led him to the closet opposite the front door to hang up his coat.

When they returned to the family room, the dog went to the rug beside the fireplace and lay down. At least for now, Amos was docile. If he could persuade Kate to let him visit a few more times Andreas thought he might cement an acceptance with the animal. Perhaps offering to help with the garden work tomorrow would be the place to start building that new relationship he craved.

Raymond Joli pulled up to the faded bungalow on Bridge Street and cut the ignition on his late model Mustang. He'd been driving steadily since leaving Winnipeg and he was tired. The road was a mess, rough and narrow. Only the fact that Klaus Tartarinov's truck was parked in the snowy driveway with its engine running prompted him to do his interview now before getting some sleep.

A middle-aged man in a plaid shirt and green twill work pants answered the knock. His tightly drawn lips suggested he was unhappy to find a stranger at his door.

"Mr. Tartarinov?" Joli began. When the man nodded, he continued. "My name is Raymond Joli. I'm a private detective looking for a man we believe visited you recently in search of your son."

He held out the picture of Vlad that Rob had faxed to him. "Have you seen him?"

Tartarinov took the picture and squinted at it, then shook his head. "No, but just hang on. Hey, Millie," he called over his shoulder. "Come here a minute."

A woman in black stretch pants and a grey sweatshirt appeared behind him.

"You ever see this guy?" Tartarinov handed her the photo.

Although she shook her head and shrugged, Joli immediately knew she was lying. It was plain to see in the way her eyes narrowed and her shoulders hunched. Was she afraid, he wondered. Thanking them, Joli retrieved the folded photo and returned to his truck. He let them see him make a u-turn in their driveway and start down the street to where a pair of tall spruces would conceal his car.

In less than five minutes Tartarinov's half-ton passed in the direction of town. Joli gave him a block head start and followed him to the railway yard. When Tartarinov parked and disappeared into the yard office, Joli relaxed. At this hour, Tartarinov must be starting his shift. Without her husband to overhear her, Millie might be more talkative.

She looked defensive when she found Joli had returned. He stuck his heavily booted foot into the door before she could slam it in his face.

"Oh, no, Millie. I came back to find out why you needed to lie to your husband. Just tell me what happened and I'll be on my way. Klaus has no reason to know we talked. When was he here? What happened?" He stepped forward, crowding her.

"Little shit," Millie grumbled, backing up to let Joli into her kitchen. "What has he done now?"

"What little shit?" Her reference puzzled Joli.

"Nick. Who else?" she muttered, and dropped onto a stool by the kitchen table. Her expression was defiant now, trying to conceal her fear.

"Who is Nick?"

"Klaus' useless kid. The bastard's always causing trouble." She picked up a cigarette smoldering in an ashtray beside her. She took a long drag and exhaled the smoke in a grey stream. "What's he got into this time?"

Unsure how her tirade connected to Horbatsky, Joli prodded. "I'm not sure what you mean."

"Well, it's got to be him," Millie blustered. "You're the third guy in two weeks to come looking for him. So, what's he done?"

Joli didn't correct her. Her remark about having two previous male visitors looking for Nick caught him by surprise. The best way to untangle this was to start at the beginning, he decided.

Depositing himself uninvited into a chair at the end of the table, he began to walk her through the part he already knew. "The house in Sudbury sold in mid-September. That's when Nick left Timmins and went back to sign the papers. Then he came here. Right?"

She nodded.

"How long did he stay?"

She shrugged. "A week, maybe. Maybe less."

"And where did he go?"

"To Sandra's, in Prince George. That's Klaus' daughter," she added as Joli opened his mouth to ask for an explanation.

"And?"

"About a week later, your guy showed up looking for Nick. Claimed he owed Nick money and wanted to find him to pay him."

"You sent him to Sandra?"

Millie nodded. "Nick never had any money to lend anyone. I didn't believe a word your guy said. But they ain't my kids. I don't interfere."

Joli nodded. "So who was this other guy?"

Millie inhaled another lungful of smoke. "Don't know. He never gave me a name. Just said Nick owed him money and he was looking for him to collect. Now that I can believe. He was a nasty looking piece of work. I wasn't about to cross him."

"So you sent him to Sandra, too."

Again Millie nodded. "Like I said. They ain't my kids. If someone's following them, I keep out of it."

"And when was this?"

"A week after your guy was here."

"So, last week?"

"Something like that."

"Did you tell your husband?"

She shook her head. "Klaus gets protective of Sandra. He wouldn't like it if she got trouble because of me. But I didn't like the look of the guy Nick owes money to. I was afraid of him."

Her defensive posture told Joli she meant it. Whoever the second caller was, he'd threatened Millie. Her reaction disgusted Joli. Some mother. Wouldn't even stick up for her own kid. Then he remembered they weren't Millie's children. All the same, lying to her husband wasn't a good sign.

He concluded that whatever Horbatsky was involved with was more complicated than his client expected. He needed to be careful. Should he warn her?

Not yet, he decided. No sense worrying her until he had facts and so far, all he had was a bunch of questions.

First he'd sleep. Then he'd head for Prince George. Maybe the situation would resolve itself there.

By the time he found a motel, he had rearranged his schedule. He'd call Sandra MacLeod after supper. Then he'd call Cameron and report. If he was heading for B.C., he might as well fly. Regardless, he was going to get some shuteye before he went anywhere.

Vlad found the drive south easier than the trip north earlier in the week. This time the sun shone most of the way and encounters with snow were brief, and only at higher elevations.

He reached the city late in the morning and after booking into a hotel near the harbor, went looking for Harro Street. Vlad was sure Ivana's displeasure at the sight of him did not rest solely on his deception. Although she said nothing, he suspected she knew his real identity and it made her nervous.

She led him to a living room that appeared cramped and dingy in the light of a single, grimy window. The overstuffed furnishings, like the area rug beneath them, were worn thin and faded to nondescript beige. Dust coated the multitude of framed photographs hung along the wall behind the couch.

Most of them showed a dark-haired girl or a heavy-set boy at various stages of their young lives. Only one showed the youngsters with a stocky man and a trim, round-faced woman. Vlad wondered whether Klaus Tartarinov still resembled the man in this old photograph.

Graying, slightly stooped and wearing glasses now, Ivana looked very little like the plain young woman in another picture seated on the front fender of her father's car. Vlad remembered Danilewski as balding, myopic, and sullen. The chip on his shoulder showed even as he posed behind the wheel of his convertible. It was the sight of the slimmer, prettier girl gracing the door by his side that surprised Vlad. He'd forgotten how attractive Nadia had been.

Ivana didn't offer refreshments. She went directly to her armchair, flopped into it and lit up a cigarette. When smoke began drifting towards the ceiling, she turned her brown eyes on Vlad and waited.

"I've got a double reason for the trip," he began. "For starters, our priest wanted to get in touch with Nick in order to find you. When I said I was coming west to visit my kids, he asked me to see if I could track you down."

Vlad braced for copious tears and wailing as he passed on the priest's message. Instead, Ivana demanded to know how a Polish priest knew which Canadian priest to contact. Ivana might look old and shabby, but her brain still functioned well. Coldly too. News of her mother's death didn't cause so much as a ripple in Ivana's expression.

Vlad shrugged and told the truth. "I haven't a clue. I didn't ask."

He feigned a grin and continued. "I told him I was coming west and asked if Nick had said where he was going. You see, I owed Nick some money and I wanted to repay him. I didn't figure it would be this much of a chase, though. But now that I'm here, where is he?"

Ivana shrugged. "I don't know. He just said he needed to get away for a while."

"And where did he go?" Vlad watched Ivana drag deeply on her cigarette butt, then stub it out.

"Down to my sister in Washington State."

"To Nadia?"

Instantly Ivana's eyes narrowed. She took her time picking a fleck of tobacco from her lip. "You know about her, then?"

Vlad could have kicked himself. Had he just betrayed his identity? "Nick used to talk about his aunt occasionally." He tried to sound nonchalant.

Continuing to watch him intently, Ivana lit a new cigarette, then leaned back and blew a smoke ring. "Yeah, he would. He didn't see her more than once or twice, but he idolized her all the same."

Vlad probed cautiously. "You don't sound happy with your son."

"What makes you think he's mine?" Ivana muttered. Her concentration shifted to depositing ashes in the brimming saucer on the table by her chair. "Klaus wanted the kid so badly, he can have him. I have enough trouble keeping myself. He can't expect me to look after the boy when he's all grown up."

Not hers? So whose was he, Vlad wondered. Had Klaus been widowed and in need of a mother for his son when he met Ivana? Was the boy a by-blow from an earlier affair? Despite his curiosity, Vlad changed the subject. "So Nick went to Washington?"

Ivana nodded again. "Yeah, that's right. He left here to drive down in mid October. Something like that."

"And do you know if he got there?"

"No."

After prying Nadia's address and telephone number out of Ivana, Vlad departed. He had remembered Ivana as having the makings of a first class bitch and time had proven his early assumptions to be correct. He felt slightly sorry for Klaus Tartarinov. He hadn't lost a thing when Ivana walked away on him, but neither had he gained anything by acquiring Millie.

CHAPTER THIRTY

Kate cleared the table while Andreas put coffee in the perk. It had been a pleasant day despite the cool temperature. They had finished cleaning up the garden ready for winter. They had shared a filling meal. Her kids might disapprove of her getting involved with Andreas again, but they weren't around to know. She felt a contentment she had not experienced in months. It was good to have a helpful man around the house again. Better yet, Andreas was behaving like a gentleman. Even Amos was relaxed with him now. When the phone rang, Kate expected to hear Alexi's voice. She braced to evade his questions as tactfully as possible.

"Hi Kate. It's me." Rob's cheerfulness conveyed good news and Kate relaxed immediately.

"Our man in Manitoba just called," he continued. "He's been one busy boy over the last two days. Thought I should fill you in. Got time to listen?" He didn't wait for her answer.

"Seems Vlad was in The Pas, all right. Claimed to be looking for Nicholas. Said he owed him money he wanted to repay."

"What? I don't believe that for a minute," Kate exclaimed. Vlad was so careful about paying his bills that she immediately knew the story was a lie.

Rob cut her off. "Neither do I. But wait, it gets better. Apparently Nicholas' stepmother told Vlad that he'd gone to Prince George, British Columbia, to see his sister. Since that's a heck of a drive, Joli figured it would be easier to go by plane if he had to. So he called the sister. Yes, Nick had been there and yes, Vlad had visited too. She said Nicholas had headed off to see their mother in Vancouver and Vlad followed him. Joli called the mother and again, she'd seen them both. When she told Vlad that Nicholas left to see her sister down in Gillingsworth, Washington, he apparently took off after him."

"My God, what's gotten into the man?" Kate mumbled, her mind racing. "It can't be money. He doesn't even know this Tartarinov."

"You're sure?"

"Yes. Eddie said Vlad didn't know Nicholas. If it were Tartarinov, the father, I'd think it might be someone from the old country. Someone he knew as a kid, maybe. But this Nicholas…" She stopped. "How old is he? Does Joli have any idea?"

"Adam's age," Rob replied, referring to his own son. "Mid-twenties."

"Then, no. He's too young for Vlad to have known him before he emigrated."

"So, was I right, then? You want Joli to keep going?"

"Definitely." There was no hesitation in her reply. "We may have a notion of where he is, but we still have no idea why he's there. This is just too weird to let it go, Rob."

"Yeah, that's what I expected you'd say. He'll catch a plane for Kelowna in the morning and rent a car. Gillingsworth is buried in the Cascades, so the best way to get there is to drive down. Even so, it's at least a good day's travel, provided the weather's with him. Apparently they've had snow in B.C. and the Cascades are bound to have had it, too. We have no idea what their roads are like."

"I don't care. If Joli's willing to go, send him," Kate insisted. Vlad wasn't following a stranger on a whim. Something was going on and she was determined to find out what.

Absently she watched Andreas find the coffee mugs and go to the fridge in search of the milk. She opened her mouth to direct him, then stopped herself. No sense letting others know of Andreas' presence.

Rob continued. "There's more. Seems someone else is following Nick. Millie had a visit from a man who claims Nicholas owes him money."

"Another man? Is he following Vlad or Nicholas?" The sudden surge of fear surprised Kate. Why did she care? Habit, she told herself. She no longer loved Vlad. Or did she?

"Who is this third man following? Nicholas, Vlad, or both of them? I mean, who visited the woman first? Vlad or this other man?"

"So far as Joli understands, Nicholas came first.

Then a couple of weeks later Vlad showed up. Finally this fellow came just a few days behind Vlad."

"So Vlad's unaware he has a tail?"

"Probably. Millie was scared of this guy, Joli said. He didn't ask about Vlad, just Nicholas. She figured he'd follow Nicholas to Prince George. I told Joli about the Russian Family Fund scam, by the way. He knew nothing about it but he'll be on the watch for connections now."

Kate was dimly aware of Rob's words as another idea formed. "Could the guy be RCMP?" she suggested. "Do you remember that Eddie told Vlad they were preparing a sting and hoping to scoop up all the scam's participants?"

"I hope so," Rob said. "Only trouble is, will he arrest Vlad too, if he finds him chasing after Nicholas? I mean, what's Vlad trying to do?"

Kate sighed. "You know, I could just shake that man until his teeth rattle. You're right, of course. They may well think Vlad's involved." Where was the damned fool now, she wondered, and what on earth was he doing?

After Kate hung up, Andreas carried their coffee to the family room and crooked a beckoning finger for her to join him.

"That was serious," he said. "What have you learned?"

When Kate finished detailing Joli's report, Andreas shook his head. "I don't like the sound of this other mysterious man. If he's chasing Nicholas, what's to stop him taking down Vlad too?"

Kate's heart did a little extra thump, remembering Insp. Davies' question about Vlad hiring a hit man to handle Andreas. Only that made no sense.

"I haven't a clue what's going on. I'm just glad this Raymond Joli seems to be pretty good at his job."

"Is it possible Vlad is after this Tartarinov to silence him?"

Andreas' suggestion shook Kate. "But why?"

"I can only guess. We know the boy was trying to get money out of Vlad for the Russian Family Fund. Perhaps he also knows something he could use to blackmail Vlad."

Again, Kate's heart gave an extra hard bump. The idea was all too plausible. Vlad would never stand still to be blackmailed. Only, what could he possibly have done to compromise himself?

"What do you know that I don't?" she demanded.

Andreas shrugged. "Nothing. I've just been thinking about Vlad's departure date. He found out about the sting at the fair on Saturday. He left the next Friday night. That would be his first opportunity if he didn't want to miss work. Had Nicholas been in Timmins, Vlad could have been up and back over the one weekend. No one would have known anything about his trip except you. And that's all the clothes he took, wasn't it? Enough for a couple of days?"

Kate reminded herself that Vlad knew she wouldn't have asked questions because they were barely speaking. While she might have been extremely curious, she wouldn't have demanded answers and he wouldn't have told her a thing, the rotten bastard.

She looked up to find Andreas watching her. "It just seems logical."

She nodded. "Only too logical, unfortunately."

Crossing the border turned out to be easier than Vlad expected but his luck ended there. The map he picked up at the first gas station south of the border showed only a handful of major roads crossing the state of Washington. Buried deep in the mountains, Gillingsworth was several miles off what the map indicated would be a two-lane secondary road. Vlad hoped the clouds obscuring much of the afternoon sky would carry only a little snow rather than the sort of road-closing blizzard he had encountered en route to Prince George.

His concern was justified. Over the next two days snow fell steadily. While it wasn't exactly a raging storm, neither was it the sort of weather in which to push recklessly forward on unfamiliar roads. He was frustrated at needing to take a break every three hours to remain alert, but he had no choice.

The storm also impeded his ability to survey his surroundings as he drove. While he'd probably have to deal with Nicholas in Gillingsworth, Vlad preferred the idea of staging a fatal accident somewhere on a deserted mountain road. Everything depended on Nicholas' gullibility.

Ivana's attitude had warned him to expect a small community. It was, but it had a friendly aura. Set in a high valley, mountains shielded it from the worst of the winter weather from the east and evergreen forests cut the winds from the north and west.

Like Prince George, timber had obviously played a major role in the town's formation and development. It was probably too isolated to attract tourists, but he could see its sawmill and a plywood manufacturing plant had made many of its citizens prosperous.

Upon arrival, Vlad immediately booked into a motel, then sought directions to Nadia's house from the desk clerk. The man's instructions were precise, and Vlad found her bungalow without difficulty.

The neat white house with bright red shutters was surrounded by a well-kept yard. Nadia took pride in her home and it showed. Not a lot like her sister, Vlad thought as he left his truck by the curb and approached the front door. He lifted the gleaming knocker and let it fall twice. The sound of a piano coming from inside ceased and the red door opened.

He found himself facing a small, shapely woman with dark hair. Gold-rimmed glassed framed her blue eyes and her tanned skin had a healthy glow.

Time had changed the little sister he remembered, but she was still very attractive. Their father would have been proud of her.

"Yes?" A touch of accent remained in her clear voice.

"Hello, Nadia," he said in Ukrainian.

For an instant she stared, then grinned and threw her arms around him.

"Vladymyr! It has been years!" Her hug was as enthusiastic as her expression. "Come in, come in."

She stepped aside, emphasizing her invitation with a sweep of her hand. "It is a pleasure to see you again. Give me your coat. How do you take your coffee? How long has it been? 1945? I cannot believe this. How did you find me?"

Chattering in their native tongue as she went, she led the way into a comfortably decorated room with a large piano against one wall and a fireplace on another. Here, too, the subtle message of cleanliness and good taste underscored the difference between the sisters.

Before Vlad could intervene she was off to the kitchen and the rattle of china accompanied the sound of running water. Her voice drifted back to him through the doorway.

"What has happened to bring you here like this after all these years? Not that I am unhappy to see you, you understand," she added. "It is just that you would not turn up out of the blue without a reason."

"I am looking for Nicholas. Is he here?"

Vlad could tell his response had caught her by surprise. She stuck her head around the doorjamb. "Nick? Yes. He arrived about three weeks ago."

"And he stayed?"

She frowned at him. "Yes. What has Nick done that you are chasing him? He is no relation to you."

Her direct approach confirmed Vlad's earlier decision not to pretend he owed Nicholas money. He'd tell Nadia the truth—or at least part of it, and rely on her family loyalty to work in his favor. She'd point him towards Nicholas so long as she thought he wanted to help the boy. He'd need to appear relieved to be so close and take the time to accept her friendly overtures.

"I know. But he has himself involved with an extortion scheme and the Mounties are looking for him. I thought he should be warned."

"Extortion?" Nadia's eyes widened. The whistling of the kettle drew her back into the kitchen. In moments she reappeared bearing a tray and set it on the low table in front of the chesterfield. She sat and resumed her interrogation.

"Now, how did you find out about this?" She poured coffee and listened as Vlad told her a streamlined version of Nicholas' attempt to extract money for Olga via contributions to the bogus Russian Family Fund.

"I could not explain this to Ivana," Vlad concluded. "Instead, I fed her a line about owing Nicholas money and needing to see that he got it in order to salve my conscience."

Nadia chuckled. "You told Ivana that?" She shook her head. "Sorry, Vlad. I know she's my sister, but she was never big on honesty or keeping promises. She would have trouble wrapping her head around that concept."

"I wondered," he said. "She gave me a strange look when I said it. I couldn't tell her the real story though, or she would never have told me how to find Nicholas."

"That's true. She pretty much washed her hands of both the kids when she split with Klaus. I suspect she just gave Nick my address because she wanted to be rid of him."

Vlad leaned forward. "But he did actually come here?"

Nadia nodded. "Oh, he's here. Arrived about two weeks ago, I guess it was. He stayed with me for a couple of days until he was able to find his own room."

"And what's he up to now?" Vlad prompted.

Nadia shrugged. "Now he goes on about his business. He got a job at the mill and looks after himself. I talked to him for a few minutes last week in the grocery store. His car has died so he's pretty much tied here until he can afford to replace it. But he's working on that, he says." She smiled. "At least he hasn't asked me for a loan."

"What I cannot understand," Vlad said, "is why Nicholas would call me to pay for his grandmother's medicine. Does he not realize if I really was connected to your mother, I would know who he is?"

Nadia nodded. "It would seem so, except that Nick is not Mother's grandson. He is Klaus' nephew."

Vlad gave Nadia a puzzled look and she continued. "It's complicated. The Tartarinovs were our neighbors when we were teenagers. Since the Russians were in charge after the war, Klaus and Ivana slipped over the border to Germany. Life there was no picnic either, so he applied to emigrate and they married as soon as his papers came through. What they didn't expect was to wind up with an infant before the ink even dried on their marriage license. You see, Klaus' sister, Anna, was so sick with tuberculosis by then that she had to be hospitalized. Since she had no one else to leave her baby with, Nick went to Klaus and Ivana and came to America with them. He has always considered them his parents even though he knows the truth. He probably doesn't realize that Olga Danilewski is Ivana's mother. When she emigrated, my sister made no effort to keep in touch with Mother. She wouldn't even have kept in touch with me, only I called her. And that was mostly so I could tell Mother about her and the children when I wrote."

"And when was the last time you did that?"

Nadia sighed. "Probably eight years now. I used to write two or three times a year, but then my letters started coming back with a stamp saying she was no longer at this address. I tried, but I was never able to track her down. You know the problems trying to find someone behind the Iron Curtain. Eventually I gave up."

Vlad understood how that went. "Then I guess I do have news for you. Bad news. I'm sorry to be the one to tell you, Nadia. Olga died a couple of years ago. My parish priest was able to find out through a friend of a friend. I went checking when the calls started because I suspected she might already be dead, and Father Darcovich's friend says I'm right."

Nadia closed her eyes. "I was afraid of that. They don't have pensions over there like we do. I always wondered how she would manage."

For several moments silence filled the room as Nadia dealt with the pain of her new knowledge. Then she resumed her story. "I wanted her to come with us when I married Joe and moved to the States. She wouldn't do it. Her own husband had just died and I was afraid Ivana wouldn't be around for long. She was still in Berlin at the time, but she was already engaged to Klaus and she married him a year or so later. Mamma has been on her own for twenty-five years.

"I wasn't too worried about her at first. She had her nursing and she could support herself because they always need nurses no matter what government is in power. But she would have been eighty last fall, and she must have retired about the time I lost track of her."

Silence fell again for a moment. Then Nadia collected herself and directed her attention to Vlad. She demanded details of his life and family. A sense of kinship was starting to build when the ringing of the doorbell interrupted them.

School was finished and Nadia's first pupil had arrived for her weekly piano lesson. Concealing his relief at the interruption, Vlad promised to call later and hurried away. Nadia had already provided him with addresses for both Nicholas' employer and his landlady.

Since he didn't know Nicholas by sight and wouldn't be able to pick him out in the flood of men exiting the paper mill, Vlad decided to approach the landlady first.

Freda Bird showed little interest in her tenant's visitor. He was working the afternoon shift, she said, and wouldn't be home until midnight, possibly later if he went to the hotel with his friends until closing time.

Vlad scribbled a message on a page from his notebook and asked the landlady to see that Nicholas got it when he came home. Then, following the woman's directions, he located the Maitland House and wasted an hour chatting up the bartender and explaining his phony errand. If he planned to tackle Nicholas in the bar at midnight, it would help to have the bartender as an ally.

CHAPTER THIRTY-ONE

Gaston stood by a pillar opposite the bus depot coffee shop and watched. In his grey wool jacket and black cord pants, he was just one more faceless individual in a building full of anonymous individuals hurrying elsewhere, ignoring those around them. The booming announcements of arrivals and departures echoed through the depot, mingling with the roar of engines and grinding of gears. Exhaust fumes belched into the main lounge each time the doors from the passenger platforms opened.

Just yards away the lunch counter where Ivana Tartarinovska worked was emptying quickly, many of her customers apparently heeding the call to board the bus to Campbell River. Gaston waited. He hoped Sandra had not told her mother about his visit. It could make her stubborn and he disliked roughing up women.

When Ivana picked up a cloth to wipe her counter, Gaston crossed and took a seat near the cash register.

"Where's Nick?" he asked in response to the usual query about what he wanted to eat.

Ivana heaved an exaggerated sigh and shook her head. "What is it with you guys? Don't you ever talk to each other? I told your partner. He took off for my sister's place."

Partner? Where did she get that idea? Gaston frowned at her.

"Where does your sister live?"

"Like I told you, ask your partner."

"I don't have a partner, Madame. Nor do I have time for games." He used his most menacing tone. "Your son owes me money. I intend to collect it. If you try to be difficult, you'll regret it."

Her grim expression told Gaston this woman was not a typical mother. If Ivana felt intimidated, her frown concealed the fact well.

"Look, buster, let's get a few things straight. Nick is not my son. He's my husband's nephew. He foisted the brat on me when his sister got sick and I spent our whole marriage looking after him. Now that I'm on my own, so is he. He doesn't pay my bills and I don't pay his. If you want money, go see Klaus."

Gaston pretended to be placated. "Okay. Maybe I will. But first, let's see if I can get Nick to pay his own bills. Where does your sister live?"

"I told you. Ask your partner." Her surly tone matched the stubborn set of her lips.

"I work alone," Gaston retorted, his icy tone underlining the earlier threat. "Who is this partner you think I have?"

Ivana's expression grew even colder. "His name is Horbatsky. Vladymyr Horbatsky. He claimed to owe Nick money."

Gaston grunted. "Interesting. Maybe he's the one I should see to get my money. Anyway, what is your sister's name and exactly where does she live?

"Nadia lives in Gillingsworth, Washington."

Gaston kept staring at her until she added Nadia's surname and street address. He rose from his stool and dipped his head in acknowledgement of the information. He could see a woman on the other half of the counter watching them. Ivana's demeanor told him she wouldn't be telling her co-worker anything about their discussion.

Back on the street Gaston began considering Ivana's news about Horbatsky. It seemed improbable that he really owed Nick money. More than likely, the story was a cover to find the young man. Why? Igor said they suspected Horbatsky of working with Tartarinov. Maybe they had collaborated and the kid had robbed him, too.

He smiled to himself as he got into his car and started it up. If Horbatsky were chasing Tartarinov, his job had just become easier. Now Gaston could take care of both hits at the same time.

#

Evening had closed in by the time Vlad left the bar. Given the hour, he felt safe exploring the town's back streets and dead ends in search of a place to deal with Nicholas.

He found it north and east of Havergill's Paper Mill where a narrow, snow-covered road wound by the bank of a river for a couple of miles before ascending the side of the valley into a stretch of rocks and scrubby Jack pine. Where it went from there, Vlad didn't know or care. It appeared to be a logging road. That would meet his needs perfectly since only company trucks were likely to be using it early in the morning.

The road's second advantage was its topography. About a mile into its climb to the forest, the road widened to a small lay-by overlooking the gorge through which the river twisted and plunged towards the mill on the edge of town. There was no fence to protect spectators from the two hundred foot drop between the parking area and the stream below. Froth topped the black water swirling around the rocks in the center of the stream. The current moved quickly here and anyone caught in it was unlikely to surface alive. Between the current, the rocks, and the remnants of a chained log boom moored in the mill's catchment pond, any body that surfaced would be so battered no one would question the cause of death.

Later, sitting in his room trying to read a local paper, Vlad couldn't concentrate. Hearing Nadia at the piano this afternoon had triggered memories of another room and another winter evening.

His mother was sitting at the piano with Nadia on her knee picking out the notes of an old folk song and trying to sing to the little girl. It was a sad song about lost love and there were tears in her voice as she sang. Their father was out somewhere with Olga and his mother was doing her best not to let the children know. Only she wasn't being very successful. He knew before she did about that night's assignation. He'd seen Olga cross the street to get into their father's car and drive away.

Nadia, too, understood that Mamma Tatiana as she called Vlad's mother, was unhappy. She was reaching up and patting her cheek as Mamma played for her.

Vlad knew the situation with his father wasn't entirely his father's fault. Dimitri Horbatsky was a product of his time and his station, but Vlad still resented his attitude on his mother's behalf.

The only son of a Cossack family with estates outside Kiev, Dimitri was fifteen or twenty years younger than his two sisters. When their father died, he was only six and his sisters, both doctors, were already grown and married.

Vlad's father had often told him about leaving home at the age of ten. "Mother took me into the parlor and sat me down," he'd say. "She told me I was going to Papa's old school in St. Petersburg. That's what he had wanted for me, and she was going to honor his wishes even though it was hundreds of miles away."

Vlad remembered the picture of his grandmother that had hung above his parents' bed. Stern-faced, small, dressed all in black like the prosperous widow she was, her eyes followed you around the room. Although he had never met her, he didn't need his father's lectures to tell him she was one tough lady.

Dimitri graduated from St. Stephen's in 1895 as the second best marksman with a rifle and the best pistol shot in all of Russia. Coupled with high marks in his academic studies, these skills landed him an appointment to the same guard regiment in which his father had been a colonel.

Vlad couldn't recall all the places Dimitri served or how quickly he moved up the ranks until he, too, was a colonel in the Tszar's guards. He was a handsome man with an eye for the ladies and sufficient money and prestige to enjoy his privileges.

Tatiana Davinsky had been a court interpreter when Dimitri met her. She had long dark hair, flashing blue eyes, and a fearless nature befitting the youngest daughter of a prominent Cossack general. Given their similar background and Dimitri's prospects for advancement, both families approved their marriage in 1898.

By the time Dimitri fought the Bolsheviks in Leningrad in 1917, he already had three sons and a daughter. Vlad was born after his father moved the family home to Kiev to take a position with the defense ministry in the newly formed government of an independent Ukraine.

When the Communists invaded in 1922, the Horbatskys, like most of the patriotic elite, were targeted and hunted in an attempt to crush any future rebellion against Mother Russia. Their position was even more dangerous because Dimitri was a born leader as well as a highly trained soldier.

The family fled to Berlin in 1923 and established a restaurant to earn a living. Vlad's elder brothers, Ivan, Mikhail, and Peter, had already finished school when the family arrived in Germany, but Natasha and Vlad received most of their education in Berlin.

Olga had been a nurse in a field hospital and Dimitri met her when he was wounded in action in 1916. He boasted about how he'd proposed to her on the operating table and she accepted. He never talked about her reaction to learning, after the fact, that he was already married and the father of several children. Nor had Vlad ever heard his mother's reaction to learning she not only had a rival, but a rival who had conceived her husband's child at the same time as Tatiana was carrying her own youngest son. It was only as an adult that Vlad came to realize how much his mother had resented sharing her Berlin home with her husband's mistress.

Dimitri was something of a community leader among the Ukrainian émigrés in Berlin. When food got scarce, he continued to pass supplies out the restaurant's back door to the poorest of his countrymen. Hitler's spies knew it, of course, and, being Slavs, the family was in constant danger the more entrenched the laws about ethnic purity became.

One day the authorities just walked in and marched all the restaurant's male staff, including Dimitri and his sons, away to the work camps. Vlad's sister and mother weren't there at the time so they managed to escape to a little village west of Berlin.

By the time Vlad got home in 1945, his three brothers and his father had all starved to death in the camps, his sister had committed suicide after being raped by soldiers, and his mother was an invalid unable to walk. Without Anna, she too, would have died before he saw her again.

He had felt no pain at leaving Europe behind. With his family all dead, Anna was his only tie and she was to come to him in Canada once he was settled. The plan had not worked out, but Kate and their children had filled the void. Once he took care of Nicholas, he could return to them.

Vlad sat back in the hard wooden chair and ignored the noise around him; his eyes focused on the dark-haired man in the shabby cord jacket seated three tables away. Nadia had pronounced him Anna's son. He did have her coloring. Other than that, Vlad could see little resemblance. The boy must look like his father, Vlad decided, stoically burying memories of their passionate times together. The relationship had never matured. He told himself her son belonged to some subsequent lover.

The friendly bartender had identified Nicholas with a quick nod of his head as soon as the group from the sawmill arrived. They had chosen a spot in the centre of the room and ordered a pitcher of draft each. Over the ensuing hour three of Nicholas' five companions finished their beer and left. Vlad waited patiently, not prepared to interfere unless he must. Better to let the outsiders drift away on their own so his conversation with Nicholas could take place without witnesses.

Vlad sipped slowly. The waiter made his round for last call. One of Nicholas' companions made his farewells and the other headed for the washroom while Nicholas placed a final order. This was the time, Vlad decided. He got up and walked to the centre table.

"Hi, Nicholas. Got a minute? I think we need to talk." The young man cast him a puzzled glance and opened his mouth to question the intrusion. "About Olga,"

Vlad added. "And the money she does not get from the Russian Family Fund."

Fear flashed across Nicholas' face and he pushed his chair back. Vlad smiled and held out a delaying hand.

"Do not worry. I am not part of the fund management team, but we do need to talk—in private. How be I drive you home? That way, your buddy does not need to hear about me." Nicholas nodded and Vlad returned to his own table.

The last companion returned long enough to sip a couple of mouthfuls from his glass, then rose. Vlad heard him offer Nicholas a lift, and saw Nicholas shake his head. Moments later the man was gone and Nicholas brought his glass to Vlad's table.

"Okay," Nicholas said as he sank into the chair opposite Vlad. "Talk. Who the hell are you and why should I want to hear what you have to say?"

"Because I could send you to jail," Vlad replied quietly. "I will not. I would not do that to a relative of Nadia. Or Olga, for that matter." He saw Nicholas' eyes widen in surprise but he gave him no opportunity to interrupt. "But I will warn you that you are in danger. The Mounties know about the Fund and they are looking to scoop everyone connected to it. That includes you."

"How do you know this?"

Vlad smiled. "A friend of mine told me. The same friend who helped me find you."

"Who are you?" Nick paled.

"My name is Vladymyr Horbatsky." Nicholas' eyes narrowed. Obviously he recognized the name. "Nadia

Dymitruk is my half-sister." Nicholas' mouth opened in surprise. Now he understood the relationship that had previously eluded him.

Vlad nodded. "Yes, Nicholas. Frederick knew why I might feel guilty enough to send Olga money even if you did not. What he did not know was how far I would go to fight his scam. I do not believe in making money from the dead."

"Olga's dead?" Nick was again startled.

Vlad nodded. "Yes. Ivana's mother is dead. You did not realize who she was, did you?"

Nicholas shook his head. "No. I just took the names I was given. I didn't ask…" He shook his head again in bewilderment, then slumped back in his chair.

"So, if you did not know about the Mounties, why did you need to come down here?" Vlad asked. "And how well have you covered your tracks?"

The younger man concentrated on his glass as though debating what to say. He didn't look up as he spoke.

"I've got this guy on my tail. I don't want Aunt Nadia knowing about him. She's way too thick with the local cops. She's dating one of them now, since Uncle Joe died. If her boyfriend found out about this guy, then he'd be after me, too. I came down here to get away from the whole thing."

"Your aunt does not know about the blackmail. Is that it?"

Vlad watched Nicholas wince when he used the term. Apparently Nicholas thought some of the money actually went to the families left behind. Vlad knew better.

None of the money Nicholas collected would ever reach the families. It disappeared into the hands of Korczak and others along the chain that gave Nicholas his orders.

"Okay, tell me the whole story, Nicholas. From the beginning. How did this guy recruit you to make calls for him?"

Vlad didn't really care how the scheme worked. He just needed to gain Nicholas' trust. Once that was established, Nicholas wouldn't question Vlad's understanding of the operation. Nor would he wonder how Vlad knew about Korczak.

"I attended a couple of meetings at college," the younger man began. "We had a history prof who had contacts with some draft dodgers in the Winnipeg area. He suggested we might want to talk to them and set up a date for a meeting. They made a lot of sense, explaining how we could protest the U.S. involvement in Nam, that sort of thing. Anyway, there was a signup sheet so they could contact us when they had connections worked out and we'd go picket the embassy in Ottawa. Only I never heard from them. Instead, this Fred who was at the meeting called me and asked how I'd like to help some of our own people behind the Iron Curtain. I knew I had family back there somewhere, so I said sure. He gave me a list of people to call and the name of the individual in their family that needed help," Nicholas finished.

"And when did you start making these calls?"

"Three years ago, I guess. About that time, anyway."

"And the money? Did Fred tell you how much to ask for?"

Nicholas nodded. "Yeah. He told me."

"And how was the money supposed to be delivered? Mailed to you, or sent directly to Fred?"

"Like I told you on the phone: I picked up the checks from a post office box, then sent them on."

"Just how much money were you collecting, Nick?"

Vlad didn't really care about the amount, but the way Nicholas avoided his gaze as he shrugged said he wasn't about to admit how much he was demanding.

"A few hundred." He tossed off the number casually, too casually to be truthful.

"Well, you wanted a hundred a month from me," Vlad prodded. "Was that more than usual?"

Again, Nicholas shrugged. "A bit more."

In a flash Vlad connected the sum and the reluctance to talk. No wonder Nicholas was worried.

"Just how much were you supposed to ask me for, Nicholas?"

The young man glanced at Vlad, then looked away again.

"Fred told you a different amount, did he not?" Vlad persisted. "What did he want? Fifty dollars? Seventy-five?"

Nicholas took a sip of beer and set the glass back on the battered table.

"You padded the amount you were supposed to ask for," Vlad persisted. "That is why you are in trouble. Fred found out you were asking for more than you were giving him. Now he is after you for skimming his profits. Is that it?"

Nicholas didn't say a word.

"You had better tell me, Nicholas, because you will not be safe here. You know that. If you are playing with the Russian mob — and that is probably who Fred works for— you are in a bind. They are bound to have their connections to the KGB. They found me. They will find Nadia, if they do not already know about her. And once they track her down, they will figure you out too."

Nicholas toyed with his glass, then got up. Vlad could see his hands trembling. He'd hit a nerve. If Nicholas hadn't understood whom he was crossing when he started stealing, he realized his error now—now, when it was too late to plead stupidity. The Freds of this world didn't allow their underlings to cheat. No amount of contrition or restitution would suffice. They'd make an example of Nicholas if they caught up with him.

"I am right, am I not?" he repeated. "Fred is looking for you to teach you a lesson. And it will not be a nice lesson. In fact, you will not survive the lesson if he finds you. Right?"

Nicholas started to walk away.

Vlad rose and followed him. "So what do you plan to do about this, Nicholas? Sit here and wait till Fred finds you? He will probably not come himself, you know. He will send someone else. Someone you will not know so you will not be able to defend yourself."

Someone like me.

Even after hearing the whole sorry truth, Nicholas still didn't understand the way the Commies worked. He was starting to trust Vlad and that trust would be his downfall. The stupid fool was already half way into Vlad's trap.

Nicholas stopped, rummaged in his pocket and produced a package of cigarettes. He dug one out and lit up.

Zipping his jacket, Vlad motioned for Nicholas to follow him and headed for the door.

"You can stay here and worry about every stranger you meet, or you can do something about it," Vlad continued once they were outside. "You can let me help you get away."

Nicholas leaned against the entry wall, and took a deep drag on his cigarette. "And why would you want to help me?" he asked.

"Because of Nadia and Olga." Vlad lied. "You see, the Mounties are watching Fred. They are trying to pick up his contact people. That is why I started out. To warn you to stop and get out before they found you."

Nicholas took another drag on his cigarette and blew a cloud of smoke. "I don't get it. You fought me all the way about the money. Why would you warn me?"

Figuring Nicholas would be more likely to cooperate if he thought no one knew his real background, Vlad made no mention of the history Nadia had given him.

"You do not understand people like me," he said. "People who put their family first. I do not want to see

Olga's grandson in jail. Let me help you get away from them."

"I'll think about it," Nicolas muttered, then added. "I left some stuff with Sandra. I need to get it if I go anywhere long term. Only my car died a couple of days after I got here and I haven't got the money to replace it just yet."

His own money, Vlad guessed. Thinking no one would look for it there, Nicholas had probably stashed much or all of his ill-gotten cash in something he left with his sister.

Vlad nodded. "I leave for Canada on Friday morning. I will take you back to Prince George on my way if that's what you want. Think about it and call me with your decision before you go to work tomorrow. We can discuss your disappearance during the drive."

CHAPTER THIRTY-TWO

Having finished his supper and his habitual evening walk, Andreas returned to the hotel for the night. His mind was busy with plans for the next project. He'd be done at Clarke's in another couple of weeks. He needed to call Gallagher's in New York to set up a timeline with them.

He wasn't ready to leave Kate. On the other hand, he could see no way to persuade her to pick up and come with him. While Vlad had been gone almost three weeks, there was still no clue either to the purpose of his departure or his fate since leaving. Andreas found the waiting frustrating and marveled at Kate's strength. By now, most women would have broken under the pressures of worry and anger.

The desk clerk called to Andreas as he passed through the lobby on the way to his room.

"A lady called you around five-thirty," she said. "Wouldn't give me a name. Just said to have you call Beacon Street, and you'd know the rest."

Andreas thanked the girl and, ignoring her obvious curiosity, turned back towards the elevator.

He knew Marie Overland's telephone number by heart. He'd been using her Beacon Street Answering Service as his business contact ever since he began consulting. These days, with his office in his apartment and him on the road so much, having a full time secretary was impractical. Marie was an excellent, very professional, alternative.

Back in his room, he hung up his windbreaker and kicked off his shoes, all the while puzzling over what was important enough to prompt Marie to break their routine. Especially since he'd made his weekly call to pick up messages the night before.

"Beacon Street," the familiar voice began.

"Hi, Marie. I hear you're looking for me."

"Actually, it's your landlady, not me," Marie replied. "She called me this afternoon in a right panic. Something about your room being searched and she couldn't stop them."

"Searched?"

"Yeah. She sure sounded shook up. I trust the lady's got all her marbles?"

"No problem there. But my apartment searched?" It crossed his mind that someone might have broken in and ransacked the place while Lois Wilson was out. Widowed and in her seventies, she would certainly have found such an event upsetting.

"She wanted me to get you to call her," Marie continued.

"Okay, will do. Thanks, Marie."

He glanced at his watch. It was just after eight. Not too late to call.

Marie had made no mistake in assessing Lois as flustered. After apologizing for tracking him down through his answering service, Lois explained that she felt he ought to know his apartment had been searched.

"It didn't seem right what with you not being home to defend yourself," Lois said. "But I couldn't stop them. Not when they had a warrant."

Her tone surprised Andreas almost as much as her message. In the twelve years he'd rented her second floor apartment Andreas had never known her to sound so nervous.

"Searched my apartment? Who did that, Lois?"

"The CIA. At least that's what their badges said."

The CIA? Andreas' heartbeat kicked up a notch. If it weren't a scam, then she had good cause to be concerned. So did he.

"Let's start over. Who came to the house? What did they want?"

"Three days ago a man showed up at the door and asked to speak to you. When I said you weren't here, he asked where you were. I told him Canada. Then, he began with the questions. How long have you lived here? How well do I know you? Do you make this trip often? Where were you, exactly? Why were you there? When did you leave? When would you be back? He didn't look happy with my answers, but he left. Then this morning he was back with a couple of other guys and a search warrant for your apartment. They were there until mid afternoon and they had a whole pile of boxes with them when they left."

The questions sounded normal if they were looking for him. The mystery was why they would want him. He'd been given security clearances for his work years ago and he'd never had any problems. So why now? What did they want with his files? Because those boxes had to be his files. He didn't have anything else up there except his clothes and some reference texts.

"Thanks for warning me, Lois. Did you get any idea why they're looking for me?"

"None, but I'm guessing that it has something to do with your work. Then Larry Campbell stopped in after supper. He wants to talk to you too. Since you two worked together…" She let the implication speak for itself.

Andreas thanked his landlady again and promised to call his old office partner.

"But not until late," Lois added. "He said he had a meeting tonight that he expected would last until well after ten. And whatever you do, you aren't to leave a phone number on his answering machine."

Don't leave a number? Curiouser and curiouser, as Alice said in Wonderland. "Okay, Lois. I'll remember. You didn't tell anyone about Marie, did you?" Reassured that his answering service remained anonymous, he hung up and began to pace.

Larry Campbell had shared a secretary with Andreas when they both worked for NASA and was as close to a friend as he had at work. Even if they no longer worked together, Larry would hear anything being whispered on the grapevine. If Larry were suspicious, Andreas would listen attentively.

Lois' call puzzled him. Larry must know something if he wanted to talk. Andreas went to the mini bar and poured himself a drink.

He was tired, but he knew he wouldn't sleep until after he spoke to Larry. He dug his address book from his suitcase and went to sit by the window staring into the star-speckled sky, nursing his drink and waiting. It was after midnight before he placed the call. Larry answered on the first ring.

Andreas could hear the strain in his friend's voice the moment he began speaking.

He didn't bother with civilities. "Okay. What's up?" he demanded.

"Nothing good, buddy. Lois was right when she said it was CIA. Someone has apparently provided the Ruskies with a copy of the plans for your fire control system."

Andreas stifled a gasp of shock as Larry plowed on.

"They think it was you. Or at least the investigators that came after me tonight think it was you. They were certainly hammering away about what I know about your background, your connections, who you know on the other side. All that kind of thing."

"But I never…"

Larry cut him off. "I know that. It doesn't matter to them though."

Andreas grew cold with fear. It was the worst nightmare for anyone working in weapons design. "They questioned you?"

"Yeah, tonight. That's why I warned you not to leave a message. My phone's likely tapped. Lois' too, for that matter."

"I don't know anything about this."

"But you do design for military manufacturers and they aren't prepared to look beyond the obvious," Larry reminded him. "The authorities always like to see traitors instead of spies. Makes their life easier."

And put designers in incredible jeopardy, Andreas realized, wiping an icy palm against his pant leg. "Damn. So the fools think it's my fault that the plans jumped the Curtain?"

"Sort of looks like that."

"That's rubbish but I suppose I'll be under arrest the minute I poke my nose into the house. Right?"

"That's my guess."

"And if I end up in jail, I won't be able to check out the real source of the leak," Andreas reasoned aloud. "Do you know exactly what the Russians got?"

"Not exactly. Just that it was some part of the control system. Whatever it was, they can now duplicate our controls."

"Was it the entire system?"

"Don't know."

Andreas thought for a moment. A good designer could duplicate his work with only some of his components. Only which ones and where were they made? If he knew that, he might be able to find the thief.

"Guess I need to figure out who the contractor was."

"That's the logical starting point for finding an industrial spy, isn't it?"

Andreas sighed. "Yup. And if I don't want to wind up in Leavenworth, I'd better find that out damn quick."

"That would be my advice, buddy. You can't just walk in unprepared. You need to lay low until I know more."

Andreas wished they could speak freely. He consoled himself with the knowledge that Larry would use public phones and go through Marie with any future messages.

"I appreciate the warning."

"Where are you going to go?"

"You're safer not knowing. I'll call you some time. Take care of yourself."

Andreas hung up the telephone and dropped against the chair's padded back. So now he was a hunted man. Larry was putting a brave face on it but Andreas knew the darker side that lay beneath. Anyone who betrayed the defense department was a traitor to the country. He'd need rock solid proof of his innocence if he wanted to stay out of jail.

He couldn't go anywhere near his home in San Antonio. Indeed, he might not be safe anywhere in the States. That would screw up all three of his next contracts. So he'd have to work fast to untangle the mess. Meanwhile, he'd stay in Canada close to Kate. Damn, this wasn't how he wanted to start their life together.

From half a block back, Joli slowed, then followed as the dark half-ton with the Ontario plates pulled into the restaurant parking lot. Pretending to fiddle with his parking, Joli watched a big man in a winter parka get out and head for the double doors. He cut his ignition and sat thinking. He hadn't seen the man's face but the size was right and the license matched Horbatsky's. Joli was almost certain he'd found his quarry.

That pleased him, given he'd been too tired to start hunting when he arrived in town the previous evening. Professional or not, tracking could be time-consuming and if he were right he'd finished this assignment in just over two weeks.

While he disliked being seen by a subject, there was no way Horbatsky could know he was being hunted. He'd have some breakfast and get a look at Horbatsky's face at the same time.

Joli found himself a spot at the counter and ordered bacon and eggs with toast and coffee. In the mirror behind the counter, he could see his man at a table in the corner, half hidden behind a newspaper. The waitress was busy taking his order when a second man arrived and slid into a chair across the table from Horbatsky. From his age, Joli surmised it might be Tartarinov, although with no photo for comparison, he had no way to be sure.

His meal was slow in coming and he was in no hurry to eat it. He cast his eyes towards the corner table frequently enough to see that the men were saying little despite their apparent acquaintance. They didn't look to be great friends.

He was working on a refill of his coffee cup when Vlad and his companion approached the cash register.

The younger one handed Vlad money and his bill. "Gotta go or I'll be late," he said.

Vlad nodded. A moment later, he looked up and called after the man. "Nicholas, remember what I said."

"Yeah, I'll be there," the younger one replied and disappeared out the door.

So Vlad had found Nick. He was up to something, Joli decided. More importantly, he needed to report his findings to Rob Cameron.

Gaston checked the license number on the navy pickup parked near the front of the Tall Pines Motel. Plate and description both matched those Korczak had provided along with the details about Horbatsky.

Could he be this lucky? Of course, Gillingsworth had a population of less than ten thousand and he had been looking around since just after lunch. It wasn't really luck. He was a professional.

Ivana's information about Horbatsky had saved him the trouble of contacting Nadia Dymitruk. He had seen her house during his pass through town, but felt no need to knock at her door. Horbatsky would locate Tartarinov for him, and the fewer people who knew he was in Gillingsworth, the better.

Realizing that two Canadian license plates at the same motel might draw attention, he drove to the Addison Place Hotel in the heart of town. It was older and probably less comfortable. Certainly it would be noisier since there was a bar next to the parking lot at the rear. All the same, he'd be less conspicuous here than at the motel.

The early twilight found him checking the menu at a nearby Chinese restaurant. The place was doing a brisk takeout business and a few patrons from the bar wandered in during his meal. The waitress greeted them like old acquaintances, her pidgin English barely intelligible to Gaston but obviously familiar to the regulars.

Fed and relaxed, he paid his bill, left a tip, and returned to the street. After walking the six blocks that comprised the town's commercial area, he collected his wagon and drove back to the Tall Pines. He parked half a block from the motel and waited. Just before six, the blue truck entered the street and drove away. Gaston followed at a discreet distance. They were almost to the town's northern limits when the truck pulled into Chuck's Choice.

So this was the diner Horbatsky frequented. Well aware that people tended to stick to familiar haunts in strange places, Gaston tucked the information away for future use.

He gave the man time to begin his meal before entering the diner and seating himself at the counter twenty feet from Horbatsky's table. He ordered pie and coffee, then inspected his quarry carefully in the mirror behind the counter. The photograph Igor had provided was a good likeness of the man.

When his cup and plate were empty, Gaston returned to his car and waited. Horbatsky appeared before long. Gaston let him lead the way back to the motel where he disappeared into the room closest to the street. A couple of tall evergreens shadowed the corner of a parking lot opposite the motel. Gaston hunkered down in the dark and waited, sleeping fitfully. Periodically, the cold seeping through his winter clothes woke him. He'd run the motor long enough to get warm, then shut it off and doze again.

It was nearing midnight when the sound of a door slamming brought him fully awake. He saw Horbatsky's truck lights come on and moments later it was heading down the main street with Gaston on its tail. The cross street Horbatsky took ended at the mill parking lot. Gaston watched him find a place near the door, cut the engine and sit in the dark.

Less than ten minutes later men carrying lunch buckets began emerging.

Gaston noticed Tartarinov the moment he appeared in the light at the top of the mill steps. He was looking around as though expecting someone. Sure enough, Horbatsky's truck lights came on and he pulled up beside the young man.

Gaston stayed well back as Horbatsky drove Tartarinov to a house on Jackson Street, then left him with a crisp "See you in the morning."

Gaston watched Horbatsky drive away. Why were his targets getting together again? Breakfast? It was the only logical reason for a morning meeting. But why?

He considered visiting Tartarinov just before dawn, then shelved the idea. Unless he wanted to kill Horbatsky in his motel room, he'd do better to wait until they got together, then take them both down at once. A truck accident with two victims would be much less suspicious than two bodies in separate accidents in the same town on the same night.

    The light in the upstairs window blinked off as he started back to his own room. It was going to be a short night. He'd need to be up and checked out before five if he wanted to ensure he got to the Tall Pines before Horbatsky began his day.

CHAPTER THIRTY-THREE

Glaring at his watch and cursing roundly, Joli scrambled out of bed and threw on his clothes. No time for a shower. He was thankful he'd paid his motel bill last night, just in case. Nor did he need to re-pack his suitcase. Just throw in his toothbrush and lock it. He was in his car ten minutes after he wakened.

He was approaching the motel just as Vlad's truck turned out of the parking lot onto the street. The road was empty at seven-fifteen. Joli made a U-turn around a set of service station gas pumps and fell into line a couple of blocks behind Vlad. Within minutes he suspected the destination—Nick's boarding house. Even before Vlad stopped, Joli could see Nick standing at the street, duffle bag at his feet.

Joli drove straight past and made a left turn at the next intersection, then stopped in the second driveway from the corner. When he saw Vlad's truck pass, he backed out and continued his pursuit.

At this hour, the men would be looking for breakfast, he decided. He needed some himself come to that, since he had no idea where his quarry was heading, or when he'd next have time to eat. That was the trouble with surveillance. Your subject called the shots and you had no choice about following, unless you were willing to risk losing him.

Near the north end of town, he watched Vlad's signal light blink and congratulated himself on guessing correctly. The only vacant parking spot he could find was against the back fence.

Chuck's menu was familiar after three days and Joli ordered the fastest, most filling meal he could get— grapefruit and oatmeal with a chaser of coffee. The waitress eyed him suspiciously, obviously not used to health-conscious patrons. All the same, Joli managed to finish eating and return to his car while Vlad and Nick were still enjoying their toast and coffee.

He hunkered down and pretended to be busy with a roadmap spread out beside him. All the while his attention bounced between the map and the rearview mirror, taking in every patron coming and going through the diner's door.

He paid little attention to the slim fellow in the grey pea coat until he crossed the street to the beige Chev wagon parked by the curb. Exactly why the man seemed familiar he didn't know. Then he remembered seeing an identical wagon across from Nick's house the previous evening when Vlad dropped him home from work. Coincidence? Maybe. Or was he the "nasty" fellow Millie had told him about?

#

Vlad ran an eye over his room checking for forgotten articles. He'd already said his goodbyes to Nadia.

He'd check out, then pick up Nicholas and get some breakfast. They should be on the road before nine and with any luck, he'd be in Canada by mid afternoon. Even if they got the predicted snow, he should be able to reach the border tonight.

Nicholas was ready for him, his belongings packed into an overnight bag. He threw the bag in the back and slammed the truck door as he settled comfortably in the cab beside Vlad.

"Looks like we have good weather for traveling," he remarked as they headed off towards a restaurant.

Over bacon and eggs and steaming coffee, Vlad pumped Nicholas for information about his plans. So far, he had fallen in with Vlad's suggestions fairly well, but Vlad felt he needed to seem genuinely concerned if he were to retain Nicholas' trust and cooperation.

"After I collect the rest of my stuff from Sandra," Nicholas said, "I'll come back here for a couple of weeks. Just long enough for people to forget that you visited me. Then I'll head out across the mountains. Hitchhike, probably. That will make me harder to follow. Once I'm down around Kentucky or so, I can hop a plane to Mexico. If I disappear there for a month or two, I can head on to South America. Argentina, maybe. I hear Slavs are welcome there."

Vlad nodded. "So I have been told."

Absently, Vlad noticed the slim man in the jeans and plaid shirt eating near the kitchen. His heavy grey jacket slung over his chair, his face hidden by the morning paper, the man seemed isolated somehow, as though he wasn't part of the community. Then, when the waitress offered to refill his coffee cup, the man refused and Vlad caught a touch of foreign accent in his voice.

Nicholas' question about how soon they'd reach the border distracted Vlad for a moment. The next time he looked, the table was empty and the stranger was exiting the restaurant, heading for a battered beige wagon parked on the street.

Nicholas accepted a second cup of coffee and Vlad went to pay for their meals. Minutes later they were in Vlad's truck, anxious to be on their way.

Gaston left the diner and slouched down behind the wheel to wait for his targets to return to their truck. He'd seen both men put bags in the back, a broad hint they were planning to leave town. He would accompany them from a distance until he found a suitable place to run them off the road. Not a terribly ingenious accident, but common enough not to raise suspicion, given the location and the season.

He couldn't believe it when Horbatsky opted for the deserted back street leading to the logging road north of the mill. He'd checked it out himself the previous afternoon while looking for a place to stage an accident. It had seemed an unlikely prospect since it ended at the company's camp in the bush with no intersecting side roads. Strictly purpose-built, it would have been a tight squeeze to manoeuvre around the loaded trucks in ordinary circumstances. Now, half blocked by drifting snow, it was a death trap. What on earth was the man thinking?

Once Horbatsky was firmly committed to his route, Gaston sped past, determined to reach the bypass he had picked as potentially suitable to his needs. Less than ten miles from town, it was designed to allow slow-moving vehicles to pull over for those capable of negotiating the tricky S-bend more nimbly. The right side of the bend was open and bore the scars of an old avalanche rolling two hundred feet to the gorge below. The bypass was partly screened by young evergreens, but offered a good view of the ascending road. Gaston left his engine running and sauntered to the edge of the drop to watch for Horbatsky's approach.

###

When Vlad turned left at the town's main intersection Nicholas gave him a questioning look.

"Thought I'd take the scenic route," Vlad explained. "Not likely to be here again so I may as well see everything along the way."

Nicholas smiled. "In this dump there isn't much to see."

Vlad started mumbling softly as the truck left the level stretch by the river and began to climb. While deliberately ignoring Nicholas' curious glances and queries, he continued to curse and apparently fight the truck, all the while keeping one eye on the road ahead for approaching traffic. When he pulled into the lay-by a couple of miles further up the mountain, tall timber, granite rock faces, and the icy chill of the morning air surrounded them.

"Damned thing," he muttered, pretending to focus on his truck problems. "What the hell is the matter with it?

I checked the tires last night when I gassed up. It should not be soft now."

"Which one?" The young man already had his hand on the door handle, ready to be helpful.

"Your side, front," Vlad replied, and took his time about applying the parking brake. He wanted Nicholas out first, busy checking the tire. By the time he rounded the hood, Nicholas was bent down running a finger along the tire's treads. Concentrating, he didn't see the rock Vlad had retrieved from under his seat.

With the solid chunk of granite cupped in his palm, Vlad struck Nicholas' temple hard. Nicholas slumped forward immediately. Blood trickled from his ear.

Vlad saw the blow had left a depression. He felt for a pulse and smiled. Good. The boy was still alive. Feeling his way carefully, he half-dragged, half-carried Nicholas to the edge of the cliff and tipped him over. He watched the body drop fifty feet or more to the first ledge, ricochet off it, and continue rolling and bouncing until it ended up on the ice at the edge of the river. For a few moments, he thought it might be hung up there: clearly visible if anyone happened to glance down. Then the ice let go.

If Nicholas were found, his lungs would be full of water. Toppling off the mountain would account for his condition if he were found here. If the river took him all the way to town, the submerged logs around the mill would be blamed for any cracks in his skull. Either way, Nicholas' death would seem a mysterious, but perfectly natural accident.

Vlad was surprised at how calm he felt. He had wondered if he'd be troubled this time. He wasn't. Like the others, Nicholas was just another threat to be removed. Whatever sentiment he had once felt for Anna was gone and her bastard child could not be allowed to interfere with his present life.

He'd killed before, of course, in the camps. His first time had been unintentional, a matter of keeping the boots that protected his feet in the winter of 1942 while he worked on road repairs. The boots were ill-fitting, worn so thin that he felt every pebble he trod on, but at least they held in the straw he used for insulation to keep his toes from freezing.

When the big gypsy two bunks down crawled out of his blanket to go to the latrine in the middle of the night, he should have been able to go unnoticed. Only some instinct wakened Vlad and he caught the fellow trying to walk away with the boots. He demanded the boots back, but the man ignored him. Vlad stabbed him with the sharpened handle of his spoon. One thrust and the man fell to his knees clutching his throat, gurgling as blood gushed out between his fingers.

Pulling his mind sharply back to the present, Vlad glanced at the trail of bloody snow leading to the cliff, then down at his jacket. Satisfied that it bore no traces of Nicholas' blood, he went to his truck to retrieve the garbage bag he had stuffed into his glove compartment.

As he scooped the snow into the bag he remembered how horrified he had been at the way the thief had bled. The stuff seemed to be everywhere. Then there'd been the terror of how the guards would react to the murder. He'd been young then, not yet hardened to the necessities of self-preservation.

The man was known for his bullying ways and the guards made only a half-hearted attempt to find the culprit responsible for his death. When no witnesses could be found, they let it go. Prisoners in the camp were dying on a regular basis from starvation and overwork, so their superiors asked no questions about an extra body.

By 1943, when he killed the second time, he was starving and desperate enough not to care that he was seen. They were receiving only one meal a day then, a chunk of moldy, black bread and a portion of thin soup made from half-rotten cabbage and potato peelings.

The scrawny fellow who tried to take his meal looked both weak and stupid. When he moved, his coat flapped as though it hung over a scarecrow and his vacant eyes gave no sign of the cunning brain that functioned behind them. No one should have feared a man of his stature, and yet they did because he was both sneaky and dangerous. Weak though he was, Vlad knew that if the man got away with taking his meager bowl of food once, he'd be back again and again. They'd been given their portions and went off to eat when the troublemaker came up and demanded Vlad hand over his bowl. Vlad refused and tried to tip the remainder of the meal down his throat in one swallow. The man yanked at the bowl, spilling the remnants of the soup. Cursing, he drew back his arm to punch Vlad. Vlad knew he was in for a battle and immediately kicked the man in the shin. Furious and unprepared, the man howled and bent to his injury. Vlad struck him in the face with the metal bowl, then dropped it and grabbed him by the throat. He had no memory of the ensuing fight, but by the time the guards hauled Vlad off him, the man was dead.

He rolled the bag of soiled snow into a ball and placed it in the box of the truck with the bloody rock on top. He'd throw it away later where no one would connect it to Nicholas' death.

Satisfied with the results of his planning, he jumped into the cab, released the brake and turned his truck back towards town to resume his journey. He felt invigorated. Even the beige wagon passing in the opposite direction didn't spoil his elation despite the fact he was sure he'd seen it in the restaurant parking lot fifteen minutes earlier.

Gaston had a birds' eye view of the road almost to the mill. Horbatsky's truck was parked at the lay-by, barely a hundred feet from where he'd passed it. Horbatsky was walking towards the edge of the cliff. Why so slowly? Then Gaston understood. Horbatsky was slow because of his burden. He was dragging Tartarinov.

Fascinated, Gaston watched as Horbatsky reached the edge and shoved Tartarinov over. The body hurtled downward, bouncing and rolling all the way to the river. In seconds, all he could make out was a dark shape bobbing on the surface of the water. Then it disappeared.

Frustrated, he watched as Horbatsky returned to his truck, executed a perfect U-turn and disappeared back towards Gillingsworth. Damn. Now where was he going?

###

While Joli wasn't about to let Vlad and Nicholas disappear on him, neither did he want to betray his presence to the man in the wagon. The fact they were carrying luggage told Joli that his quarry was leaving town, probably returning to Canada. If his suspicions were correct, the wagon driver would be on their tail, too. He'd just hang back for now and get his answers within a few miles.

Vlad appeared first, started the truck, and had it warmed up by the time Nicholas joined him. The speed with which he shot out of the lot reflected impatience. Joli started his car but made no move. Before Vlad was a block down the street, the wagon too, pulled away. Joli gave them another two blocks, then joined the parade.

Given existing road conditions, he hadn't expected Vlad to pick the northern route back across the Cascades. Little snow had fallen since his arrival, but he'd overheard plenty of speculation as to how soon the mountain road would be closed for the winter. It seemed a foolish choice when the highway to Ossoyoos had been in such good condition when he used it earlier in the week.

He was even more startled when Vlad turned onto the river road at the northern edge of town. It was such a deserted stretch. Joli wondered how he was going to remain unobserved. Then the wagon accelerated past the truck and he decided his original suspicions were wrong. Joli let Vlad pull well ahead so that he was just beyond the mill when his quarry pulled into the lay-by.

Determined to remain hidden, Joli slammed on his brakes and slid to a stop behind a clump of young evergreens sprouting from the rocks. He cut his ignition and stepped into the pines for a better view.

Moments later, he stumbled back to his car, stunned and fighting nausea. Having seen Vlad return to his truck and start it, instinct told him he needed to move too, if Vlad were to presume he was just passing through.

Common sense told Joli the murder had happened too fast and he was too far away to have stopped it. All the same, his conscience said he should have screamed, blown his horn, done something—anything—that would have prompted Vlad to hesitate because he had a witness. He felt sick at his own inaction.

His mind raced as the two vehicles passed. He needed to turn around or he'd lose Vlad. He drove on, desperately watching for a wider section. A beige wagon sped by, heading for town. He barely had time to register the vehicle's identity before he saw—through a whirl of flying snow—that the road forked right.

Praying he wouldn't flip, Joli swung his car into the fork, stomped on the brakes and spun around twice before winding up on the verge of the road back to Gillingsworth. Taking only a second to catch his breath, he hit the accelerator and started after Vlad and the beige wagon. It had to be the same one that had tailed Vlad out of town.

CHAPTER THIRTY-FOUR

Kate set down her morning coffee and grabbed up the ringing telephone. Gerry was expecting a call from Osbourne about the results of a contract bid and everyone was anxious. Not that the situation was critical. Thanks to the Americans, production remained steady and Clarke's bottom line was good. Still, awaiting the results on any contract bid always produced some tension.

Rob's voice caught her by surprise. "We've found him. Or rather, I should say Joli has seen him in Gillingsworth."

For an instant, relief flooded Kate. "He's seen him. So, obviously he's still alive." Then, just as quickly, anger followed. How dare Vlad be alive and well while she was worrying about him? She heard the sharpness in her tone as she demanded details.

"It took Joli the better part of the day to drive down to Gillingsworth," Rob explained. "He saw Vlad at lunch yesterday. He was with a young man and he called him Nicholas. So we have to assume they've met up. But Vlad isn't leaving. He seems to be just hanging around, killing time. Joli feels he's waiting for something."

That startled Kate. "Waiting? For what? If he's already contacted Nick, why the delay?"

"Hey. What do I know?"

"Sorry. I'm just confused. We need to find out what's going on."

"Yes, we do. Question is whether you want Joli to bring in the cops. Vlad is a missing person."

Kate's reaction was immediate. "No. He hasn't done anything except disappear. And if Joli could track him, then he isn't missing any more. Right? So if the cops approach him, it'll just put his back up. We won't get answers that way."

"Yeah. That would be my guess. So, do you want Joli to keep poking around? Or do you want me to take a couple of days and fly down? I'm your brother. It would be logical for me to be concerned on your behalf."

"No." Again Kate's reply was instinctive. "He's as apt to take offense at your intervention as he would at Joli's. If anyone goes, it will have to be me. I need to think this through. Can we get back to Joli tonight? I want to talk to Andreas before I give you a final answer."

"That should work," Rob said. "He usually calls me last thing before he turns in for the night. And then there's a three-hour time difference."

"Give him my number," Kate said. "I think I need to talk to him directly. It doesn't matter how late he calls."

Satisfied, they both returned to work. Throughout the remainder of the day, questions interfered with Kate's concentration on her work. There was no help for it. She couldn't accept such cockamamie behavior until Vlad explained his reasoning to her. The big question was whether he'd ever tell the truth.

The more she thought, the more suspicious she became. If Eddie and Father Darcovich were right, this Nicholas was involved in some sort of extortion scheme. Extortionists didn't fool around. She had always assumed them to be secretive, and vicious if discovered. So why was Vlad hanging around if he had actually met up with Nicholas? She would have expected him to point the man out to police, then head for home at top speed.

Once again, she recalled Andreas' suggestion about blackmail. What grounds would anyone have to blackmail Vlad? Apart from his irrationally bad temper—which had never been displayed in public—he was a model citizen. Or at least he had been, until he became so jealous he began attacking Andreas.

The problem had to stem from his past, something he'd done as a youth in Germany. But what? Despite twenty-three years of marriage, there were still large gaps in her knowledge about that part of his life. Damn the man's secretive nature.

She'd always taken that reluctance to share his early experiences as a need to forget them, perhaps a desire to shield her from the horrors he had endured. Now she was forced to view it differently. The man with whom she had been living was obviously very different from the man she thought she had married. The sudden vicious streak, the uncontrollable jealousy, the storms of rage, the murder attempts, all bordered on psychotic.

She even toyed briefly with the idea of Vlad being a Communist spy, a sleeper agent sent into the West to await orders from his control in Moscow. Her own experience told her it could have been done. What spoiled the image was Vlad's apparent hatred of everything even faintly tainted by Communist doctrine. Good spies moderate their reactions to blend with their surroundings. Vlad couldn't have faked his vitriolic outbursts for all these years. Could he?

Poking and twisting her theories only increased her anger. A man who genuinely loved her would have explained his fears, shared his worries, revealed his reasons. That Vlad had not, simply underscored the gulf between them. She had been reluctant to hurt the father of her children, while this man obviously didn't give a damn about her. He had his own agenda and she was supposed to accept it blindly.

Her sudden desire to hurt him as he had hurt her was dangerous. While it was probably understandable, the fact he could make her this angry said their marriage needed to end.

Nor would separation be good enough. She might be able to simply cut Vlad out of her life and continue living in Milton, but he would never let her go. To be free she would need to divorce him and disappear completely.

###

Vlad drove east from Gillingsworth with the intention of turning north when he reached the road to Ossoyoos. He'd overheard someone in the restaurant yesterday saying that road was still in good shape despite its mountainous terrain. It would get him back to Canada in a few hours and out of reach of American authorities. Things had gone so smoothly he had no worries. All the same, it would be good to get across the border again.

Despite the cold, the sun was glinting off the snow, making his eyes water behind his sunglasses. It was a fine morning and he was well pleased with himself. His task was complete. It had taken him four weeks, but it was done. Nicholas would never betray him to the Mounties and without Nicholas as a link, they wouldn't connect him to Korczak.

Vlad's next major task was to devise a sufficiently strong reason for his absence to gain Gerry's sympathy. That shouldn't be hard. He was smart. He had three, maybe four days to work things out before he got back to Milton. He'd have his story ready by that time. Besides, Gerry considered him a highly valued employee, a significant part of the Clarke team.

Idly, he wondered how long it would take the Americans to find out that the Russians had their plans. He must be patient. It might take months before all the connections were made and Andreas was arrested. He might not even be in Canada by the time it happened. Perhaps that would be a good thing, Vlad decided. While he'd love to see the Kraut squirming and protesting in vain, it might be better if Kate knew nothing until it was all over. That way she couldn't get involved.

He reached Omak just before noon and stopped in dismay where the road forked north. Police barricades blocked it. A state trooper leaned against his patrol car beside the barrier.

Having nothing else to distract him and seeing Vlad's blinker indicating his intention to turn north, the man shook his head and ambled towards the truck where it sat at the stop sign.

Nervous, Vlad rolled down his window.

"Good morning, sir." The cop smiled broadly. "Can't do that, I'm afraid. We've got a big rig off the road about ten miles up. It'll take most of the day before things are cleared away. Where you heading? Back to Canada?" He was looking at the truck's Ontario plates.

"Yeah." Vlad nodded. "I was going up to Osoyoos to catch the Trans Canada."

"Well, you won't be doing that today. But if you head on east a bit you can pick up a good road at the Colorado River. That will take you up around Trail. There's a road before that, just east of Grand Coulee, but it may not be as well plowed. I'd advise you to take the main highway at Davenport. Neither route will delay you if you're heading all the way east to Ontario."

Vlad thanked the trooper, crossed the highway and continued east as advised. While he disliked having to change his plans, the cop was right. Both roads would get him home with an hour or less difference in the travel time.

He stopped to eat at a diner near the Colorado River. The television mounted near the ceiling by the cash register, was tuned to the early afternoon news. Vlad had little interest in the reporter's comments until he started talking about the storm coming down from Canada.

"They're getting hammered up there already," the anchorman said. "Lots of road closures. Anyone going that direction might be smart to call their destination to see if they can get through. Being stuck on a mountain road in the dark's no fun, folks. Better check things out first."

Snow again, Vlad cursed inwardly. Here he was all done and ready to go home, and the weather was deliberately playing games with him. He decided not to take the trooper's advice after all. He had plenty of choices. He'd keep going east instead. If things got bad, he could hole up in Spokane for the night, let the storm pass.

\# \# \#

Gaston stopped for the state trooper, listened to his advice and nodded agreeably. If the cop were telling him to head east, then Horbatsky would have received the same message. He couldn't be far ahead.

By killing Tartarinov, Horbatsky had done half Gaston's job for him. It didn't much matter where Gaston finished the assignment. He'd stay on Horbatsky's trail if possible. If he lost him, so be it. The man was obviously making tracks for home, unaware that he was being followed. Gaston could always make the second hit in Milton. Igor had specified no location, only that the job be done. Gaston relaxed and concentrated on the road twisting downward off the mountain in the late morning sunshine.

\# \# \#

By five fifteen the rest of the office staff had gone and Kate was engrossed in finishing a letter confirming Clarke's acceptance of the contract with Osbourne. The touch of lips on the back of her neck brought her half out of her seat with a startled exclamation.

She rounded on the intruder in shock. Discovering it was Andreas, she relaxed and shook her fist at him, cutting off his apology. "You startled me half to death. What are you doing here at this hour?"

Then, giving him no time to explain, she announced that Vlad had been found.

"Found? My God, he's there?"

Kate repeated her brother's information and explained about Joli's request for direction. "Now I need your advice on whether to have Joli poke around for further answers or go and face Vlad myself."

Andreas dropped onto the edge of Kate's desk and swung the steno chair around so that his hands rested on her shoulders. "My vote has to be for Joli. He must know what he's doing. He's in the business, after all. You, on the other hand, could put yourself in danger. If Vlad's chasing an extortionist, he's dealing with tough thugs. I don't want you anywhere near that sort of scum."

"But…"

"No." Andreas cut off her protest. "I can't go down there right now so that's the end of it. You aren't going anywhere that I can't go to protect you."

"That's silly. I…"

Andreas pulled her up from the chair to rest against him. His lips closed over hers, stopping her words and her breath in the same moment. In seconds, her hands curled into the front of his jacket, clinging to him instead of pushing him away.

She knew she should be resisting him. They had been discussing a serious topic. Only she no longer had the will to resist.

Andreas' embrace tightened and his mouth became more demanding against hers, then slid sideways to nibble her neck. He murmured coaxing words and pulled her closer, his hands wandering over her back and hips, feeling her response, growing more insistent as she weakened in his arms.

"I need you, Kati," he whispered against her cheek. "Come back to me. I've been patient. Please. Come to the hotel with me. Now."

She could feel his heart hammering into her breast. Her own breathing was erratic and shallow.

Before she could answer, Gerry's voice called out. "Hey Kate, are you still…ah, ah…"

Red-faced, he stood in the hall doorway, stunned, then realized he was staring and bolted into his own office.

Kate buried her face in Andreas' shoulder, and they stood rigid together fighting to control their laughter.

They could hear him opening drawers and banging things. He seemed to be taking his time over his search.

Kate straightened up and looked at Andreas. Still grinning, he nodded. He put his arm around her as they crossed to Gerry's partially open door. Kate knocked.

Gerry straightened up from a file cabinet drawer and turned to look at them. His expression was grim as he fought to control his emotions.

"This isn't exactly what you think," Kate said. "The emphasis being on *exactly*. The special circumstance here is the fact that Andreas is Ruth's father."

"Your first husband? My God!" Gerry's jaw dropped. Abruptly he shut it and swallowed. "No wonder… I mean…oh, hell."

Kate couldn't help herself. She started to laugh again. "It's not that bad. Getting caught kissing my husband shouldn't be cause for that much concern."

Gerry blushed. "I'm sorry," he stammered. "This is really awkward."

"No one knew, Gerry, including my family. We didn't tell anyone because we're in rather a box about it. I mean, if I confess Andreas is my husband where does that leave my marriage to Vlad? If I maintain my marriage to Vlad is legal, what does that make Andreas and me? So we took the route of least confusion and kept our mouths shut."

Gerry nodded. "That makes sense. Who needs to know anyway?" He looked up. "So this is why Vlad left?"

Andreas shook his head. "No, we don't think so. Vlad suspected who I was and he wasn't happy about it. At first we thought his disappearance might be an attempt to teach Kate a lesson. But Kate has new information today that changes the picture."

Kate nodded, then repeated what she had learned about the extortion scheme from Eddie and Father Darcovich. She concluded by saying she wanted to personally follow Vlad to Gillingsworth in the state of Washington.

"I don't know what he's up to, but I want answers," she said. "I'm not going to leave this to a P.I. if I can do it myself. It was all well and good having him track Vlad down, but if this is the end of the line, I should finish it in person."

"That could be dangerous," Gerry cautioned. "You should let the police do it."

"True," Kate nodded. "But he's done nothing illegal for them to act on. They might be able to trail him as a missing person, but with no criminal connection, where does it fit in their list of priorities? I'm not prepared to wait that long. If I confront him, Vlad will talk to me."

Worry lines creased Andreas' forehead. "That's dangerous, Kate. Vlad is unstable. He's already tried to kill me several times. We have no way of knowing when he might turn on you, too."

"Kill you?" Gerry dropped into a chair. "You're kidding."

Kate shook her head. "I wish he was. I can't prove it, but tampering with his car and an explosion that almost killed the man in the soldering booth Andreas could have been in? What do you think? Especially given Vlad's position here and access to tools."

"I think Andreas is right," Gerry muttered as he struggled to absorb what he'd been told. "If Vlad is that jealous, he's unbalanced. He could easily turn on you."

Kate protested. "But I'm the only one he will confide in. The police certainly won't get anything out of him. I have to try."

"Not on your own," Andreas said. "If you go after him, I'm coming with you."

"That would just make him more jealous," Kate warned.

"True, but I won't let you face him on your own. Washington is pretty remote. I should be safe there."

That was when Kate picked up on Andreas' earlier references to not going to the U.S. "What do you mean, *safe?*" Kate's tone was sharp. "And what about work? You can't just take off like this."

Andreas sighed. "Yeah, well, I haven't told you yet, have I? Seems the Russians have got hold of my fire control designs and now the CIA wants to know how that happened. If I show my face south of the border, I'm likely to be arrested. That's why I'm staying here. The info probably came from a supplier somewhere, but I need freedom to trace the source of the leak myself because they won't look beyond me."

"Control plans?" Gerry blanched.

"Control plans? Oh, my God!" Kate stood looking at Andreas as the missing piece of Vlad's puzzle fell into place. *How dare he? And all over his bloody pride. The rotten, selfish bastard.*

"Are those the same plans we use here to manufacture components?" she asked.

Andreas nodded. "Some of them. What about it?"

Kate moved to the corner of Gerry's desk and sank down heavily, gripping the top to stop her hands from trembling. Even the Nazis hadn't been able to drive her to such fury. Right now, were Vlad to appear in front of her, she was so angry she just might kill him. Tear him limb from limb or run him down with her car.

"I think I know how the Russians got your plans," she said, and turned to Gerry. "What was the date of our burglary? Mid-June, wasn't it? And we thought nothing was taken except a bit of petty cash. But something could have been removed and photocopied, then returned to its file. If that happened, no one would have been any the wiser."

Both Gerry and Andreas were staring at her.

"What if Vlad copied the plans and handed them over to the Russians in order to incriminate Andreas? I mean, he tried to murder him and that didn't work. Sending Andreas to jail for treason would remove him just as effectively as murdering him."

"Oh, shit," Gerry said. "If that's what happened, it's one hell of a way to get rid of the competition."

Andreas stood, shaking his head. "I wish I didn't believe it. I didn't know about any break-in here."

"You wouldn't have," Kate said. "You were gone before it happened and I don't think I mentioned it when you came back. I didn't think it was important. We decided some competitor had stolen a contract bid so they could undercut us. I put the incident out of my mind after that."

"But how would Vlad even get in touch with Russian agents?" Gerry asked. "He always seemed so set against anything involving Communism; I can't imagine him knowing anyone connected to Russian espionage."

"I'm betting that's where the Russian Family Fund comes in," Kate replied.

By the time she finished explaining Bell Canada's investigation into the extortion scheme and Nicholas Tartarinov, Gerry was shaking his head, looking dazed.

"He was such a hard-working, loyal guy, I just can't believe he'd turn like that. But even if it's true, how do you prove anything that will help Andreas?"

"That's why I have to go to Gillingsworth and tackle Vlad myself," Kate said.

Gerry looked worried. "After what you just said? That's too risky. Leave it to the police."

Kate shook her head. "No good. As I said, he won't talk to them. I'm the only one who can get a confession out of him."

"And how will you do that?" Gerry demanded. "Even if you succeed, it would just be your word against his. The police interrogate for a living. Leave it to them."

"The Nazi's used torture, Gerry. They couldn't break him. Rule-bound Canadian cops can't top that."

"And you can?"

Kate's smile was cold. "With proper prodding he'll be only too glad to boast about how he tricked Andreas with his superior planning."

Andreas agreed. "I think she's right, Gerry. She can tape it. Put that with the circumstantial evidence we already know and the police should be able to lay charges that stick. And there's no question of her being alone. I need my name cleared and him off my back. We can fly out tomorrow morning."

Gerry found his missing papers while Kate cleared her desk and prepared to leave. She and Andreas were at the door when she realized they had a telephone problem.

"We can't call Air Canada from my place. Davies has my line tapped," she exclaimed. "We can't let him know what we've discovered this afternoon."

"Not if we don't want him making it official police business and telling us to stay out of it," Andreas agreed.

"Yup. And it gets worse. The Mounties deal with espionage, not the locals. They won't go over the border without co-operation from American authorities, probably CIA, maybe FBI, possibly both. In other words, you'll be arrested before they even get to Vlad. And when they can't break him, they won't worry much because they'll already have you. So, sir, you call Air Canada from here. I'll have to call Rob from here. Somebody has to look after Amos in our absence."

CHAPTER THIRTY-FIVE

Having seen no sign of any storm by the time he passed through Spokane, Vlad continued into Idaho, heading north towards Boddington. He'd use the good weather and the daylight while he had them. He knew he still faced mountains no matter which way he went. He also felt faintly uneasy about being in the States where his Ontario license plate stood out. Down here, with traffic offense fines going to local coffers, there was always the danger of running into a rogue cop. Now was not the time to wind up in jail on some trumped up misdemeanor.

He passed through another blink-and-you-missed-it community and started to climb. The road was narrower than before and Vlad slowed on the ascent. Because it was late afternoon, not even school buses were using the roads, let alone whatever passed for commuter traffic in the area.

He was about five miles into more rugged terrain before he noticed the beige wagon exiting a series of turns on the edge of the village he had just left. Considering the isolation of the place he was surprised to see another vehicle. It was moving quickly too. Must be someone local who knew the road well. Too bad. He wasn't familiar with the road so he wasn't comfortable with increasing his speed. The guy would just have to learn patience.

The road was cut into the side of a mountain. The off side, hidden in the growing darkness, dropped sharply away to the valley below. No guardrails protected unwary drivers from the mile-deep decent they faced at the slightest miscalculation.

With the wagon rapidly closing in behind him, Vlad rounded a steep bend and found himself bumper to tailgate with a dump truck loaded with gravel. Of necessity, he braked sharply, then glanced in his rearview mirror. The wagon was clearly visible now, less than a mile away. He was going to wind up like jam in a sandwich with the truck in front of him and the wagon behind.

Inexplicably nervous, he inched forward, his attention torn between the creeping truck and the headlights of the approaching vehicle. He was sure it was coming on too fast. Couldn't the driver see the damned truck blocking the way?

There was no sound of brakes and no apparent decrease in speed, just a blinding flash of headlights reflecting from his rearview mirror. The wagon had arrived, inches behind him, threatening his tailgate with the slightest mistake. As he cursed silently and waited the chance to pass, he could feel the wagon driver's impatience as keenly as his own.

Unexpectedly, just as the road made a sharp turn, the truck ground to a halt, shuddering. Gravel dribbled from the tailgate and plinked merrily onto the pavement.

Vlad virtually jumped on his brake to avoid colliding with it and laid on the horn. Despite his lack of speed he skidded to within inches of the box before his vehicle stopped. Only then did he allow himself to glance into his rearview mirror. The wagon appeared to be touching his back bumper.

He gave himself a moment to calm down, then blasted the horn one more time. Was the trucker ill? Was there something wrong with his motor? There was no response from either the trucker or the driver behind him. He swore, slammed into park, stepped down from his truck and walked forward.

"Hey," he yelled up at the truck. "Hey, what is wrong? Why did you stop?"

At first Vlad thought the driver hadn't heard him. Then the glass was slowly lowered in the window. He could see the man staring down as though unsure where the voice was coming from.

"Hey, bud. What is going on?" he yelled again, then swung himself up onto the truck step. "Hey, are you okay?"

The man wore a plaid mackinaw and a grubby toque. His five o'clock shadow was heavy around a thick jaw.

"Is something wrong?" Vlad demanded. "Why did you stop here?"

"Can't go no further," the trucker replied.

Exasperated, Vlad waited for an explanation. When he got none, he probed again. "Why not?"

"She stalled."

"Obviously," he muttered to himself. "So what do you plan to do? We cannot get around you."

"Then you'll just have to sit, I guess."

At the speed this fellow thought, they could be sitting all night. Disgusted, Vlad jumped down and headed back towards the wagon.

Rather than an open window and a stream of questions as he expected, Vlad found the driver staring forward, his hands clasping the steering wheel, dash lights casting his face in shadow. The window was firmly closed.

Vlad rapped on the glass and waited. The man rolled it down only a couple of inches. Although he partially turned towards him, Vlad did not get a clear look at his face. When he did not speak, Vlad explained that the trucker wasn't going to be moving.

"I am trapped," he said. "You will have to go first."

The man made no reply, dropped the gearshift into reverse, and began backing up before Vlad had time to move. Then the wagon shot forward, barely missing Vlad with the right front fender. Instantly the taillights blinked and vanished around the next bend.

Shaking, Vlad returned to his cab and cranked up the heater to full. The man was a maniac. He should have seen the problem coming. It wasn't his fault they'd got caught behind the truck.

After a few moments Vlad's nerves settled and he was ready to move on. Carefully he backed up, then eased out to creep along the left side of the gravel truck, scraping off its grey paint with his side mirror.

Just as he came even with the rear of the cab, the driver's door shot open. Vlad heard the impact of metal on metal as the corner of the truck door ripped into the cap covering his truck box. For an instant his truck hesitated, then it lurched forward and swerved further into the opposite lane. The cap fell off onto the pavement.

He was lucky. There was no oncoming traffic. The road ran straight ahead for several yards before it began a sharp sweep to the right to continue its upward climb.

No sooner did he have his truck under control, than he pulled to the side of the road, shaking. He was going to go back there and teach the idiot a thing or two about driving. Maybe he'd get the message about how to treat fellow drivers when he was dangling over the cliff begging for mercy. The fool had bloody nearly killed him.

Vlad's hand was on the door handle when another thought struck him with the impact of the aborted collision. Was that the purpose of the near accident? Was he supposed to loose control and drive over the cliff?

He had embellished Nicholas' fears by saying the Russian mob would put a hit man on his tail. What if it were true? What if Korczak had marked him for elimination as well as Nicholas?

Vlad grabbed the key and re-started the truck. He wasn't taking any chances. Trembling, he slammed the vehicle into gear and burned rubber with the speed of his departure. He'd gone nearly ten miles before he stopped checking his rearview mirror every few seconds.

###

When Kate and Andreas left the factory, they found the threatening skies from earlier in the day had begun delivering snow. The flakes were still small and light, but the weather forecast was for a heavy snowfall over the next twenty-four hours.

"Isn't it the truth though?" Kate grumbled. "The only times they get it right is when the weather's bad. I just hope it clears by tomorrow so our flight won't be cancelled."

Confronting Vlad would be difficult at any time. Knowing she wanted a divorce just made it worse. Somehow, she couldn't face the thought of an evening alone even though she should be busy packing and doing her weekend cleaning. When she suggested Andreas come for supper and bring his laundry, he accepted quickly.

While Kate got their food on the stove, Andreas threw his clothes into the washer and took Amos for a long run in the snow. Supper was ready by the time they returned, both panting from their exertion and covered in melting flakes.

They were half way through their dessert when the telephone rang. "Kids?" Andreas asked.

Kate glanced at the clock. It was after seven. "Maybe." She headed for the telephone in the family room.

She noticed static, then an indrawn breath punctuated several moments of silence. Finally a deep, male voice with a heavy Slavic accent asked to speak to Vlad. She explained he wasn't home and offered to take a message.

"Tell him Olga is gravely ill," the voice said. "She needs medication and we can't afford it. She's counting on him for another shipment we can sell to raise the money she needs to buy it. I haven't the heart to tell her the colonel's son is so cruel and neglects his duty to his family. The disappointment might be fatal."

Her mind whirling in search of a way to probe her caller's identity, Kate pretended Vlad had confided in her concerning his dealings with Korczak.

"He isn't here at the moment but I'll tell him you called, Mr. Korczak. It is Mr. Korczak, isn't it? He'll get back to you the moment he returns. Or he'll give me a message for you. I'm sure he has your number but I'll take it again as a precaution."

The click of the receiver falling into place and the hum of the dead line answered her.

As she came back to the kitchen, Andreas' look of concern told her the shock must be showing in her own expression.

"That wasn't your son, was it?" Andreas said.

Instead of sitting down, Kate turned to the desk by the back window and began to write. She needed to record the conversation before she forgot it. The police should already know the content of the call if their wiretap was working properly. All the same, she was taking no chances.

Andreas came to read over her shoulder. He smiled approvingly as she dated the notes, recorded the time and signed them. He filled both their mugs with coffee and they returned to the table together.

"I guess that confirms what Vlad's mysterious telephone calls were all about, doesn't it?" he said. "Just like Pasternak told you."

Kate chewed her last bite of pie and sipped her coffee. Thinking aloud, she said, "And the remark about needing another shipment. A request for more stolen plans?"

"Probably, but I think we have a bigger problem at the moment," Andreas said. "Korczak now considers you part of whatever Vlad did. You only found out about the Russian Family Fund in the past few days but Korczak doesn't know that. From the way you spoke, he'll assume you and Vlad were in this together from the start. That's not good. You shouldn't be here alone. And then there's the matter of the police monitoring your line. If they're doing what they said, that call is going to set them wondering. They're going to be looking for an explanation. The best we can hope is that the storm will keep them too busy to do it before tomorrow."

"For goodness sake, Andreas," Kate protested. "I've been on my own here ever since Vlad left. No one's going to come hunting for me tonight. Not in a near blizzard."

"Maybe not. Then again, we don't know anything about this Korczak. I'm not happy with this arrangement, storm or no storm. Pack your bag and let me take you and Amos to your brother. Now. Please, Kate. Humor me."

Kate opened her mouth to argue, then stopped. Andreas's expression was grim. Clearly, he was frightened for her. She'd hurt him enough over the years. It wasn't fair to worry him even more when she knew she was always welcome to use Rob and Rachael's spare room.

Kate nodded and began to clear the table. She could be ready to leave within the hour.

# # #

Gaston was still swearing ten minutes after he passed Vlad and the stalled truck. He'd been lucky to see Horbatsky take the road north to Boddington as he left Spokane. Gaston had expected him to stick to the expressway where he could make better time. It had seemed a positive omen. Only, when they reached a nice series of twists appropriate for nudging his target over a cliff, they'd encountered the damned underpowered truck.

Up to that point, he was sure Horbatsky had had no idea he was being followed. He might still be oblivious, but Gaston couldn't take the risk. Now, Horbatsky would be sure to recognize the wagon if he ever saw it again. Even worse, he might have seen Gaston's face.

It was time to find another vehicle. It needed to be fast, easy to control, and inconspicuous. It also needed winter tires, given the storm they were apparently about to face.

He was on the edge of a village when he noticed a roadside diner to his left. It was attached to a small store with a set of gas pumps out front. His stomach rumbled at the thought of food but there was no time for that. He had to locate a car, hot wire it and be ready to follow the moment Horbatsky passed. Or drove in. Horbatsky hadn't eaten for a good while either. Maybe he'd be ready for a meal too.

Gaston pulled up to the pumps and prepared to fill the tank, then remembered he was about to dump the wagon. He moved to the side of the building away from the glare of the overhead lights and parked in the shadow of a big rig.

The lot contained a handful of vehicles, most parked in front of the restaurant. An older model red sedan nestled between the dumpster and the back door offered possibilities. Its location betrayed its ownership as that of a staffer rather than a customer. Perfect. He'd leave the wagon and pick up the car. If it belonged to someone living in the mountains he had no qualms as to its winter readiness. His only worry would be the amount of fuel in the tank since he dare not fill up here.

The plan for exchange completed, Gaston snuggled back to wait for Horbatsky's appearance. His quest ended moments later when Vlad pulled up to the pumps, filled his tank, then moved his truck a few feet further to park before the restaurant. Gaston shook his head in disbelief. Fortune didn't smile on him like this very often. He'd get his meal after all.

#

Kate closed her suitcase and went to the closet for her coat. They'd be on the road in minutes. Andreas was already in the yard giving Amos a final run for the night before they loaded him into the car for the trip to Rob and Rachel.

The phone began ringing as she was making her last survey of the house. Fearing it would be the police, she was inclined to ignore it. She had expected the storm to keep them so busy they wouldn't call before morning. By the fourth ring she remembered Joli and her afternoon conversation with Rob. Was Rob impatient to find out what she had decided? She should answer it and tell him she was on her way over. That wouldn't be incriminating. He'd learn the rest when she arrived.

"Madame Horbatsky? Thank God your brother gave me your number. This is Raymond Joli," a heavily accented voice announced immediately. "I tried to call Rob but I keep getting a busy signal and I can't talk for long."

Kate tried to interrupt him but Joli ignored her. "Vlad is eating and I have to be ready to run when he finishes. I've got some terrible news. He killed Tartarinov this morning, then set out east through the mountains. We're in Idaho now. I don't know where he's headed. Looks like he could be coming home but I can't be sure. I couldn't stop to call earlier or I'd have lost him. I just reported him and I'm expecting the state troopers will catch us on the road. Sorry to hit you with this but I felt I owed you a warning."

Kate stumbled back into a chair, the telephone receiver clutched so tightly she couldn't feel her fingers. Her mind was reeling. Vlad had killed Nicholas? He had finally snapped. The Americans would arrest Vlad but they'd never get the truth out of him about the espionage. Andreas would never be exonerated.

"Wait," she gasped, sensing Joli was about to break the connection. "There's more to this than just murder. Not that the murder should be ignored. I mean, you have to stay with him, keep me informed. It's vital I get to Vlad before the American cops do." She was begging and on the verge of tears.

"This afternoon I discovered he passed over plans for computerized guidance systems, the kind the U.S. uses to direct bombs on their fighter planes. I found out because a friend of mine is being blamed for the leak. I can't let my friend go to jail for Vlad's treachery. I must talk to him. He'll tell me. We need that confession."

"Whoa boy." Joli whistled through his teeth. "Okay, I see what you mean. But it's too late. The authorities are already onto him. I can keep an eye on him as long as possible and I can call when they bust him. That's the best I can promise you."

Kate explained how she and Andreas had been about to join him in Gillingsworth.

"Don't come," Joli advised. "We have no idea where he's headed or how fast he'll travel. I can't begin to contact you if we're both on the road. Stay put and stay packed. I'll give you a destination the moment he's nabbed."

Kate sighed, knowing the damage was done. The police listening to her tapped telephone now knew both her plans and the extent of Vlad's villainy. All they lacked was proof of who had actually stolen and passed on Andreas' plans. "What happened? Was there a fight or something?"

She could hear the reluctance in his voice.

"No, no fight. In fact, Vlad picked the kid up at his rooming house this morning and they went out for breakfast. I'd seen him put his bag in the truck so I suspected he was checking out. Then, when Tartarinov was carrying a bag, too, it was obvious they were heading out somewhere. I followed them north along a road by the river behind the mill. Vlad stopped the truck and when Tartarinov joined him, he hit him with something and tossed him into the river. It's deep there and flows down to the mill holding yard. No question of the kid surviving. Nor will anyone ever see it as anything beyond an accident. He fell into the river and drowned and the bruise on his skull will be attributed to a close encounter with a log after he died."

She couldn't blame Nicholas' death on Vlad's stress, anxiety, depression, or extenuating circumstances. Nicholas' *accident* had to have been deliberate. Just finding a place to stage it required too much planning to be anything else. There was no getting around it. Vlad had shown his willingness to kill months ago when he attempted to kill Andreas. Now he'd followed through with a different victim. The man had to be stopped. Only not before Andreas was exonerated. Now Andreas came first.

CHAPTER THIRTY-SIX

Although the rest of the drive to Boddington proved uneventful, Vlad's nerves were still jumping when he reached the gas station and adjoining restaurant at the edge of town. Even though he was too agitated to stop for long, he needed to pee. He decided to gas up and grab some supper. He'd find a table near the window where he could watch for the truck to pass. Then he'd head out again—in another direction. He should be able to make it over the border in an hour or two.

Annoyed to find the only vacant tables were back by the kitchen, he placed his order and headed for the washroom. He was on his way back to his seat when the door opened with a bang to admit a couple dressed in skidoo suits and heavy boots. Snow filled the creases in their clothing and the frigid outdoors seemed to have followed them inside. Muttering, the man struggled against the blast to get the door closed behind them.

"Hell, will you look out there?" someone at an adjoining table muttered. "Guess they weren't kidding about that storm."

Vlad glanced towards the window onto the parking lot and swore silently. The gas pumps out front had disappeared into a wall of driving white. The overhead sign rode horizontally on the wind. His earlier plan ruined, he knew he had no option now but to spend the night in whatever accommodation the town could offer.

The waitress on cash directed him to The BonAire Motel on the north side of town. She warned him not to expect big city accommodations. One look at the old house covered in green clapboard with a boxy wing of eight units attached to one side told him she was right. It would keep him out of the wind though and reasonably warm—provided the heating system worked.

A young woman with a baby in one arm and a bottle in the other hand answered the bell on the office counter. She glanced at Vlad's license, told him the price and nudged the register in his direction with her elbow. When he laid cash on the desk, she picked it up, lifted the infant to her shoulder to burp him, and spared a moment to hand Vlad a key.

"You're two doors along," she said with a toss of her head to her left. "There's extra blankets in the bottom drawer of the bureau if you need them."

She had already disappeared back into her private quarters by the time Vlad reached the office door.

He drove to his unit and left the headlights on so he could see the lock in the doorknob. He let himself in and switched on a light before returning to his truck for his duffle bag. Fumbling in the dark box behind the cab, he found a bag and dragged it forward. Halfway to the motel room door he realized the bag was not his. He'd forgotten he still had Nick's things. He threw it into his room and returned to collect his own luggage, thankful no one had seen his mistake.

Despite his satisfaction with earlier events, it had been a long day. Vlad cranked up the heater, dug out his shaving gear and toothbrush, then undressed. The room was cool, but he could hear the electric heating element ticking as it warmed up. He was surprised to discover no draft from the front window. With an extra blanket and the heat turned up, he just might have a good night after all.

# # #

Andreas let Amos into the hall ahead of him and paused to step out of his boots. He got no response when he called Kate's name. Her suitcase was waiting by the closet door. He picked it up to take to the car, then set it down again. He suspected she was in the washroom, but Amos had gone towards the kitchen. Knowing the animal had superior instincts, Andreas followed him. Kate was seated at the telephone, staring into space, tears rolling down her cheeks.

He hurried across the room and crouched in front of her. "What's wrong," he demanded.

"Vlad killed Nicholas this morning."

"What? How do you know? Are you sure?"

"Joli just called. He saw it happen. Now they're on the road somewhere in Idaho."

Andreas stood up and pulled Kate into his arms. Even distrusting Vlad as he did, it came as a shock to hear the man had actually succeeded in committing murder. He could only guess how it had shaken Kate. They clung in silence for several seconds before she continued.

"It gets worse. Joli had to report the murder to the police. That means they're on his tail too. We can't possibly get to him before they do."

Andreas stayed silent, unwilling to point out how this worked in their favor by freeing Kate from a marriage she claimed to want to end. Her next words warmed his heart.

"There's no way I can get a confession out of him once he's been arrested. If I tell the authorities what he's been up to, there's no question that they'll interrogate him. But he'll just lie and implicate you, probably send them here to look for you."

He hugged her to him. "It's not your fault. We'll find a way to get the proof. Does Joli know where Vlad's heading?"

"No. Hasn't a clue. That's why I have to stay here so he can get in touch with me as soon as the police pick Vlad up."

"Right." After a moment he added, "We have a new problem. Since your line is tapped, the cops are going to know about this now. We have to talk to Davies."

Kate nodded. "Yeah. First thing in the morning I'll call and arrange an appointment."

"What about Rob? He expected you to be there tonight."

Kate nodded. "I know. The trouble is, I don't want to tell him this yet. And how am I going to tell the kids?"

Andreas nodded. "I understand that but you can't avoid it. Rob and Gerry are your backers with the cops and they have to hear it all tomorrow."

Andreas watched Kate talk to her brother. Obviously the latest developments shocked him too. After a few minutes Kate handed Andreas the receiver.

Rob was blunt. "Are you staying with her tonight? She shouldn't be alone."

Andreas didn't need to consider his answer. "Of course. I won't leave her from here on."

"This does explain Vlad's disappearance," Rob continued. "My fear now is whether this Korczak thinks Kate knows what Vlad was up to."

"I agree. She got a call earlier this evening asking for another shipment for Olga."

"Hell, she didn't tell me that. Make sure the cops know about it. It smells of blackmail or a hit coming on. Either way, Kate's in danger."

"I'm afraid so, and she's stubborn enough to try to stand up to them herself."

"True. The worst part of it is, she is more capable than most. She was a crack shot at one time, and she had combat training. Obsolete now, of course, but still very useful in a tight situation because no one would expect her to know what she does. Unfortunately, that just means she'll take chances she shouldn't, with—or without— police protection."

That Rob shared his opinion of what Kate was likely to do, offered Andreas no comfort. He could see a battle coming on and he wasn't sure how to handle it. He didn't want to try laying down boundaries. That was Vlad's way and Kate defied him. Normally, Andreas appealed to reason and in the past that had worked. This was different.

He found her in the family room by the fire. Kate seemed to have retreated into herself. She was knitting a sock, mechanically working row after row, not speaking and paying no attention to Andreas. Amos laid his head on her knee, then, when she ignored him, too, curled up by her feet.

After an hour of silence, during which Andreas had unsuccessfully attempted to read the daily paper, he went to the kitchen and made a pot of coffee. He'd reached some conclusions and he needed to test his theories on Kate.

Setting a mug beside her, he took her needles from her hands and laid them on the table by her chair.

"Break time." He smiled and backed to his own spot on the couch. "We need to make some decisions before we see Davies tomorrow. We have to ask Davies for protection for you."

"Protection? Don't be silly, Andreas. I'm in no more danger that I was all along. All that's changed is that now we know what's going on. And I'm a lot more comfortable knowing than guessing."

"So, you admit you probably upped the ante tonight by letting Korczak know you are aware of his identity?"

Kate ignored the censure in his voice. "And you know a better way to bring him out of hiding?"

Andreas fought down his temper and managed a reasonable tone. "If Vlad's so spooked that he killed Nicholas, then we have to presume he had a damned good reason. Was it just to ensure Nicholas couldn't betray him to the cops? Or did Korczak order him to take care of Nicholas? And if Korczak ordered Nicholas killed, what do you bet he'll want Vlad dead too? Which is what scares me. After tonight you're just as big a threat to him as your husband is. I know why you did it. The trouble is, it put you in serious danger."

"We have to connect Vlad and Korczak." Kate was angry.

At him or at the situation? Andreas tried to keep control. "Making a target of yourself won't help. Now the police have to worry about protecting you instead of concentrating on finding Korczak."

"If Bell has evidence of a fraud scheme, they already have Korczak's address," Kate countered. "They know where to find him. They just have no reason to connect him to Vlad and the espionage. They need that reason. Without pressure, he's not going to just roll over and admit Vlad gave him plans he could flog to Russia. If he has to take a swipe at me to make them see the seriousness of his involvement, then so be it."

"Damn it, Kati, that's no excuse to be reckless. Proving I'm innocent is no consolation if you're dead."

"Now you're being ridiculous. I can take care of myself."

"Correction. You *could* take care of yourself," Andreas snarled in exasperation. "That was then—when no one knew you were a problem. This is now, and they're certain you're dangerous. What are you going to do if Korczak comes gunning for you?"

"I'll fight back." Kate was defiant. "I have my gun. I know how to use it."

"You *knew* how to use it." Andreas again stressed the past tense. "When was the last time you fired that gun? Is it even in operating condition any more, or has it seized up in its hidey-hole after all these years?"

"It's fine," Kate snapped. "No, I haven't used it much for the last ten years. But there's nothing to stop me getting it out and doing some target practice. Since I have to sit around here and wait, I guess it would be sensible to make sure my aim is as good as it used to be."

"Stop it, woman! That's what the police are for." He was furious by this time. Kate's reaction was exactly what Rob had predicted and what Andreas had feared.

She ignored him and continued in a perfectly reasonable tone. "The police don't have the manpower to guard me. If they put me in protective custody, I'll wind up in a hotel somewhere where Joli can't find me when he needs me. I have to be free to move when I get the call. The real problem will be to get Davies to agree with letting me talk to the American police when they grab Vlad."

Andreas stood up. "I love you but *Gott,* you're an infuriating creature! You just won't see reason, will you?"

"I see reason. It's just a different reason from yours. I see you packed off to jail for something you didn't do because of my husband's madness. I won't sit around wailing for help when I can help myself. I won't turn my back on the cops. I'm not that stupid. But I won't sit back and expect them to do everything. I have to be prepared to look after myself. And that's all I plan to do. Believe me. I love you too, but there's no point arguing about it, Andreas. My mind's made up."

Kate rose and collected the empty cup from Andreas' hands and headed for the kitchen. "I'm tired. Morning will come soon and just getting out of here could be a struggle after all this snow. We should be at the police station early, before Davies gets immersed in other things."

Angry as he still was, Andreas had to admit defeat. All he could do was beg Davies to reason with her. He turned out the lights and headed for the bedrooms behind Kate, then stopped. His suitcase was still in the car ready for their flight. Quietly he turned around and went out to retrieve it.

The house was silent by the time he returned. He went directly to the bedroom Kate said belonged to Alexi. Since he found running water to be soothing, he decided to take a shower before turning in. Kate's bedroom light was out when he came back down the hall. Realizing he couldn't check whether she was actually sleeping without opening her door, he went straight to his own bed leaving the nightlight glowing in the hall.

CHAPTER THIRTY-SEVEN

It was daylight when Vlad awoke. The first thing he noticed was the brightness in the room. The sun was reflecting off the snow through the curtains.

The room was warm now but he felt none of the usual lingering lassitude from a good sleep. He wanted to get back on the road. Padding to the window in his bare feet, he revised his opinion of the motel. The baseboard heaters might have warmed the air, but they'd done little to raise the temperature of the linoleum flooring.

Shoving the curtain aside, he found the snow had stopped but not the wind. Drifts encircled his truck as high as the hood. The street beyond the parking lot was barely visible through a swirling white mist. The message was clear. He wasn't going anywhere until the wind calmed and the plows got to work.

Cold now, he returned to bed and snuggled in. Five minutes of flailing about left him frustrated and wide awake. Knowing he was temporarily stranded, he determined to fill the time formulating his story for Gerry.

Nadia made a good beginning, he decided. He'd say she had called in a panic about her mother. The Russian Family Fund was pestering her and she was afraid they were interfering in Olga's care. No, Father Darcovich would blow that tale out of the water if he ever heard it. So how else could he twist things?

No matter how he juggled his story, it didn't quite work. Someone was always in a position to reveal his lies. Besides there was Kate. Reluctantly, he admitted she would question him more precisely than Gerry and be even more skeptical of his answers. It hurt to admit their relationship had deteriorated this far. Nor was it going to be easy to repair the damage.

Lying under the blankets, he wished Kate were beside him. He was in the mood to make love to her this morning. He wanted to run his hands over her hips, feel the warmth of her skin, watch her eyes open slowly, see the smile on her lips. Yes, he had to admit it. He had come to love his wife. She was stubborn, wrong-headed in fact, but he loved her.

Four solid weeks without her had reaffirmed that point. He had married Kate because she met his needs better than any other woman. She was attractive, smart, hard working, a good homemaker, and a good mother. Marrying her had given him a place in the established community and brought him prestige. He had had no desire to live alone then, and still didn't.

He sat up and threw aside the covers, determined to take a shower, dress, and find some breakfast.

When he finished shaving, he returned to the bedroom in his underwear to collect his jeans and a fresh shirt. He'd done laundry at Nadia's on Thursday so all his clothes would be clean for the trip home.

Cleanliness was almost an obsession with him after living in his own filth for months at a time in the concentration camp. Even the smell of a dirty diaper could turn his stomach, and he had no respect for lazy men who ignored basic hygiene despite having all amenities available to them.

Rummaging through his own suitcase reminded him that Nicholas' carryall still lay by the door where he had tossed it the previous night. Another problem to be dealt with. He straightened the bedding and dropped the bag on top. He had every intention of chucking the bag and its contents into the first dumpster he saw. Regardless, he should check through it. He didn't want anyone finding the clothes and connecting them to Nicholas.

Vlad hauled out underwear, socks, a shaving kit, slippers, several sweat shirts, jeans and a heavy sweater. The moment he saw it, he knew the sweater was handmade. Nice work, too, he thought as he examined it. Then he saw the label below the neckband. Made with love by Mamma, it said—in Polish.

The message puzzled him. Ivana had insisted that Nicholas was not her child. So why sew in such a sentimental label if she cared as little for the young man as she intimated? In fact, why make the sweater at all?

Curious, Vlad turned the bag upside down and shook it. A rectangle of white in a tattered plastic sleeve dropped onto the blanket. The numbers 1958 were written on it in faded blue ink. Vlad turned it over, wondering whose photograph would be so important to Nicholas that he needed to bring it along while he ran for his life.

For an instant he didn't recognize the face. She was thin, gaunt almost. Her hair hung like a droopy rag over her ears. Her cheeks were lined and the chords of her neck were plainly visible above the high-collared dress. Only the eyes were the same, brown, sparkling, mischievous despite the general tenor of neglect about her appearance.

Anna Tartarinovska had changed drastically between their last meeting in 1949 and her encounter with the photographer in 1958.

Stunned, Vlad sank onto the bed and stared at the snapshot in his hand. Although he'd known from the moment he'd first heard Nicholas' name that Anna and Nicholas might be connected, he'd rejected the idea. Even when Nadia confirmed it, he'd refused to believe it. He couldn't ignore this. Why else would Nicholas carry Anna's picture?

Then he realized there was a man beside her smiling into the camera. He was a healthy-looking fellow with ruddy cheeks and good teeth. He had an arm around Anna and she appeared to be leaning against him.

So, she'd found some other sucker to look after her. Vlad's shock turned to anger. He'd always known she was a flirt. He'd seen it often enough. Even as a sixteen-year-old waitress at the *Jar am Zoo* in Berlin, she earned her tips more from smiles and wiggles than exemplary service. He remembered his father had once considered firing her as a threat to the restaurant's reputation for respectability.

    He chose to forget how useful that personality had been in the early days of Berlin's occupation when she used it to protect both herself and his mother from the Russians. Of course he knew how she kept the roof over their heads, the fuel in their wood box, and the rations on the kitchen shelf. At the time, he hadn't cared. He hadn't been above a few questionable acts himself when health and safety demanded it.

    But this? The rage built. She had deliberately sent him off to Canada while she stayed behind and lived it up. She had rejected his offer of marriage in favor of a good time in familiar haunts. She had ignored his letters. She'd taken the money he sent her, but she hadn't come to join him. She hadn't even bothered to tell him she wasn't coming. She'd just disappeared.

    Who was Nicholas' father? Certainly not the man who raised him. Both Nadia and Ivana identified Klaus as her brother from Poland.

    He shivered at the narrowness of his escape. He had loved her deeply, thought her a generous, beautiful woman with a kind heart, treasured the joy she had given him in his youth. Although he had forced himself to bury her memory in favor of his new life, he had always respected her as an honorable woman. Now, he knew differently and his stomach churned with the pain of her treachery.

    Anna was a user. She had used him for her pleasure. The Russians might bring her supplies, but his American

GI's pay packet brought her prestige as well as real money with which to buy goods.

He wondered if she had found someone even more useful before he emigrated. Was that why she stayed behind? So she could live it up with this man?

And Nicholas. Had his father not wanted a woman hampered with a child? Vlad felt a twinge of sympathy for the boy. His own mother had dumped him on her brother so she could run off to play. Damned bitch!

Then Nadia's words echoed through his head again. *His sister was hospitalized with tuberculosis and couldn't look after the baby so she gave him to Klaus.*

Could it be true? He had to admit she did look ill. Such a thing was possible. But likely? No. It was too convenient. Anna just wanted to be rid of a burden. If she really had been ill, why hadn't she told him? He'd have gone home to be with her. No, maybe not. All the same, he'd have sent her money to help with her medical bills.

So where did Nicholas fit in? Was Nicholas his son? Mentally, Vlad shook his head and dropped the thought. She'd become ill after he left. She'd become pregnant after he left too. No. Nicholas could not possibly be his child.

He stared at the photo of Anna, then slipped it into his shirt pocket.

Grabbing up the jumble of clothing, Vlad shoved it back into the bag, zipped it, and heaved it towards the door. His stomach was too riled now to tolerate even the thought of food. As soon as the weather cleared enough, he was getting into his truck and heading east. He needed to get home to Kate.

#

Andreas came awake instantly with no idea what had disturbed him. The room was dark and quiet. The luminous dial on the bedside clock told him it was shortly after three. He lay absolutely still, listening. Because Amos was silent, he knew no one had entered the house. Unless the intruder was a member of the family. He dismissed that possibility too, because even friendly greetings caused some commotion. About to turn over and shrug off his disturbed sleep as imagination, he heard Kate cry out. Then there was a thump. It was followed by a soft whimper from Amos and the sound of his claws on the hardwood floor.

Andreas didn't need an invitation. He leapt from bed and crossed the hall in three long strides, only to discover her door still closed. Then he heard Amos whine and another soft bump jolted Kate's door.

What in hell was going on in there? He turned the doorknob noiselessly and stepped into the moonlit room. Amos met him and licked his hand. He started to walk around the dog and tripped. *A book? In the middle of the floor?*

Kate's voice was low and full of anger. She was flailing at the air and tossing around in the bed. "Get off me, you stupid oaf." The blankets were half on the floor except for a corner wrapped around her hips, trapping her legs. She threw herself sideways, muttering another curse and striking the mattress with her fist.

"Kati." Andreas scooped up a pillow and moved to lean over the bed. What was she dreaming about? "Kati," he repeated and placed a gentle hand on her shoulder. "You're dreaming, *Liebling*. Wake up. It's just a dream."

Her eyes flew open, unfocused and blank. Her fist clenched automatically, then gradually relaxed as she realized who he was. "Andreas. Was I yelling? Did I disturb you? Sorry."

He stepped back. Grabbing the blankets, he pulled them onto the bed, then sat down and asked about her nightmare. "It was about Vlad, wasn't it? What did he do to you?"

Kate turned her face into the pillow and shuddered. "I don't want to talk about it."

"Not good enough. How can I help if I don't know your problem? Come on, Kate. This is me. I don't shock. You know that. You can trust me."

That was when she started to cry.

The tears infuriated Andreas. What had that bastard done to her? He knew the risk he was taking when he slid under the blankets and took her into his arms, but at the moment, stopping the tears was more important.

"Come here, Kati. You're safe with me," he murmured. He pulled her closer, rocking her gently and running a soothing hand up and down her back. The moments ticked by. Ever so slowly he felt her relax. Finally the damp spot on his shoulder began to cool. She had calmed down but her breathing told him she was far from asleep.

He tried again. "Okay? Good. Now tell me what that was all about. What were you dreaming?"

She sighed and pulled back to the other side of the bed. "I knew he had the capacity to be violent. When you sent me the roses—he lost it that night. He raped me. I could have stopped him, probably. But I didn't try. I think I knew deep inside that any resistance would wind up in a fight to the death. And now he's killed Nicholas."

She began to shake. Andreas knew there wasn't a damned thing he could say. Indeed, he was so angry he, too, was trembling. He wanted to strangle the arrogant idiot.

Silently, he hauled Kate back into his arms, tucked her head into his shoulder, and waited for the warmth of his body to soothe her. Given how much she'd been hiding, it was no wonder she'd had a nightmare. What shocked Andreas was discovering that Vlad had attacked her. She seemed so vulnerable, soft, and clinging as she lay against him. What man in his right mind mistreated a woman? Especially a woman like this.

However, that was the key, wasn't it? Vlad wasn't in his right mind. If he attacked Kate for receiving a bouquet, how would he react to hearing she planned to leave him? A cold wave of dread swept over him. He had to get her to a safe place until Vlad was arrested.

Andreas began thinking of hiding places, then remembered the other problem. Kate wouldn't hide. She'd try to face Vlad and get him to admit he'd framed Andreas. Foregoing that confession would probably put paid to any chance of clearing his name, but he'd live with that to protect Kate.

Kate sighed and turned, her steady breathing telling Andreas she had fallen asleep. Her back fitted snuggly against his chest, her bottom nestled in his lap. Quite naturally his arm draped over her waist and his hand clasped her breast. Dear *Gott*, she felt good. It was like old times. Aroused, he leaned over to press his lips to her neck, then stopped.

What in hell was wrong with him? He'd been pursuing this woman for months. Now that she had finally come to trust him again, was he going to pull a Vlad? Take her in her sleep? He loved her, for heaven's sake. He could wait.

While his intentions might have been good, the situation was not. Holding Kate was torture. She needed comfort; he needed space. His slightest movement would disturb her. He gritted his teeth silently and forced himself to lie still, despairing that morning would ever come.

CHAPTER THIRTY-EIGHT

Joli stirred and listened to the wind howl around the corner of the motel. The luminous dial on his watch showed four a.m. At that moment the alarm began beeping. He shut it off and went to the window. In the fury of the storm, he could barely make out the streetlight across the parking lot. At least two feet of snow surrounded his car and Horbatsky's truck.

When he checked in he'd asked the desk clerk to call him the moment the plows arrived. They hadn't come. Nor had anyone entered or left that parking lot in the night. It was strictly training that drove him to confirm his observations. He opened the door enough to stick his head out and see Horbatsky's truck still parked four doors away. He ducked back inside and shivered. His face was wet and he could feel snow on his eyelashes. He took a few moments to dry off, then crawled back under the covers. It looked as though he could grab at least another couple of hours of sleep. No one would be leaving this place anytime soon.

When he awoke again the room was bright, but he knew instinctively that it was from the reflected snow. Breakfast would be a good thing. On the other hand, considering what he'd seen earlier, he was in no rush to move.

He rose slowly, yawned and went to the window. The depth of the snow took him by surprise. His hometown of Timmins didn't usually get this much accumulation even by winter's end. And this was only November.

He dressed and struck off for the front office, wading through the thigh-high drifts, the tops of his ankle-length boots picking up a fresh load of snow with each new step. As he passed Horbatsky's door, Joli saw his truck was buried to the door handles. The unblemished banks told him he was right in assuming Horbatsky had made no effort to depart.

A middle-aged male manned the front desk this morning. He directed Joli to the Eagle's Nest three blocks west of the motel.

"That's the closest eating place," the man said. "And this morning distance counts because you'll be walking. They may have the main drag plowed out. Then again, maybe not. The way that wind's roaring through here things will fill in as fast as they open 'em up."

"How about the road out?" Joli asked.

The other man just shook his head. "They'll need a full day after the wind dies down before things are squared away. The cops won't be lifting the barricades until then."

By the time he reached the diner, Joli's legs ached and his feet were freezing. Snow had blown into any available crevice. Tiny crystals caked his eyebrows, matted the fur on the hood of his parka, and froze the strings that tied it. He leaned against the doorway to yank off each boot and dump the snow packed around his ankles.

The room was warm and the atmosphere friendly. The waitress told him to find himself a seat as she hurried by with a coffee pot in one hand and a plate of bacon and eggs in the other. Hoping to remain inconspicuous in case Horbatsky arrived before he finished eating, Joli opted for a booth near the kitchen entrance.

He was draining his second cup of coffee when a man in a grey wool jacket entered and shook the snow from his hair. There was nothing to distinguish him from other diners lounging at their tables, discussing the storm over a final coffee. Lean, dark, bare-headed, dressed in cords, blowing on his cold hands. Only he wasn't just anyone. He was the man Joli had seen following Tartarinov and Horbatsky from the restaurant in Gillingsworth the previous morning. The one who, according to Millie, might have been following Tartarinov. Only Tartarinov was dead. So why was the man now following Horbotsky? Could it be linked to the espionage thing Mrs. Horbatsky had mentioned? If it were, then the man was probably a pro.

Joli kept his face averted and pretended to be engrossed in the newspaper he had picked up on the counter on his way to his table. He considered leaving, then thought better of it. Despite the protection of a booth, there was a better-than-even chance the man had seen him. Joli could do nothing about it. Having promised to follow

Horbatsky, he could only hope the stranger would not decide to broaden the focus of his undetermined mission.

He ordered a third coffee and headed for the washroom figuring a call of nature would allow him to waste another few minutes. As he exited the washroom, his heart sank. Horbatsky was seated at the booth next to his.

Instinct warned him the situation was dangerous. Horbatsky would be safe so long as he was among others. The attack—if one were planned—would come when he was alone, probably on his way back to the motel.

Much as he was loath to make a target of himself, Joli must keep his promise to Mrs. Horbatsky. There was no avoiding the need to stretch his meal still longer. He ordered a second helping of toast and coffee and settled in to wait out Horbatsky and his tail.

Joli was finishing his toast when the unidentified man left his table and paid his bill. Vlad was mopping up egg yolk and munching the last slice of bacon. He seemed to be barreling through his meal. Joli wondered why he was hurrying. The wind had not abated. He wouldn't be going anywhere soon.

Joli waited five minutes more, then he too, rose and went to the cash register. Once outside, there was no sign of the stranger, but the blowing snow offered plenty of cover. He could be hiding between buildings anywhere between the diner and the motel.

While he had no wish to make his presence obvious, Joli decided he needed to stick close to the diner until Vlad began his return trip to the motel. He crossed the street to the deserted hardware store and inspected the items in its front window without interruption.

He pulled back the cuff of his parka and checked his watch. He'd only been outside for a few minutes but already his ears tingled with cold despite his hood. Judging by Timmins standards, the temperature here was in the forty below range—and that was ignoring the effects of wind chill. Not a day for dawdling outdoors.

Finally, Horbtsky appeared in the diner doorway and struck off towards the motel.

Times like this were when Joli wished he were licensed to carry a gun like detectives on American television. Something told him he might need one. Keeping his head down so that his face was hidden, he let Horbatsky get fifty feet ahead of him before setting out in pursuit. He prayed he wasn't the monkey in the middle.

Joli cursed the storm silently, feeling the cold bite through his slacks despite his long underwear. At the cross streets, the gusts coming down between the buildings almost took him off his feet. Even though Horbatsky was not far ahead of him, at times the blowing snow obliterated him.

The streets were empty of vehicles and foot traffic was negligible. Even the community's dogs were doing their business in the shelter of their owners' back porches.

After a gust died down, the mystery man appeared abruptly, walking some yards behind Horbatsky.

Joli kept his eyes glued to the pair across the street as they all struggled through the drifts. He didn't think the mystery man had seen him. Then again, if he had, he was unlikely to act in front of a witness.

They were almost at the entry to the motel when the stranger closed in until he was only a couple of steps behind Horbatsky. He raised his arm swiftly and swung at Horbatsky's head.

The wind shrieked around the corner of the motel creating another whiteout. Joli couldn't see the front of his own jacket let alone any activity involving two men fifty feet away.

As unpredictably as it began, the wind died. The silence was eerie. Vlad lay on his face, half hidden under a snow-laden shrub. The mystery man was gone. All that remained was a trail of half-filled prints in the snow leading off towards the rear of the motel.

Joli was torn. He had no wish to get sucked into Horbatsky's scheme. Neither would he feel right about leaving the man to freeze in the storm.

Horbatsky groaned and struggled to his knees as Joli arrived behind him. At least the man was alive. While it went against the grain to ignore Horbatsky's condition, endangering his own life made no sense. Joli circled wide and strode on. At the parking lot entrance he stepped behind a cedar shrub and watched.

It took Horbatsky a couple of minutes to get on his feet and a second whiteout obscured his movements. By the time it cleared, he was staggering forward, one hand holding his head as though to ease the pain.

While Horbatsky seemed intent on watching his footing, Joli took no chances on being seen. He moved further behind the evergreen and waited until Horbatsky let himself into his unit before wading the rest of the way to his own door.

###

Kate came awake slowly, warm, and contented with the feel of an arm across her waist. It was a natural reaction to ease closer to the solid bulk of the man behind her.

Then Joli's message filled her mind. Vlad had killed Nicholas Tartarinov and was apparently heading home.

The comfort Andreas had provided through the night was gone in a flash, incinerated by thoughts of Vlad's deceit. To claim he loved her when he was involved in a scheme like this was beyond bearing. She wanted to take her fist to him, rip his hair out, kick him in the balls. He wasn't here though. Frustration boiled up. She needed to do something—anything—to dispel her rage. She'd take Amos for a walk.

She could feel Andreas' warm breath on the back of her neck. He was sleeping. Cautiously, she slid out of his grasp and lay still. He didn't stir. She waited a moment or two to be sure his deep, regular breathing continued, then slipped out of the covers. She saw Amos' ears pick up expectantly when she grabbed up slacks and a heavy top from a chair by the bed. He beat her to the bedroom door but contained his good spirits in silence.

The storm had ended in the night, but several more inches of snow covered the ground. Despite having long passed the puppy stage, Amos jumped and frolicked in the cold fluff. Kate couldn't share his joy at the beauty of the morning. She trudged through the drifts with a determined

Love, Obey & Betray

stride, her hands buried in her jacket pockets, cursing Vlad with each step.

Where was he? How soon would he return? Would the American police catch him before he crossed the border? Her circling thoughts distracted her and she was nearly a mile from home before she realized how far she'd gone.

By the time they returned to the house Amos was soaked and Kate wanted a shower. She set the table, plugged in the coffeemaker, and put the bacon and eggs on the counter before heading for the bathroom.

She had turned off the water and was reaching around the shower curtain for a towel when she heard the toilet flush and the bathroom door close. So Andreas was awake. There was no need to be quiet now. Then she realized that her housecoat and fresh clothes were in the bedroom.

She smiled. Modesty had never been an issue between them and she knew what she wanted. With the towel wrapped carelessly around her, she followed Andreas across the hall.

She found him sitting on the edge of the bed, staring out the window. When he heard her, he looked around, surprised.

"Are you planning to get back under the covers or are you ready for breakfast?" Kate asked.

"You've already sneaked out with Amos. How cold is it?"

She ignored the question and came to stand beside him. "Dry me off." She turned her back and handed him the towel. For a moment there was no response. Then his arms folded the cloth back around her and he pulled her down onto his knee. He brushed his beard along her ear.

"Are you sure, Kati?" His voice was barely above a whisper.

She pulled away and looked at him. His expression was so solemn it hurt.

"Having second thoughts?" she teased.

He didn't smile back. His eyes rested on the chain holding his wedding ring around her neck. He shoved her hair aside, found the clasp, undid it, and caught the ring in his palm. He took her left hand, grasped Vlad's ring and waited, his eyes studying her face.

She nodded. "Yes, Andreas. You win. It's over."

He removed Vlad's ring and reached around her to set it on the bedside table, then caught her hand again. He slid the old ring onto her finger very slowly, whispering the words he had never been allowed to use to her.

"With this ring, I thee wed. For better, for worse, for richer, for poorer, in sickness and health, as long as we both shall live."

She wasn't sure the order was right. It didn't matter. Tears streamed down her cheeks as she removed her ring and slid it onto his finger as far as it would go while repeating his words back to him.

It was hard to tell whose emotions were the shakiest as he wrapped her in his arms and kissed her. The kiss ended way too soon when he pulled back.

"But this isn't enough, you know," he said. "Until I get your name on the paper and my ring blessed by a priest I'm not going to trust this happiness."

Kate leaned forward and nibbled his lip. "That's going to take time. And I don't want to wait. How about you?"

There was no hesitation as he lay back on the bed and pulled her down beside him.

CHAPTER THIRTY-NINE

When Vlad dragged himself out of bed at mid morning, the wind had died down but the sky was still heavy with clouds. His belly reminded him that he hadn't eaten for hours and his head was still sore to the touch.

He had heard heavy trucks in the night and assumed the plows were busy. Then, shortly after daybreak he heard another familiar sound, that of a snow blower practically coming through his door.

When he finished dressing he opened his curtains and saw that both the motel parking lot and the sidewalk in front of the units were thoroughly cleared of snow.

While checking out, he learned that the road north was still closed. Unwilling to wait for them to get it open, he decided to cross the mountains into Montana and head home that way.

He'd had a bad night wrestling with the question of how he'd struck his head. Since he couldn't remember slipping or tripping, he could only assume someone had hit him. That left the issue of who and why. The only logical answer seemed to be that Korczak had sent someone after him. He'd need to be more cautious.

As he waited for his vehicle to warm up, Vlad glanced down at Nicholas' bag lying where he'd dropped it onto the truck floor. Hungry or not, he didn't want to make any stops until he was rid of it.

The clear condition of the street confirmed how active the snowplows had been throughout the night, pushing back the snow banks and opening up the drifts. Everything considered, he should have a decent drive today. He switched from defrost to heater and put his truck in gear.

He followed the street out of town until it intersected with the road to Montana. It seemed clear, and in no time, he was twisting his way through still more mountains. Wary of being followed, he kept glancing into his rearview mirror. He saw no one. Less than an hour after leaving Boddington, he hit a stretch of road cut into the rocks on one side with a long, steep drop on the other. He stopped and heaved the navy canvas bag over the side. The snow would hide it until spring. By then, everything should have rotted away.

A few miles further east he found a gas station with an attached diner advertising all-day breakfasts. He ate a filling meal and followed it up with two cups of coffee to wash down his headache pills.

When he came back out of the diner, the light reflecting off the snow bothered his eyes even though there was no actual sunshine. He dug dark glasses out of the truck's glove compartment and settled down for eight hours behind the wheel. It shouldn't take quite that long to get to Great Falls. He'd eat there, then take the intersecting northern road to Canada.

Watching for pursuit grew tiresome, especially when traffic was so sparse. Perhaps that was why it was mid afternoon before he first noticed the two vehicles a couple of miles behind him. One, a newer model black American car, resembled one he had seen at the motel. The other was an old red sedan. When they were still there half an hour later, he began to panic. He reminded himself he was on the interstate. Of course there'd be other vehicles behind him. Moreover, there was no reason to expect them to catch up with him given that he was speeding. Speeding? Cops. Damn it. He eased off the gas in case one of them was an unmarked cruiser, then remembered that there were no posted speed limits in Montana. All the same, this was no time to test some state trooper's definition of a safe and prudent pace.

When the red car passed the black one and began to gain on him, he tensed, braced for trouble. Was Korczak's man about to attack him again? He debated increasing his speed, then decided against it, loath to attract attention if the driver was merely a fellow traveler in a hurry. Only after the car caught him, passed, and eventually disappeared into the horizon did he realize he was wringing wet and his clenched fingers ached from gripping the steering wheel.

He checked on the black car, realizing he had ignored it while concentrating on the red one. It had gained a little but was still more than a mile behind him.

The sun was sinking into the clouds when Vlad crested a hill and saw the red car parked by the side of the road ahead. He was about a quarter of a mile from it when he heard the first crack. Something hit the front bumper. His first thought was that a flying stone had struck him. Only there were no passing vehicles.

He panicked. A second crack sent shards of windshield flying onto the dashboard. A neatly punched hole appeared in the glass to the left of his face.

Dear God! He was being shot at! Was the marksman behind a snow bank? If so, which one? Or was he in the stopped car?

Fear clawed at the back of his throat. Vlad could barely breathe. He had no place to hide. Braking would only make him slower, and therefore less maneuverable.

Nor would he benefit from turning around. He'd passed no intersecting roads for miles. Crazy or not, he had no option. He must continue towards his attacker. He stomped the gas pedal and began to weave up the road, jerking back and forth across the pavement in hopes of presenting a more erratic target.

He caught no glimpse of the car's driver when he roared past it, but a third pop told him another bullet had found its mark. He was far enough up the road to wonder if he was safe when yet another bullet pinged into metal somewhere behind him.

Over the next hour he drove with one eye on his mirror and the other on the road, terrified lest the red car reappear. While the vast spaces seemed deserted, he took no comfort in that illusion. There was just enough roll to the countryside to conceal a tail, especially in the gathering darkness.

His mind in turmoil, Vlad considered his situation. In retrospect, the gravel truck incident could not be dismissed as a mere coincidence. Nor had yesterday's head injury resulted from any accident. He had warned Nicholas that stealing funds destined for the KGB was dangerous. Now he, too, was caught in their trap. All because of one stupid kid who thought he could outsmart his masters.

His foot to the floor, Vlad raced east through the darkness, his mind busily reviewing his options while his eyes darted repeatedly to the road behind him. He needed to shake off his tail. But how?

He could head for home as fast as possible. The Canadian border was only a couple of hours north of him along flat, open roads that invited speed. Unfortunately, those empty stretches would provide him with no concealment while offering his pursuer ample opportunity to finish his job without witnesses. The shooter was bound to have noticed his Ontario plates and he would expect that move.

Vlad concluded that his best chance of escape would be in doing the unexpected. Instead of bee lining for the border, he'd head for Great Falls. It was fairly large and only a couple of hours south. Then he'd work his way to Chicago. It would be a long drive, but traffic was heavier that way, and he'd have more opportunity to lose the red car.

He kept his foot to the floor until the glow of streetlights on the horizon told him he was approaching

Havre. While the town was small, it would have a gas station and he'd need more fuel before he reached Great Falls.

The first gas pumps he saw sat in front of a general store with a service station attached to one side. Thoughts of food made Vlad realize he had not eaten since breakfast. He was too tense to be hungry, but he was thirsty. He left his truck with the attendant filling it up and hurried inside to pick up some fruit and a bottle of pop.

His purchases hastily picked out, he turned towards the cash register and stopped short. Directly above the burly cashier's head hung a sign that read HUNTING LICENSES AVAILABLE HERE. The glass showcase directly below the register was stocked with ammunition of various calibers.

Feeling his guardian angel had directed him to the store, Vlad made his decision instantly. He'd pick up a pistol and ammunition. He needed to protect himself. He'd have to sleep at least once before he reached any major cities big enough to hide in and having a gun under his pillow would make him feel a lot safer in whatever motel he chose for that stop.

The store clerk grinned and shook his head. "Handgun? Nobody tries to bring down antelope that way. You're not from around here, are you? You want game, you want a good old thirty-thirty."

He turned and motioned for Vlad to follow him around a corner to the rear of the store where a rack of hunting rifles was mounted on the wall.

While this wasn't the type of weapon Vlad wanted, he apparently had no choice if he intended to arm himself. Common sense said he should. He hefted three of them quickly to check their balance and sighted down their barrels before deciding on a Remington. He would like to have tried it out before making a final choice, but that, too, was impossible. He needed to get back on the road. He handed over cash for his purchases and waited impatiently for the receipt needed to get the gun across the border, then almost ran back to his truck.

There was no sign of any red car. Relieved, but not convinced he was safe yet, Vlad got back behind the wheel and took the highway south. Once he hit the big city he'd go to ground someplace where the gunman wouldn't even think of looking. He hoped he could figure a way to get his newly purchased rifle into his room for the night.

Gaston cursed softly as he drove through the twilight. He was furious with himself for his poor choice of location earlier in the afternoon. He should have known better than to try aiming directly into the setting sun. Now his target was warned. He'd be more difficult to trap in a situation that could be made to look accidental.

Gaston glanced once again at the map of Montana spread out on the seat beside him. It showed no intersecting roads until well past Havre. That's where Horbatsky would probably turn north to Canada. Then again, he was a tricky bastard. He might not. He just might head south to Great Falls and continue eastward through the U.S.

While he didn't want Horbatsky to see headlights tailing him, neither did Gaston dare let him get too far ahead. Traffic was so sparse he felt safe to shut off his lights whenever he crested a rise. Once he was sure Horbatsky couldn't spot him, he'd turn them back on and press on as fast as the little red Toyota would go.

He needed a different vehicle, too, since Horbatsky was sure to recognize this one now. The empty road offered no place to ditch the car and replace it with something else. He was getting frustrated by the time the dim glow in the sky announced his approach to Havre.

When he began to see buildings, he slowed down. Now he must blend with any passing traffic while keeping watch for Horbatsky.

Seeing the well-lit gas pumps, Gaston looked at his gas gauge and decided to fill up while he could. He had his signal on to turn in when he recognized Horbatsky's truck at the pumps. Changing his mind, he slowed to a stop in a driveway some yards further along the road. The truck appeared empty. Gaston drew back onto the road and continued driving until he spotted another gas station. He filled up and continued east.

He was almost at the intersection with the north-south throughway when he saw the large parking lot of a truck stop. Finding a vacant spot between two semis, he turned off his lights and waited. A few minutes later Horbatsky's truck pulled to a stop at the intersection, then turned south.

Gaston was about to turn the key in the Toyota's ignition, when he noticed a blue half-ton pull away from the pumps and circle the lot looking for place to park. The truck was barely stopped before the driver's door flew open and a blond stepped out. Her short jacket hung open revealing a small apron and she carried a matching cap in one hand. Gaston didn't need to see her saunter casually towards a side door to realize she was a waitress starting her shift.

He wasted no time folding his map and lifted his duffle to his shoulder. Glancing around to be sure he was alone, he got out and crossed quickly between the parked vehicles. He opened the truck door and grinned at his good fortune. The woman had left the key in the ignition. He took a moment to adjust the seat and mirrors to his liking before starting the truck. Then, comfortably settled, began heading towards Great Falls mere moments behind his quarry.

###

Morning found Vlad rested if not relaxed. He was sure Koczak's hit man was still out there. He just had no idea where. Indeed, he feared the accursed bastard might keep hunting him even after he got home. At least in Milton he could go to the police and spin them a line that the assailant couldn't refute without exposing himself. All he had to do was get home safely.

Vlad paid little attention to his fellow patrons when he entered the hotel dining room before sunrise. He had decided to push hard today and aim to make Fargo by midnight. He'd stop for a few hours rest there, then get up early again and strike off for Minneapolis and Chicago. He'd feel safer once he had more traffic to hide in.

Knowing he wouldn't be making extra stops, he forced down a bacon and egg breakfast he didn't even taste and set out. Traffic across Minnesota was heavier than it had been the previous day, but thankfully there was no sign of the red car.

Mid morning he spotted a black car that looked suspiciously familiar. Worried, he checked his mirrors more frequently over the next half hour. Then the vehicle turned into a driveway and he scolded himself for being so suspicious. The road was full of black cars. It was red cars he needed to worry about.

Having stopped for gas and a sandwich only twice during nearly eighteen hours of driving, he reached the western edge of Minneapolis exhausted and nervous. He knew he needed nourishment or he'd collapse. He circled several blocks before finding the sort of motel he wanted. Most of the units were filled and there was a twenty-four hour diner across the street.

He asked for a wake-up call when he checked in, tossed his bag into his room and headed off to get food. He'd bring the rifle in from the truck on his return. Worn out mentally and physically, he barely noticed the patrons around him as he wolfed a hot beef sandwich washed down with a cold beer. Feeling more tired when he finished than when he began eating, even the cold air couldn't revive him as he left the diner and staggered back over the snow banks to his room. He collapsed on his bed, still planning to be on the road by four a.m.

CHAPTER FORTY

Joli turned left into a plaza opposite the Triple M Motel and parked at a convenience store. Through his back window he could see Horbatsky's truck in front of the motel office. He was hungry and exhausted after hours on the road employing every trick he knew to conceal his surveillance. Horbatsky must be just as tired. Joli wondered how long he'd allow himself to rest.

In a matter of minutes Horbatsky returned to his truck and moved it to a spot near the rear of the building. Joli watched him carry his bag from the truck and toss it into his room, then cross the nearly full lot, and disappear over the snowbank towards the diner across the street. Now it was his turn to check in.

Joli crossed to the motel and circled past Horbatsky's truck before entering the office. While it was a step above the cheap joints available in most cities, it wasn't high class either.

"I see my buddy in room 15 has already arrived," he said as he finished signing the register. "Just so I'm ready, what time did he put in for our wake-up call?"

"I've got him down for four am," the clerk replied.

Joli groaned. "Damned early bird. Probably wants a leisurely breakfast. Okay. Give me a call at three forty-five, so I can at least have my eyes open before he starts pounding on my door."

Joli eased his rented car into his assigned spot and walked the few yards to where Horbatsky had parked his truck. One look at the hole in the windshield explained Horbatsky's erratic maneuvers the previous day. He'd guessed right. Horbatsky had been avoiding a gunman.

He had no doubt that the driver of the red car he had seen parked by the road was the culprit. Moments after Horbatsky raced off, that same driver had recklessly pulled back onto the road directly in Joli's path, forcing him across the centre line to avoid a collision. Then he, too, had roared off into the early evening. Although Joli had his suspicions about the driver's identity, he'd been too busy avoiding an accident to get a look at the man's face. He could only speculate it was the same guy who had attacked Horbatsky in the snowstorm.

Joli returned to his car, collected his belongings, and entered his room. He threw his case down by his bed and looked at his watch. Since it was too late to call Mrs. Horbatsky, he decided to visit the diner across the road. The place was unlikely to be crowded at this hour, but so far, Horbatsky had had no reason to identify him. Besides, he must be worn out. Joli had no fear he was exposing himself by eating in the same restaurant with his target.

He saw Horbatsky sitting by the kitchen doorway when he entered the diner. Joli was still eating when

Horbatsky walked to the cash register, then moved unsteadily toward the exit. He looked so exhausted Joli wondered if he'd be able to get up when he got his call at four am.

#

Vlad woke before the desk clerk called. Refreshed by six hours of solid sleep, he showered, and planned his drive. He'd check out and grab a sandwich at the diner across the street. Then he'd be on his way.

His bag slung over his shoulder, he opened the door, and stopped in mid stride. His truck was gone. He had parked right outside his unit. Hoping he was just confused, he scanned the row of vehicles either side of his door. It wasn't there. It had disappeared. But how? Surely he'd have heard anyone tampering with it. He didn't sleep that soundly. Did he?

His mind raced as he tried to remember hearing any sounds during the night. Nothing. Frustrated, he returned to his room and sank into the chair by the bed, his keys in his hand. Someone had hot-wired his truck and stolen it. Damn his luck! Now how was he going to get home?

He could always buy another vehicle of some sort. Perhaps an old clunker that would survive the trip. That would be expensive, however, and he was starting to run low on cash. Besides, he must report the theft to city police if he wanted to make an insurance claim for it.

Panic struck when he recalled the rifle under the seat. The police would be full of questions when they found that. Not if it hadn't been fired, he reassured himself. Lots of Americans kept firearms in their vehicles, especially if they travelled long distances alone. He mulled his options for several more minutes before deciding not to make a purchase here. He would shop at home so he could count on service later.

So what other options did he have? He considered calling Kate to come and get him, then rejected the notion. It was too far. It would take too long. He needed to get over the border as quickly as possible.

Joli awoke early, scurried into the shower, and finished shaving before he heard the phone ringing. He dressed and donned his boots, planning to leave when Horbatsky did. Though he'd like a bite to eat before he started his day, that wasn't likely to happen. Then he remembered the coffee and snack table he'd seen in a corner of the office when he'd checked in. Maybe he could grab something there.

He pulled back a corner of his curtain and peeked across to where Horbatsky's truck was parked. It was gone. The wake-up call had been set for four, and it was only three fifty-five.

Joli grabbed his coat and hefted his bag to his shoulder. He was still fiddling with buttons as he rushed out the door. He had just thrown his bag into his trunk when Horbatsky's door opened. Startled, he jumped in behind the wheel and waited. Horbatsky's bewilderment was apparent, even from across the parking lot.

So only the truck was gone. Was the theft strictly coincidence? Had Horbatsky been so tired he left his keys in the ignition when he turned in, and that made it too tempting a target of opportunity for some local thief to resist?

Joli considered calling in the cops in case it was a setup preparatory to killing Horbatsky, then discarded the idea. He hadn't seen the guy in the red car. Only instinct made him connect the missing truck with the previous attacks. He had no desire to open that can of worms with American authorities.

Besides, Mrs. Horbatsky was his client and she wanted her husband home to answer for crimes he had committed in Canada. While he would have preferred to keep his distance, playing Good Samaritan shouldn't get him seriously involved. Frustrated, he got out and crossed the parking lot.

"You look troubled," he said as he stepped up on the sidewalk in front of Horbatsky. "Is something wrong? Can I help?"

Horbatsky shot him a suspicious look. "My truck's gone." He held up his hand with the keys. "Somebody must have hot-wired it. Did you hear anything in the night?"

Joli shook his head. "Nope. But then, I sleep pretty sound." He hesitated, then continued. "You need a lift to the police station?"

Horbatsky eyed him seriously, then shook his head quickly. Joli was relieved to see he had no interest in involving the police.

"I can't wait around for them to find the two-bit punk responsible for this. I need to get home," he said. "I'll report it here, then grab a bus."

"I'm leaving too, but I'm not on a tight schedule," Joli said. "I can take you to the station. The desk clerk can probably direct us."

As Horbatsky stared at him, Joli could almost see the wheels turning in his mind. Finally, he nodded and began walking towards the motel office. Joli retrieved his car, parked it by the office door, and went inside. He could hear Horbatsky on the phone as he checked out.

The clerk seemed flustered at the theft. "We never have trouble," he kept repeating. "We're a respectable place. Nobody's had anything stolen from here in all the time I've been working. That's fifteen years."

Joli interrupted him long enough to get directions to the bus station, then headed for the coffee and rolls.

Horbatsky finished his call and turned to the desk clerk. After returning his key, he asked about transportation. "What's the best way to get east?"

"East where?"

"Toronto."

"Where?"

Joli could see the clerk had never heard of the place. The man frowned as Horbatsky explained that it was a Canadian city east of Detroit. He considered before replying. "Don't know for sure, but my guess would be the train. Schedules may be less frequent, but they're faster, and with yesterday's storm around Chicago, highways east may not be so good just now."

The advice made sense given the snow they had encountered in the past couple of days.

#

They went out the door together. Vlad watched his new friend carefully, suspicious in case he were actually Korczak's hit man. If that were the case, keeping him close was pure self-defense.

As they started down the steps a dark cab pulled out of the parking lot across the street and slowed to a stop at the motel door. The driver rolled down his window and called to them.

"Which one of you guys called for a cab?"

Vlad shook his head. "Not us."

The cabbie eyed him suspiciously. His displeasure showed as he put the vehicle in park and went into the motel office in search of his passenger.

"Let's get going," Vlad urged his new friend as soon as the motel door closed on the cabbie's heels. "No sense paying him for a trip he doesn't have to make."

He was pleased that Joli took the hint. His vehicle already sat at the curb by the office door, and they were pulling into the street by the time the cabbie reappeared.

The telephone rang twice as Kate set the pot back in the coffeemaker, lowered the heat under the frying pan and turned off the radio. At this hour it could only be Joli. Why was he calling again? They'd already talked at suppertime.

Hearing Vlad's voice caught her completely by surprise.

"I haven't got long," he began. "I have to catch a train. That's why I'm calling. I can't get a connection straight home but I can get to Toronto by noon on Wednesday. I need you to meet me."

He sounded a bit stressed, but not enough to make up for his assumption that she'd drop everything and fly to his command. Kate wanted badly to refuse and hang up, but that wouldn't solve her problem. She needed to portray complete ignorance. All the same, she could let him hear some annoyance in her tone. That would seem natural.

"Oh, so you've decided to come home, have you? Where the hell have you been for the past four weeks? And what's happened to your truck? You drove away. Drive back." Not terribly sympathetic of her, but she was controlling her voice so that it betrayed only a bit of her anger.

"Somebody stole my truck last night," Vlad replied, ignoring her temper and her curiosity.

"Stole your truck? How did that happen?"

Vlad's explanation was cryptic. Kate wanted more. "Just what are you doing in Minneapolis, anyway?"

"I'm hiding. Some madman is trying to kill me."

So Vlad shared Joli's interpretation of the incidents earlier in the week. Kate continued her feigned ignorance. "And what did you do to upset someone that badly?"

"I don't know."

Liar. He knew all right. The trouble was getting him to admit it. He didn't know she knew the truth about his father's mistress. Could she break down his guard by pretending to be jealous over Olga?

"Might it just possibly have something to do with Olga?" she asked sarcastically.

She heard his breath catch and there was a pause before he replied. "Olga? Who is this Olga? What would she have to do with me?"

There was tension in his tone but he was sticking to his story. She pressed harder.

"That's what I want to know. Why would some man call here asking for you and saying that Olga needed another shipment?"

"I know nothing…"

Kate cut him off. "Might he have been referring to the break-in at work in June? It wasn't a competitor trying to find out our prices. It was you stealing part of Andreas' blueprints for the Russians, wasn't it?" Silence. She continued her accusations. "When you couldn't kill him in the *accidents* you rigged, you framed him for treason. What good would that do you? Did you think I wouldn't find out what you'd done?"

"You don't know anything," he snarled. "All you see is your wonderful German. Well, not again. This time the German won't get my wife."

He changed the subject. "My train gets to Toronto around seven Wednesday morning. I will expect you to meet it."

"Given that you framed Andreas, why should I care about you?"

"Because if you don't, the whole town is going to know their precious Kate Cameron isn't any wonderful war bride. She was a German whore." There was only an instant's pause before he continued. "And don't even think of trying to run off with the bastard. I will kill you both before I allow that. Understand?"

Even though she could clearly read between the lines, there had been no confession. The police might not even take his threats seriously unless and until he actually attacked her. Obviously she was in for a fight if she wanted out of their marriage. That battle would come later.

Right now, it was one step at a time. Davies seemed to believe her. What Joli had seen should give the police grounds to charge Vlad with Nicholas' murder. Bell had evidence to link both Vlad and Nicholas with Korczak. Surely the police could play one off against the other until one of them cracked. If they couldn't actually prove Andreas innocent of espionage, they could at least raise huge doubts about his involvement. Eventually, Vlad would have to be handed over to the Americans, of course. For now, all she could do was get him home to start the whole process.

"Okay. You win," she said. "What train are you on? I'll need to know which platform to go to."

He took her defeat in stride and told her to meet the Chicago train. The line went dead without so much as closing words, never mind any words of endearment.

Andreas stood in the doorway unzipping his jacket, Amos' leash draped over his arm. Amos pushed around him, leaving a trail of wet paw prints across the kitchen floor. "From your end of that conversation I'd say you were talking to Vlad. What did he want?"

"Me to come and get him in Toronto on Wednesday morning."

Andreas frowned. "Why did you agree?"

"So we can get him back this side of the border."

"And what about the police? At what point are you going to get them involved?"

"As soon as I can speak to Davies," Kate replied. "It's over between us, but the only way to clear you is by breaking him."

Andreas didn't try to hide his concern. "I don't like it. You'll be in danger all the way from the station to wherever the police arrest him. And what about during the actual arrest? Do you think he's going to just sit there and let them take him? Don't be silly. He'll explode, and you'll be his first target because you betrayed him."

"We'll leave it to the police to solve that," Kate said and picked up the telephone receiver again. "Good thing Davies is working days this week. We won't have to waste time explaining the background to a stranger."

CHAPTER FORTY-ONE

Gaston followed the black sedan from a secure distance. When he saw the driver pull into the train station parking lot, he left his hijacked cab by the curb and walked the final block, his suitcase in his hand.

He saw the driver drop Horbatsky at the station door and drive away. Inside, he watched while Horbatsky made a telephone call, then went to buy a ticket. The departure schedule posted on a sign hanging from the ceiling told Gaston which train he needed. It didn't leave for nearly an hour.

He went to the coffee shop and bought a pre-breakfast snack. He took his time over it, concealing his face in the depths of an old newspaper when Horbatsky's friend came to buy coffee and a doughnut. Now that was interesting. What was he doing here?

The train arrived late from the west. Getting a seat was easy before dawn. Everyone was still asleep. Gaston tucked himself into a corner by the door to the car in which Horbatsky and his friend sat.

His mind rolled possibilities like dice. Was this friend just happenstance? Someone who had accidentally seen Horbatsky pick himself out of the snow at the motel? Or was he a cop watching Horbatsky because of something else?

In setting up their contract Igor had not referred to anyone else being involved with the two men. Did he know more than he was telling?

Gaston disliked dragging in superfluous targets. At the same time, he knew he'd be a fool to ignore a witness. He decided to wait and watch. He needed to understand the relationship between Horbatsky and his mysterious friend.

It was mid afternoon before the train arrived in Chicago. Darkness had closed in and passengers were pushing and scrambling to disembark. Everyone seemed unhappy because of the late arrival. The station was crowded and luggage slowed Gaston down as he elbowed his way after his target into the reception lounge.

He noticed and ignored a cop near the ticket counter talking to a Redcap. The interesting part was Horbatsky's reaction. He, too, saw the uniformed officer and immediately ducked into the men's washroom. The lawman was gone when Horbatsky reappeared ten minutes later. Then he approached the counter and purchased a ticket to Toronto.

Horbstsky and his friend had taken separate seats for their ride to Chicago. Once off the train, they'd gone different ways. In the station, too, they had remained apart. Either they were deliberately isolating themselves from each other, Gaston concluded, or they truly were just passing acquaintances.

With a couple of hours to kill before the Toronto Amtrak left for Detroit, Gaston decided to call Frederick and ensure he had received complete details about his mission.

"Just got a few minutes to spare before we continue our trip," he announced when Frederick answered his telephone. "The major component of the assignment has been completed. The second half will be dealt with between here and home. I'm calling because a third party has appeared on the scene in the past couple of days. I'm saying *appeared* because it could be total circumstances. Was anyone else involved that you failed to mention when we began this arrangement? Anyone else I should be aware of?"

The answer was immediate, but not what Gaston expected. "The wife is apparently aware of her husband's activities," Frederick said. "We want her added to the contract."

Gaston was startled. Only once before had he been asked to remove a female.

"Very well. I assume the same conditions and payment schedule applies. Do you have pertinent information available for me?"

"At this moment, no," Frederick replied. "However, I believe you can collect your own material based on what you know about her husband. For starters, you have addresses for both work and home."

Gaston remembered the description of Horbatsky's lifestyle that he had originally been given. They lived in a secluded country house and their children were grown and gone. Husband and wife worked in the same company in a nearby town. Yes, removing the wife too, should prove simple enough.

"Very well," he said. "The new goal should prove as achievable as the original ones. I just wanted to be sure about this third party. I don't believe in complicating things unnecessarily. Likewise, loose ends can be a nuisance."

"That will have to be your call," Korczak told him. "I have no additional information to offer that will help with your decision."

Gaston left the phone booth and returned to the waiting area adjacent to the boarding platforms. Picking up a newspaper and a paperback from a newsstand, he found himself a seat and pretended to become engrossed in his reading. Horbatsky was settled on a bench near the boarding platform doors with a magazine.

The first call for the Toronto train was echoing over the public address system when Gaston saw the mysterious unidentified man lingering by the phone booths. If he were not involved somehow, Gaston reasoned, he should not still be here.

Horbatsky had chosen a nice window seat in the middle of the car and stowed his suitcase overhead. He had eaten and appeared to be engrossed in his magazine.

Gaston again placed himself near the doorway in the adjoining passenger car. Through the glassed doors, he could see passengers moving around, changing seats, making trips to the washroom, generally settling in for a lengthy journey.

It came as little surprise when Horbatsky's friend appeared seconds before the train doors closed and positioned himself at the rear of the car. Gaston wondered if Horbatsky realized the man was still with him.

Passengers relaxed over the next couple of hours. One by one, conversations died away, reading lights blinked off. Near midnight, Gaston shuffled slowly through two cars to a washroom. On the way, he saw only a handful of fellow passengers were still awake.

Back in his seat he snuggled into his jacket, pulled the collar close to his neck so it partially concealed his face, and set his mental alarm for four o'clock. That was when people slept soundest—their body rhythm at its lowest.

When Gaston roused, the place was silent except for half-strangled snores from someone at the other end of his car. The only illumination was from small lights near the floor designed to help passengers reach the washroom safely.

He let himself into Horbatsky's car silently and closed the door. Here, too, all was quiet and dim. He could see no signs of wakeful passengers as he made his stealthy way down the aisle.

When he arrived where he had last seen Horbatsky, he almost gasped. The seat was empty. The man in the aisle seat was still there, wheezing quietly, but the place beside him was vacant.

Squeezing past his companion would likely have wakened the man, Gaston realized, so Vlad had chosen not to return and disturb him again.

Cautiously Gaston worked his way on towards the door to the next car, pausing by each seat to ascertain that Vlad was not its occupant. He repeated the process throughout the next car and the third. He passed the washroom and opened the door to yet another passenger car. Vlad was tucked into the corner of the car's last seat. As far as Gaston could tell, he was sleeping.

Gaston pulled on his leather gloves and flexed his fingers to stretch the material comfortably. The carpeted floor made no sound. He moved forward purposefully as though on a perfectly normal task, and eased into the seat opposite Vlad. This was the tricky moment when instinct might warn his target of danger.

He was barely in place when Vlad sighed heavily and uncrossed his legs. Gaston froze, his hands poised to strike. Vlad relaxed. So did Gaston. He inched forward until he was directly across from Vlad. One hand covered his mouth. Simultaneously, the fingers of the other violently gripped his throat, pressing on the carotid artery, shutting off the flow of blood to the brain. Vlad went limp almost before Gaston finished counting off the mandatory seconds required for the hold to cause death.

The faint sound of a door closing behind him warned Gaston that he was no longer alone. Thankful the high seat backs would conceal him from whoever was approaching, Gaston dropped back and feigned sleep.

Moments later the conductor passed, entered the next car, and closed the interconnecting doors.

Gaston glanced around. The surrounding passengers slept on, oblivious. He needed rid of the body. Outside, the darkness hid all details of the passing countryside. It also told Gaston they must be in an isolated location since there were no lights. The train was rattling along at speed, obviously far from a station.

He removed his coat, dragged Vlad to the aisle seat, then stood up, and propped him against the doorjamb. With one arm under Vlad's arms and the other hand manipulating the door latch, Gaston hoisted him out into the alley between the cars and closed the inner door. Then he opened the outer door to the steps. The wind whistled around the cars. The wheels clacked softly, their rhythm deadened by the snow covering the steel rails. A fine mist of white drifted up to engulf him in dampness.

Gaston let his eyes adjust to the moonlit world beyond the swiftly moving train. They appeared to be in a rural area. The track was surrounded by trees. Gaston hauled Vlad closer to the door, steadied himself, then heaved the body out into the darkness. In seconds it was left behind, probably crumpled somewhere at the base of a tree, ideally mangled beyond recognition.

Gaston closed the outer door, then brushed the snow from his face. No one stirred when he opened the inner door and returned to where he'd left his coat. He shrugged it into place and began walking back to his seat. The cars were silent. The passengers slept peacefully.

Horbatsky's friend shifted in his seat and grunted softly as Gaston paused beside him. He appeared to be sleeping soundly. What would he do when he discovered his travelling companion was gone? Or were they actually together? Gaston still had no proof of that. Since he had witnessed nothing, there seemed to be no reason to remove this stranger, too. Gaston opened the door to his car and passed on.

Smiling at the confusion that might ensue, he eased carefully back into his own seat. No one had noticed his absence. He checked his watch. The job had taken less than twenty minutes. Two down and one to go, he told himself. The woman' death should be even easier to arrange since she had no reason to suspect she was in danger.

Horbatsky's absence would go unnoticed until they reached Detroit in a couple of hours. Maybe even longer than that. Then with only hand luggage, he'd be off and gone before they thought to question passengers. Gaston curled comfortably into his corner and closed his eyes.

Joli stood by the door leading to the next car and watched passengers stepping down to the platform at the Detroit train station. He glanced at his watch, debating whether to get off and call Kate Horbatsky now, or wait until the train arrived in Toronto. He'd been searching for her husband since shortly after six a.m. It was now seven-thirty. In that time, he'd found no sign of the man, although his carry-on was still stuffed onto the shelf above his seat.

Joli had, however, seen the same man he'd first encountered the morning Nick died: the nameless man who appeared to be following Horbatsky. At daybreak, the man had been tucked up in a corner of the next car with his eyes closed. Ten minutes ago, he'd left the train with an overnight bag in his hand and disappeared into the station waiting room.

The train would depart in less than five minutes. Unless he was prepared to stay behind, there was no time to prod authorities into investigating Horbatsky's disappearance. Since Kate Horbatsky had already reported her husband's activities to local police, it seemed more sensible just to keep going. Joli moved to the seat Horbatsky had vacated and stashed his case alongside Horbatsky's abandoned bag on the overhead shelf. Instinct told him the man wouldn't show up. Common sense told him to be there anyway, just in case.

Vlad regained consciousness slowly. His throat ached abominably and he was having trouble breathing because of a stabbing pain in his side. He seemed to be rolled into a ball somehow, with his knees practically in his face.

Gradually he realized he was cold. And sort of wet. At least his cheek and neck felt wet and his hands were freezing—literally. He could barely force his fingers apart. Uncurling his legs took concentrated effort and he couldn't feel his toes. When he finally straightened to his full length, he realized he was wedged between a tree and a large rock. Wiggling into a sitting position exhausted him. He leaned against the tree trunk to catch his breath and take stock of his situation. Twice now, he'd escaped death.

His cheek was stiff where it had lain against the snow. His bare hands were icy and he was shivering despite his exertion, his open coat providing no protection from the weather. His neck and throat hurt like hell and his head throbbed. When he raised his hand to it, it came away bloody. He must have struck his head and split the skin somewhere. When he tried to zip his parka he almost yelped at the pain. His right hand wouldn't work properly. His wrist must be broken.

With his back braced against the tree and his feet jammed against the rock, he began working his way upright. By the time he was on his feet, he was dizzy from the pain in his side. Or was it from the blow to his head? He couldn't be sure. Gritting his teeth to prevent them chattering, he leaned heavily against the tree trunk until his world stopped spinning and he figured out his next move.

He took his time looking around. Day had just broken. The wind was bitterly cold, raising tiny funnels of fine snow where the latest layer had not yet frozen into place.

He couldn't stand around expecting to be rescued. No one even knew he was missing except Korczak's hit man, and *he* wouldn't be sending out any search parties. If he didn't start moving, he would freeze to death.

Vlad cursed his own carelessness at letting the man catch him sleeping. At least, that must have been what happened since his last recollection was of a trip to the washroom around two-thirty. The man must have found him, knocked him out, then thrown him from the train.

He dug his gloves from his pockets with his left hand and gritted his teeth against the pain as he worked them onto numb fingers. With better protection from the elements in place, he took time to examine his broken wrist more thoroughly.

It wasn't his wrist, he concluded. Since his whole arm bent in the wrong place leaving his hand dangling like a limp glove, he must have broken both bones in his forearm. The least movement caused excruciating pain. The break needed support to prevent the bones from shifting.

He was in a forested area littered with broken branches. Improvising a splint would be time-consuming but not impossible. Bending stirred the pain in his side and he was panting by the time he had collected a dozen or so branches the thickness of his thumb. Then, using his foot to snap off excess length, he arranged them about his arm, with one end shoved into his glove and the other held in place by the cuff of his jacket. He rummaged through his pockets until he found a cloth handkerchief to wrap about the makeshift splint.

The next trick would be to support the whole arm so that the hand was upright. So far, the cold had kept the swelling to a minimum. Once he started moving around, jostling the break, his fingers might puff up like sausages. He laid his arm across his chest and hooked his fingers into the neck of his jacket to improvise a sling. It was crude, but it was the best he could do for now.

He couldn't stand around indefinitely, despite how much pain resulted from every move. He had to get to a road.

Now he realized how suspicious he'd look in the middle of nowhere without luggage. He didn't even have much money. Or any? Had the man taken his wallet before throwing him off the train? Panic gripped him.

He managed to unzip his coat and dig into his shirt pocket. Thank God! His wallet was just where he had put it for safekeeping when he left Minneapolis. He wondered at the hit man leaving it. To make it look like an accident? Like a vagrant perhaps? No, not with money. A drunk who stumbled and fell from the train? Yes, that would seem logical.

So now he needed a road, a kindhearted motorist who would pick up a hitchhiker, and a doctor who would accept a check to pay his bill. Shivering and wincing with the pain, he began climbing the embankment to the tracks.

CHAPTER FORTY-TWO

Wednesday morning Andreas insisted on driving Kate to meet the train. Despite her best efforts to remain calm, she was edgy. She only hoped Vlad wouldn't notice.

Insp. Davies agreed that having Kate meet Vlad's train was the best solution to their problem. She would be the bait to lure Vlad onto the platform. Then the police would scoop him as they crossed the station to her car.

At the appropriate time, Andreas slipped away to mingle with the travelers while Kate went to the arrivals platform. She leaned against a pillar where she would be clearly visible to passengers coming in from Chicago. She saw the train pull in and felt her tension grow as people began disembarking. She shifted her gaze along the doorways, seeking Vlad's dark head amid the crowd.

Ten minutes later, the train stood silent, its cars deserted. Except for a handful of people holding suitcases and glancing at watches or pacing impatiently, the platform was empty. There was no sign of Vlad.

Kate waited another ten minutes before heading back towards the car park. Her nerves were wound tightly now and she could feel eyes watching her every step. She knew both Andreas and the police were somewhere in the crowd, but she was glad she couldn't pick them out. If she couldn't see them, neither would Vlad. Any second, she expected him to step out from behind a pillar or appear around a corner.

She was almost back to her car when she heard herself being paged to come to the information booth. For an instant, she froze. It had to be Vlad. Why was he doing this instead of just walking up to her? Was he suspicious? Had he seen Andreas?

Reluctantly, she turned and made her way back into the terminal. Near the ticket counter she saw a corrugated glass door with the word INFORMATION printed on it in black letters. She breathed deeply and turned the knob.

A man in a navy parka stood by the counter on which a microphone sat. He had a suitcase at his feet and a duffle bag over his shoulder. He looked worried. Another man in an official-looking uniform busied himself behind the desk. Both men turned to look at her when Kate entered the room.

The man in the coat barely allowed her to say her name before giving the official a nod and grabbing up the suitcase. He took her elbow with his other hand, and steered her back into the waiting room.

"I am Raymond Joli, *madame*," he began. "I am sorry to do this, but we need to speak before you leave the station."

"How did you know I was here?"

"I tried to call you, and when I couldn't get an answer, I called your brother. He told me about the police coming with you this morning to arrest your husband."

Kate shook her head. "It didn't happen. Vlad didn't show up."

Joli nodded. "No. He disappeared in the night. I saw the man who was following him get off the train in Detroit shortly after seven this morning, but there is no sign of your husband." He shrugged the bag off his shoulder and dropped it beside the suitcase. "This was in the rack over the seat in which he was sitting during the night. It's his, isn't it?"

Kate glanced at the dark green bag, then grabbed the zipper and opened it. She recognized the shaving kit and a sweater, as well as the smell of the dirty laundry. She nodded. "It's his. So what's happened?"

Joli bit his lip, then took a deep breath. "My guess is that the hit man succeeded."

Fighting tears, Kate nodded. "So all this was for nothing."

"I am afraid so, *madame*."

Kate didn't notice Insp. Davies approaching until he was standing by her side. "What's up?"

"Looks like Vlad's dead," Kate replied, fighting to get the words around the lump in her throat. While she regained control of her emotions, the two men introduced themselves to each other.

"Come and sit down," Davies urged Joli and led the way towards the coffee shop. "I need to hear what you can tell us."

When Andreas found them minutes later, they were cradling cups of coffee in a quiet corner of the restaurant.

Joli ordered a sandwich, then began to explain the events he had witnessed over the past week. "I stayed away from Vlad on the train," he said. "I didn't want him to see me and get suspicious. I saw the man from Boddington driving a taxi as we were leaving the motel, but I didn't know he was with us on the train until late last night when I saw him leaving the washroom. Then he got off in Detroit this morning."

"So he's gone," Davies said, and glanced at Kate. "I don't like to think of him getting on a plane out of here until we find your husband."

He turned back to Joli. "Do you know where you were the last time you saw Vlad Horbatsky?"

"Not precisely. Just somewhere in western Michigan. But I'm sure an engineer could give us our location at two fifteen. I believe we were on schedule."

Davies nodded. "Right. So I'll have a chat with the Amtrak security people. We might as well get the search started. Normally, I'd ask you to go through our mug books, but something tells me that won't help. This guy isn't local. We do need a statement though, so that still means a trip to the station." He looked pointedly at Vlad's duffle bag. "We need to look at that too."

Joli nodded. "I expected that. I'll need a lift since I left my own car in Winnipeg."

Kate spoke very little during the drive back to Milton. Her mind was occupied with the practical details of her situation. She would need to arrange a funeral for Vlad but that couldn't happen until his body was found. Father Darcovich and Eddie should hear an edited version of the situation since they had been peripherally involved.

Gerry already knew a lot and would need to hear the rest since he was likely to be dragged into any American investigation to clear Andreas' name. He also needed to get on with replacing Vlad as the firm's maintenance supervisor.

Telling her family was the real sticking point. Rob, Rachel, and Ruth already knew most of the story. Her father would be saddened, but he'd accept the truth. He'd even work on her mother until she learned to cope.

It was Alexi and Tanya who really worried her. Tanya in particular, was her Daddy's girl. At twenty, she was far too young to believe the truth. To her, Daddy only got mad when people deserved it. Most certainly, she would refuse to believe him capable of treason, let alone murder. Alexi, on the other hand, was not so naive. He had seen his father's rages. He was training in criminal law. All the same, knowing the truth wouldn't ease the pain of losing their father.

Kate was torn over calling Nadia. She had never met Vlad's half sister, hadn't even known she existed, in fact. Should she be told about Vlad's death and what he'd done to Nicholas? If she'd had a hand in connecting the two men, then she'd be saddled with guilt as well as grief. What kindness was there in that?

#

Vlad stopped on the diner's front step and looked around. He'd walked most of the morning before an older man gave him a lift for a few miles. He'd been dropped at the man's farm gate and walked for another hour before getting a second ride, this time with a couple heading to town to shop for groceries. And so it had gone. An hour of walking for twenty miles of riding with strangers. His progress had been painfully slow.

His arm was throbbing and his hand was purple. His fingers were badly swollen. He needed to see a doctor—soon. Fortunately, it wasn't life-threatening and that meant he could delay treatment until he got home. His OHIP card would not be accepted here in Michigan. Even if it were, Ontario Hospital Insurance most certainly wouldn't cover American medical costs.

By now, the shock had worn off. He realized just how close to death he'd come. He'd felt chilled when he returned from the washroom in the middle of the night so he'd unrolled the parka he'd been using as a pillow and slipped into it. Except for that, he would be dead. Frozen in a snow bank or fatally battered by the fall.

It was like running to the Allies in 1945. His life now depended on his adaptability. In those days everyone knew the end was upon them and they were all fleeing. Only the Germans hadn't known how to escape whereas Vlad had his route mapped out. As a dispatch rider, he went wherever his orders sent him. That was the key. In the turmoil, most dispatch offices were empty. He simply went in as though delivering a message, looked around for a blank order pad, wrote himself fresh orders that sent him south and continued towards the army that would release him from his enemies. It had seemed a pitifully slow process, but in the end it worked. Convincing the sergeant who found him that he was really an escaped prisoner rather than a true German soldier had proved difficult. Convincing the hard-ass colonel of his worth as an interpreter had been even trickier. He managed that too, and in the end the Americans put him to work as an interpreter at the naval war crimes trials.

He shook off his memories and started walking out of town, following the highway east. At least he wasn't hungry any more. He'd have to be careful. He was running low on American cash and not even banks were willing to exchange Canadian money in small communities. Nor could he count on his check being accepted. It baffled him how a country as large and as modern as the United States could have such a disjointed banking system.

He had gone a mile or more with no sign of passing motorists. His nose was beginning to pinch in the cold. The sun was sinking slowly. If he didn't get a lift soon, he'd find himself walking in the dark and perhaps spending the night on his feet to keep from freezing. Then he heard the roar of a heavy motor. He turned towards the sound and stuck out his thumb. It was an eighteen-wheeler loaded with lumber.

The trucker slowed as quickly as he could. Even so, Vlad ran to climb into the cab before the man changed his mind and drove on without him.

"Too cold to be out there tonight," the man said as Vlad clambered onto the bench seat. "You'll need to give it a good slam," he continued, seeing Vlad's unsuccessful attempt to close the door gently. "Where you headed?"

"Windsor, actually, but anywhere that direction is good."

The man clutched and set his truck in motion. He talked as he checked his mirrors and returned to the road. "I only go to Ann Arbor, but that's not far from the border. You should be able to get another lift from there."

Vlad leaned back and made himself comfortable. "Thanks a lot. I was starting to get cold."

The trucker didn't ask personal questions as they headed east into the gathering darkness. Vlad stuck to general topics. They'd been travelling a couple of hours before the man Vlad now knew as Bill Watson asked what had happened to his arm.

"I fell off a train," Vlad replied, giving him the semi-believable half of the story. Then added, "I wasn't feeling well so I went into the doorway to get some air. I don't know whether I passed out or we hit a bump or what. Next thing I know I woke up in a heap in a ditch with this arm all banged up."

"You need to see a doctor. Looks like it could be broken."

Vlad nodded. "That's part of the hurry to get home. I can't afford your hospital charges here when my own medical insurance will cover this when I get back to Ontario."

Bill nodded and started in on a series of stories concerning the horrors of American medical costs. An hour later they were seeing signs directing them to Ann Arbor.

The sky was brighter ahead and Bill soon pulled in at a truck stop with a huge parking lot and a restaurant attached. There were at least two dozen rigs parked to one side of the buildings and Vlad could see three bearing Ontario plates.

"This is the end of the road for me. Why don't you go see if any of those Canadians are heading home?" Bill said.

It didn't take long for Vlad to discover the Canadian-licensed rigs were empty. Disgruntled, he entered the restaurant.

Bill was sitting at a table with two other drivers working on coffees and waiting for their orders to arrive.

"Here's my passenger," he announced as Vlad approached. "Vlad, come and sit down. George here, says he's heading for Ontario."

Vlad took the empty chair and introduced himself. As Bill had indicated, George was willing to take him as far as London. Vlad accepted the offer immediately.

"London would be great." He thanked his new acquaintance. "I'll get my arm looked after there, then call the wife to come get me. That's only a couple of hours from home. She'll have no trouble with a drive like that."

CHAPTER FORTY-THREE

Andreas pulled the car into the garage and Kate forced herself into the house. It was still early afternoon, but she was in no mood to go to work. She'd set off in the morning with such high hopes things would be over by the time she returned. Instead, nothing was resolved. She found herself wandering aimlessly around the kitchen, almost in a daze.

Andreas took her arm and guided her towards her armchair. "Sit. I'll make coffee." Then he headed for the kitchen. Kate sat, suddenly cold and trembling as reaction took hold.

When he sat down across from her, his expression was sober. "What are you going to do about being alone here?"

Rubbing her arms to increase her circulation, Kate shrugged. "Nothing. I've been on my own for a month now."

"*Ja*, but that was before you got the call from the Russian wanting more money for Olga. Ever since, we've been so busy worrying about Vlad that we sort of overlooked him."

Again, Kate shrugged. "Vlad was the one he dealt with."

"True. But he didn't know how much you knew until after your conversation the other night. Now he does. I don't want you out here all by yourself."

"Is that a hint? You want to move in?"

Andreas shrugged. "Not exactly. I was thinking about you coming to stay with me at the hotel."

"Oh, sure. And we're going to keep *that* quiet. Besides, what about Amos? I can't just abandon him." She shook her head. "If our living arrangements are to change, you'll have to come here."

"Are you sure?"

"No, but it's the best we can do for now."

"Fine. Then I'll go get my stuff. Which bedroom do you want me to use?"

"Ruth's closet is empty. You can store clothes there until I clear out Vlad's things." When Andreas opened his mouth to protest, she cut him short. "I know, I know. I won't be doing anything like that until his body is found."

Just saying the words seemed so final. His body. He'd been alive and ranting the last time she'd seen him. Now, she was talking about him as if he were dead. But was he? Somehow she couldn't accept that yet.

She trailed Andreas to the hall closet and watched him put on his coat and boots. Amos perked up his ears expectantly, then sank down again by her chair when Andreas left without him.

Alone, Kate wandered into the living room and picked up the empty mugs. There wasn't much to be done around the house. Still, she needed to find something to keep her busy. While rinsing the crockery, she mulled Andreas' concerns about her safety. If he were right, then perhaps it was time to take precautions. Making her decision steadied her.

Leaving the mugs to drip, she took a key from the kitchen cupboard and went to the basement where Vlad kept a rifle and a shotgun in a gun locker. She inspected them to make sure they functioned properly, then brought them upstairs. She put one in the broom closet at the end of the kitchen counter, and the other in the front hall closet behind some coats.

Her cedar chest sat by the wall opposite the closet. Buried in the bottom was a carved wooden box her grandfather had given her when she returned from the war. He'd made it especially to fit her Luger and that's where the unused memento of her youth had been stored ever since. Memories flooded back as she dug it out. There had been a couple of close calls on her return trip to England, but she'd never actually had to kill anyone with it. Now, after all these years, she couldn't imagine needing it again. Just the same, her brain on autopilot, she took the Luger apart, cleaned it, oiled it, and re-assembled it as she had been trained to do so many years ago. She picked up the carton of bullets from her grandfather's box and loaded the weapon. Then, gun in one hand and bullets in the other, she went to clear a space in her night table.

When she turned to leave the room she saw Vlad's bag at the foot of the bed where Andreas had left it. Davies had glanced through it, then handed it back to her. It needed to be emptied and there was no point in delaying the chore. Kate set it on the bed and began removing garments, absently rolling the soiled things into a bundle for the laundry hamper.

Despite her anger at Vlad's stupid jealousy, tears welled up. If Joli's suspicions were correct, this would be the last time she'd wash Vlad's clothes. His scent clinging to the fabric brought memories flooding back.

Memories of him in a t-shirt, sweat trickling down his back, the shovel in his hands gleaming in the sunshine as he broke up the sod for the flowerbed by the driveway the first spring after they built the house.

She added his favorite bulky sweater to the heap. He'd worn that over his flannel shirt and wrapped himself in an afghan last spring when he spent three days on the couch with a fever.

She was annoyed with herself for crying. After what he'd done the bastard didn't deserve her tears. Still, the images of a younger Vlad working on the car, playing ball with the kids, covered in gold speckles from painting the kitchen, dancing at the church hall continued to roll past her mind's eye as the tears scalded her cheeks.

It was strictly routine that prompted her to run a hand through the pockets on each piece of clothing to ensure that they were actually empty. Without that habitual thoroughness, she would never have found the picture tucked into the pocket of his grey flannel shirt.

She was still staring at it when Andreas walked in.

"What is that?" he asked.

She shook her head and handed it to him. "I've no idea."

"It doesn't look like Vlad."

"Nope. Nor any of his family or friends, either," she replied. "All it says is 1958—written on the back."

"So he got this while he was away? But who is it?"

Kate shrugged. "Haven't a clue. Unless it's his sister and her husband. Maybe Nadia gave it to him."

"Yeah, that would make sense." Andreas handed the picture back. "She sure doesn't look like Vlad."

Kate laid the picture on the dresser and put the suitcase back in the closet. She wasn't sure what she'd do with the photograph. Maybe Tanya would want it.

With the work completed, Kate went to make their evening meal. Andreas took Amos for a walk. They had agreed to call Rob and Rachel after they ate. Ruth, too, would need to hear the gist of Joli's report and Gerry would be briefed when they returned to work the next morning. Only Alexi and Tanya would be kept in the dark as much as possible until Vlad's body was recovered.

The telephone rang while Kate was cleaning up the kitchen. From the timing, she suspected it was Ruth checking up as she did most nights.

The woman who asked if she was speaking with Katrina Horbatsky spoke clearly, but with a marked accent. It took Kate a moment to realize she sounded much like Vlad.

"I am Nadia Dymitruk. Is Vlad there?"

Vlad's sister? Why would she be calling? "No, Nadia. I'm sorry to say that your brother hasn't got home yet. Can I help you?"

"Oh. So you know about me," the woman said. Immediately, her voice was warmer, her speech less hesitant. "My brother-in-law wanted to speak to Vlad. Just a moment while I put him on."

The man identified himself as Klaus Tartarinov. His accent, too, was Slavic, and he hesitated as though unsure how to say what was on his mind. "Nadia says your husband met Nicholas. I was hoping he could tell me when. You see, the police found Nicholas' body in the river. They suspect he may have been murdered."

So the investigation had begun after all. Although he wasn't actually asking, Kate wondered if Klaus knew Vlad had killed his son. She decided to leave it to the authorities to give Klaus the details.

"I would help you if I could," she replied. "Since you know Vlad was looking for Nicholas, then I may as well fill you in. I've had a private investigator looking for Vlad. He says another man was also looking for him. He first saw the man in Gillingsworth when Nicholas and Vlad were having breakfast together on Friday morning. The man turned up a couple of times as Vlad drove east. Vlad called me from Minneapolis to say his truck had been stolen and he was coming the rest of the way by train. My investigator saw him on the train, but last night he disappeared somewhere in Michigan. I've been told the man who was following Vlad left the train in Detroit this morning."

"So your husband may be dead too? Is that what you're saying?"

"I don't know. We suspect so, but until they find his body…" She trailed off. She knew about Nicholas' death but unless the Gillingsworth police questioned Joli they might never identify Vlad as the killer. She decided it wouldn't help anyone to make that connection now.

"So Vlad may well have been the last person to see Nicholas alive," Klaus continued after a brief pause. "I suppose that is appropriate since he was Nicholas' father."

"What?" The information took Kate's breath away. "Nicholas was my husband's son?"

"*Da.* Anna never told Vlad she was pregnant. By the time he sent for her, she was in hospital with tuberculosis. Since she was too ill to look after him, she gave Nicholas to Ivana and me to bring with us to Canada."

He fell silent.

"Would Nicholas have told Vlad who he was?" Kate asked.

"Nicholas never knew who his father was."

"Did he know he wasn't your son?"

"Oh, yes. He knew Anna was his mother."

"Did he have a picture of her? Taken in 1958? With a well-fed, good-looking fellow? Was your sister very thin, and dark-haired?"

Her questions surprised Klaus. It took him a moment to speak and he was wary when he did reply. "Anna sent Nicholas a picture of her husband when she married in 1958. How would you know about that if you didn't know about Anna?"

"My investigator brought home Vlad's suitcase and I found a picture in it when I was emptying it."

"But why would Nicholas give Vlad his mother's picture if he didn't know the connection?"

Kate wasn't about to voice her suspicions. "I don't know. I just know I found the picture."

"This is very strange."

Kate could hear Nadia's voice in the background. A moment later she took over the conversation.

"I told Vlad about Nicholas being Anna's son. When he came here the first day I told him that Klaus was Nick's uncle. He also knew that Nick's mother was so ill that she gave the boy to Klaus when Nick was very young. I should have guessed the connection.

"Klaus and Anna's family lived in the flat below us when we were in Warsaw. Anna wanted to find a job away from her family. My mother sent her to the *Jar*, to Vlad's father in Berlin. I gave Anna the letter of introduction that my mother wrote for her. There's no question he would remember Anna."

She broke off and Kate could hear muffled sobbing. Klaus came back on the line.

"I did not know your husband was Nicholas' father. After they found his body, I called Anna to tell her what had happened. That was when she told me that she had been supposed to join Vlad Horbatsky in Canada. Only she was sick by then. The immigration authorities would not have permitted her to enter the country. She says she never did answer his letter. She didn't want to ruin his chance at a new life and she was afraid he'd come back if he knew about Nicholas. Instead, she just disappeared."

Disappeared? Dear God. Exactly what she'd done to Andreas. No wonder Vlad suspected her of betraying him. Anna had walked out on him. Why wouldn't she?

The instant of sympathy waned as quickly as it had come. Hate and mistrust of Anna was no excuse to kill their son. Unless Vlad told him, Nicholas wouldn't even have known that Vlad was his father.

Klaus was still speaking. "That's why we called. Anna wanted me to tell Vlad who Nick was. Since he'd met their son, she wanted him to realize who he'd been trying to help."

Kate felt her own eyes fill with tears. She was glad she'd kept silent about what Joli had seen. Revealing it would be cruel. She'd leave it to the police whether they ever learned the truth. She finally forced words around the lump in her throat.

"I don't know what to say. I am so sorry this has happened."

Klaus' voice, too, was choked as he thanked her and hung up.

Andreas was beside her by the time she settled the telephone receiver back in its cradle. One arm circled her shoulders and he turned her to lean against him.

"Okay. Now what's happened?"

They were sitting on the family room couch when she finished her explanation. Andreas stroked the back of her head and let her cry away her pain and rage.

"The bastard killed his own son," she whispered over and over. "I knew he was sick, but this...this is more than that. It's..." She stopped, clenching and unclenching her fists, unable to put her feelings into words.

"It's not your fault, Kati," Andreas comforted her. "We knew nothing of this. Joli didn't know. There was no way anyone could have stopped him."

Andreas finished loading the dishwasher and wiped down the table and counters. Kate was still sitting on the couch staring into space when he returned to her. He put an arm under hers and led her to the bedroom. "You're going to bed now. I will join you a bit later. Try to go to sleep. You must see your brother tomorrow and the police have to be told what we've just heard."

He waited while she undressed and crawled under the covers.

"I need to go to work," Kate said as he snapped off the light. "I can't let anyone know what's happened until they find his body. Besides, if someone is watching, we can't alter our routine or he'll know we suspect something."

Her practicality jolted Andreas. Was this what spy schooling did? Made you think rationally despite your emotions being in turmoil?

"We'll see in the morning," he said and closed the bedroom door.

CHAPTER FORTY- FOUR

At last he was nearly home. Vlad eased himself over the tailgate and dropped to the ground. It was covered in a light layer of snow, nothing like the amounts he'd encountered in the west. The early afternoon sun warmed his face, and he walked with loose, easy strides. He was only half a mile from the house if he used the shortcut through the fields but he'd stick to the road because that made for easier walking. Even so, he'd be home in fifteen minutes.

Now, with home so close, he felt exhausted. He'd had five long weeks on the road and the last three days in particular had been physically grueling. George had dropped him at the hospital in London to get his arm set. Then he'd managed to catch a bus to Toronto and hitchhiked back to Milton the previous evening. Getting those last few miles home had been the hard part.

He didn't want to be seen around town looking like a tramp. He could have called Kate, of course, but if she were fooling around he didn't want to warn her. He preferred to catch her in the act.

That was when he thought of Chris Hadley, the neighbor who worked nights at the glass plant down the road from Clarke's. He'd crawled into the back of Chris' truck, covered himself with the tarp he found there, and waited. It had frustrated him when Chris went to the barber, the bank, and did half a dozen other errands after he left work. The worst had been lying in the back of the truck while Chris stopped at the Chinese restaurant in the plaza for lunch. His stomach was rumbling so loud he expected Chris to hear it when he returned to his truck.

The house looked quiet, deserted even, as it should with Kate at work. He could see the front flowerbeds had been emptied of dead plants for the winter. He didn't bother to check the garden. Kate was good at keeping things in order.

He put his key in the front door and smiled a greeting at Amos when the big dog met him in the hall. Amos wiggled happily, smelling his boots, and whimpering softly. Vlad patted the animal's head, then knelt and hugged him, receiving a tongue along his cheek in return.

"Are you glad to see me, fella?" he asked quietly. "I'm glad to see you."

Still prancing, the dog watched as Vlad hung his coat in the closet, carried his boots to the tray by the back door, and went to the sink for a drink of water.

Glancing around, he saw meat thawing on a plate in the oven beyond Amos' reach, the way Kate always left it in preparation for the evening meal. Nothing had changed in his absence. Nothing obvious, at least. But then, he hadn't really checked yet.

He stood in the middle of the living room and scanned for anything out of place, any new objects, a favorite pipe maybe, unfamiliar glasses on the end table, slippers by the couch. There was no sign of Wachter in this room.

He went to the bedroom and opened the closet. Finding no strange jackets or slacks on the hangers, he began systematically checking dresser drawers. Still nothing. He had to give him credit. The man was careful.

Lastly, Vlad went to the bathroom. An electric razor. Yes! His euphoria died as quickly as it appeared. It was his own razor. Now how had that happened? His razor should be in the suitcase he'd left on the train.

Puzzled now, he turned to the laundry hamper and found two shirts and several pairs of socks and underwear that had also been in his case. Quickly returning to the bedroom closet, he now noticed his missing duffle back in its customary place on the floor behind his shoe rack. Somehow his suitcase and clothing had been returned to Kate. But how?

Had his assailant from the train returned them? If that were the case, then he was connected to Kate, and she knew all about his ordeal. It also meant that she wanted him dead. He couldn't believe that. Not Kate. She might be angry with him for taking off without telling her, but angry enough to kill him?

About to dismiss the idea, he had a sudden vision of Wachter's furious face the night Vlad had tried to cut his brake lines. The thought struck Vlad as hard as any physical blow. He staggered to the end of the bed and dropped onto it, his stomach queasy with shock.

All the time he'd been blaming Korczak he should have been looking closer to home. He should also have realized that if *he* wanted the German dead, Wachter would just as happily see *him* gone. What better way to achieve it than to have him murdered? While his instinct was to absolve Kate of any involvement, he knew that could not be true. Their hired killer had brought his suitcase back to her.

The realization of his wife's apparent betrayal left him numb. He sat motionless for several minutes, trying to think. Finally, hunger pangs forced him to the kitchen.

His body now as shaky as his mind, Vlad took a can of vegetable soup from the cupboard. Usually Kate made her own soup but she always kept emergency supplies, and right now Vlad's hunger constituted an emergency.

He heated the soup in the microwave, ate it all, then found a plastic bag to cover his cast and had a long, warm shower. He needed sleep and the bed beckoned like a mythical siren in the silence of the empty house.

However, his safety had to take priority. Resolutely, he went to the kitchen for his key, then down to the gun locker in the basement. Fear washed over him in a cold wave when he opened the cabinet and found it empty.

Slamming down the lid, he thundered back up the stairs, almost tripping over Amos in his haste. He drew up short in the centre of the kitchen and looked around, his mind racing. Only one cupboard was long enough to hold his guns. He crossed to the broom closet and yanked it open. The mops were neatly arranged in snap holders around the walls. The shotgun nestled between them. He grunted in satisfaction and withdrew it carefully. He broke it open and nodded. It was loaded.

Cradling the gun in the crook of his arm, he went searching for his deer rifle. Amos stood back and eyed him warily.

"It's okay, boy," he muttered. "She won't be using these on me if I find them first."

Methodically checking as he went, Vlad found the second long gun in the hall closet at the front door. Content now, he relaxed and headed for his bedroom. He dare not sleep long, but he absolutely had to get some rest. He laid one gun on the floor and the other on the bed beside him. No one would catch him by surprise even if they did get into the house.

###

Gaston pulled into the deserted driveway on the back road he had used the day before, then turned off the truck's ignition and glanced at his watch. It was nearly four-thirty. The sun had set, but he still had enough light to pick his way through the brush along the fence line. He wanted to be in place before the woman got home from work. He buttoned his coat to the neck, turned down the earflaps on his newly purchased hat and slung his rifle case over his shoulder. The wind was rising. It would be a cold night. It pleased him to think of returning to his warm motel room and a good night's sleep while others toiled over the results of his handiwork.

Spending the previous day watching the house from a sheltered corner of a neighbor's field had confirmed Korczak's original information. The Horbatskys did indeed have a large dog and the wife returned from work around five-thirty. What Gaston hadn't expected was to see a man in the car with the woman when she arrived home. Nor had he expected the man to walk her dog and stay the night.

Gaston had first planned to take the woman down while she was out with the dog. One quick bullet for the dog and a second for the woman. Alternatively, he had considered striking just before dawn, when sleep was deepest and the dog was least likely to succeed in waking her over an intruder.

The unidentified man's presence complicated things. Had her husband's disappearance made her suspicious enough to hire a bodyguard? Or did she have a lover? Either way, he had settled on an uncomplicated hit—when the man had the dog away from the house.

Ignoring the previous day's observation point, he continued around the edge of the field until he reached the tall cedar hedge that encircled the Horbatsky property. Having already carved out a hiding place in the shrubbery, he eased into it and set down his gun case. Then the hard part began—the waiting. He could make no move until the man and the dog were well away from the property.

###

The house was as dark as the night sky outside when Kate arrived home from work. Amos met her at the kitchen door, his stubby tail wagging happily in anticipation of his evening walk. She picked his leash off the hook by the kitchen door and turned back into the garage.

For propriety, Andreas was using his car and left work a few moments behind her. He pulled into the driveway as she and Amos came back through the garage to close the outside door.

Stepping out of his car, he handed her his briefcase and said he'd take Amos out. "I'm starving. If you get supper ready while we're gone, we'll be back within the hour. Remember to lock up when you go in. I have my keys."

Kate nodded and watched Amos lead him quickly off into the night. Abruptly, she shivered. Realizing she'd been standing, staring into space for some time, she turned and hurried inside.

She spotted the boots the moment she stopped at the boot tray to drop her own. For an instant she froze, undecided about what to do. They couldn't belong to the hit man. Amos wouldn't be calm and happy with a stranger in the house. Nor would an intruder be stupid enough to leave things in plain view in her kitchen. They weren't Vlad's though. Or were they? The size looked right, and Joli said they'd encountered blizzards a couple of times. Maybe Vlad had been forced to buy winter boots.

So if Vlad was home, where was he? Kate changed into her house shoes and walked to the hall closet to hang up her coat. An unfamiliar parka of the right size to fit her husband hung on a hanger beside his spring jacket. Her gaze automatically went to where she had propped the

Winchester .3030 in the corner behind her trench coat. It was gone.

Fear rippled down her spine. Why would Vlad take the gun? She quickly retraced her steps to the broom closet. The double bore 12-gauge she had placed there was also missing.

She walked quietly to the drawer by the sink and sighed in relief to find the new carton of shells was still where she'd left it. Only the two shells were missing that she had loaded into the shotgun. The box of rifle bullets appeared equally untouched. So he hadn't taken extra ammunition. Not that that would protect her when he had both guns and eight rounds between them with which to shoot her.

Kate returned to where she had dropped her purse on the counter and removed her Luger. She hadn't wanted to take it out of the house but Andreas had insisted she carry it everywhere she went. Now she was thankful for his persistence. She dropped it into the pocket of her suit jacket and stopped to think. The extra ammunition was still in her nightstand, but the Luger's clip carried almost as many rounds as Vlad had at his disposal with the two long guns.

She had never considered pulling a weapon on Vlad and she still rejected the idea. Given he'd taken the guns though, she couldn't risk facing him unarmed.

She racked her mind trying to determine what had caused this lunacy. First killing Nicholas. Now collecting up their guns. Something was very, very wrong with Vlad.

The next task was finding him. Since his coat and boots were here he must be somewhere in the house.

Quietly, one hand on the pistol in her pocket, she crept from the front hall around the corner towards the bedrooms. Because Amos roamed the house in her absence, she kept the doors closed. Now the door to the master bedroom stood ajar. While she hesitated, debating whether to open it all the way and confront him, a soft rumble welled into the silence. Then another. Vlad was snoring. The familiar sound tugged at her memory—fleetingly.

He was probably exhausted and might stay asleep provided she made no noise that wakened him. What did that tell her? Could she be wrong in presuming he would attack her? Maybe he thought being left alone had frightened her so she'd put the guns where they'd be handy —just in case.

If that were his mindset, pulling out her own sidearm would just set him off. Maybe bring about the very confrontation she needed to avoid. Not the right way to handle this. She might have to let him make the first move. Meanwhile, there was one thing she could do.

She went to the telephone in the living room and called the police. She could hear the loudspeaker echoing Davies' name into the general commotion of shift change.

"It'll take us about twenty minutes to get there," Davies said. "And you're right. No sirens. Just unlock the back door and expect us to let ourselves in."

"Well, remember I have a Rottweiler. He's out walking right now but if he gets back before you arrive he's going to kick up a ruckus."

Kate glanced at the clock and wondered how long it would be before Andreas and Amos returned. She needed to head them off. In fact, since Vlad would explode if he saw Andreas, she should send them away until Vlad was in custody. So how was she going to keep Vlad from noticing Amos' absence?

Her stomach in knots and her nerves pinging like taut wire, Kate began hunting for the tape recorder in the drawers of the entertainment unit. The likelihood of her getting him to confess to stealing Andreas' plans was slim, but she had to try. Besides, it gave her something to do while she waited for the police.

CHAPTER FORTY-FIVE

Vlad woke gradually. For the first seconds, he didn't know where he was. Slowly, he realized he wasn't dreaming. He was really in his own bed, in his own house. He glanced at the clock. Kate should be home any time now. Then he remembered the guns she had stashed around the house.

He slid off the bed, put on his slippers, and stood a moment, thinking. Should he take the rifle with him? He'd be awkward handling it with his arm in a cast. If she wanted him dead, he needed it. Did he want her to know he saw through her scheme? Better safe than sorry. He grabbed the gun by the barrel and started for the kitchen. Tiptoeing down the hall, he could see Kate's reflection on the television screen in the family room. She was fiddling with something at the counter beside the sink.

He stopped by the closet to set the gun in the corner between the wall and the doorjamb. It slipped and landed on the hardwood with a hollow thunk.

He saw her turn and frown in his direction, then move a step away from the counter. He could see the tension in her posture. Her hands trembled. His element of surprise gone, he walked around the corner to confront her.

"What in hell are you doing sneaking up on me?" There was neither welcome nor pleasure in her tone.

"I would think you should be glad to see me after all this time," he shot back. "What is the matter? Got Wachter living here already? You do not need me any more?"

"No, that's not the problem," Kate snapped, her voice raised to match his. "Thanks to you and your antics, I may have a hit man after me. For a second there, I thought he'd got into the house somehow."

"Hit man?" The very word sent a chill up Vlad's back. Was he wrong? Did the man who threw him from the train not work for her? Was his danger not over? He must brazen it out. "Who is this hit man? What have you done now to get yourself into a mess?"

"Me? Done? What have I done? I haven't done a damned thing." Vlad could see fury sparking in her eyes and tight lines around her mouth. "I have apparently got caught up in your fancy machinations with this Korczak. He called here right after you left looking for another shipment for Olga. Another shipment, Vlad? What were you going to steal for him this time? More of Andreas' plans?"

"Of course not. There are…" He caught himself.

Kate nodded, glaring at him. "That's right. There are no more. You already gave him everything we had."

"I do not know what you are talking about." He heard himself speaking very precisely, and cursed silently.

Kate would know he was nervous. "How is Korczak connected to this hit man you claim is chasing you?"

She pounced on his words immediately, ignoring his question. "So you admit you know Korczak."

"I never said that," he protested. "You are putting words into my mouth."

She resumed her attack. "Well, obviously he knows you or he wouldn't have called. That's why the police suggested I put the guns where they were handy."

His stomach churned. His chest felt tight. "How did the police get into this? Did you tell them about the call?"

"I didn't have to. Since we had no idea whether you'd been kidnapped, they put a tap on our phone. They heard the call."

She spoke so calmly that Vlad's rage dropped like a stone. "Oh." Infuriating as it was, it was also logical. Why hadn't he considered that possibility before he left? He changed the subject. "How did you get my suitcase?"

"My private investigator brought it back on Wednesday."

Private investigator? When had he caught up with him? What had he seen? Before Vlad could formulate a new question, she resumed her attack.

"What possessed you to hand over Andreas' designs to the Russians? You hate Communism. How much did Korczak pay you to turn into a traitor?"

In one sentence she had swept aside all the pain and worry he'd endured for months to concentrate on the Kraut. How dare she!

"You want to know how much?" he screamed, all attempts to be rational cast aside. "I'll tell you how much. Nothing. He did not pay me a penny. I am your husband. I have almost been killed protecting you from vermin like Wachter. And what thanks do I get? You babble on about your precious lover. Not a thought for my pain and suffering. For you, everything is about Wachter."

"So I was right," Kate snarled back. "First you tampered with his car, then you blew up the plant to kill Andreas. And when that failed you broke into the plant and stole his plans. All because you're a jealous fool."

"Jealous?" he bellowed. "You expect me to stand idle while Wachter takes you away from me? Wrecks our family? I did what I had to do."

"You had to blow up the plant. You had to sell Andreas' plans to the Russians." Her sarcasm sailed right over his head.

"Of course. I am a Cossack. No one destroys my family."

"While you, of course, are quite free to destroy it yourself," she snapped. "Including your own son." She shook her head, disgusted at his warped logic.

"My son? Alexi?" Panicked, he repeated his question. "What has happened to Alexi?"

"Your *other* son." She hurled the words. "Nicholas."

"Nich...He is not my son." The denial was out before he even had time to question how she knew the boy's name.

"That's not what Anna says."

Vlad waved away the accusation. "She lies. Always."

How in hell had she connected with Anna? He had no time to question that as Kate plowed ahead with her cross-examination.

"Why would she want you to know Nicholas was your child if it weren't true?"

"Money. She probably wants money."

Kate snorted in derision. "Not after all these years. And especially not with Nicholas dead."

She knew the boy was dead? "She didn't care about the boy," Vlad began.

Kate cut him off. "Oh, no? Then why did she send him her picture? And why did he carry it with him?"

So that was it. She'd found the picture. Of course! Fool that he was, he'd left it in his pocket. "If she cared so much why did she give him away?" Vlad countered.

"Because she was too sick to look after him. Nadia told you that."

Vlad shook his head in denial and started to turn away, bewildered at the facts she had somehow uncovered. The sudden softening of her voice stopped him.

"You really don't understand, do you? Tuberculosis is highly contagious. In her condition—so sick she needed hospitalization—it's a wonder the baby didn't catch it from her. The only way to protect him would have been to give him up. Poor wee tyke. The choice must have been heart breaking for her. She was lucky she had a brother to take him."

Vlad couldn't ignore the scenario Kate painted with her quiet words. Anna did look ill in the photograph. Well, maybe not sick, exactly, but certainly not healthy. That was eight years after they had separated.

The war dragged everyone down, he reminded himself. The last time he'd seen her, Anna had been thin, worn-looking. At the time, he attributed it to caring for his mother during her final days. Could there have been more? Could she have been pregnant? Kate had looked a bit off during the first weeks of her pregnancies. She hadn't experienced morning sickness the way many other women apparently did, but she had been lethargic, exhausted over nothing. Maybe Anna…

He buried the thought. It couldn't be true. Nicholas couldn't have been his child. He was born after Vlad emigrated. Yes, but how long after, an inner voice whispered? He didn't know the answer.

What if he were wrong? What if Nicholas truly was his child? His stomach lurched and his knees went weak. He reached a hand to grasp the end of the counter for support as the kitchen did a slow spiral in opposition to the whirling of his head. He hadn't killed his own child. Surely, God would not be that cruel. It was a man's obligation to take care of his family—even its illegitimate members. Nicholas couldn't be his child. Kate was not a gullible woman, however. Nor did Nadia live in fantasy. If they believed Anna's tale…

Kate mustn't know the strength of the doubts she had planted. He took several deep breaths to steady his trembling legs, then turned towards the hall.

Kate's nerves were doing handsprings. Where the heck were the police? They should have arrived by now. The fact she knew about Nicholas seemed to have shaken Vlad. How long would that last? Also, how much longer would it be before he realized that Amos was missing? Then he'd start asking questions.

When the phone rang, she almost crossed the room to grab it, then stopped herself. If they were coming in quietly, the cops wouldn't be calling her. It was probably one of the kids. Let Vlad be the one to make the explanations. In fact, she wanted to hear what sort of line he was going to use to try to cover up his absence. There was no doubt he'd wind up in jail, but for now, she wanted to see him squirm.

After five rings Vlad walked into the living room and picked up the receiver. His second sentence told her it was Tanya.

"I went to see my sister," he explained. "No, Mom didn't know about it. Nadia is my half sister, actually. I didn't know she was living in Washington. No, Washington State. In the mountains. When Father Darcovich said she was looking for me, I decided to go. It was a spur-of-the-moment thing."

He laughed so naturally that Kate wanted to kick him. Poor Tanya was going to get a horrible shock when she learned the real story. There was no doubt she'd find out. By the time Vlad was tried for murder and espionage the whole country would know what he'd done.

"She wants to speak to you," Vlad said. Handing Kate the receiver, he went to the hall and collected the rifle, then carried it across the kitchen towards the broom closet.

Not sure how to avoid the whole issue of her husband's deception, Kate dropped onto the couch and prepared to let her daughter do the talking.

"Isn't it great?" Tanya's voice bubbled. "Daddy's home and safe."

The bang drowned the rest of her words.

Kate dropped the phone. She threw herself flat on the cushions, then rolled onto the floor, and crawled to the end of the couch. She couldn't see the gunman. A spider web of cracks surrounded the hole in the patio door. Vlad lay face down on the kitchen floor, the rifle clutched in his hand, blood pooling on his right side. Where the hell were those cops?

"Where did you put the other gun?" she called in a low voice.

"Bedroom floor," Vlad wheezed. "Get it. I'll distract him."

Immediately he opened fire, raining a series of shots in a precise pattern across the back yard. Although the light from the kitchen revealed her and concealed the shooter, Vlad's barrage would at least make him duck for cover temporarily.

Kate was down the hall by the time Vlad was out of ammunition. She raced into the bedroom and grabbed the shotgun, then dropped it onto the bed.

In this situation her handgun was more useful. She ran around the bed and grabbed the box of bullets from the nightstand drawer. Dropping it into her pocket, she pulled out the Luger and went to the window overlooking the back yard.

She could see nothing in the circle of light from the patio doors. Then a second shot cracked into the silence and she saw the muzzle flash near the back fence.

She needed to get out into the yard before she fired. Reasoning that two weapons were better than one, she again grabbed up the shotgun and raced back to the front door.

Now she could see blood puddling further away from Vlad. He had lost his grip on the rifle. His eyes were closed.

She yanked the door open, then hit the storm door handle and crashed into the glass. The metal door wouldn't budge. Ice built up on the doorstep? She hadn't used the door since the last storm.

After three fruitless kicks, she whipped the shotgun up and smashed the butt through the glass. Taking care to avoid shards still stuck in the frame, she stepped through the opening.

The evening air bit at Andreas' nose and a cloud of steam rose with each breath. Light from the rising moon made their surroundings surprisingly bright. Amos was anxious to run despite the hour and Andreas was happy to oblige. Waiting for trouble to strike had him so wound up he needed the exercise.

As they hurried along, his mind wandered through the tangle of law enforcement agencies Vlad had dragged into their lives. Tallying them up in his head, he reached a total of seven between the two countries. He wondered if any of them was communicating with any other. Probably not, or somebody would already be on his doorstep hauling him away to face charges of treason.

His biggest worry was how he'd ever prove his innocence given that the man at the heart of the whole mess was gone. If Korczak could be made to talk...but why would he? What incentive could be offered that would work that miracle?

Thanks to Vlad, he knew he'd never work in his field again, but at his age that mattered less than losing his good name. Most important of all was the fear of losing his freedom now that he and Kate were reunited. They could run, of course. He had the money and it could be shifted to someplace where the U.S. couldn't reach them. All the same, hiding wasn't his way. Nor could he ask Kate to share a fugitive's life. The whole mess made him furious. He could cheerfully have wrung Vlad's neck if he could just get his hands on him. The irony of the thought almost made him smile. If he could just get his hands on Vlad, that would solve the whole problem.

For the first time since Amos had led him down the driveway out onto the side road, he became aware of their surroundings. They were jogging along towards the crossroad half a mile away. Farm fields, almost hidden by brush, lined the road on both sides. Part way to the next road, a strip of bush bisected the adjoining farms and followed a stream that meandered east over the horizon.

As they neared the bush, Andreas noticed a dark pickup parked almost in a snow bank adjacent to the trees. Immediately he was suspicious. He knew it was deer hunting season, but something about the way the truck was concealed made him uneasy. There was no sign of life around the vehicle, and when he laid his hand on the hood, the motor was barely warm. It had been off for some time.

Then he found the footprints leading across the ditch and along the fence in the direction of the house. His suspicion turned to certainty. Amos sniffed them, then looked up, waiting for permission to head off after the maker of the prints.

Andreas struggled through ankle-deep snow over uneven ground. Between the snow masking the roots and rocky outcrops and the shadows under the trees, he stumbled frequently. It was hard to say whether the sweat trickling down his back was from exertion or fear. Meanwhile Amos charged ahead, stopping only occasionally to sniff a track, then dash on.

They were almost out of the bush when Andreas heard a barrage of evenly spaced reports. Even after years of peace, he clearly remembered the sound of gunfire. The question was, who was firing that gun?

He began to run. Amos led the way.

While it was only a few hundred yards, he was winded by the time he reached the rail fence and the cedar windbreak surrounding three sides of the Horbatsky lot.

Andreas stopped to catch his breath. Amos was nowhere in sight. Nor could he see the house through the

Love, Obey & Betray

thick shrubbery. The silence terrified him. Where was Kate?

He had no weapon capable of inflicting injury from a distance. Desperate, he felt around in the snow. His fingers closed around a stone twice the size of his fist. Now, if he could just get close to the gunman...

Andreas stepped quietly down the east side of the lot. Paw prints lead in the same direction. Had Amos seen something?

He was almost opposite the end of the house when he heard a sharp crack. Then a yelp. Amos!

Instinctively, Andreas ducked. The direction of the sound put the killer somewhere in the shrubbery behind him.

He raced to the end of the hedge. Light from the patio doors off the kitchen reflected into the yard but did not illuminate all of it. Where was the gunman? He couldn't wait to find out. He had to be sure Kate was okay.

He sprinted across the space to the front of the house heading for the front door. He didn't see Kate concealed in a juniper bush until a hand grabbed his coat.

"He's somewhere along the back fence," she said. "Or at least, he was."

He almost choked on his relief. "I'll go get the gun from the hall closet."

Kate cut him off. "I have it here." She handed it over.

"Then I'll go up the other side of the house. See if we can smoke him out. We have to get a fix on him to know where to aim."

"You only have two rounds. I've got plenty here." She jiggled the box of shells in her pocket. "Let me draw his fire. Once you know where he is, the shotgun will take him down."

"I don't…"

Kate cut him off. "There's no time to argue. Go. I'll give you a couple of minutes to get in place."

Knowing she was better with the Luger than with the long gun, Andreas turned to obey.

Shadows made an inky alley of the yard between the hedge and the house. Beyond the patio, the yard was bright. He couldn't imagine the gunman risking exposure in that light. All the same, he eyed his dark path carefully before running up it to the back of the house.

Part way to his goal a soft whine stopped him. Amos limped out of the shrubbery, nursing a bleeding paw. Andreas stopped to pat his head and order him back onto the ground, then rushed on.

He had barely settled and drawn the gun to his shoulder when Kate let off a couple of rounds that thudded into something solid, probably a post. The silence stretched for what seemed like minutes, broken only by his own labored breathing. Then Kate's third round followed the first two.

Again the silence scraped along Andreas' taut nerves.

Then a fourth shot rang out. This time he saw a muzzle flash. Instantly, Andreas aimed just below the flash and squeezed the trigger. Even as the recoil jolted into his shoulder, another report from Kate's pistol shattered the darkness. He heard a sharp cry. A dark silhouette seemed to slide down through the shadows where he'd seen the flash of light. Before stepping forward to inspect the heap, he snugged the stock firmly back into place, ready to let off the second round if necessary.

"Careful," Kate cautioned in a low voice from the other corner of the house.

Andreas saw her emerge from the shrubbery. The pistol in her hand was pointed towards the shape on the ground. Following her example, he stayed out of the light as he walked to their downed assailant. The man wasn't moving.

Andreas kept his gun trained on the man while Kate jerked the rifle from his limp hand, then checked his neck for a pulse.

She stood up. "He's alive, but just barely. We need an ambulance."

An explosion of flashing lights and sirens in the driveway drowned out further conversation.

"So much for a silent arrival," Kate exclaimed. "They were supposed to have been here ages ago."

CHAPTER FORTY-SIX

"You aren't safe here."

Vlad could feel people around him and hear their jumbled voices, but the dominant words came from somewhere overhead. He couldn't see the speaker's face.

"City hall is built on the bridge in the centre of the river," the voice continued. "It will survive this attack. You'll be safe there."

The advice was sound. Unless a bomb struck it directly a brick building many yards from other structures and surrounded by water had the best chance to remain standing after an Allied raid.

Vlad opened his eyes and tried to rise. He couldn't. He was surrounded by men in navy uniforms. Above them, red and yellow flashes cut the night sky. His belly burned as though the fire had already reached him. Only that couldn't be. The rest of him was cold. Freezing, in fact.

Hands were moving down his body, probing his back and arms. He heard someone say, "He's gut shot." The speaker was very calm, not the least upset.

Then he was being lifted onto a flat surface. He wanted to scream with the pain. He could only grunt. He was shivering. Strong hands wrapped him in warmth.

"You have to move." Her voice came again. "They'll find you if you stay here."

He turned his eyes skyward in search of the speaker. She was there, just on the edge of his vision, silhouetted by the dancing light. For a moment, he didn't recognize her. Dark hair fluffed around her face casting shadows across the high cheekbones, concealing her eyes. Then he recognized her voice. "Anna? What are you doing here?"

He saw her smile. "I came to tell you, you have a son named Nicholas," Anna replied.

"But I killed Nicholas."

The face drew nearer as though she bent over him. In a flash, the smile was gone. Anger laced the firm tone. "Yes, you did. You had no right to do that."

His breath caught and pain radiated from his belly. "I'm sorry."

"So you should be," the voice hissed. The dark eyes bored into his. "He was only a boy. He was no match for you."

"But I feared he would betray me."

"And so he should have. What were you doing, dealing with men like Korczak? What was wrong with your head?"

"I had to protect my family."

"At the expense of your other family? That's not protection, Vladymyr. That's cheating. Playing the Cossack noble. At least your father wasn't too proud to acknowledge his mistress and her child. You were ashamed of us."

He heard the anger in her tone and protested. "No. I loved you."

"Not enough to trust me. I couldn't tell you I was pregnant. You needed a new start. If you stayed with us, you'd have lost that chance for a better life. I had to let you go."

"But I betrayed you. I was wrong. I know that. Forgive me."

"Only God can forgive you." The message didn't come in Anna's voice. In fact, he felt the words rather than heard them. Sudden fear set him trembling.

"Anna." He could barely whisper her name, pleading for forgiveness. He felt weak, so tired. He tried to ignore the burning in his stomach. His stretcher was moving, bumping over steps.

He needed to rest. The November wind knifed through the blankets. He shivered. Doors banged shut. The sounds of an engine drowned out his voice.

He closed his eyes and felt a woman's hand on his cheek. Anna's touch comforted him. He wondered what had happened to Kate. He tried to open his eyes but they refused to cooperate.

"He's lost too much blood." A man's voice made the statement just as he heard a thump and the growl of a motor accelerating. His world began to jolt and sway, rocking him to eternal sleep.

About the Author

Writing was Maggie Petru's secret solution to boredom and loneliness from her early teens onwards.

That love of language pointed her towards Sheridan College's journalism program, and started her on a lengthy career as an award-winning reporter/photographer for assorted daily and weekly newspapers in the Toronto area.

Years in a one-person bureau saw her covering everything from municipal council meetings, to court cases, school activities, murder investigations, fires, car accidents, natural disasters, visiting prime ministers and all manner of human interest events in two counties. Now she says she can't just waste all that experience when it could be turned into so many great yarns.

Made in the USA
Charleston, SC
01 March 2013